D1507022

The Glory Road

THE GLORY ROAD

Catherine Gavin

GRAFTON BOOKS

A Division of the Collins Publishing Group

LONDON GLASGOW
TORONTO SYDNEY AUCKLAND

Grafton Books
A Division of the Collins Publishing Group
8 Grafton Street, London W1X 3LA

Published by Grafton Books 1987

British Library Cataloguing in Publication Data

Gavin, Catherine
The glory road.
I. Title
823'.914 [F]   PR6013.A83

ISBN 0-246-12989-1

Typeset by Ace Filmsetting Ltd, Frome, Somerset
Printed in Great Britain by
Robert Hartnoll (1985) Ltd, Bodmin

To Margaret Mary Foedisch

CONTENTS

PART ONE

*'The French call their army
the Great Unknown'*

1

The colossal head of the Statue of Liberty towered above the Paris show grounds.

"It throws the whole exhibition out of proportion," said Baron Hubert de Grimont. "Which doesn't say much for Monsieur Bartholdi's notions of perspective."

"I suppose he wanted his work in progress to be seen," said his son Alain. "I think it's wonderful."

They were uncomfortably close to the railings surrounding the Head of Liberty, in a crowd of sightseers enjoying the rare sunny day of a wet July.

"It would be more wonderful still if it had been done in time to be a real centennial gift to the United States. Two years late already, and how many more years will it take to finish the thing?"

"But when it *is* finished it won't be out of proportion in New York Harbour," Alain said.

At eighteen he was growing bolder in argument with his father, whom he saw only once a year, and who liked to disparage other men's work. He had heard de Grimont sneer at the whole idea of the Universal Exhibition, at which the

Liberty head was on show, although in this year of 1878 the exhibition was the triumphant affirmation that after a lost war, a siege, and the carnage of the Commune, Paris was herself again.

He looked up at the noble bust, armless like the Venus de Milo and constructed of hammered copper which glowed in the late afternoon sun. The face was a woman's, calm and triumphant, crowned with a pointed diadem.

"They'll have trouble getting it across the Atlantic," his father said. "I hear Monsieur Eiffel's having problems with the armature. But I must admit, it grows on one."

"I'm glad you think so. It was good of you to come with me today."

"But you've found Bertrand a knowledgeable guide?"

Bertrand was the baron's valet and confidential man. He had escorted Alain on all his visits to the Universal Exhibition, whether as guide or as keeper it was hard to tell.

"Bertrand knows the show inside out," said Alain.

"Quite so. Has it always been as disagreeably crowded?"

"I rather like the crowds."

Next to the Head of Liberty, Alain had enjoyed the shifting scene in the international buildings which filled the Champ de Mars and spread out into the side streets. He had not been in Paris since he was ten years old, in the summer of the Franco-Prussian War. At the first defeat of the invincible French Army his parents sent him to his mother's brother, the Duc de la Treille, at Hyères in the south of France, and there he had lived ever since. Once a year, with his two elder cousins, he had visited his father at the de Grimont château in the Sologne during the shooting season. The three boys had been put into the care of the head keeper, and after the long days of sport they were glad to eat an early supper by themselves. They saw very little of their host, preoccupied with his adult guests; if they did dine alone with him he confined himself to sarcastic questions on their studies. This year all was changed. The de la Treilles had started on their chosen careers, and Alain was invited alone to the Paris exhibition. He had begun to feel like an exhibit himself. He had been shown off everywhere from the presidential palace to the concerts at the Trocadero, which had been specially built for the exhibition.

One day he had been taken to the Chambre des Députés, where his father sat with the Centre Party, and listened for two hours to a debate on the Congress of Berlin which had just ended. When the Chamber rose he was presented to the prime minister, Jules Dufaure, aged eighty. Most of the men at two dinners the baron gave for his son, at the Jockey Club and the Café Anglais, were in their sixties. Tonight the baron was entertaining a small party of notabilities in his private dining room, to complete Alain's introduction to Paris society.

"Have you feasted your eyes on the giantess long enough?" asked Hubert de Grimont.

"I'm ready to go if you are."

They had lived so long apart that they were in the habit of speaking abruptly; it was not easy to use the *mon fils* and *mon papa* of affectionate family style.

"Then we'd better leave now, before we're submerged in a flood of English trippers."

The tours organised by Thomas Cook and Son were a feature of the exhibition summer, and an omnibus had just set down a load of chartered tourists at the nearest gate. Monsieur de Grimont would have been surprised to know that he interested them as much as the Liberty head. They had just arrived in Paris, and muttered "Look! A typical Frenchman!" as he made his way through the crush. At fifty-three he was not a handsome man, being corpulent, bald and a head shorter than his son, but so dapper from silk hat to patent leather shoes with white spats, from waxed moustache to the red rosette of the Legion of Honour in the lapel of his frock coat that he was like any London cartoon of a 'Froggy' to the insular arrivals. Alain, tall and fair, and wearing a blue suit, might have been one of themselves.

"Now where the devil has my driver got to?" fretted the baron, when they were clear of the Champ de Mars and in a street full of stationary cabs and carriages. "I don't want to take out my watch in this swarm of pickpockets, but it must be after six o'clock."

"We're in good time for dinner, surely!"

"Yes, but I've letters to write before I dress."

Half an hour would do it, Alain thought. Half an hour to stroll alone on the boulevard, to feel himself what he was – a Parisian born. He had hardly been let off the leash since his visit began.

"Here's the coupé," he said thankfully, catching sight of the vehicle which his father rented by the month from the livery stable of the Grand Hotel.

"On the wrong side of the street, as usual! Etienne, back to the hotel as fast as you can."

"*Bien, monsieur le ministre*," said the man. "But the traffic on the right bank's very bad."

'*Monsieur le ministre*' was the usual form of address for anyone who had ever held ministerial office, as Alain knew quite well. He had no idea what made him blurt out, as soon as they were settled in the coupé:

"Are you sorry you're not still the Minister of Justice, instead of a Deputy for the Loiret?"

De Grimont waited for a calculated moment, long enough to make his son wonder if he had been impertinent, before he said, "That's something I've been meaning to talk to you about, before you go back to Hyères. We might discuss it this evening, after the guests have gone."

The coupé made its slow way down the Quai d'Orsay and across the Concorde bridge, where two carriages with their wheels locked were slowing up the traffic. It was the hour when fashionable Paris was returning from the afternoon drive round the lake in the Bois de Boulogne and down the Champs Elysées, and as well as the fiacres and carriages the Place de la Concorde was congested with the regular omnibuses and the lumbering 'exhibition vans' which carried fifty passengers. Sightseers were coming back on foot from the Champ de Mars, laughing and dodging under the noses of the horses, and Alain looked enviously at the escorts of the pretty girls tripping along with their parasols tilted against the late sunshine. It was hard to believe in that scene of youth and gaiety that only seven years earlier Frenchmen had fought Frenchmen in that square and in those narrow streets until the Seine ran red with blood, while palaces and the homes of the people exploded in flaming ruin. Then the coupé came abreast of the statue of Strasbourg, draped in mourning black for the lost provinces of Alsace and Lorraine. As they turned into the Rue de Rivoli Alain's mood changed, and a certain resolve grew stronger in his heart.

When his wife Elvire, born Princesse de la Treille, died in the Commune, Hubert de Grimont sold his great Paris mansion in the Rue St Florentin, and removed the valuable contents, with his carriage and horses, to his château in the Sologne. As Minister of Justice he had to remain at Versailles, the seat of the National Government which had defeated the Commune, and thus, he said, he became accustomed to hotel life. The Grand Hotel in Paris had been a hospital during the war with Prussia and the Commune. As soon as it was renovated de Grimont moved into a handsome suite on the second floor. It was an unconventional step for a man of his age and position, and one of his first guests, a pretty lady called the Comtesse de Lhomond, told her husband after their visit that obviously the baron didn't mean to marry again.

"A bedroom for himself, two reception rooms and a place for his valet," she said, "and nothing at all for the boy?

Hubert means to lead a bachelor existence, and I don't blame him!"

"If he finds another woman with a title like Elvire's and a better dowry, he'll marry as soon as convention allows," predicted the Comte de Lhomond. "A hotel suite isn't a permanency."

"He had a dozen years of Elvire, didn't he? Enough to put a man off matrimony for the rest of his life."

"What cats you women are, Sylvie! Elvire was reckless, but she was clever enough to avoid an open scandal. And her end was terrible, poor thing."

His wife was silenced. The Lhomonds had escaped to England during the Commune, but Sylvie knew the victims of those three tragic months were only to be mentioned with pious sighs. In the east end, where the Communards fought the government ferociously and paid a terrible price in defeat, the Red Spectre still walked and the names of the executed and exiled were revered. In society the rule was that the dead past should bury its dead. Hubert de Grimont's new way of life was soon taken for granted, and the child in the south of France as quickly forgotten as his headstrong and lovely mother.

"Well, here we are," said de Grimont, as the coupé drew up in front of the hotel on the Boulevard des Capucines, "later than I expected. You'd better dress for dinner, Alain, and remember I want you to make a good impression on the men from Cairo."

The young man had received a similar order many times during his two weeks in Paris. He had been required to make a good impression on the President of the Republic, Marshal MacMahon, and on leaders of society as dissimilar as Princess Mathilde Bonaparte and the Duc d'Aumale, whose father, King Louis Philippe, had given the de Grimonts — plain Grimonts then — their title of nobility. Now he had to confront a regent of the Banque de France and two representatives of the French presence in Egypt, both on leave in Paris. Monsieur Dubosc was a director of the Suez Canal Company, Monsieur Regnier an official of the Dual Control. How was an eighteen-year-old, ignorant of high finance and Egyptian affairs, to talk to men like that? At least he would be properly dressed for the occasion. His first dress suit, made by his father's tailor, was a perfect fit.

Before he began to change Alain stood for several minutes at the open window. His room on the fourth floor looked down on the Rue Scribe, not as congested as the boulevard on the other side of the hotel, but busy enough to make Alain feel as lonely as in the days when, like most rich people's children, he was left to servants and tutors in the bare attics of the Rue St Florentin. There was no time to waste in wishing himself down there with people of his own age, however, if he wanted to take a bath in his own white marble bathroom. It was luxury to someone accustomed to the wooden tub at Hyères, which a garden boy filled from a pottery jar while the little gecko lizards snapped at flies on the red tiled floor. First he had to insert the new studs and cuff links into the stiff shirt his father's valet had laid out for him. They were single pearls in a setting of mother of pearl, a gift from his uncle and aunt for his eighteenth birthday in June. Half an hour later, bathed and dressed, Alain tied his white tie satisfactorily, and hurried down two flights of stairs to join his father.

2

The baron's suite was in the middle of a landing with a parquet floor carpeted in red, where palms and aspidistras stood in tall brass pots, and over a marble balustrade the fashionable throng was seen moving in the foyer of the Grand Hotel. From the hallway of the suite Alain could hear the valet quietly directing the hotel servants as they put the finishing touches to the dining table. The folding doors to the salon were closed, and de Grimont was there alone. He was standing in front of a fireplace filled with ferns, immaculate in a dress coat adorned with the inevitable red rosette. Giving Alain an approving nod, he complained of the noise from the boulevard, and asked his son to close the louvred shutters.

"Won't it make the rooms terribly hot?"

"Perhaps, but otherwise we shan't be able to hear ourselves speak. There's a brass band playing in the Place de l'Opéra, that's something new."

When the *persiennes* were closed the salon had a wintry aspect. The purple carpet and curtains and the green velvet upholstery looked hot under the light of two flaring gaseliers. A bust of Julius Caesar stood on a marble pedestal, a green malachite clock with side ornaments was on the plush draped chimney piece. A few books in morocco bindings lay next to the silver ashtrays on the mahogany tables, and the pictures were sepia reproductions of battle pieces by Meissonier. There were no portraits. The writing desk was bare of anything personal except a small pile of stamped envelopes which showed that the former minister had found time to deal with his correspondence.

The guests were punctual, arriving almost on each other's heels. The two officials from Cairo were stiff, portly, bearded men who greeted Alain with formal handshakes; he was more at ease with Monsieur Imbert of the Banque de France. While apéritifs were served he talked pleasantly to the boy, telling him he had known the Duc and Duchesse de la Treille when they were first married and lived in Paris, and asking about their sons and their home in Hyères. Alain felt relaxed before the words *monsieur le ministre est servi* summoned them to the dining room.

The first course was on the table before Monsieur Dubosc, the Suez Canal director, deigned to address Alain directly.

"So you've come to see the great exhibition, *jeune homme*," he said. "Have you enjoyed all the novelties on the Champ de Mars?"

"Very much, monsieur," said Alain. He hated being addressed as 'young man': it was what people said to thirteen-year-old boys whom they wanted to tease or flatter, and he disliked the way Dubosc, with his napkin tucked into his collar, allowed flecks of lobster mousse to spatter his beard. Imbert spoke up at once.

"Monsieur Alain de Grimont has gone further than the exhibition grounds," he said with a smile. "I saw him a few days ago at a levée in the Elysée Palace, having quite a conversation with the President of the Republic."

"Really?" said Monsieur Regnier. "What did the great man say to you?"

"He was very gracious, monsieur, even though I made a stupid mistake. I called him *monsieur le maréchal* instead of *monsieur le président* — "

"My son has been brought up to admire military glory."

It was a typical de Grimont sarcasm. Alain flushed, but he went on with a smile for his father:

" — but the president didn't seem to mind. He said, 'So you are the nephew of my old comrade in arms, Gilbert de la Treille. I hope he has long ago recovered from the wound he got by my side at Magenta?' I thanked him and said my uncle was very well. Then the president said, 'Give him my best regards, and tell him we need men like him in Paris now.' "

This boy can stand up for himself, the banker thought. He's a true de la Treille as far as looks and spirit go. Is that why Hubert kept him hidden for so long? Or because he couldn't bear to be reminded of what happened to Elvire? "I imagine if your uncle came to Paris now," he said, "the president would find him an inconvenient supporter of the Comte de Chambord, the Bourbon claimant to the throne."

"I think not, monsieur," Alain spoke respectfully but firmly. "My uncle taught his sons and me to be loyal to the Third Republic. He said three pretenders to a non-existent throne made France ridiculous. Especially when the Comte de Chambord wanted to abolish the Tricolore and bring back the white flag and the lilies."

"That's all so much water under the bridge, my dear Imbert," snapped de Grimont. "The Comte de Chambord and the Comte de Paris withdrew their claims to the throne years ago."

"But what about the third pretender?" The French commissioner in Cairo was not above baiting his host a little. "The two other gentlemen are out of the running, certainly. But the late emperor's son is only twenty-two. Now that he's graduated from the English artillery college, mayn't he think of crossing the Channel and trying a *coup d'état* like his father? He might turn out a force to be reckoned with."

"Not he!" growled Dubosc, whose napkin was now spattered with sauce from the duckling *à l'orange*. "He was only admitted to Woolwich to please his mother and her crony Queen Victoria – Empress of India as she calls herself now. It was a clear case of favouritism."

"However he went in, he passed out of Woolwich seventh in his class," said Alain, but Dubosc blustered on.

"The English cooked his marks, just to stir up trouble here," he said. "He'll never make a soldier, let alone an emperor. He hasn't got the stamina. Remember, he was a delicate child – "

"Not too delicate to go to war against the Prussians at fourteen," said Alain. He had no special enthusiasm for the exiled Prince Imperial, but he instinctively defended youth against the sneers of an older man. "When I saw the prince last he was in excellent health and spirits."

There was a burst of agitated questions.

"You've seen him?"

"Are you in touch with him?"

"Do you know his friends in Paris?"

Alain de Grimont said without a smile, "I saw the Prince Imperial once, and that was at the Tuileries. It was at a party for his thirteenth birthday, and I was nine."

The palace of the Tuileries had been fired by the Communards, and now stood, a burned-out shell, under a long postponed demolition order. All the four older men at the dinner table had begun their careers under Napoleon III, all had many times been his guests at the balls and glittering soirées of the Tuileries. There was a moment of silence, a tribute to memory, before de Grimont motioned to the waiter to refill the glasses of champagne.

"I imagine the ex-Empress Eugénie is more discussed in

Cairo than her late husband or her son," he said. "Her brilliant performance when she opened the Suez Canal hasn't been forgotten, eh Dubosc?"

The former minister had turned the conversation into the channel in which he intended it to flow. The men from Cairo needed no prompting to discuss the Egyptian problems which had followed that French triumph, the construction of the Suez Canal, and Alain de Grimont, after his little show of self will, prepared to listen and to learn.

He learned that the Sultan of Turkey was still the paramount ruler of Egypt, and that his viceroy, or Khedive, was that Ismail who had so lavishly entertained the Empress of the French and other foreign royalties in 1869. His prodigality, continued for years, had brought a potentially rich country to the verge of bankruptcy. Egypt had passed under the Dual Control of Britain and France, Britain – according to Monsieur Regnier – presuming to act as the senior partner. Ismail had sold his shares in Suez Canal stock to Britain for £4 million, which – according to Monsieur Dubosc – gave Britain complete control of the great new route to India.

Over the Paris dinner table, where gas lights in ruby shades fell on a stiff arrangement of flowers set between two epergnes of fruit, the story of eastern folly and western jealousy was gradually unfolded. The recital continued when the party returned to the salon, where coffee and liqueurs were served by Bertrand. There were few interruptions. Once the banker took issue with Dubosc when he said Egypt had been 'pawned to the bondholders', and de Grimont asked if the American mercenaries employed by the Khedive as army instructors were speculating, through nominees, in Egyptian cotton futures. Alain listened to them all in silence.

Much of the financial detail was above his head. The only history he had been taught at Hyères was French history, and that by a refugee from Alsace; he was unable to detect the many omissions in the Egyptian story. Neither Regnier nor Dubosc had begun to understand the strange, antique civilisation on the banks of the Nile. To them the inhabitants of the land were 'natives', exploited by corrupt masters but incapable of independent action. Nor had they assessed the awesome power of Islam, the religion professed by nine million Moslems, whom they called 'heathen', from the Delta to the utmost limit of the Sudan.

Alain was quite alert enough to see that far more interesting to the French administrators than Egyptian affairs was the rivalry of Britain, perfidious Albion, the hereditary enemy.

He thought he had failed to make a good impression, but it seemed that in this case silence was golden. When the guests left, and he and his father were alone in the salon after Bertrand had picked up the coffee tray and the letters for the post, the baron positively smiled.

"A thimbleful of cognac, Alain? A cigarette? You did quite well tonight. Showed them you had a mind of your own. Only you shouldn't have teased Monsieur Dubosc about the Prince Imperial's birthday party. Older men don't like that sort of thing."

"Monsieur Regnier laughed."

"Yes, well, Regnier has a sense of humour, and he was pleased with you. When I walked out to the landing with him he said to me, 'You've an intelligent boy there. He can talk clearly and listen quietly. Let me know if I can be of service.'"

"What did he mean by that?"

"That he was willing to help in planning your career."

"A career in Egypt?"

He was quick, the son of Elvire de la Treille, as quick and perceptive as his mother had been! The father said, "It's a possibility," and watched his son. Alain was sitting on the sofa, with a cigarette between his long fingers, and his

23

shoulders well braced against the green upholstery. He never fidgeted, but also he never relaxed, never seemed at ease in his father's presence! As a little boy he had been the image of his mother, with golden curls and delicate features. Now the hair was severely cropped and light brown in colour, while the clean-shaven mouth, wide and narrow, was quick to set in a stubborn line.

"I hope you told Monsieur Regnier that my career is planned already," said Alain de Grimont. "All my life I've meant to go into the army."

"All your long life! I know you had a schoolboy fancy to become an army officer, just as your cousin Armand used to chatter about joining the navy."

"He *did* join the navy. He's with his ship off Tahiti now. And it wasn't only when I was a kid that I talked about the army. I told you as soon as I came to Paris that I hoped to enter St Cyr with the next *promotion*."

"I remember your saying something about it," said the baron negligently, "but I hoped to show you other and more rewarding ways of life. I talked to Regnier at the club before inviting him to dine tonight. Now that he's interested in you, a clerkship in the Commission of the Public Debt could be yours in November."

"Sitting on an office stool in Cairo and doing sums all day?"

"That's only the beginning. Your cousin Maurice has the same sort of job in Saigon now, though since he's the heir to a dukedom, even a penniless dukedom, it's called an assistant secretaryship."

"Maurice joined a commercial mission to Saigon because he wanted to see the world. He isn't going to spend his life in Cochin China."

"No? From what I saw of Prince Maurice de la Treille at the Sologne shoots, I think he'll take very kindly to colonial life anywhere in the Indo-Chinese peninsula. There he's part

24

of a privileged society where he can make his fortune. As you can do in Egypt if you choose."

"But how?"

"For one thing, by speculating in cotton futures, like those American soldiers of fortune the Khedive hired."

"I don't even know what cotton futures are."

"You'd soon learn." De Grimont studied his son's downcast face. "This has been a surprise to you, I know. You must think it over carefully, and have another talk with Monsieur Regnier. All I wanted for you was the opportunity, but if Egypt doesn't appeal — and I admit I would prefer to have you in Paris, in a serious profession — that can be even easier to arrange."

"How?" said the boy again.

"You could enter politics."

"But I'm only eighteen!"

"I didn't mean you could become a Deputy next year, or even for a few years. But when you went to Toulon and passed your baccalaureate — with honourable mention, too — you became eligible to enter law school in October. You could have a share in a law practice within three years, as I did. You would soon be deeply involved in politics. Wasn't that at the back of your mind when you asked if I regretted being a mere Deputy instead of the Minister of Justice?"

"You couldn't be a mere anything."

De Grimont shrugged. "Look at it this way. I knew I would have to give up the Justice Ministry when Thiers fell from power. MacMahon didn't want me in his cabinet; he's no politician, though he was the figurehead we needed in 1873. I'm sure he was far happier today, presenting the Gold Cup at the Deauville races, than when he had to listen to the latest reports from Cairo. But that's beside the point. When a parliamentary seat in the Loiret fell vacant, my friends urged me to contest it for the Centre party, which is a check and balance to the royalists and the Reds. When I won the seat I was thinking of your future as well as my own."

His son raised dulled eyes to his. Alain looked weary and defenceless, like a schoolboy again instead of the handsome youth of the dinner party.

"You never talked like this before," he said. "You never came to see me at Hyères or showed you cared what became of me – "

"You were better off in your Aunt Blanche's care while you were a child. Now you're a man and a de Grimont. Enter law school now, and in a few years you could be the Deputy for the Loiret."

"I haven't the brains to be a politician, or the patience to sit in the Chamber day after day, listening to debates on the Congress of Berlin."

"Three years of law school, competing with men of your own age, would soon sharpen your wits, and I think you've the patience to listen to the country people you would represent. At the château you'd meet the men who count in national politics. The Loiret's within easy driving distance from home, and you'd make a start in local elections, parish council first, then district, then cantonal, until the voters know you as well as they know me. I'm sure of a seat in the Senate when I turn the constituency over to you. There you are, Alain: what do you think of my idea?"

"I – I don't know what to say."

"Then don't try to say anything now. Think about both my proposals carefully – and," de Grimont added, "I suppose you'll want to talk them over with your uncle – before we meet again. You know there won't be any shooting parties at the château this year? My doctor wants me to take the cure at Vichy as soon as the Chamber rises."

"Yes, you told me. I'm sorry you aren't feeling well."

"Come and join me at the Hôtel du Parc. At Vichy we'll have leisure to thrash the whole thing out, and decide if it's to be Cairo or Paris."

26

Alain's reply was irritatingly inconsequent. "Do you mind if I open the shutters? It's stifling in here." The salon was heavy with cigar smoke.

"Open them if you want to listen to the band."

Alain had been dimly aware that a brass band was playing on the boulevard. When he flung the shutters wide and the noise grew louder, he could distinguish the patriotic strains of *Sambre et Meuse*. As he stood looking down into the street, decked with streamers and banners, his father came softly up behind him.

"Did you expect to see a *military* band, Alain?"

Marching in ragged formation along the boulevard were five or six men dressed as clowns, with a pierrot turning somersaults at their head. From their instruments hung advertisements of the next day's special attractions at the Universal Exhibition. The sightseers crowding into the roadway to applaud them had to dodge one of the huge exhibition vans lumbering along behind the clowns.

"It's too late for those monstrosities to be on the streets," complained de Grimont. "That thing can't even be plying for hire. What's that they've got on the windows?"

"More advertisements, probably."

All the windows of the van were covered with posters of the various sights to be seen on the Champ de Mars.

"And to think this nonsense will go on for weeks yet!" said de Grimont. "For God's sake close the shutters, Alain. We're in the middle of a serious conversation. Sit down and don't be so restless."

Alain obeyed. He felt as if he had been seated for a fortnight, listening to old men pontificating on every subject from the Congress of Berlin to the Egyptian Public Debt.

"*Monsieur mon père*," he said formally, "I'm grateful for your interest, and I'll join you at Vichy if you wish. But don't expect me to change my mind. I mean to join the army and I will."

"Why?"

The peremptory question, the icy tone following his father's reasonable and almost coaxing arguments unnerved the boy. It was a technique which the former minister had employed many times. But Alain had the courage of strong convictions. He instinctively stood up like a man in the witness box, and said, "I want to be ready for the day when France can challenge Germany again. When we can win back Alsace and Lorraine. When we get our revenge for Eighteen Seventy."

"So that's it," said de Grimont slowly. "I see I've underestimated you, Alain. I thought you wanted to enter St Cyr because you'd look well in a fancy uniform and a hat with feathers. Or because your uncle and that Alsatian tutor, what's-his-name – "

"Monsieur Scherer."

"Scherer, yes – had stuffed your head with their own brand of patriotic claptrap. Now I see it goes deeper than that. You want revenge, *la revanche*, which may well turn out to be the curse of our country."

"Most men of my age feel the way I do."

"By 'men' you mean your cousins, and the young fellows you know in Toulon and Hyères?"

"I don't know any young fellows in Paris."

De Grimont's face, always sallow, seemed to turn yellow at the sarcasm in his own style. "No, perhaps not," he said suavely. "I assumed you'd want to meet men of solid achievement while you were with me. In Paris, where we had to fight the Commune after we fought Prussia, we have no such exalted ideas about the military. Do you know what people here call the French Army? They call it the Great Unknown. Out of sight and out of mind."

"That could be changed by a modern officer class."

"Which you won't find at St Cyr. I know the commandant, old General Hanrion, who's still fighting the Algerian battles of forty years ago. Even for a military college the teaching is obsolete, and what you youngsters who want to take the glory road don't realise is that if we went to war with Germany one year or five years from now, we would lose as many lives, as much territory, and even more money than we did before. Now that monstrous war indemnity is paid in full we have a free hand in the world's markets. That's where you young men can beat Bismarck and his *junkers*, in trade and colonisation. Not by drilling sullen conscripts on some dusty barracks square."

"They have to be drilled before they can cross the Rhine."

"France's future lies overseas, not on the Rhine. Come, Alain, be sensible! Whatever worthwhile career you choose, at home or abroad, I'll be behind you to the full extent of my influence and fortune. I'm not sure I'd want to subsidise a second lieutenant, frittering away his life in a garrison town like Limoges."

"Then I'll be a sullen conscript myself when I'm called up with my class. I believe it's still possible to rise from the ranks."

It was de Grimont's turn to get to his feet, and take a few angry paces through the room before he poured himself another glass of cognac. "Don't be a fool," he said thickly. "If it's revenge you want you ought to enter politics, if only to avenge your mother's death."

"What have politics to do with my mother's death? I know she died in the Commune – "

"Did anyone ever tell you how?"

"Certainly *you* didn't. I didn't even see you for more than a year after it happened. It was Aunt Blanche who told me mother had been nursing the wounded, and died of hospital fever – "

"Dear Blanche," said de Grimont, biting his lip, "always sentimental. Elvire never went near an army hospital. Her interests were social, not humanitarian."

29

Her son flushed. "Then was it something that happened in what's called Bloody Week?"

"She died in April, a month before Bloody Week, when the Commune still ruled in Paris. They were defeated at the end of May, and Monsieur Thiers's campaign of expiation wiped out most of the rank and file. Many of the leaders escaped across the frontier, and only some of the most vicious were executed or transported to New Caledonia. That firebrand Gambetta's back in the Chambre des Députés now, and planning to push through an amnesty bill for their pardon and return to France. That's why we need young men like you, to fight the Reds before they become too powerful."

"Was it some of those men who were transported who were – responsible for my mother's death?" Alain was shaking uncontrollably, whether with rage or grief his father couldn't tell.

"The man who murdered her was Théophile Ferré, the Communard Prefect of Police. He was in prison near Versailles for six months before I had the pleasure of signing the warrant for his execution."

"But why – why was she murdered?"

"As I heard the story she was trying to cross the Rue de Rivoli, where the Reds had erected a barricade across the Rue St Florentin, when she got into a row with this lunatic Ferré. There were other people involved, accused of sheltering a deserter, and without trial, point blank, Ferré ordered them lined up against the barricade and shot. They were buried where they fell – in quicklime."

The boy had his hands over his eyes now, but his eyes were dry.

"You say 'as you heard the story,'" he got out. "Where were *you*?"

"At Versailles with Monsieur Thiers and his cabinet."

"Why didn't you take her with you?"

"I took her mother there, a paralysed old woman, but

Elvire refused to leave Paris and care for her. She stayed in the Rue St Florentin, and there she died."

Alain was not listening. He whispered, "Buried in quick-lime!" and when his father offered him a glass half full of cognac, he struck his hand away.

"You'll see worse horrors if you go to war," said Hubert de Grimont.

"In war, yes! But this was my mother – your own wife!"

De Grimont's control broke. He was shaking, like his son, when he spat the words at him:

"She was not a faithful wife to me!"

"That's a lie!"

"She betrayed me in my own house, with the knowledge of my own servants. Would you like to know the names and dates?"

He was accustomed to bully and browbeat, but almost for the first time in his life de Grimont quailed when he saw the naked rage in his son's eyes. Of the two it was Alain who recovered a kind of composure first.

"I've had all of this I can stand," he said. "Will you excuse me now – monsieur?"

He was on his way to the door when his father said,

"Are you going to your room or going on the town?"

In an exact echo of his own jeering tone he heard Alain reply:

"Which would you advise?"

3

Servants had been in to tidy the fourth floor room and turn down the bed, and because of a short squall of rain had closed the windows as well as the wooden shutters. It increased Alain's claustrophobic sense of being his father's prisoner. He pulled everything open, and while the night breeze cooled his burning face he kept gasping "The swine! Damn the murdering swine!" He could not have told if he was cursing Théophile Ferré, who had ordered his mother's execution, or the husband who had abandoned her to danger.

The long sobbing breaths were the sole physical evidence of Alain's emotion. He had only wept for his mother once, on the day when Aunt Blanche, in her boudoir at Hyères, had taken him in her arms to tell him gently that 'dear mamma had died in Paris, helping poor people' – a version of the truth which had developed into the fiction of hospital nursing and the fever. He had cried his heart out on Aunt Blanche's soft breast while she caressed and lulled him like a baby, as he had never been comforted by his mother while she lived. He was crying not for what he had lost, but for what he had never had.

His aunt kept him close by her for the next few days, and his boy cousins considerately kept away, until by degrees Alain slipped back into the routine of games and school books, so much happier than anything he had known in the Rue St Florentin. The priest who heard him say his catechism taught him to pray for the repose of his mother's soul, and gradually she became idealised in the boy's memory as a vision of beauty, insubstantial as a wraith.

His uncle and aunt had so completely taken the place of his parents that Alain's childish grief had been transmuted long ago. Not two hours since, when he had enjoyed teasing Monsieur Dubosc about the Prince Imperial's birthday party, he had felt no sentimental pang because his mother took him there. Elvire de Grimont had not often given her little boy the treat of a drive in the great carriage with the two matched bays in which she took the air nearly every afternoon in the Bois de Boulogne, but an invitation to the palace of the Tuileries was something special, and he could remember every detail of their departure from home, with a footman respectfully arranging his mother's crinoline on the floor of the carriage beneath a fur rug, while Alain in his velvet suit stood waiting in the courtyard to be lifted to the opposite seat. He remembered the party, and the boy they expected to be emperor one day, and how the boy's mother, in her imperial glory, had been outshone by the Baronne de Grimont, with her golden hair brushed into one long curl on her slim shoulder. And all that beauty had been defiled on a madman's order, and buried in quicklime like a common criminal at the foot of a prison wall! At the corner of the Rue de Rivoli, he thought, we drove over the very spot today, and how many more times since I came to Paris!

Suddenly the impersonal hotel room became a prison in itself, and Alain began to undress rapidly. The white tie came off, the pearl studs, the stiff shirt; the new suit was flung across a chair for Bertrand to pick up in the morning,

33

when he was sure to appear with the orders for the day. There were other new suits in the wardrobe, but Alain pushed them aside to take out the light grey suit in which he had travelled from Hyères. As he dressed he heard the brass band playing, further away, and now the music was the *Marche Lorraine*.

He remembered to put money in his pocket, but forgot to wear a hat, so that well dressed people entering the lobby of the Grand Hotel turned to look after him as he reached the pavement. Once on the boulevard he was not conspicuous, for the warm, humid summer night seemed to have made the tourists a little crazy, and any extravaganza of dress was acceptable. Some of them were even dancing in the roadway, blowing toy trumpets or flying baloons under the brilliant gas lamps which had given Paris the name of the City of Light. The outdoor terrace of the Café de la Paix was crowded when Alain hurried past, and the waiters were carrying out extra tables for the throng of arrivals from the Opéra.

There a performance of *Aida* had just ended, but the lamps still shone on the façade of Garnier's masterpiece completed since the days of the Commune, when the unfinished building was hemmed in on three sides after the government troops entered Paris. The Marine sharpshooters, firing from the surrounding housetops, had picked off the revolutionaries with ease. So said Bertrand the valet, who as he escorted Alain to and from the exhibition never failed to point out the landmarks of the terrible days of 1871.

"Where were you, Bertrand, while those horrible things were going on?"

"I was a prisoner of war in Germany, Monsieur Alain."

He was like the slave in the Roman triumph, whose grim *memento mori* reminded the victor of his mortality. Alain turned away from the Place de l'Opéra. Now that he had his wish, and was alone and free in the streets of the capital, he had no idea which way to turn. In a state of shock he had

34

retrogressed to the Paris of 1871: the street lamps were the flares of the *pétroleuses*, and the dancing figures seemed to be brandishing the rifles which had killed his mother.

He crossed the boulevard to avoid the Grand Hotel. Ahead, and not far distant, lay the Rue Royale, the scene of some of the fiercest fighting of Bloody Week. Between the hotel and the Rue Royale was a network of narrow streets which included the Rue St Florentin. Early in his visit he had proposed to his father that they might drive that way and look at his birthplace.

"There's nothing to see. There's nothing at all as you remember it, because the house is a government office now, with solid iron gates and no flowers in the courtyard. Nothing on the street side but two guards on duty."

"Oh well, in that case!"

– My father was ashamed to pass the gates, he was afraid to pass the gates –

Nonsense. He has driven over the place where she died twenty times with me, and how many times in the past seven years?

Alain realised that he was talking to himself, and people were beginning to look round.

He crossed the boulevard again and turned into the Rue Vignon, a street of little shops, hand laundries and unpretentious bars. The latter were as crowded as the Café de la Paix, but with a very different class of customer: light women and their bullies, sporting characters of the prize-fighting sort, and punters disputing the result of the Gold Cup Stakes at Deauville. The stop press sheets of the racing papers lay in tatters on several floors.

Alain de Grimont had drunk two glasses of champagne at dinner and declined cognac. Now he wanted spirits, something to drown the confusion in his mind, something like the fiery *grappa* his uncle's Italian gardeners drank when their day's work was done. He turned in to the first bar on the corner, where the barman took a bottle of *marc* from the shelf behind his head and filled a glass for Alain.

He tossed it off and asked for another. The second he drank more slowly, letting the liquor do its work, and becoming aware that some of the girls sitting at the marble topped tables were eyeing him; so young, so dishevelled and hatless, he should be an easy mark. They smiled their professional invitation. Alain had no intention of accepting it. He was not an innocent, for his cousin Armand had seen to his sexual initiation when they were both studying at Toulon, Armand in the naval college and Alain taking special coaching in higher mathematics. He knew the difference between the attractive young ladies of Madame Cosette's discreet establishment and the smirking prostitues of the Rue Vignon, and left the bar without responding to the smiles and winks. But the little interlude had had its effect: it had cured him of the morbid fancy to visit the Rue St Florentin.

He walked on towards the Place de la Madeleine, which stretched between the boulevard and the Rue Royale. There stood the great church which had been another strong point during the battles of the Commune and still bore the marks of heavy shelling. Protected by its railings and shaded from the garish lights of the boulevard, the church of the Madeleine was the expression in stone of the same victorious calm as Alain had felt in the head of the Statue of Liberty.

The square was so dark and still that the slightest movement was noticeable, and Alain's attention was caught by footsteps and quiet voices in the place where a flower market was held by day. At that hour of the night it was represented by empty stands and a smell of rotting vegetation. Now under the awnings of the two central stands he saw the exhibition van which had rumbled down the Boulevard des Capucines an hour ago. Behind the posters covering the windows it had not been empty. A dozen men dressed in

36

black stood whispering with the clowns of the brass band and the pierrot who was their leader.

There was something so furtive in the gathering, so odd a contrast between the black clothes of the one group and the motley of the others that Alain stopped to watch. In a moment the sinister impression vanished as two of the men unslung the nosebags from the horses harnessed to the van. "They stopped to give the poor brutes a feed," he thought, and walked on past the bullet-pocked steps of the church to the far side of the Place de la Madeleine.

"Are you looking for somebody, monsieur?"

It was a girl who had accosted him, coming out of the darkness at the corner of the railings, and looking up at him with a confident smile. Taken aback, Alain stammered that he was a stranger in Paris, knew nobody – and then, more boldly, added "Perhaps I was looking for you."

"I hoped you were."

He had very little worldly wisdom, but it was not too difficult to see what this solitary young lady was doing in the dark square at midnight. She was about twenty, he judged; not too heavily rouged, and wearing a modest dress of grey alpaca swathed and moulded to her slim figure in the new fashion which Alain found far more seductive than the crinoline. She was probably a *midinette* from one of the dressmakers' workrooms, making a little extra money from the traffic of the night.

She laid her gloved hand on his arm. "So you're all alone, like me?"

Desire stirred in the boy's body at her gentle touch. This was what he had wanted since he fled from his father's presence: a woman's hands, a woman's body clinging to his own. He drew her close to him and kissed her eager lips.

"You're sweet," he said. "What's your name?"

"Alice."

"Well, Alice" – looking over her flowered bonnet at the

37

lights of the Rue Royale — "suppose we go across to one of those cafés and have a glass of wine?"

She hung back. "I'm not smartly dressed enough for a grand café. I know a quiet hotel on the Rue Tronchet where we can have a cosy supper, and no one will disturb us . . ."

"Are you hungry?"

"Very."

Like the van horses, needing a nosebag! It disarmed the young man, now prepared to ignore all the good advice his cousins had given him. Never risk a street pickup. Never go to a back street hotel room with a strange girl, whose pimp may be hidden in a closet ready to steal your wallet and leave you with a broken head. At that moment his only concern was where to find the Rue Tronchet.

"This way," said Alice, as if she read his thoughts. "It isn't far. But listen to the band!"

The Rue Tronchet was at the other side of the Madeleine church, and just as they reached it the brass band came out of the deserted flower market with the exhibition van lumbering behind. Above the music they heard another sound. The jingle of harness, the roll of carriage wheels and the shouting of a military command indicated to the spectators in the Rue Tronchet that the President of the Republic was driving back to the Elysée from the Gare St Lazare, after attending the races at Deauville.

The president, Edmé Patrice MacMahon, Marshal of France and Duc de Magenta, settled back on the cushions of his carriage with a sigh of relief. For a man of seventy it had been a long hot day, and the train journeys to and from Deauville had been tiring, but the races had been enjoyable and he had been cheered to the echo as he drove down the racecourse. That didn't often happen in Paris now. Even the crowd at the railway station had not been enthusiastic.

"This was intended to be a private occasion," he grumbled

to the officer riding close to the carriage. "Who ordered a military escort?"

"With great respect, *monsieur le président* – the order came from Madame."

MacMahon grunted and smiled in spite of himself. Madame his wife was inclined to meddle, but she was always concerned for his safety, and an escort of half a dozen mounted men was not excessive.

"What's your name, lieutenant?" he asked the boyish officer.

"Scheffler, *monsieur le président*, 88th Lancers."

Scheffler, an Alsatian name. Probably vowed to the liberation of his native province. The commander-in-chief found it in his heart to envy the lieutenant, with all his life before him and a career to make. He looked back to the days more than thirty years ago when he trod the glory road, winning victories in the Crimea, in Algeria, in Italy, before the shattering defeats of the Franco-Prussian War and the blood-letting of the Commune. In victory or defeat he had been happier as a soldier than he was now, torn between the quarrels of the Senate and the Chambre des Députés, escorting the Shah of Persia round the Universal Exhibition in the pouring rain, or trying to unravel the problems of the Dual Control in Egypt. That man Regnier had asked for another audience tomorrow.

The carriage swung out of the Rue de Rome and into the Rue Tronchet, and the major in command of the little escort ordered it forward. One of the exhibition vans had pulled squarely across the road and was blocking the way.

"The president! Clear the way for the president!"

"Oh look! It's Maréchal MacMahon!" exclaimed Alice, clinging to Alain de Grimont's arm. They were within a few paces of the quiet hotel where the supposed *midinette* was accustomed to take her clients.

But Alain was not listening to the girl. He was watching

39

the band of clowns and the tumbling pierrot who was now close to the presidential carriage. He saw that the mounted escort had been blocked by the manoeuvre of the van. He dropped Alice's arm and ran into the roadway, cutting off the pierrot in whose hand a pistol had appeared. He fell on the man an instant before he fired, pinning his wrist to the ground so that the bullet skittered between the wheels and sent the horses plunging and rearing, while MacMahon clung to the coachwork, while the driver and the footman on the box tugged desperately at the reins. He was not aware that the escort was galloping back along the pavement, for the assassin was strong and supple, and writhing like an eel beneath his weight. But he had relaxed his grip on the pistol and it was in Alain's hand. Before he could turn it on his enemy he heard the man scream as a soldier's sabre struck him on the head. Then he felt a heavy blow on his own head, and as he collapsed in the dust Alain felt nothing but thankfulness that the wretched night was done.

4

The Duchesse de la Treille was pouring tea for two unexpected and unwanted guests. The visit of Madame Barthou
and her pretty daughter Henriette was badly timed, for the
duchess had wanted to have her nephew Alain for the sole
enjoyment of herself and her husband after his startling
adventure in Paris. The callers had appeared five minutes
before the duke drove off to meet Alain at the railway station,
and she had rung for tea immediately. It was far too early,
but she wasn't going to have the boy's welcome home spoiled
by the ritual of passing silver cake baskets and generally
dancing attendance on a mother and daughter who should
have had the good taste to stay away.

The duchess was not a snob, and did not condescend to
Madame Barthou because her husband had been 'in trade',
the partner in one of the new Paris department stores before
his retirement to Hyères. But there was too much of the eager
saleswoman about his wife for a country lady's taste, and
Madame Barthou, who had found prosperous husbands for
her two elder daughters, was all too obviously on the lookout
for a third. Little Henriette, poised on the edge of a chair to

41

accommodate the fashionable bustle of her new faille dress, and wearing a stylish flower-pot hat, had been the hoydenish playmate of the de la Treille boys and their cousin not so long ago. She was now a self-conscious coquette of the sort which flourished in the relaxed atmosphere of Hyères, long established as a health resort on the Mediterranean shore.

Madame de la Treille, born Blanche de Laghet, had never been a hoyden or a beauty or a flirt. She was brought up in the tumbledown castle of Laghet, high in the mountains above Nice, which had once been a watch tower against the Saracens. When her mother's cousins gave the blushing awkward girl a season in Paris, she had no jewels, no adornments, and only one evening dress suitable for her presentation at the court of the Tuileries. There Prince Gilbert de la Treille, one of the most attractive young men in attendance at the palace, had sought an introduction, had invited Blanche de Laghet to dance, and to the astonishment of the generous cousins, had promptly fallen in love. Their happy marriage had now lasted for over twenty years.

"Another little cake, madame?" proposed the duchess. "Alain's train must be over half an hour late."

"Detained at La Pauline, no doubt," said Madame Barthou, declining cake. "After the night journey from Paris to Marseille, it's too maddening to have to wait at the junction on the branch line to St Raphael. My husband has protested to the railway company more than once. Has Alain been sending you good news of his dear papa?"

"Not very good," said the duchess coldly. "Monsieur de Grimont has been advised to take the cure at Vichy this year. Some trouble with the liver, I believe."

"Then perhaps it's nothing very serious," said Madame de Barthou.

It was a reasonable comment in France, where a liver complaint, or *crise de foie*, often meant nothing worse than an upset stomach.

"I hear wheels!" cried Henriette.

"Here they come!" said the duchess joyfully.

She was a tall woman, growing stout in her middle years and not given to rapid movement, but she hurried across the salon as eagerly as a girl to greet Alain. Henriette, so recently his playmate, started up too.

"Dearest Aunt Blanche!" He kissed her on both cheeks, sketched a kiss above Madame Barthou's hand, and when little Henriette breathed "Our hero!" told her not to be a silly kid.

He was changed; they all saw it, and when his uncle coming in after giving orders about Alain's baggage, said cheerfully, "Well, what do you think of him?" none of the women knew quite what to reply. Alain had been gone for less than three weeks, but he was no longer the boy who went away. In a dark suit cut by a Paris tailor, a high starched collar and cuffs with new gold links, with a wide silk cravat, he was a man of fashion: with a look of fatigue for which even a long night in the train could not be held responsible, he was quite simply a man.

"Why shouldn't my little girl call you a hero?" said Madame Barthou. "You saved the life of the President of the Republic — it was in all the papers!"

"Do tell us about it!" begged her daughter.

"There's nothing to tell, madame," said Alain. "I had the luck to be in the right place at the right time, that was all."

"And you were nearly killed yourself, when that officer struck you with his sabre."

"It was an accident," said Alain. "No harm done. He's a thoroughly good fellow, Lieutenant Scheffler."

"The president must have been *so* grateful," cooed the girl. "What did he say to you?"

"Nothing at the moment," said Alain with a grin. "But two days later he invited me to luncheon at the Elysée."

"Your father too?" said his uncle swiftly.

43

"No, just me. The president's lady was there, she was very kind to me. Oh, and General Hanrion, the commandant of St Cyr."

"How in the name of good fortune did he get there?" asked the duke.

"I told them at the police station I was a candidate for St Cyr. I suppose it was in the report to the president."

"With that sort of an introduction to the commandant you'll have a head start as a cadet."

"I still have to pass the entrance exam," Alain reminded his uncle.

His aunt beamed. "It'll be child's play, darling, after your success in the baccalaureate."

"But please," begged Madame Barthou prettily, "you're going too fast for me! What in the world were *you* doing in a police station, Alain?"

"I was arrested," he said. "There was a good deal of confusion at the time, and some of the bodyguard thought I was involved . . . that I was as guilty as the clowns . . . I don't know what they thought. But at the *commissariat* the name of the former Minister of Justice worked wonders. I was escorted back to the hotel and turned over to my father."

"And wasn't your dear papa terribly proud of you?" gushed Madame Barthou.

"I don't know."

"And were all those vile men captured?"

"I'm afraid I don't know that either, madame."

"Is it true they were all anarchists?" ventured Henriette.

"Oh, come on, Henriette!" said Alain impatiently. "What do you know about anarchists?"

"Alain dear!" his aunt remonstrated, and Henriette blushed under the snub. The added colour was becoming to a pretty girl in her teens, overdressed for an afternoon call, but her lower lip trembled as she looked appealingly at her mother. Madame Barthou rose gracefully to her feet.

"We have to be going, *chère madame*. We've had a glimpse of this brave boy, and now I'm sure he ought to rest after that miserable night journey."

Alain began to protest, but his aunt made no effort to detain the unbidden guests. "You must come again soon," was as far as she went in affability, and Alain and his uncle went out to the gravel sweep before the front door to help the ladies into the low basket carriage which Madame Barthou enjoyed driving herself. They watched it disappear down the avenue fringed with palm trees, like so many of the carriage drives and streets in Hyères-les-Palmiers, and when they went back to the salon Alain flung himself down on the sofa beside his aunt and looked about him with a sigh of pleasure.

It was a delightful room in its old-fashioned way, with french windows open on a flagged terrace, and bowls of roses on the ornamental tables among the family photographs and miniatures in silver frames. All the furniture had seen long service, but was covered in fresh *toile de Jouy*, patterned in a blue which matched the silk of the duchess's equally old-fashioned dress. Alain declined her offer to ring for a fresh pot of tea.

"Only if my uncle wants some too," he said. "I've had the queerest assortment of food and drink in the last few days, and I'm not a bit hungry. Tell me what *you've* been doing while I was in Paris."

"Having the painters in, and turning the old schoolroom into a sewing room. I couldn't bear to see it standing empty, with all three of you gone away."

"But here I am back again!"

"Not for long, my dear."

"No, not for long . . . Any news of Maurice and Armand?"

"Nothing from Armand, but a splendid long letter from Maurice, all about the gaieties of life in Saigon. I'll show it to you by and by. Your own letters weren't nearly so informative. Didn't you enjoy the exhibition?"

"It was all right, if you care for displays of American watches and English mustard." He was going on to describe the great Head of Liberty, when his uncle, who had been watching him gravely, interrupted.

"You liked the English guns, didn't you? The Purdey guns with the maple stocks?"

"My father sent to London for a Purdey gun for me." There was no relaxing of the set young face. "He called it a belated birthday present – but he had it sent to the Sologne."

Exactly Hubert's idea of a backhanded gift! "Too bad you can't have a day with the guns now," he began, and then remembered that the boy had had a night with the guns less than a week ago. "I'll tell you what would do you good – a stroll in the garden. Nothing like fresh air to clear your head after the train."

"And nothing I'd like better, if you'll excuse me, aunt." Alain kissed her hand, and said penitently, "I'm afraid I ruined my grey suit, rolling about in the Rue Tronchet."

His aunt shuddered. "Thank God you weren't hurt yourself. Are you really all right, dear?"

"Of course I am."

"Do you realise how proud of you we are?"

He received that with an embarrassed laugh, and said to his uncle, "I'll be quick!" They listened to his footsteps crossing the hall. Then Blanche de la Treille said, "That was clever, to propose the gardens. He'll talk freely when he's alone with you."

"He already asked if we could have a private talk. I didn't reckon on the Barthous staying on."

"Something's wrong, isn't it? More than the attempt on the president's life?"

"I'm afraid so. I saw how tense he was as soon as he got off the train, and I was sorry I hadn't gone alone. But we needed Jacques and the waggonette to handle the mountain of new luggage he brought back, and of course Jacques was listening

46

to everything we said. Poor old fellow, he was very excited about how *le petit Alain*, as he still thinks of him, had saved the life of *le maréchal MacMahon*."

"He doesn't seem to want to talk about it."

"Not to the Barthous, obviously. He gave me some of the details on the way home. He suspected something was up when he saw those villains lurking in the flower market – "

"Did he say what he was doing alone in the market at midnight?"

"I believe we can lay that to Hubert's address."

"Exactly what I thought myself."

"The truth about Elvire's death, told as brutally as possible. They say murder will out, my darling Blanche; perhaps we kept that murder to ourselves too long."

The house where the owners were worrying about the past had been known to the postal authorities for some years as the Château de la Treille. This was a courtesy title only, for with the exception of an ancient watch tower in one angle the dwelling was a quaint blend of Provencal *mas* and Genoese villa, put together by more than one generation of Blanche de la Treille's own family. It had been made over to her husband and herself by her eccentric old father, the Comte de Laghet, when his son-in-law came out of hospital in Milan, invalided out of the army and shattered in health after the chest wound he received in the battle of Magenta.

"I didn't give you much of a dowry," said de Laghet to his daughter, "so I'm turning over that place at Hyères to you and Gilbert. Never cared for the coast myself, and your brother will get the Château de Laghet when I'm gone."

Blanche was overwhelmed. "It'll mean life to Gilbert," she said. "Another winter in Paris would have killed him, the doctors say."

"Doctors always make the worst of it," said her cross-grained father. "Mind! It isn't an estate. Barely fifteen acres. When Gilbert's fit again, you'd better find some sensible thing for him to do; he's too young to retire at twenty-five."

Prince Gilbert, as he then was, had found the occupation for himself, by laying out twelve of the fifteen acres in carnation fields, and growing flowers for the Paris market. Even when his father died, leaving him a title encumbered by debts, and his own health had been restored on the Riviera, he had no desire to return to Paris. He was perfectly happy at Hyères with Blanche and the boys.

The house had so many small rooms, winding corridors and unexpected staircases that guests without a sense of direction often complained that they lost their way, but whether they fetched up in some boxroom or attic, or even in the dungeon of the old Tour de Laghet, they all praised the mingled scent of flowers and the sea which was everywhere. Alain de Grimont breathed it in as he changed out of his formal clothes and into a pair of white linen trousers and a much laundered cotton shirt, with a fisherman's red kerchief taking the place of the silk cravat, and it was not until he had gone down to one of the many half landings that he felt the vanishing but distinct smell of fresh paint.

He went along a corridor and opened the door of the schoolroom he had shared with his cousins. His aunt had made a good job of turning it into a sewing room, for it contained a sewing machine and a dressmaker's dummy as well as a table covered with sheets of fine linen, cut and ready to be hemmed. The table stood where the *estrade* had stood, on which the visiting tutors lectured to three docile heads, and the resident tutor, Monsieur Scherer from Alsace, had instructed them in French history and English literature. Alain advanced into the room where a gay flowered wallpaper had taken the place of whitewash on the walls, and looked out of the familiar window.

It was probably the only window which gave no view of the Mediterranean, for views were held to be distracting to boys writing a *dictée* or studying algebra, and an uninspired

48

sight of the kitchen garden was all it commanded. Even that was partly obscured by the blackboard, which had now disappeared. Alain remembered the day when Monsieur Scherer wrote on that blackboard the title of a new story which the boys were to study. *La Dernière Classe, par Alphonse Daudet*, was written in the Alsatian tutor's flowing script, and he read with emotion — it was only four years since Alsace was lost — the story of Monsieur Hamel who had to give up his school to a German.

'Monsieur Hamel took the chalk and wrote in the biggest letters possible:

'VIVE LA FRANCE —

'Then he stayed where he was, leaning his head against the wall, and without speaking he made a sign with his hand,

'*"It is finished . . . go away."*'

The Last Class, thought Alain. I was about fourteen then, and I suppose that was the kind of 'patriotic claptrap' my father sneered about. But I haven't forgotten, and I never will.

He ran down the shallow oak staircase. There were family portraits on the walls, three of which had been sent to Hyères by the Baron de Grimont when he gave up his house in Paris. They were portraits of three young de la Treille princes guillotined in the French Revolution, and in satin, lace and powdered hair they looked very like the present duke in his old jacket, examining the flowers in Biot jars on each side of the open front door, and also like Alain himself in his red neckerchief. He wondered, as he had never done before, what had become of the portrait of his mother at twenty, painted by Alexandre Cabanel.

"There you are, my boy, that's right! Now you look more like yourself!" said the duke heartily, as his nephew joined him on the gravel sweep. "Shall we have a look at the roses first? Your aunt's flower beds are doing splendidly."

"Aren't we going to the carnation fields?"

49

"Not unless you want another cross-examination on the events in Paris. The men are just as excited as old Jacques about the boy who saved the president."

"Then for heaven's sake let's see the roses."

The magnificent blooms which were Blanche de la Treille's pride were duly admired, and the men had reached the secluded pergola which gave enchanting glimpses of the blue Mediterranean before Alain took the plunge.

"Uncle, I wanted to speak to you . . . there's something I must tell you . . . I may have to go back to Paris fairly soon."

"Already? I thought the St Cyr exam wasn't held until September."

"No, it isn't. This is — something else."

"Something to do with your father?"

"*He* wants me to go to Vichy instead. But — the two men they arrested after — that night, will probably be brought to trial soon. And I'll be required to give evidence. Father wants to get me out of that."

"Why in the world should Hubert want any such thing? You're the one who'll come out of it covered with glory — "

"According to him it's not as simple as all that. He thinks the trial will be too political."

De la Treille stopped on the flagged path. His handsome face was a study in perplexity.

"Alain," he said, "we live out of the world here. We get our news from the *Figaro*, and it comes in forty-eight hours late. If it hadn't been for your telegram telling us not to worry, we would have known nothing about the attempt on MacMahon's life. Now the *Figaro* hints that it was a Red plot, the overture to a new Commune. Considering how hot your father was against the Reds while he was in office, why should he object to the trial of a new group of Communards, if that's what they are?"

"Well, that's just it," said Alain ruefully. "They aren't. I mean they aren't French. Four of the men they caught were

Russians, they came into France through Switzerland. Uncle Gilbert, you may say you live out of the world, but you read and study so much, you're far better informed than any of the *mandarins* I met in Paris. Have *you* ever heard of the Narod-niki?"

"The Party of the People's Will," replied his uncle. "It's something new in Russia, a split from Nihilism. I didn't know the Narodniki were operating in western Europe yet, but Nihilism was the creed of Bakunin, who made no end of trouble in Lyon during the Commune. Bakunin died two years ago, but Karl Marx is very much alive in London, and so is the Idea of revolution by murder . . . Is that what you wanted to know?"

"It's what my father would like to know, before the MacMahon *attentat* comes to trial."

"Does Hubert think your appearance at the trial would bring the vengeance of the Narodniki down on your young head?"

"Not on mine. His own."

The duke whistled. "A former minister isn't quite as important a target as the President of the Republic."

"He was the minister who signed the deportation or execution orders for hundreds of men and women after the Commune ended. That's why he was so furious with me for going out alone and getting mixed up with a gang of anarchists."

"Yes," said the duke. "Why did you? You *were* alone, I suppose?"

"I went out because I had a row with my father. And yes, of course I was alone."

They had all lied to him about his mother, so he could tell an untruth if he pleased. And anyway it was a white lie, for he *had* been alone when he launched himself at the would-be assassin. As soon as he dropped her arm the girl Alice had disappeared into the shadows from which she had come to accost him: the Alices of the boulevard avoided any clash with the law.

A row with his father— just what the duke and his wife had feared! It looked as if the bad moment was upon them, and in an attempt to stave it off de la Treille tried a diversion.

"'Mixed up with a gang of anarchists' eh? It seems as if Mademoiselle Barthou was right after all."

"Henriette? She probably reads the *Figaro* too."

"You shouldn't have spoken so sharply to the poor little thing, Alain. Remember she's only sixteen — "

"Yes," said Alain. "My mother was only sixteen when I was born, wasn't she? And twenty-six when she was shot dead by order of Théophile Ferré, and buried in quicklime at the corner of the Rue de Rivoli?"

His uncle, speechless, laid a hand on his arm, but Alain shook it off.

"Why did you let Aunt Blanche tell me that fairy story about mother helping poor people, and dying of the hospital fever? Why did you let me believe she was buried in the de Grimont vault in Père Lachaise?"

"Because you were only ten when it happened, my boy. Far too young to be told the terrible truth."

"You preferred to leave it to my father? Quite right. He has a brutal style you couldn't beat."

"That was why you quarrelled, the night you went out alone? That was the only reason?"

Alain resented the probe. Not for the world would he have told his mother's brother about that slur upon her honour: *she was not a faithful wife to me*.

"The only reason," he said savagely. "Wasn't it enough?"

"Yes," said the duke. "It must have been a fearful shock. You'll have to forgive us for our silence, Alain, we acted for the best."

The boy's harsh defiance melted at the word 'forgive'.

"Forgive you and my aunt!" he cried. "You've always been

so wonderful to me – Maurice and Armand too – "

De la Treille took his arm again, and this time his hand
was not rejected. "I don't know what your father told you,"
he said, "but I would like to tell you the truth as I know it,
and it won't be in a brutal style. Will you listen to me
quietly?"

Alain nodded, and they left the rose-hung pergola to cross
an open terrace above the sea.

"Your father was twenty years older than your mother,"
said the duke. "She was fifteen when she was taken from
her convent school to marry Hubert de Grimont. He
paid my father a handsome sum in settlement – it was soon
lost at the gaming tables – and bought a princess for his
bride."

"I think that was horrible."

"It happens every day in Paris society."

"Didn't you speak out against the match?"

"I would have, but I wasn't there. I was fighting in Italy,
when the emperor went to war with the Austrians for Italian
unity, and Blanche was alone in Paris with our two baby
boys. She went to the wedding in St Philippe du Roule, and
said my sister Elvire looked very happy."

"Were they ever happy? I can hardly remember seeing
them at home."

"We thought when you were born it would bring them
closer together, and perhaps for a time it did. Here at
Hyères, after the Comte de Laghet gave us shelter, we heard
of my sister as a brilliant political hostess, a great asset to her
ambitious husband, and a great favourite of the Empress
Eugénie. Then the war with Prussia came, and you were sent
here for safety; then the Commune, and then their fatal
quarrel."

"About what?"

"I have not the faintest idea," said de la Treille with
emphasis. "I only learned too late that Elvire refused to

accompany her husband when Thiers and his cabinet moved to Versailles."

"He should have forced her to go with him when there was fighting in Paris."

"One didn't force Elvire," said her brother. "But de Grimont did his best. Did he tell you that he took her money and her jewels, closed the house, dismissed the servants, took the carriage and horses to Versailles and left her alone to face the Commune?"

"My God, no!" said Alain. "He didn't tell me that! Left her alone in that great house?"

"There was a kitchen maid and a boy, and just enough cash to feed them for a month. That was where Elvire made her mistake, poor darling; she genuinely thought that because the Communards had closed the Gates of Paris and cut all communications with the south, she was a captive in the city. Of course it was possible to leave, because both sides took bribes, and at last she went to our family solicitor – you've heard me speak of Maître Gaucher – and told him she wanted to come to Hyères and be with you."

"With me!" The shadow of a smile flickered on Alain's face.

"Yes, with you and all of us; she was on her way to a rendezvous with what Gaucher called a *passeur*, a man who would get her out of Paris and on to Orléans, when she ran into trouble at the foot of the Rue St Florentin. And she did die helping poor people, as your aunt said: she defied that madman Ferré for the sake of two poor little shopkeepers and their son, a government soldier; the charge against them was 'complicity with Versailles'. They were all shot without trial, and buried – you know how. I heard the whole story when I reached Paris after the Commune was defeated, and I told your father I would let the world know what he did unless he left you with us while you were a child."

"Thank you." Alain's voice was muffled, for he had laid

his head down on his arms, crossed on the top of the terrace wall. "Thank you for telling me the truth."

"My dear boy, I stood beside the place where your mother was buried, less than six weeks after her death. The men were pouring new cement into the gaps in the street where the barricade had been. I told myself that she was not there. You must think of that, rather than of vengeance. Our good Father Gillet would tell you so. You've prayed for the peace of your mother's soul for years. Some day you'll be able to pray for your father too."

"Can you?"

"I try. Tell Father Gillet about this new trouble, and he'll help you, but all the time hold on to this: your mother did die for the poor and the rejected, and that last day she was on her way to you."

5

The accused in the Rue Tronchet Plot, as it came to be known, were not brought to trial as soon as Alain de Grimont had expected. His uncle had to remind him that the law courts never sat in August, and that according to the *Figaro*, the police were still searching for the men in the stolen exhibition van. In their black garments they had disappeared in the gathering crowd.

After that announcement all mention of the attempt on the president's life disappeared from the Paris press. It was believed that attendance at the Exhibition would fall off if visitors from foreign countries knew that ten or a dozen terrorists were at large in the city.

The British trippers continued to arrive in strength. Terrorists did not scare them, and where the Prince of Wales and his beautiful princess went, his mother's subjects followed. The Prince of Wales was president of the British section of the Universal Exhibition, and took his duties very seriously, visiting the city he loved many times. The Rue Tronchet Plot was replaced in the public interest by the arrival of the Prince and Princess of Wales to open the Hertford Hospital, which had grown out of the British ambulance given by Sir Richard Wallace for service in the war and the Commune. Through a broiling August such occasions added to the prestige and glamour of the City of Light.

There was another reason for the silence in the press, shrewdly guessed at by the Duc de la Treille. The Czar's government was demanding the extradition of the four Russian 'clowns' who belonged to the Narodniki, and whose fate in Russia as members of an anarchist sect was easy to imagine. "The guillotine in Paris or the gallows in St Petersburg," said the duke, "those fellows haven't got much choice!"

"The Russians are making a great mystery about their nationals," wrote the Baron de Grimont, in one of his rare letters to his son, "and the trial will not take place until the end of September at the earliest." The Chamber had risen and de Grimont was leaving at once for Vichy, but Monsieur Imbert would look after Alain when he came to Paris.

"Your prowess in the Rue Tronchet," the letter continued, "has convinced me that the army is the right career for you. I have instructed Monsieur Imbert to pay the annual fee of fifteen hundred francs for your board and tuition at St Cyr. While you are a cadet he will pay an equivalent sum, quarterly, as a personal allowance to yourself."

"'Prowess!'" said Alain bitterly. "He knows how to put in the knife!"

"He's treating you handsomely," said the duke, ignoring the bitterness. "Is this Monsieur Imbert the banker you told us about?"

"He's a regent of the Banque de France."

"Do you like him?"

"He's all right."

"He seems to be taking over my rôle as your guardian."

"I don't see why he should. I don't care for being handed about like a parcel. I can look after myself."

"Can you really? You're going to live under military discipline for the rest of your life."

"That's quite different." Alain folded up the letter. "Thank heaven he's given up the idea of Egypt or law school. And he doesn't say he's expecting me at Vichy."

The older man spoke urgently. "He's agreed to St Cyr — that's so much gained. If he invites you again to join him at Vichy I think you ought to go. Don't deliberately alienate your father, Alain. Remember he's a very rich man, and you're his heir-at-law."

"I didn't know money meant so much to you."

"I've learned what it means to be without it."

They seemed to have lost the power to communicate with each other. Alain's sullen answers betrayed his resentment at what he thought of as his uncle's failures: first to prevent his sister's marriage as a child, and then to give her a brother's support in her Paris life. "He should have told me the truth about her death years ago," thought the boy. "How was he to know my father wouldn't ram it down my throat in the Sologne last year, when I was seventeen? Why didn't Aunt Blanche do something about it?"

In a day or two it was Aunt Blanche's turn to encounter Alain's sullen mood, when he was invited to a small dance at the Barthou villa, organised by the indefatigable Madame Barthou's young married daughters.

"It's much too hot for dancing. I don't think I want to go."

"Oh, don't be silly, Alain. You know you always enjoy their summer dances, and the suppers in the garden. Go, and be specially nice to little Henriette. I think you hurt her feelings the day you came back from Paris."

"Please don't try to pair me off with a sixteen-year-old girl."

"Alain!"

"I apologise, Aunt Blanche. Truly, I didn't mean to be impertinent —"

"I think Paris must have gone to your head."

The duchess walked away in dudgeon, but when she was alone with her husband she confessed that within five minutes she felt like apologising herself. "I should have made allowances for all the shocks he had in Paris — and now this worry about the trial . . ."

"He's growing up, that's all," said the duke. "He's on an emotional see-saw, just as Maurice was a few years ago. And he's lonely without Armand, they were always very close."

"Too bad Armand isn't here now, instead of keeping station off Nouméa in case some more of those rascally Communards try a jail break to Australia."

Alain himself regretted Armand's absence. If his cousin had been at home they might have gone to Toulon on some naval pretext or other, and paid a visit to Madame Cosette's discreet 'maison tolérée' — an expression which sounded so much better than 'brothel'. Alain was not sophisticated enough to visit Madame Cosette's by himself. He thought her young ladies might laugh at him, but his whole starved young body was on fire for sexual satisfaction. He tried to sublimate the passion without an object into outdoor occupations, from hard work in the carnation fields to puttering round the rose garden with Aunt Blanche, dead-heading the flowers; he drove his uncle in the pony carriage, he took the ferry to Port Cros and tramped miles across the island, where he swam naked in a secluded cove. He went to the Barthou party and danced with Henriette, but there his body was unresponsive, nor could he have explained to himself why he recoiled from the soft arms and softer breast of a girl of sixteen.

It was a relief when the call to Paris came, although Alain knew, and so did his aunt and uncle, that he was bidding them a long goodbye. On the way to the junction at La Pauline, and in the westbound train from St Raphaël, he still felt his childhood ties with the red rocks and the blue sea, but once at the Gare St Charles in Marseille and embarked on the long night journey he felt the renewal of the strong bond with Paris, and the train's whistle in the night was like the sound of a bugle.

He did not expect a regent of the Banque de France to meet him at the Gare de Lyon, but he was approached by a polite bank messenger with a note from Monsieur Imbert inviting him to luncheon at the Continental Hotel.

"A reservation has been made for monsieur at the Continental," explained the messenger. "The Grand Hotel is so full of foreigners that it was impossible to obtain a vacant room."

Which meant that the Baron de Grimont's apartment was not available to his son. Alain shrugged; the new Continental suited him very well, and the view over the Tuileries gardens made up for the simple *cabinet de toilette* which replaced the marble bathroom of the Grand. He felt vigorous and eager, but he stayed in his room until it was time to go down to the foyer and meet Monsieur Imbert, who appeared punctually at one o'clock.

The banker, as pleasantly relaxed as when they first met, began by assuring Alain that he had 'all sorts of affectionate messages' from the Baron de Grimont. Perhaps it was because he was leading the way into the restaurant, and nodding to several friends among the pretty women and distinguished men who were already seated, that the banker failed to convey any of the messages in so many words before he gave his attention to the menu and the wine list. When the all-important choice was made and the waiters had stopped bustling round their table, Monsieur Imbert asked Alain 'if he were nervous about tomorrow in the Palais de Justice'.

"I think I am, a little," Alain confessed. "I mean, I hope there won't be another fuss with the police, like there was that night — "

"Of course not. You ought never to have been taken to the *commissariat*, especially when you had a slight concussion, but there will be no difficulty today. Your father has instructed his attorney to be present in court, to hold a watching brief on your behalf. You'll meet him, of course, before the proceedings start at ten o'clock tomorrow morning."

"What's his name?"

"Maître Leboyer." Monsieur Imbert hesitated. "I'm sure your father would have wished to be with you himself, but his doctor insisted that he leave for Vichy . . . Did he ever discuss the nature of his ailment with you?"

"A liver complaint, he said, but the cure at Vichy would put him right."

"It may be more complicated than that."

"In what way?"

The banker saw that the boy had no idea of the hint. He said, "I'm only guessing, because his doctor wants him to have a good rest at the château after he completes the cure. Meantime I'm sure he'll want to hear from you as soon as the trial is over . . . He's very proud of you, you know."

"Proud? Of me? At least he's given his consent to my going to St Cyr."

"Of course you're looking forward to that." The talk was pleasant until Monsieur Imbert rose to go, saying that Madame Imbert intended to send him an early invitation to dinner at their house.

So there was Alain alone at last, and free to roam the streets of Paris as he pleased. He left the Continental by the Rue Castiglione, and after admiring the restored statue of Napoleon which the Communards had toppled from its column, struck away through the side streets to the Champ de Mars. The exhibition grounds were crowded in spite of the great heat, and there was the usual throng in front of the Head of Liberty. That was what Alain had come to see, the majestic head with its coronal of seven spikes for the seven continents and the seven seas. It had become a symbol to him, not by its future and grandiose title of Liberty Enlightening the World, but of calm and assurance in all his perplexities.

Alain was pleased that he had not been 'handed about like a parcel' to his father's attorney, Maître Leboyer. He drove alone in a fiacre to the law courts, down the Rue de Rivoli and across the Pont Neuf, but the mere sight of the Palais de Justice, rising like a cliff beside the Seine, was enough to intimidate a country-bred boy. He asked usher after usher where he was supposed to go, and where to find Maître Leboyer; he was directed at last, and on the stroke of ten, to the Assize Court of the Seine, where the attorney was waiting for him in an anteroom. Leboyer was a grey man: grey of hair, of complexion and of a voice devoid of colour – "exactly the sort of man my father would choose as a solicitor," Alain thought. In a monotone Maître Leboyer introduced himself and told Alain the judges were still in the robing room, so that he could count on half an hour's grace before being called as a witness.

Only two men were to go on trial, the Russians having been extradited to their native land – "to Siberia, if they're lucky," said Leboyer – the two Frenchmen being the man Alain had disarmed, named Olivier, and one of his accomplices. Both had criminal records, both had refused 'under a certain degree of persuasion' to name the men behind the plot to kill the President of the Republic.

"The Public Prosecutor will demand the death penalty for Olivier, and I believe he'll get it," said the attorney. "The other may get away with transportation to New Caledonia, where he'll have other anarchists to keep him company. It's a clear cut case, and won't take long."

"Monsieur Alain de Grimont!" cried an usher.

The Assize Court of the Seine was half empty and half dark. It was a sunny morning, and the only gaseliers lighted were those above the three judges in their red robes and the Public Prosecutor, also robed in red. The windows were wide, and the sun streamed in, but between the windows the carved oak walls were dark, and the two men in the dock stood in this shadow, with jailers between and behind them. The desks of the clerks of the court and the press tribune were in a striped mixture of light and shade.

The prisoner at the bar, Olivier, stared incuriously at Alain as the young man who had brought him down answered the questions of the Public Prosecutor. He was taken through the whole story, from his first suspicions when he saw the meeting in the flower market to his flinging himself on the man with the gun, and concluding with the scuffle in which he had been injured. He annoyed the Prosecutor by amending this to 'slightly injured', was complimented by the senior judge and permitted to stand down. Whereupon the second of the two accused, a thin young man with a wispy beard, shouted out that all they had heard was a pack of lies, to be expected from the son of 'Killer' Grimont, who had hunted the Friends of the People to their deaths in '71.

The judges cried "Silence!", the jailers struggled with the prisoner, and even Olivier laid a restraining hand on his arm. The voice of the usher calling the name of the next witness was inaudible, and he had to repeat the summons twice:

"Lieutenant Robert Scheffler!"

A man in his early twenties, immaculate in his uniform and extremely serious, came to attention in the witness box. Alain recognised the officer of the bodyguard who had struck out with the flat of his sabre both at himself and the man he was struggling with on the roadway of the Rue Tronchet.

63

Better than that attack in the semi-darkness he remembered coming to his senses in the gaslit police station, and his embarrassment at finding his head on the shoulder of Lieutenant Scheffler, who was looking after him, and apologising, until the police surgeon could be found. Although the lieutenant, in the Assize Court of the Seine, was a model of military bearing, he allowed his eyes to rove along the public benches, and when they alighted on Alain, the ghost of a smile twitched the corners of his mouth.

He agreed with the Public Prosecutor that he was Robert Antoine Scheffler, born in Mulhouse in 1855, "fifteen years before the German annexation," he added quietly, graduated from St Cyr in 1876, and presently on the staff of the Military Governor of Paris. It was the governor whom Madame Mac-Mahon had requested to supply a mounted escort on the night of the president's return from Deauville.

No, there had been no sign of trouble until they turned into the Rue Tronchet. He, Scheffler, had been riding by the side of the presidential carriage, until the officer in command had given the order to advance and clear the street of an obstructive van. Hearing an outcry from the coachman and the footman on the box he had turned without orders and seen two men struggling on the ground. A shot was fired. He attacked both men with the flat of his sabre; in the case of Monsieur Alain de Grimont (again the sideways smile) he now regretted this very much.

The Public Prosecutor approved the conduct of Lieutenant Scheffler, relaxed him to the discipline of his superior officers and permitted him to leave the witness box. His place was taken by Major Vernet, in command of the bodyguard, who with an extremely sour expression admitted that he had left the presidential carriage to pursue, with no success, the occupants of the van. Lieutenant Scheffler had acted on his own initiative in returning to the scene of the crime.

Major Vernet joined the other witnesses, seated at some

distance from each other, and the red-robed judges conferred at length on the problem of the van. The two accused made no demonstration, Olivier in particular studying the vaulted ceiling and whistling soundlessly as he had done during Alain's testimony.

It was different when he rose to speak. Olivier had chosen to conduct his own defence, and that of his comrade, and where no defence was possible he decided to attack the man he tried to murder. MacMahon deserved to die, he said, because he had led innocent men to death in the wars of Napoleon III, and worse still, as leader of the Versailles forces of oppression, he had plunged Paris into the bloodbath of the Commune. The Public Prosecutor tried in vain to stem the flow, and the shouts of approval from the public benches showed that the Red Spectre still walked in the Assize Court of the Seine. But when Olivier plunged into a defence of anarchy from the days of Pierre Proudhon to Bakunin and his Russians, he was stopped in a eulogy of Karl Marx and ruled unfit to plead.

The expected verdict was not long in coming. Guilty as charged, and the only surprise was that instead of the guillotine Olivier was given transportation for life to New Caledonia. His accomplice drew ten years at hard labour, and was dragged howling from the court.

Maître Leboyer accompanied Alain to the anteroom. "Very good, monsieur," he said deferentially. "You gave your evidence clearly and well, as I shall say when I write to *monsieur le ministre*."

"I didn't like it when that villain called him Killer de Grimont. Will it be in the papers?"

The attorney smiled thinly. "I think not," he said. "You must have seen how few reporters were in the press tribune. I'm sure I can persuade their editors – for a consideration – to omit that particular item from their pages."

He produced a slip of pasteboard. "My card, with the

address of my office, monsieur. I'm at your service on any future occasion. An honour to have met you – and I think Lieutenant Scheffler wants to speak to you."

The Lancer had entered the anteroom quietly, but he now came forward and took Alain's outstretched hand.

"Monsieur de Grimont, I was glad to see you in court, and looking so well," he said. "None the worse for my banging about, that night in the Rue Tronchet?"

"None at all, and I don't think Olivier was either, unless that healed cut on his cheek came from the edge of your sabre and not the flat."

"To hell with Olivier. I thought he'd get the chop, didn't you?"

"The guillotine? Yes, I did."

"Lieutenant Scheffler!" boomed a voice from the door.

"There's Vernet; he's got it in for me now. Look here, I owe you a dinner. You free tonight, by any chance? Good man! Meet me at Ledoyen in the Champs Elysées at nine o'clock."

Lieutenant Robert Scheffler arrived at Ledoyen a little before nine o'clock, just as the place was beginning to fill up. The restaurant had been opened during the Second Empire, and some of the older patrons thought, while dining at Ledoyen, that Sedan might never have been fought, Alsace and Lorraine never lost, and that Napoleon III was still secure on his throne. The place was a little jewel set in a garden, itself secluded in a leafy parterre of the Champs Elysées not far from the Place de la Concorde, where illuminated fountains were playing. There was a rosy fountain in the garden terrace of Ledoyen too, splashing gently into a lighted pool. Lieutenant Scheffler chose a table near the pool, gave his Lancer *schapska* to a page, and called for wine.

He was a dark haired young man of medium height, whose keen face was good-humoured rather than good-looking.

66

There were several other officers dining on the *terrasse*, all in uniform as army regulations required, but only one was accompanied by a girl. The expensive courtesans who expected to be shown off at Ledoyen preferred to dine indoors. Even in a breathless September they feared the puff of wind which might disarrange their elaborate coiffures, and liked best to be seen under the gaslight which reflected the sparkle of their jewels. Scheffler remembered that it was an argument about a jewel which had prompted his invitation to Alain de Grimont. Not that his mistress would have been with him at Ledoyen, because Faustine was playing in vaudeville at the Alcazar, but he would have been lounging in her dressing room, petting and teasing her whenever she came offstage, if she hadn't set her heart on an amethyst bracelet which cost more than he could afford to pay.

Faustine's sulks were a good enough reason for having dinner with another man. Especially when that man was Alain de Grimont, whom – as the Military Governor of Paris had furiously declared – he might easily have killed. "The son of the great Baron de Grimont! – the nephew of the Duc de la Treille!" Then why hadn't the baron or the duke been with the kid that morning, instead of the fusty old lawyer snuffling round him in the Assize Court of the Seine? Young de Grimont had looked forlorn and 'out of his plate' in the dingy anteroom: the music of Ledoyen's orchestra might cheer him up.

Alain arrived in a few minutes, shook hands with his host, looked round the *terrasse* admiringly and accepted a glass of wine. "This is wonderful!" said Alain, and he was not forlorn at all when he smiled.

"You haven't been here before?"

"Never. I'd only been in Paris for a couple of weeks before the night we – met, shall I say?"

"You've been a good sport about that, you know! Don't I

67

wish old MacMahon had ordered an escort of the Garde
Républicaine to meet him at the station!"

Alain laughed, but going straight to the point he said,
"Tell me what it's like to be on the Military Governor's
staff."

"It's better than being stuck in a *bled* like the Sahara,
smoking out the Kabyle rebels. I say, shall we order, and
dine out here? I wasn't able to get a late pass tonight."

While food and wine were brought they talked about the
trial, about Olivier's luck in escaping the guillotine, the
escape of the van men and the failure of the police to capture
any of them. But when the coffee was brought Lieutenant
Scheffler changed the subject and said, regarding the tip of
his cigarette, "You didn't look as if a posting to Algeria
would appeal to you, when you graduate from St Cyr."

"Hunting the Kabyle rebels – no. But how did you know
I'm going to St Cyr?"

"You told the police all about it in the *commissariat* when
we brought you in."

"I think I was a little bit off my head that night. Nothing
to do with what happened in the Rue Tronchet."

"Well, never mind that; what are you aiming at?"

"I'd like to serve on the eastern frontier."

"What do you mean by the frontier?" the Lancer asked.

"The new line of fortifications between Belfort and Epinal."

"You might as well be in the Sahara as at Epinal."

"I'm not sure I understand you, *mon lieutenant*," said Alain
stiffly. "The Belfort–Epinal line divides us from the enemy.
And you come from Alsace."

"That's true. You heard me say in court today that I was
born in Mulhouse. But I'm not a professional Alsatian, like
so many politicians who never set foot in the lost province."

Alain remembered Monsieur Scherer, reading *La Dernière
Classe* with tears in his eyes. But Monsieur Scherer was born

68

in Strasbourg; professional or not, he was genuine.

"I suppose it depends on a man's feelings," he said.

"Or how much he lost when the Germans took over. My father was one of the smart ones, he lost very little. His glass factory had to go, of course, that couldn't be helped. But the moment war with Prussia was declared, in July '70, he sold our house, transferred all his liquid assets to Switzerland, crossed the border and entered into partnership with a Swiss glass manufacturer he'd had some dealings with. We were all in Basel a month before the disaster."

"You were fifteen then?"

"Just fifteen. Are you wondering why I didn't stay safely in Switzerland?"

"You were too young to fight."

"Then I was. But I've a brother, he's twenty now, with a better business head than I'll ever have, who's working with my father. Of course they've all become Swiss citizens. I didn't feel the same way, so I joined the army for the usual reason, *la revanche*. I believed in all of it at first. I even believed the great Victor Hugo, when he preached a return to the France of an Idea with a sword. France and the Alsatian mystique! It took me nearly two years to realise how wrong he was. You can't go back to 1793 when you're living in the 1870s, and serving in an army nearly thirty years behind the times. The Germans had twice as many effectives in the field as we had in '70; they've probably three times as many today."

"Even now, when we've got universal conscription?"

"Even now. And forgive me, I didn't mean to give you a lecture on military theory. You'll have to listen to plenty of them in a month or so." And with a gesture of apology the Lancer looked at his watch.

"*Mon lieutenant*, I know you want to get back to your quarters. May I ask you one more question: do people really call the French Army 'the Great Unknown'?"

"They do, and I don't blame them. Don't worry about the time. I'll have them call a fiacre and drop you off at the Grand Hotel," said Scheffler.

"I'm not at the Grand any longer. I'm at the Continental for the next few days."

Scheffler whistled as he motioned to the waiters. "The Grand first, and now the Continental! I wonder how you'll take to dormitory life at St Cyr."

"When we meet again I'll tell you," said Alain, and the Lancer thought the kid had class. "Only next time you must allow me to be the host."

The great garden of the Tuileries was still brilliantly lit when Alain returned to his hotel room, half elated and half depressed by his dinner with Lieutenant Scheffler, who had said, almost in so many words, the same things as the Baron de Grimont had said about the frustrations of army life. He was nearly asleep when he realised that on the way to Ledoyen he had twice crossed, without thinking, the place where his mother was buried.

6

At the military college of St Cyr each new intake was called a
promotion, and each *promotion* was given a special name. Many
of the four hundred and fifteen cadets who passed the entrance examination in 1878 wished that the great name of
La Revanche had not been pre-empted by the students who
passed through the college from 1870 to 1872: the name
chosen for their own class seemed to have nothing to do with
their desire for vengeance on Germany or even with the
history of France. *La promotion des Zoulous*: it had to be
explained to the young entry that in Africa the Zulu tribe,
ruled by a warrior king named Cetewayo, was preparing to
challenge the greedy and overbearing British. In November
Cetewayo disregarded a British order to disband his *impis* of
black fighters armed with spears and assegais. This made him
a hero to young Frenchmen who believed that if Germany
was the conqueror to defeat, Britain was still the hereditary
enemy. That was all the Zulus meant to France in the late
autumn of 1878.

By that time Alain de Grimont had settled down happily
to life at the *Ecole Militaire Supérieure*. Robert Scheffler had

warned him that to enter St Cyr as the hero of the Rue Tronchet might be a handicap. "If the place is anything like it was three years ago," he said, "you'll come in for a lot of chaffing and even a bit of horseplay from the other fellows." Alain was grateful to King Cetewayo for taking the fellows' collective mind off jokes and jeering at his own expense, and after all the ragging hadn't lasted long. His classmates were only promoted schoolboys like himself, each trying hard to adapt to a new and austere way of life. General Hanrion, the commandant since 1871, who never played favourites and never alluded to meeting Cadet de Grimont at the Elysée, was as successful in keeping the horseplay to a minimum as he had been in quelling the near-riots in the college which followed the defeat of the Franco-Prussian War. He had been a cadet in the *promotion* of 1839, and while his military thinking had not advanced since then, he was a firm believer that an overload of work kept the juniors out of mischief in the first difficult weeks.

St Cyr, as an impressive collection of buildings, was nearly two hundred years old, established by Madame de Maintenon as a convent school for girls. It had been a military college since 1808, when Napoleon moved his own military school from Fontainebleau, and very little had been done to modernise it since. Gas lighting had been installed in 1861, and there were washbasins in the dormitories, but the water had to be carried from a tap on the second floor, and the diet in the refectory was Spartan. The classrooms and the riding school were too small for modern needs, and the facilities for heavy artillery practice, granted in that same year 1878, consisted of four days at Fontainebleau, where the seniors lived under canvas in the forest. The lecture curriculum consisted only of military theory, topography and geography, and administration and law practice.

Alain was blind to all the drawbacks. He was genuinely proud when he first put on the uniform, a short blue tunic with a double row of brass buttons, and red epaulettes. The trousers were red with a blue stripe, and when he donned the shako with its plume of red and white feathers, and the sabre belt with the buckle engraved *Ecole Militaire Supérieure*, he thought it suited him far better than the white tie and tails of his introduction to Paris society.

Paris society was only twelve miles away, but Alain saw nothing of it in the first hectic weeks of hurry from the Polygone to the Champ de Tir, from the Champ de Tir to the riding school and from there to the parade ground. *"Prenez sabre! Présentez sabre! Au drapeau!"* The shouted commands rang through the mornings, the Tricolore burned on the October mists. Presently some Paris leave was granted, strictly regulated by the time-table of trains to Versailles, three miles away, though some of the wealthy fathers wanted their sons to be fetched by carriage. One wealthy father was not forthcoming, for the Baron de Grimont's convalescence in the Sologne had been prolonged. There he obviously read the papers carefully, for when the St Cyr pass list was published he wrote a dry note to his son congratulating him on passing-in twenty-fifth. "Let us see how you pass out, two years hence," the letter ended. "I shall want an account of your progress when I return to Paris after the New Year."

Not until after the New Year? The Deputy for the Loiret absent from the Chamber which had resumed its sittings? For the first time, Alain put a sinister interpretation on Monsieur Imbert's hint about his father's health. If he dared, he would have asked for leave to visit the Sologne, but he knew that nothing short of death (Death?) would cause it to be granted. His first half day's leave in Paris came in December, when he gave Lieutenant Scheffler luncheon at the Café de la Paix. This time their talk dealt more with the stage and the stars of the *café concerts* than with *la revanche*. Before the meal was over they were Alain and Bob to each other, the Lancer having a fancy for English nicknames, and when the bill was paid Scheffler said casually:

"I know a girl who's playing at the Alcazar, and it's a matinée day. Shall we go along and see the show?"

"She's playing in the orchestra?"

"You really *are* green, aren't you. She doesn't play any instrument, she's a vaudeville artiste. Actually she's the lead singer in this show."

"Sounds exciting. What's her name?"

"Faustine de St Amand on the playbills, Marie Something-or-other when she's at home in Brittany. She can be good fun when she wants to be; we'll go round and see her after the show."

"Shouldn't I be in the way?"

"In the stalls?"

"In the dressing-room."

"You'll fit in."

Mademoiselle Faustine was changing from one costume of pink sateen and sequins into another of blue sateen and strass, when Lieutenant Scheffler's *billet*, in the shape of a cocked hat, was brought to her at the intermission. She sat frowning over it while her dresser waited, and then said roughly to the woman, "I'm expecting visitors. Go and ask M'selle Minette to speak to me, and then get out."

As the door closed Faustine was throwing her own petticoats, not as fresh as they might have been, behind a screen, and pushing towels stained with grease paint into a drawer. She was a handsome girl of twenty-five who had clawed her way out of the chorus line after she grew too tall for ballet but was not yet top of the bill at the Alcazar. The friend who now sidled in had not Faustine's ambition, but was content to be a neat little ballet dancer in a pink tutu, answering to other pet names besides Minette: Mimi, Minouche, and even Minet for little pussy cat. In a pussy purr she asked "Did you want me, darling?"

"Yes. Look, Minette, my Lancer's out front. I saw him in the stalls with a kid in uniform, and they're both coming round after the show."

"I thought you were going to chuck the Lancer."

"I didn't invite him to the matinée, *or* his college boy friend. That's his way of getting out of the evening show and giving me supper at the Café Anglais."

"What do you want *me* to do about it?"

"Take care of the friend while I talk to Bob. Oh my God, he must realise I can do better than a mere lieutenant who's a you-know-what . . ."

"Too bad he's not a Rothschild, darling. There goes the bell, we'll have to run."

When Alain de Grimont emerged from the red and golden setting of the music hall, intoxicated by the wild abandon of the can-can and the risqué songs, he was surprised to find the singer so dignified in a close-fitting wrapper of dark China silk trimmed with swansdown. She gave him her hand to kiss with the style of his Aunt Blanche, and seemed too grand for the shabby dressing room, which smelt of scent and sweat. But she relaxed when two bottles of Scheffler's champagne were brought in with a tray of little pastries. When Alain saw her licking mushroom sauce from the corners of her mouth, he thought that away from the allure of the foot-lights she was nothing but a *cabotine*.

Scheffler was the man in possession, that was obvious, but for how long and on what terms Alain was too inexperienced to guess. He felt that it was an intimate but not an easy relationship. There was bad temper in Faustine's flashing black eyes and her slangy banter: he much preferred Minette, younger and gentler, and with the fair curls which always appealed to him. They were seated together on a sofa so small that their hands touched as they lifted their glasses, and it was an easy step from caressing her little hand to slipping his arm round her waist.

Somehow it was from the shy Minette that the suggestion came to hold a New Year's Eve party in Faustine's apartment. They were well into the second bottle of Veuve Clicquot by that time, and everyone was enthusiastic. "You can get leave, can't you, Alain?" Scheffler asked, and Alain said he already had leave to dine that night with Monsieur Imbert and his family.

"*They* won't keep it up till midnight," said Bob Scheffler. "In the Parc Monceau, aren't they? You can drive from there to the Rue d'Amsterdam about the same time as the girls get back from the theatre. Now, who are we going to ask?"

"I'd have to catch the first morning train," protested the St Cyrien.

"You soldier boys really are a bore," said Faustine crossly. "Always fussing about leave, and duty — "

"Oh, shut up, Faustine," said Scheffler. "The kid's all right. You have to be on time at the Alcazar, haven't you?"

Under cover of their squabble Minette whispered,

"I'm sure we can arrange a bed for you."

"Is that a promise?"

The Rue d'Amsterdam was a long grey street running arrow-straight from the St Lazare station to the Place de Clichy on the frontier of Montmartre. It was doubtful if it had ever been decorated or brightly lit during the Universal Exhibition, but on 31 December 1878 the exhibition had long been over, and the great Head of Liberty had gone back to Auguste Bartholdi's workshop to await the completion of the Statue destined for New York Harbour. Even on New Year's Eve the *grands boulevards* had lost their sparkle, and under an icy December rain Paris was no longer the City of Light.

Alain's fiacre deposited him at the concierge-guarded door

of a respectable tenement halfway up the dreary street. 'Madame de St Amand', as the concierge called her, had an apartment on the second floor. "Are you paying the rent?", Alain had bluntly asked Bob Scheffler, who had replied with an oath. "Is it likely? I've been losing at the tables, and it's as much as I can do to pay for the supper."

"Can I help out?"

"I'm not reduced to sponging on my friends."

In spite of this unpromising beginning, Scheffler was a cheerful host when an elderly maid of all work, got up in a white cap and apron, showed Alain into a little parlour, where a blazing wood fire and cleverly arranged wax candles hid the deficiencies of the furniture. There was a polished upright piano covered with framed theatre programmes, and on the draped mantel a glass bell covered a gilt wreath presented to 'Madame Faustine de St Amand' for a concert appearance at the Universal Exhibition. Bob Scheffler gave Alain a boisterous slap on the back and introduced him to a group of men lounging round the fire with glasses in their hands. All were in uniform: three from the 88th Lancers and two from the Engineers.

"Is this an officers' mess or is it a party?" demanded Alain, and there was a general laugh.

"There's plenty of food and drink in the dining room," said Bob, indicating gaslight beyond an open door, "but we can't start on supper till the girls get here. And the girls are always late."

"Probably celebrating at the theatre," said someone.

"It's ten to midnight now. Same old story, every *réveillon*."

It was twenty minutes into 1879 when the girls from the Alcazar arrived, breathless, blaming their delay on the holiday audience, the manager, the door keeper and the cab drivers. The complaints were soon forgotten in a flurry of New Year wishes, the popping of champagne corks and indiscriminate kissing. Alain smelt brandy on Faustine's breath when he kissed her cheek, but she had not dropped her *grande dame* manner when she thanked him for his New Year *étrenne*, a swan of Sèvres china whose hollow body was stuffed with chocolates. He turned with relief to Minette, delicate in a white dress with tiny blue bows from neck to hem, and gave her a china kitten in exchange for a real kiss.

Within half an hour ten more people arrived from other theatres, and the *réveillon* supper was eaten with the men waiting on the ladies and the maid pouring the wine. Then a youth with long hair sat down at the piano and the singing began. Alain sat on the arm of Minette's chair while she leaned against him, exciting him with every movement of her pliant little body.

"You're beautiful tonight," he murmured under cover of a shouted chorus, and when she answered "Am I?" he said "Darling! Are you going to keep your promise to me?"

"What promise?"

"A bed for the night."

"I said it could be arranged – no more. And look!" Minette's whisper was so low that Alain pressed his cheek against her blonde curls to listen. "If you're a good friend to Bob Scheffler, you'll get him away from here before there's a terrible row with Faustine."

"But why?"

"She wants him to set her up in a better flat, and he won't play."

"I shouldn't think he could afford it."

"Not afford it! Don't you know who his father is?"

"A glass manufacturer, living in Switzerland since the war. What are you laughing at?"

"S-sh! We mustn't talk any more, because Faustine's going to sing."

She stood up with her back to the fireplace, so that the gilt crown of her singing triumph seemed to be reflected on her black hair. The smile she gave her lover as she shook out the red feather fan which matched her dress held no hint of coming trouble, and his applause was the loudest of all. Faustine sang *Rien n'est sacré pour un Sapeur*, an old favourite of the Second Empire which was a special tease for Engineer officers. The Engineers present applauded too, for Faustine sang well, though with a coarseness in her high notes which suggested that she might never reach the top of the bill at the Alcazar. Nobody was inclined to compete with her, and somebody suggested a dance.

"There isn't room to dance in this hole," Faustine said crossly, but when the furniture was pushed out of the way, and the dining room door left open, there was quite enough room for a waltz and a polka, and the wine they had all drunk copiously did the rest. The revellers danced until some of them began to stumble and collapse into laughter; the weary maid crept off unnoticed to her garret on the sixth floor, and at last a couple of the men went off to hunt up several fiacres from the all-night cab rank at the St Lazare station. Then the departures began, somewhat subdued on the landing, because the neighbours downstairs had begun to rap on the ceiling. The last '*Bonne Année!*' echoed up the stairwell, the front door slammed, and nobody was left in the flat but Faustine, asleep in her lover's arms on a sofa drawn up in front of the fire, and Minette, tiptoeing out of the room with her hand in Alain's. Scheffler looked up as they passed, and whispered "Sleep well!" Perhaps he woke Faustine, perhaps she was only feigning sleep, for as soon as he and Minette entered a back bedroom furnished with nothing but a big bed, a wardrobe and a rush-bottomed chair, Alain heard the parlour door open and close, and footsteps crossing the lobby.

"They're all right now," he said, and by Minette's pout saw that he should have been telling her how much more than all right she was, as each silken garment came off and each part of her slender body yielded to his kisses. To a boy

79

who had known nothing but the gymnastics of the skilful whores of Madame Cosette's house in Toulon, Minette was a revelation. She was just as skilful, but she could act loving, with sudden reticences, advances and retreats, bridal protests and murmured surrenders, until all the ardour of youth and starvation was poured into the guarded treasury, and they slept.

Sleeping with a girl, Alain discovered after an hour of oblivion, wasn't all it was cracked up to be. Perhaps it was because this was the first time for him, but he found it hard to adapt his own long body to Minette's graceful little form. Her slender arm, when it lay across his chest, seemed to have the weight of a blacksmith's; her knees were all bone, and painful. He tried easing her gently on to her back, and then she snored – a kitten's snore, but regular. He tried kissing her, and that woke his own desire again, but Minette was fast asleep and he was growing more wakeful, perhaps because of the feeble gaslight on which Minette had insisted. She said she was afraid to go to bed in the dark.

It was this wakefulness which made Alain aware of voices in another room. They were subdued at first and then grew louder, punctuated by a woman's sobs. Next came the sound of a man's booted tread in the lobby, followed by the swish of a woman's robe, and then the rising scream of Faustine's hysteria. Alain sat up in bed to listen. He heard the noise of a heavy blow which could only have come from a man's hand, and then a louder crash and a splintering of glass.

He was out of bed in an instant. He had learned about fast dressing at the college, and he scrambled into his uniform and even tied his bootlaces before Minette was fully awake.

"What are you doing, *chéri*? It isn't time to go yet – "

"It's time to stop whatever's going on next door. They may be killing each other for all I know. Or jumping out of the window."

"Not Faustine, I can hear her screaming. Don't interfere, she'll calm down very soon – "

Alain paid no attention. In the parlour he found Scheffler, in his shirt, breeches and boots, holding a handkerchief to a cut on his cheek. Faustine had flung the glass bell at his head, and it lay in splinters on the floor between them. Scheffler kicked the gilt wreath out of the way when Alain came in.

"*Bonjour*," he said in his most matter-of-fact voice, "You look as if you're ready to go."

"Ready when you are."

"Then be a good fellow and get the rest of my stuff from the other room. I've got to try and calm this woman down – "

Minette was in the lobby, dressed as far as her petticoat and camisole, but with bare feet. "Put your shoes on before you go in there," Alain said, more roughly than he meant. "Faustine's in hysterics, and some glass got broken."

"What time is it?"

"Just after five."

"Then I'll dress and go up for the maid. Jeanne always knows how to deal with hysterics."

So prompt, so practical, so unlike the soft little creature he had possessed! Alain picked his friend's dark blue cutaway from the back of a chair in the disordered bedroom, looked about for more 'stuff' and found nothing, and went back to the parlour. He tried not to look at Faustine while Scheffler pulled on the cutaway – their overcoats, képis, and gauntlets had been hung in the little *entrée* – she was writhing and moaning on the sofa, calling the man who had been her lover a pig, a miser, a coward, a bastard, a dog. He bent over her, not tenderly.

"Now that's enough, Faustine," he said. "Stop that racket. You'll have the neighbours in."

She pulled herself up on all fours, like an animal, and spat at Scheffler:

"Get out, you Jew!"

81

He flung a latchkey on the table, and got out.

The grey Rue d'Amsterdam was as black as pitch on the freezing winter morning, for every second gas lamp had been switched off, and only a few lighted windows where early workers lived threw a little illumination on the icy pavements. The only sound was made by two pairs of army boots moving in cadence, until Scheffler broke the silence.

"Sorry to let you in for a sickening scene like that."

"Would you mind telling me what it was all about?"

"Faustine wanted me to set her up in a smart flat in the Faubourg St Honoré, and I wouldn't play. So, one thing led to another, and when the hysterics began I slapped her face to bring her round, and then she threw that damned glass bell at me. Thank God the women can't throw straight."

"Your cheek's bleeding, though."

"Damnation! The metal wreath did that. I'll get it cleaned up in the station, we're nearly there. And they'll have some coffee going for the *cheminots*."

The *lavabos* of the Gare St Lazare provided nothing sanitary but running water, but it stopped the trickle of blood, and Bob Scheffler kept his face turned away from the railway workers who were gathering round a zinc counter and a coffee urn. They obviously resented the arrival of two young swells in regimentals, but nothing was said, and the swells were given thick mugs of scalding coffee, bitter with an infusion of chicory.

"Did you give Minette any money?"

"Yes," said Alain, "but she doesn't know it yet. She'll find it when she opens the china kitten, looking for bon-bons."

"Then you're quits. Look here, I don't expect you to take any advice from me, because I got you into it, but don't get sentimental about Minette. She and Faustine hunt in couples; they're the perfect foil for one another."

"How long were you with Faustine?"

"Six months. Six months too long." And Scheffler looked

at his bleeding cheek in the scratched mirror behind the counter.

"She certainly used some vile language tonight," said Alain tentatively.

"Well, I may be a miser from her point of view, but I'm not a bastard; what you really want to know is, am I a Jew?"

"Are you?"

"My father's Jewish, and I was brought up in his religion. My mother's a Catholic. That suit you?"

"It doesn't make the slightest difference to me," said Alain in distress.

"I suppose you're wondering how I got into St Cyr, and was commissioned."

Alain was silent. During his first term at the military college he had learned from boys with older brothers or fathers in the Service that the army, by tradition royalist and Catholic, was in a covert way antisemitic.

"You must have done damned well," he compromised, "to get on to the staff of the Governor of Paris."

"That was a real stroke of luck, because the Governor's a friend of Clemenceau and Gambetta, and holds very liberal opinions. Besides, my father was one of the largest private contributors to the fund for repayment of the German war indemnity."

Alain thought of the Jewish Alsatian who had scented danger, and sacrificed his house and factory to cross the border into Switzerland with his fortune intact. "The glass business must be very profitable," he said drily.

"My father has other interests."

A bell rang in the distance, and the railwaymen drained their mugs and glasses and hurried off to work. The first train of the day was steaming into the Gare St Lazare, the smoke billowing out beneath the high glass roof. Alain had never taken his eyes off his friend. "He doesn't *look* like a Jew!" he thought. His only idea of how a Jew should look came from a villainous picture of Shylock in his French translation of Lamb's *Tales from Shakespeare.*

"But I've had enough of this — this favouritism!" Scheffler was saying violently. "Easy duty in Paris — playing *écarté* at the Jockey Club and dangling round the music halls. I'm going to apply for an overseas posting — "

"Overseas?"

"I'm in the mood to go as far as Indo-China. But it'll probably be Algeria. I'll be more use fighting the Kabyle rebels than slapping hysterical women."

"Well," said Alain de Grimont, "let me know what you decide . . . When you get back to barracks, have the surgeon take a look at your cheek . . . I'm going to miss the Versailles train."

"Not you," said Robert Scheffler, with the ghost of his cheery smile. "You're on the way to being General de Grimont, who catches all his trains on time. Good luck to you!"

"Good luck to you too." They shook hands, and as Alain turned away the Lancer called after him:

"Happy New Year!"

7

Scheffler was as good as his word. Before the New Year was
two weeks old it was announced in the *Gazette* that Lieutenant Robert Scheffler, 88th Lancers, had exchanged into the
33rd Tirailleurs, stationed at Algiers. On the same day Alain
de Grimont received the new Sharpshooter's visiting card
with the conventional *pour prendre congé* – 'to take leave' –
scribbled across it. That was all, and Alain guessed that
Scheffler was too ashamed of the Faustine episode to send a
more personal message. As ashamed as he was himself when
he remembered his feelings during the post-coital depression
of his three miles' tramp from Versailles to St Cyr on New
Year's morning. Uppermost in his mind had been distaste for
the astute father who had emigrated to Switzerland before
the 'Disaster' with enough money and influence to get a
commission for his elder son. Smart work – but then the Jews
were supposed to be very smart! Alain pulled himself up
short before he reached the college gate. That's just the way
some of the fellows talk, and I won't do it, he decided.
What's old man Scheffler's religion to me?

Before young Scheffler left Paris, however, Alain had

received one lengthy personal message, in the longest letter he ever had from his father. After formal New Year wishes, the baron condescended to explain to his son why he had stayed so long away from Paris. It was nothing to do with his health, which was now excellent. The autumn elections had kept him busy in his constituency, and these had been followed by the problems of the estate. Here followed a description of the property in the Sologne so detailed that it read like the advertisement of a sale. It was, 'as Alain knew', a sporting estate, with only four farms, excluding the home farm, rated as arable land. But the estate agent, having antagonised the farmers, had to be dismissed, and the head keeper — 'Alain would remember old Samson?' — was too old for the job at seventy, and had been retired on a pension. Interviewing candidates for the two jobs, and visiting every one of the farms, had taken time, but the land was in good heart, and Alain might expect to see his father in Paris soon.

Always suspicious of the baron as country gentleman, Alain felt there was something false in the whole tone of the letter. A major political crisis was brewing in the capital, and it was very unlike a man who had thriven on crises to bury himself in the country — unless it was a case of falling back for a better jump?

He read the papers carefully. Léon Gambetta, the fiery leader who proclaimed the Republic after the defeat of Sedan and inspired the continuing war against the Prussians, was now leading an attack on President MacMahon. He demanded that five generals, well over the age limit of service, be relieved of their commands, the implication being that the venerable President should go too.

"Here I am and here I'll stay!" Marshal MacMahon had cried when he stood victorious on the Malakoff. But the Crimean War was twenty years back, and he was no longer able to defend the palace of the Elysée. He resigned the presidency with more than a year of his mandate to run, and was succeeded in office by Jules Grévy.

For the St Cyr cadets the chief interest of the crisis was that their commandant, General Hanrion, was one of the veterans to be placed on the retired list. Boys who had called him an old fool, or worse, a month before, now said he was a fine man, badly treated by the infernal radicals, and there was anxious speculation about his successor. For Alain de Grimont the crisis had only begun with the new president's choice of Monsieur Waddington as his prime minister, and the latter's attempts to form a government, such being a perennial delight of the politically minded French. When the *Figaro* announced that the Baron de Grimont had returned to Paris for a midnight consultation with the new premier, Alain saw what the end would be. His father invited him to luncheon at the Grand Hotel on the very day his appointment as Minister of Justice was announced.

"Congratulations!" was an easy word to say, and an easy bridge over the gap which opened between father and son with the ugly revelation of the mother's death, and de Grimont's fury at his son's involvement in the affray on the Rue Tronchet. There were smiles and handshakes, even a paternal slap on the back for the cadet. All was warmth, even to the blazing fire which had replaced the summer greenery in the salon grate, even to the demure gaiety instead of the old death's head look on Bertrand's face. "Monsieur Alain looks very well," said the valet, bringing in a decanter of porto by way of apéritif. "Does *monsieur le ministre* think he's grown?"

"Broadened, certainly," said the minister affably. Drill and physical training had squared Alain's shoulders and made his spine ramrod straight: wry and unbidden came his father's thought, *a son to be proud of*.

"Congratulations again, and good luck," said Alain,

raising his glass in salute. "It's what you really wanted, isn't it – much, much more than a seat in the Senate?"

"Yes, it is," confessed the minister. "I admit I'd hoped for it, because in France any politician worth his salt is pretty certain of a second chance. But nothing could be done until we'd got rid of MacMahon. That's why I stayed down in the country and let Gambetta do the dirty work. I was pretty sure of Waddington, and sudden as the call was, I was ready for it."

"But it's a terrific job for a man of your age," said Alain tactlessly. "Are you positive your health will stand it?"

"You must have heard some of the rumours going about Paris, that I was suffering from cancer of the liver. Not a word of truth in it! The Vichy cure and a good rest was all I needed. As for my age, I'm fifty-four. Just the right age to get back in harness."

"Back at the Place Vendôme," said Alain. He remembered how often, as a little boy, he had asked his nurse, "Where's my papa? When's he coming home?" and was told not to be a nuisance. "Your papa's a very important man. He's at the ministry in the Place Vendôme."

"I'll tell you who's feeling his age since they turned him out to pasture," said de Grimont with a smile. "MacMahon. Were you sorry when you heard about his fall? Considering you saved his life . . . "

"That was a lucky accident. My friends at St Cyr are more concerned with who's going to replace General Hanrion. I suppose *you* know?"

"I'll tell you about that over luncheon."

Bertrand, who was waiting on table, presented a very short menu: oysters, *vol-au-vent*, *crème brûlée*. Before the muscadet was poured, de Grimont said confidentially, "Your new commandant will be General Cholleton. Never heard of him? Doesn't matter. He's only a stop gap, until they find an officer with some modern ideas on fire power and weaponry."

"I'm very glad to hear it."

"You are, eh? Do I detect a slight note of disillusion with the Premier Bataillon de France? Too out of touch with reality, even for a *revanchard* like yourself? You haven't told me what progress you're making in your studies — if any?"

It was the old sarcastic note of the Sologne questionnaires, which the de la Treille boys had hated.

Alain replied serenely, "I was first in topography in the term exams."

"*First?* First in the whole *promotion*? Well done, my boy; that *is* good news!"

And the Minister of Justice positively beamed.

"That extra coaching in maths at Toulon helped a lot," said Alain modestly.

"Or the head for figures you inherited from my father."

"From my grandfather? Not from you?"

"Words, not figures, were my forte. But my father, in his day, was something of a financial wizard."

"I don't know much about my grandfather de Grimont," said Alain. "Except that he built the château, and helped old King Louis Philippe — "

"That came later. He started life as plain Henri Grimont, born in one of the little back streets which were swallowed up by the Rue de Rivoli. *His* father was a cobbler, and my father was his errand boy."

"A — cobbler? You mean he made boots and shoes?"

"Nothing so grand. Patching, soling and heeling were more in his line. But they both worked hard, and my father began to speculate with his earnings at just the right time, when the railway development began. He was well off by the time I was born, and able to send me to the Lycée Louis-le-Grand for the education he never had himself. Is all this news to you?"

"Absolutely."

"I thought the Duc de la Treille would have revelled in the story of the cobbler's shop!"

"He never mentions the Grimonts," said Alain coldly. "But I think it's a story to be proud of."

"Do you indeed?" the baron smiled at the dark flush on the boy's face. "It certainly brought rich rewards, including the château. That's what I want to talk to you about, but not today. I must be back in the Place Vendôme by half past two to discuss some of the château problems with Maître Leboyer. Then next week we can all three meet in his office, where the estate maps and deeds are kept."

"If I can get a Paris pass."

"I think you'll find General Cholleton generous in that respect. And in your summer leave you'll come to the Sologne and meet all the farmers, who are forever clamouring for either improvements or reductions in their rent."

"I think I've met most of them already, and they were always very nice to me."

"Of course they were *gentil*, as you call it, to a boy larking about with a sporting rifle. Now you must be serious with them. Because the whole place will be yours some day."

The men who knew him best, like Monsieur Imbert, declared that his reappointment as Minister of Justice had made a new man of Hubert de Grimont. He looked younger, moved faster, and conducted the business of his high office with the same energy he had shown under Napoleon III. In a government devoted to colonial expansion, he pursued domestic policy by harassing the police, and taunting them with their failure to arrest a single one of the van conspirators in the plot to assassinate MacMahon. In the Chambre des Députés he issued warnings about the Russian infiltrators of the French Left, begun during the Commune, and attacked Gambetta for the amnesty bill which was about to become law. He clashed with the Minister of the Interior and the

Prefect of the Seine, both of whom considered the police to be under their authority, and he set up his own network of informers, who failed to smoke out any Russians, but did discover two clubs called respectively the Friends of Louise Michel and the Friends of Henri de Rochefort, the most vociferous of the Commune convicts at present in New Caledonia. These were the two whose amnesty and return to France were the most dreaded by de Grimont.

So much activity meant that the conference with Maître Leboyer had to be postponed for a couple of weeks, and by that time Alain had himself well in hand and adjusted to the idea that he was the grandson of a cobbler's errand boy as well as of the sixteenth Duc de la Treille. He began to learn how to dissemble, so that both his father and the attorney were pleased with his intelligent comments on the boundaries, rent roll, rateable value and agricultural workers on the Sologne estate, in which he had no real interest at all. His mother had laughed at the château, designed by the first Baron de Grimont as a reduced version of one of the châteaux of the Loire, so Alain laughed too, though apart from the bastard architecture and the *nouveau riche* taste, Alain began to think rather well of 'old Grimont'. He had started from nothing, and worked like the devil to make a fortune; Alain decided that work should be his own salvation. He took a higher place in class than ever, and his report from the commandant read 'Promising officer material'. Life under canvas, during the short four days the *promotion des Zoulous* spent in heavy artillery practice at Fontainebleau, suited him exactly; it was only after they came back to St Cyr that the *promotion* started taking its disparaged name too seriously.

The African Zulus had been a topic of great interest ever since their warrior chief, Cetewayo, inflicted a crushing defeat on the British in an ambush at Isandhlwana, in which eight hundred British and five hundred African troops were killed. That was entertaining news for the French, but the real sensation came later, when it was announced that the Prince Imperial would end his English exile by going out with his own battery to join the punitive expedition. Bonapartist or royalist, most of the St Cyr cadets identified with the emperor's son who wanted to see action, because action – preferably in Alsace – was what they wanted to see themselves. The Duke of Cambridge would only allow 'young Louis Bonaparte' – the Prince Imperial – to go out to Africa as a spectator, but when the troopship reached Cape Town he could put on his uniform and join Lord Chelmsford's force.

Monsieur Déléage, war correspondent of *Le Matin*, sent home encouraging despatches. The Prince Imperial was brave and distinguished himself in the minor actions of the beginning of the campaign. He was cheerful, amusing, and popular with officers and men. He was a magnificent horseman, having bought and mastered a vicious horse called Fate. The small Bonapartist party in France exulted. The young gunner was proving himself a true descendant of a Corsican gunner of the glory days.

Then came the terrible news. On 1 June Lieutenant Carey, in command of a patrol which included the prince, fell into a Zulu trap while bivouacked on the road to Itelezi, and fled on horseback without a thought for the young man in his especial charge. The Prince Imperial's own escape was undone by a broken strap on Fate's harness. On foot he turned, alone, to face the Zulus, and died, the only casualty, beneath their assegais.

The story stirred the whole of France to anger. It was a British plot, it was said: Queen Victoria had planned it herself to rid Europe of the Bonapartist claimant. It was a plot laid by the Freemasons, said the clerical party. It was not Queen Victoria, came the contradiction. It was her Jewish prime minister, Benjamin Disraeli, who had incited 'International Jewry' to plan the death of the future Emperor of the French.

The reactions at St Cyr paralleled those in the country as a whole. Many of the cadets believed in the 'British plot' theory, while a vocal minority put the blame on international Jewry. The covert antisemitism shown in the past by a few sneering remarks now became a spate of insults and accusations, driving Alain de Grimont to protest. "What infernal rubbish!" he said. "What the hell have the Jews to do with the Zulus? The only one to blame for the prince's death is that damned coward Carey, who deserves something worse than a court martial. Leave the Jews out of it, for heaven's sake."

"Are you a Jew-lover, de Grimont?" asked a cadet called St Etienne.

"I'm not a Jew-hater, at any rate."

"Are you implying that I am? Shall we continue this discussion in the Bois de Boulogne?"

"And get ourselves expelled for duelling? Don't be a fool!"

That was a typical exchange of the time, but it was nothing compared to the free fight which broke out in the mess hall after a royalist cadet proposed a toast to Cetewayo, whose men had rid France of the last of the Bonapartes. The commandant called it riotous assembly, and retaliated by confining the whole corps of cadets to barracks for two weeks, the period immediately preceding the summer examinations. Alain had to write to his father excusing himself from another meeting with Maître Leboyer, while saying as little as possible about his own share in the quarrels. The Justice Minister's reply was sharp and to the point.

"You're a bigger fool than I thought if you imagined freedom of speech would be tolerated in the army. Keep your mouth shut if you want success in the Great Unknown."

While his son endured a confinement to barracks filled with close-order drill, hours of target practice and double periods in study hall, the Minister himself was extremely vocal. He organised a police raid on a Montmartre tenement where the Friends of Louise Michel were having a secret meeting. They were all survivors of the Women's Battalion which Comrade Michel had organised when the National Guard rose against the government, and which had fought like wildcats until the day of the Commune's defeat. They had escaped justice in 1871, but warrants had been issued for their arrest and were still in force; de Grimont had six of the Friends of Louise Michel imprisoned until they could be brought before the Assize Court of the Seine on charges of treasonable conspiracy.

Whereupon Léon Gambetta, the sponsor of the amnesty bill, demanded their release, and was vigorously attacked by de Grimont in the Chamber.

As a topic it shared the headlines with the ceremonial return of the Prince Imperial's body to his sorrowing mother, and the final defeat of Cetewayo and his Zulus at the battle of Ulundi.

That was on the fourth of July, and a few days later Alain de Grimont, examinations behind him, received a Paris pass and made for the Grand Hotel. The impersonal hotel suite was just as it had been a year before, with greenery in the grate, the bust of Julius Caesar not an inch out of place, and the malachite clock ticking time away. *"Monsieur le ministre* expected to be detained," said the deferential voice of Bertrand. "May I bring you something to drink, Monsieur Alain?"

"It's too hot for anything but seltzer water, thanks, Bertrand."

As he stood at the open window, with the tall glass in his hand, Alain thought hopefully of the holiday ahead. He and his father had achieved an armed neutrality which promised well for their visit to the Sologne, and then he was going to Hyères and the dear familiarity of life with the de la Treilles. Released from the monastic existence of St Cyr he would find girls, pretty and charming girls, but above all willing girls, who whether for love or money would grant him the favours of his rampant imagination, and he smiled in anticipation at the Parisiennes two storeys beneath him, studying the shop windows of the Boulevard des Capucines.

He saw the coupé from the Grand Hotel livery stable come up to the door and stop. Alain hastily buttoned his tunic, unfastened because of the July heat: he saw that his father's frock coat, as he got stiffly out of the coupé, was as tight as ever, his hands in dark kid gloves. At that moment, before he reached the pavement, a woman sprang forward and called out his name.

"De Grimont! Assassin!"

The Minister of Justice tried to brush her aside. But the woman was armed. She drew a pistol from the folds of her black silk cloak, and with a cry of "Remember Louise Michel!" she shot him down.

Alain rushed out of the salon. He shouted to Bertrand in the little service kitchen, "Quick, Bertrand! My father's hurt!" and side by side they ran downstairs into the hall.

As usual at that time of day it was crowded, and the crowd were saying all the usual things at the pitch of their voices. Get a doctor, give him air, he opened his eyes then, the police are here, they've got the woman ... but Alain, kneeling on the floor by his father's body, said only "Is he dead?"

A hand gripped his shoulder and a voice above his head said, "No, no, monsieur, the Minister is regaining consciousness. He must be taken to his rooms at once!"

Rising stiffly to his feet, Alain recognised one of the under managers of the Grand Hotel, a careful Swiss called Müller who, after the bad publicity of attempted murder on the doorstep, wanted to avoid the presence of a corpse in the foyer. He gave some terse orders to the two hall porters who had carried de Grimont inside the hotel.

"A doctor!" said Alain hoarsely. "A doctor's the first thing – "

"One of our present guests is a medical man. I shall send to his room immediately . . . Quick, you men!" The two porters appeared with a long, hard sofa to serve as a stretcher, and gently lifted the inert body on to the cushions. Alain followed them slowly upstairs. When they reached the suite he found that Bertrand, who had rushed ahead, had brought a pile of towels from the bathroom and stripped the pillows and brocaded cover from the baron's four-poster bed.

"Lay him down quite flat," he said with authority, and the porters, their task done, hurried back to the entrance hall, where half a dozen policemen were now taking depositions from anybody who could qualify as a witness to the crime.

"We must cut off monsieur's clothing," said Bertrand. "I have a good pair of scissors in the kitchen. You put a cold compress on his forehead." Alain obeyed. He did more; with a damp towel he wiped the bloody froth from his father's moustache, for the man was bleeding from the mouth now as well as in the spurts from the chest which deepened the red of the rosette of the Legion of Honour in his lapel. Alain reached for a linen towel and turned to soak it in the pitcher of water Bertrand had brought. Only then he saw the portrait of his mother by Alexandre Cabanel, painted when Elvire de Grimont was twenty, and in all the splendour of her beauty, as her son first remembered her. It was hung on the wall opposite the foot of the bed.

"Quick now, Monsieur Alain," said Bertrand, arriving with the scissors. "Try to draw off his gloves, will you?"

"I wish the doctor would be quick."

He arrived just as Bertrand had cut through the layers of coat, waistcoat, shirt and vest, and held another wet towel on the bullet wound, pressing on the side nearest the heart. The valet muttered "Thank God!" as Monsieur Müller entered on tiptoe and introduced Dr Dandieu.

The doctor was middle-aged, short and dark, with an abrupt manner of speaking.

"Sorry for the delay," he said. "Was in the restaurant. Had to go back to my room for my bag. Bad business, eh? You're the son? And you?" (to the valet) "you seem to have kept your head."

"I was a medical orderly in the late war, monsieur."

"Humph! Well, let's have a look at him. Heart-beat feeble but distinct. Heavy loss of blood, prognosis bad. Have to extract the bullet, and I'll need some help."

"Can I do anything?" said Monsieur Müller.

"Better get back to your office and handle the police. You'll do, my medical orderly, and as for you, *jeune homme*, wait in the next room. Don't want a crowd in here."

There it was again, that hateful *jeune homme*, the 'young man' he thought he had outgrown! Feeling utterly useless, and in a turmoil of pity, shock and anger, Alain returned to the salon. The hands of the malachite clock had moved on only half an hour. Alain picked up the glass which had held the seltzer water, without remembering when he dropped it on the rug. Down in the street the police were still interrogating passers-by, and while Alain watched a man in a blue smock emerged from the hotel with a little bucket and sprinkled ashes on the puddle of de Grimont's blood.

How long he sat with his head in his hands Alain could not have told, but at last Bertrand came to his side, the slave in the Roman triumph, whose grim *memento mori* was justified at last.

"Monsieur Alain," he said, and there were tears in his eyes, "it's very bad. The doctor got the bullet out, but the right lung was damaged, and the haemorrhage can't be stopped. Dr Dandieu says a priest should be sent for, if such is your desire."

Alain thought of the good Father Gillet at Hyères, and Aunt Blanche's gentle piety: he knew what they would say. What he felt bound to say was, "Would it be my father's desire, if he could speak?"

"He can speak, he has said your name more than once. And monsieur has always practised his religion faithfully."

"Then ask Monsieur Müller to send to the Madeleine, that's the nearest church. Wait, Bertrand! Before you go, tell me how long has that picture of a lady hung at the foot of Monsieur de Grimont's bed?"

"The portrait of madame la baronne? Ever since I entered his service in this very place, back in 1873."

Six years of looking at the lovely face of the wife he had deserted and called unfaithful! Six years of remorse, perhaps, of proof that he must have loved Elvire de la Treille! How little I knew him, thought their son. I didn't even know he was *pratiquant*. And now he's dying as my mother died, from the bullet of a fanatic. Remember Louise Michel! That damned Commune, will France never hear the end of it?

The door opened a crack, and Dr Dandieu said in a staccato whisper, "Well then! Priest been sent for?"

"Yes."

"Don't think he'll get here in time. Father's been asking for you. Wants a few minutes – mind, no more – with you alone."

The bandaged figure on the bed was lightly covered with a sheet, but there was intelligence in the dying man's eyes, and the faintest movement of his right hand. Alain knelt down at the bedside and took the limp hand in his own. From the wall the beautiful young face looked down on them both. Cabanel was a flattering painter, but he had allowed the faintest tinge of mockery to flicker in Elvire's smile.

"Alain." His father spoke faintly, and with pauses between each word. "Alain, I'm sorry . . . for . . . all of it."

"Father, I'm sorry too."

Before the tinkling of a silver bell announced the priest, the hand in Alain's hand was cold.

PART TWO

The General

8

It was the beginning of March 1884, and General Georges Boulanger had been the commander of the French Army of Occupation in Tunisia for less than a month. He had made it his custom to begin the day at his Tunis headquarters with a relaxed discussion, over cigars, with his military secretary.

"I find these informal chats with you invaluable, major," he liked to say. "I learn more about my staff from you than from all the official records. But then you've been here since the beginning, haven't you?"

That could mean 'here since the invasion' or 'here since the start of the Occupation', but in any form it was a flattering reminder that the major was a veteran of the Tunisian war. Not that it had been much of a war. Merely a step forward in the colonial development which was giving France back the prestige lost in the Franco-Prussian War.

Major Millet, a cool and competent Norman, had not quite made up his mind about the informal chats. He thought uneasily of them as gossip, or even tale-bearing beyond the call of duty. He felt that 'informality' was one of the new-fangled ideas General Boulanger had brought back from the United States.

The major would have been shocked at the mere idea that he admired masculine good looks, but he was aware that Boulanger's looks were impressive. The troops were aware of it too. When he rode on to the parade ground they snapped to a *garde-à-vous* which vibrated with enthusiasm; Millet thought it was due as much to his youth as to his bearing in the saddle and the blond beard which suited his well-cut features. Officers and men alike had been accustomed to old generals, men in their sixties or even seventies, the men who had lost the war with Prussia, and Boulanger, when he went to Tunis, was only forty-seven and looked younger. Even in undress uniform, relaxed in his desk chair and facing an audience of one, he looked like what some soldiers already called him: the man of destiny.

General Boulanger, perfectly aware of the major's scrutiny, smiled inwardly. The son of an impecunious solicitor at Rennes, he had not done well at St Cyr, but what he lacked in class marks he more than made up for in physical courage. He had fought in Algeria and Cochin China, was wounded at Magenta in the war for Italian unity, and in the war with Prussia made a sensational escape from Metz, where Marshal Bazaine had allowed himself to be besieged. He joined Thiers in opposition to the Commune. In all these fields of action he had developed his power over the minds of men, so that he seemed the logical choice to head the French military deputation to the United States in 1881, when the centenary of the Battle of Yorktown was celebrated. Successful in all he undertook, the general was aware of only one serious mistake, his arranged marriage with his cousin Louise Rénouard from whom he was now separated. She lived with her daughters in what had been the family home at Versailles.

"I was rather interested," the general began casually, "in something Lieutenant de Grimont said in the mess last night."

"Lieutenant de Grimont is fond of saying interesting things, *mon général*. What was it this time?"

"He said the native insurrection against the French protectorate was called by them a *jehad*, or holy war. As it happens, I had never heard the word *jehad* before."

"That young man is fond of showing off his knowledge of the dialect."

"How did he acquire it?"

"In the usual manner, sir — in the arms of his Moslem mistress."

"Aha! So the female natives don't carry on a holy war with their conquerors?"

"An unholy war, if all I hear is true."

"De Grimont can afford to indulge his fancies, major. He's a rich man, and a landed proprietor, no?"

"*Was* a landed proprietor," the major emended. "Do you remember when his father was murdered by one of Louise Michel's viragoes, back in '79?"

"I remember something about it. What did the woman get? Transportation to New Caledonia?"

"Gambetta got her sentence reduced to five years in prison. No point in sending her to New Caledonia, her comrades were packing up to return to France under the amnesty bill."

"And what happened to the landed property?"

"That's where de Grimont shows his eccentric strain. He likes to pose as the champion of the underdog. That talk about the *jehad* — and it's not the first time *I've* heard him on the subject — might even make you think he sympathised with the natives. Then, when his father was killed, he announced that he didn't mean to use the title, and after he'd paid for improvements to his farms, he put the whole estate up for sale."

"What, right away?"

"No, he was a minor then, with a trustee. He sold the place as soon as he came of age."

"Who was his trustee?"

"His uncle, the Duc de la Treille."

"De la Treille, eh? We were in the same hospital ward in Milan after the battle of Magenta. I wouldn't have expected *his* nephew to be a radical."

"But no, *mon général*," said the major in a hurry, "the lieutenant's no radical. He's a dependable officer, and fought well after Sfax, but he does tend to be ... shall I say controversial? He's obsessed with Alsace-Lorraine, which I suppose is to his credit, but I never feel his heart's in Tunisia."

"Only his body," said Boulanger with a smile, and changed the subject.

The body of Alain de Grimont was at that moment in a version of the Moslem paradise, except that instead of being caressed by half a dozen houris he was in the clasp of only one, and lying on a silken couch— the silk frayed and tattered— in the ruins of what had been a palace. A light breeze from the Mediterranean blew through the fretwork frame of an empty window, and on the carved table level with the couch were wine and sherbet, fruit and Turkish cigarettes in a jewelled box. Everything in the room, from the hanging lamps swinging on gilt chains from the high roof painted in red and green, to the mosaic jars where incense burned, had been salvaged by the girl from the evacuation of the Moslem quarter of Tunis.

Melissa, as Alain de Grimont called her, was twenty now, which meant that she had been seventeen when the French invasion of Tunisia took place. That was after the Société Franco-Africaine purchased a vast tract of land called the Enfida and proceeded to exploit the property and the people, thus checkmating the Italians, who had to confine their own expansion to Tripoli across the eastern border. Melissa's marriage was arranged when the bridegroom whom she had never seen was killed in the *jehad*, the holy war proclaimed by the followers of Islam when the French announced their regency over Tunisia, a Beylik of the Ottoman Empire once enriched by piracy but fallen into decay. The *jehad* had not lasted long after the French sent gunboats to bombard the port of Sfax and invaded the town, although with heavy losses to their land forces, before advancing on Tunis.

Melissa was one of the lucky girls who had been neither raped nor abused by the conquerors before the French protectorate was established, and of the three French officers who had been her lovers she liked Alain de Grimont by far the best. Some girls she had known were prostitute to the French NCOs, living in the *fondouks* divided into mean little rooms with tiled floors, and foraging for food round the French camps. She was living in her own home, with an acquiescent mother in the background, servants to wait upon her, and a pillared marble patio where she waited for Alain. She had known how to adapt herself to the misfortunes of war.

She hung over Alain now as he woke from sleep, not drowsily or grumpily as so many did, but at once alert and aware of her. She wiped the sweat of the siesta from his brow with her long black hair, opening her mouth for his kisses and shuddering with pleasure as he parted her thin robe and pulled her body above his own.

"*Viens, mon adorée*!" She understood French as well as he understood Arabic, and the command was part of their ritual of love. "*Viens, Melissa, jouis!*"

She straddled his body, which she loved for its smoothness, and prolonging the pleasure bent forward to lick the triangle of fair hair growing on his breast, and waited for the moment when he turned her on her back, the moment of the deeper, plunging strokes of their mutual *jouissance*. He lay beside her then, enjoying her submissive beauty, and smoothing over her golden shoulders the iridescent gauze robe so much more practical for love-making than the voluminous garments of his Paris mistress.

Alain de Grimont, at nearly twenty-four, was far more sophisticated in his sexuality than the inexperienced youth who had gone to bed with a little dancer in the Rue d'Amsterdam. He had steered clear of the *coulisses* of the theatre since that New Year's morning, once his inherited wealth and title gave him the entrée to Paris society. He had freedom of movement in the capital now, for when he passed out fifth from St Cyr and was gazetted second lieutenant, he was made instructor in topography at the *Ecole Militaire Supérieure*. As a staff member he was often in Paris, and there he made the delightful discovery that society women, known as 'ladies', were just as willing to take a handsome young man for a lover as the soubrettes of the Alcazar. Many a pleasant *cinq à sept* he passed in the boudoirs of the Parc Monceau or the Porte Dauphine. Many a time he wondered, as he struggled with layers of cambric and lace, why the 'ladies' who were so willing to grant their favours never had the sense to take their corsets off when they had given him a *rendezvous* for five o'clock. Sometimes, when he met one of the cuckolded husbands, who had probably spent the traditional 'five to seven' with another woman, he hoped the man would never say of his spouse *she was not a faithful wife to me.*

Alain saw Melissa again next day, but on the day after that Major Millet announced at luncheon in the officers' mess that General Boulanger would be received in audience by the Bey of Tunis at five o'clock. "An appropriate escort will be required," he said, consulting a paper in his hand. "The two ADCs will accompany the general, of course, and two acting ADCs as well. Lieutenant Picquet and Lieutenant de Grimont, report for duty at half past four o'clock. Dress uniforms and swords."

"What's up now?" grumbled Lieutenant Picquet as they

rose from table. "The general paid his state visit as soon as he got here, only a couple of weeks ago."

"Probably the Bey's found something new to complain about," said Alain. "Anyway, it'll pass the time."

The *jehad*, or holy war, was so thoroughly forgotten that many of the natives actually applauded the showy French contingent on its way to the Dar-el-Bey. The four young officers, and the trooper escort carrying guidons, flanked the striking figure of Boulanger on his charger, wearing a blue uniform with gilt epaulettes and glittering with medals. They were almost too splendid for their shabby destination, for the Dar-el-Bey now housed some of the offices of the protectorate, with the apartments of the Bey himself restricted to the ground floor. The Tunisian army was reduced to one battalion, a mere token of honour for the Bey, and two men in makeshift uniforms presented arms as the Frenchmen rode up to the door.

They were received ceremoniously, and in the room where the Bey, in embroidered robes, was seated on a divan, a cushioned armchair had been placed ready for General Boulanger, with leather stools for his four officers in a semi-circle round it. Coffee was served in tiny golden cups, and a native interpreter appeared to translate from Arabic. Whether the Bey understood French or not, he never spoke it.

He was a miserable little man, who seemed to have shrunken under his misfortunes, and it was soon clear that he had nothing new to say to the commander of the army of occupation. He only wanted to repeat an old story about the transaction with the Société Franco-Africaine, which had brought the French into his country. "Enfida was *his* property!" he claimed. "He ought to share in the profits of the company. He had been cheated by a man he called his friend, Kheir-ed-din Pasha, who had since fled to Constantinople. He entreated the French to give him back his rights."

"But I understood Your Excellency *gave* land to the pasha," said Boulanger. "A princely gift, but a free gift, surely?"

"It was intended for his own use and profit, sir! Not for sale — at an enormous price — to a foreign power!"

"I understand Your Excellency's concern," said General Boulanger, "but the Société Franco-Africaine is not under my command. You should address yourself to Monsieur Paul Cambon, the Resident-General. It's he who represents the civil power in the protectorate."

"I've complained to Monsieur Cambon a dozen times," cried the Bey. "*He* suggests I address myself to the Sultan. Who despises me since I surrendered the Beylik! Who has taken Kheir-ed-din under his protection!"

"I will have a word with Monsieur Cambon, Excellency. I'm sure he regrets, as I do, this unfortunate situation."

A few more platitudes were exchanged, a few empty compliments, and then the Bey gave the signal for the ritual coffee of departure, after which the Frenchmen took their leave. When they rode across the courtyard and through the rusty gates, the general halted.

"The smell of scent, as well as incense, in that room was overpowering. I need fresh air. I need a gallop. Lieutenant de Grimont, will you show me the way to the Goletta, and then point out the shore road to me?"

"*A vos ordres, mon général.*"

The Goletta was the port of Tunis, now filling up with mercantile traffic. There was no French naval presence, but far out in the Gulf of Tunis two British ironclads were keeping station, their silhouettes just visible from the land.

"Our guardian angels," said Boulanger sarcastically. "Are they always here?"

"If it's *Monarch* and *Condor*, they've been here as long as I have, sir. Since the summer of '81."

"Ironclads. Hanging about, just as they did off Alexandria

at the time of Arabi's rebellion, waiting for a chance to interfere. Well, Tunisia is not as great a prize as Egypt, but I won't give them that chance . . ."

They had been riding round the harbour road at a walking pace, and Alain thought the general was talking to himself. But he seemed to dismiss the British ships with a shrug, and as the young man pointed the way to the shore road, he broke into a canter, with Alain at his horse's heels.

When the shore road became a mule track, and they had to walk again, the general showed where his thoughts had been. "You came out in '81," he said. "So you were a St Cyr instructor for just one year. Why was that?"

"I wanted to see action, *mon général*. I didn't want to become a fixture at St Cyr, teaching topography — the same old *topo et géo* — to new generations of cadets."

"Generations, I like that!" smiled Boulanger. "You didn't give it much of a trial. Where did you want to go on active service — Egypt?"

"God forbid!" said Alain fervently. "Anywhere but Egypt." The general's manner was so encouraging that he felt bold enough to speak bluntly. "What really made me ask for a posting was the death in action of a friend of mine, Captain Robert Scheffler. He fell in Algeria, in the Touareg massacre of 1881."

"I'm sorry, de Grimont. Was he a close friend?"

"I only met him a few times, but I admired the way he gave up easy duty and volunteered for active service. So — I joined the second expeditionary force ordered to Tunisia."

"I see," said General Boulanger, and pulled out his watch. "This road's impossible; it's time to go back." He wheeled his horse, and checked him again. The riders were now face to face and Alain, as yet unaware of the general's gift for melodrama, thought this was one of the most dramatic moments of his life. The sun was setting, and the golden light was tempered by a violet mist rising over the Mediterranean. Alone on the wild seashore, with his back towards the sunset, General Boulanger was a more than striking figure. His trained capacity to convey his exclusive interest in the person before him dictated his next words:

"Tunisia or Egypt, it didn't matter which. Tell me, where do you really want to see action?"

"In Alsace."

"Do the other young officers feel the same way?"

"I don't know, *mon général*. We never discuss it. Our duty is here in Africa, and we all remember what Monsieur Gambetta said about Alsace-Lorraine before he died."

"What was that?"

" 'Never talk about it. Think about it always.' "

"And you have?"

"Ever since I was a child."

"De Grimont, the day is coming – soon – when you *will* talk about it. When everybody will talk about *la revanche*. When you go back on leave to France you'll find many changes. The army is no longer the Great Unknown. There are new plans, new weapons, new inspiration. Men are only waiting for the Leader who will take them into Strasbourg, into Metz, and across the Rhine to Germany."

"*Mon général!*"

The young man's sudden flush, his indrawn breath, told the future Leader that he had been understood. He said, in a less exalted tone:

"Ride on, de Grimont. You know this vile track better than I do. You lead the way."

The mist on the sea had become a violet crown as they rode back to Tunis. The general kept his eyes on the stony track and a tight rein. But now and again he looked at the rider ahead of him and thought, "You'll do. A tragic family background, a difficult nature, a gift for loyalty and a fixed obsession. You're just the sort of man I'm looking for."

9

Boulanger had not set a time for approaching the Resident-General on the Bey's behalf, but he was anticipated. When he came off parade next morning he saw drawn up, near the parade ground, the *calèche* used by the Resident, with himself and his driver inside, and no other footman or groom in attendance.

That fellow has no sense of style, thought Georges Boulanger, and with his own inimitable sense of style he spurred his charger across the dusty parade ground, up to the carriage, and saluted.

"To what do we owe this honour, Excellency?"

"The need for a word with you, *mon général*."

"I'm entirely at your service."

Paul Cambon, the French Resident-General in Tunisia, was at the beginning of the extraordinary career in foreign politics which he was to share with his brother Jules. He was not yet a polished diplomat, and he was irritated enough to show it in his face and voice when he declined the glass of wine Boulanger offered as soon as they were alone in his private room.

"I don't drink wine so early in the morning."

"Neither do I," approved the general, and put the bottle back on the table which stood beneath a portrait of President Grévy, the only picture on the whitewashed walls. "I'm all attention, monsieur," he said.

"Why did you ask for an audience with the Bey yesterday without informing me?"

General Boulanger raised his eyebrows. "*I* ask for an audience? It was His Highness who sent for me."

"That's not what I was told."

"Told by whom?"

"That's my business."

He probably has his spies inside the Dar-el-Bey. "Ah well," said Boulanger aloud. "You politicians are sticklers for precedence. What is important was what the Bey had to say to me, which indeed I promised to communicate to you: it was the Enfida business all over again. He wants compensation from the Société Franco-Africaine for the property he gave to a certain pasha, now in Constantinople."

"Oh, that was it?" said the Resident in a more pacific tone. "He probably thought he had found a new and sympathetic listener in you. Enfida, what a nightmare! Of course there's nothing to be done. Kheir-ed-din Pasha was perfectly within his rights in selling to the Société. The Bey's transfer of Enfida to him was legalised: I have a copy of the deed of gift in my office. It was a bit of sharp practice, if you like, but the Bey has only himself to blame."

"That's what I thought," said Boulanger. "His ancestors did better out of piracy."

"You are pleased to be facetious, *mon général*. The Bey is in an awkward position, caught between the protectorate and the Ottoman Empire. And we're in enough trouble in Cairo without arousing the enmity of Constantinople."

"Civilians are always looking for trouble, and then expect the military to set it right."

"That's a soldier's viewpoint. Very well, *mon général*, there's no harm done this time, but for the future I must insist that you have no more conversations with His Highness unless a member of my staff is present."

"Are you serious?"

"Perfectly."

"You believe that the commander-in-chief of the Army of Occupation should be subordinate to Paul Cambon?"

"Not to Paul Cambon the man. But to the representative of France in Tunisia. Or so I understood when I received the appointment. If necessary I'll get confirmation from the Quai d'Orsay."

"While I can refer you to the War Ministry, or to the Elysée Palace, if I must."

"You have powerful friends in Paris, *mon général*. From the Duc d'Aumale, who got you your promotion to brigadier general, to the prime minister, Jules Ferry, who sent you here as a *général de division*. Monsieur Ferry might do the most for you — as long as he remains in office."

Boulanger's eyes blazed at the sneer. But his self-control never failed him. "Come, Excellency," he said, "we're making too much of a very slight misunderstanding. I assure you I'm too much concerned with the efficiency and well-being of my troops to wish to intrude on your sphere of influence. Let us try in future to work as colleagues, not as competitors."

"Very willingly." Both men stood up and bowed, but without shaking hands. The Resident took his departure, and the general accompanied him to the *calèche* drawn up outside the door.

"The representative of France deserves a better vehicle," he said by way of parting. "Can't the Quai d'Orsay rise to a carriage and pair?"

"No carriage springs would last long on Tunisian tracks. Didn't you see how bad the shore road was, when you rode there yesterday?"

The Resident was driven away, the general automatically acknowledged the sentries' salutes as he returned to his office. No one saw the face convulsed by rage and ambition, or the hands clenching and unclenching, or heard Boulanger mutter, "That jackanapes the representative of France! France shall be *mine*!"

Presently he began to think about the shore road and its sorry state. He made a long entry in his official diary. Then he wrote a much shorter directive, marked it 'Action this day', and rang for his military secretary.

Day had turned into evening before the order for action went down the echelons as far as Lieutenant Alain de Grimont, who was sent for by the colonel of the Line regiment to which he had been posted when he gave up his instructorship at St Cyr.

"Eh well, my poor de Grimont," said the jovial Colonel Chaudron, who like all the other officers at GHQ had smartened up considerably since Boulanger took command, "you didn't do yourself any good when you showed the general the shore road yesterday."

"With respect, *mon colonel*, it was he who asked to see it."

"And now he's seen the map you made of it after the so-called *jehad* was over."

"I mapped it as far as it went, sir. To the point where we had to turn back yesterday."

"Yes, well, now he's seen the place and seen the map, and he wants the road prolonged to the Algerian border. Which might take years, with the labour force at my disposal. It isn't as if we had *one* battalion of Sappers here. Only our tame topographer, Lieutenant de Grimont."

"Am I to do the surveying, link by link?"

"A higher fate has been reserved for you. You're to go to work on the road from Bizerta to Tunis. Working out of Bizerta, far from the temptations of Tunis."

Alain swallowed. "I've been over the road to Bizerta," he said. "It's a track, but it's complete, and it's not as rough as the road along the shore."

"Could it take a big military convoy?"

"Oh! certainly not."

"Well, there you are. The C-in-C has this tremendous conception of a great military highway between the desert and the sea. If the Italians attack us out of Tripoli, our transport could go right at them – "

"Or they could walk right in."

"Don't look so glum, man!" said the colonel. "Bizerta itself is to be strengthened, and that's where you come in. The present garrison is below strength, and as well as acting topographer you'll have the command of a half-company. If the natives attack, and you chase them back into the desert, you'll get your captaincy out of it, I promise you."

"When do I leave, sir?"

"That's the spirit! In about a week, I should think. That'll give us time to plan a farewell dinner, and for you to say a tender adieu to Tunis."

He was probably joking about the farewell dinner, for the week's plans would be concentrated on logistics, transport and supplies for the increased garrison of Bizerta, but he wasn't joking about the tender adieu. It was adieu to Melissa he meant, for talk about the native girls was free and loose, and as he lay wakeful in his army cot that night, Alain thought about the silken couch and the exotic girl in the iridescent gown. The affair, he knew, was over. Melissa would pass on to another man who would pay for the kohl for her eyes and the henna for her nails, the necklaces and the little gold slippers with the upturned toes. She thought she was old at twenty, and couldn't afford to lose time in fidelity to a man who might not return for months from the *bled* they called Bizerta. Adieu Melissa! Somehow he couldn't be too sorry. An hour in her arms had suddenly become less important than those few moments on the shore road with the general, and the promise Boulanger held out for the future.

He was with Melissa twice in the busy week which followed, and she wept real tears when the time came to say goodbye. She even asked him to take her with him to Bizerta, though she must have known it was impossible; nor did she really want to leave her mother and such comforts as they had gathered around them. He gave her a good present and lay with her one last time on the silken couch before going back to the mess and the farewell dinner.

General Boulanger was at the dinner and proposed the toast of the French Republic. He had been eating apart with his staff for the past week, and Alain had begun to wonder if he would see him again before he left, but there he was, raising his glass and nodding pleasantly when Colonel Chaudron, very informally, proposed "Good luck to Lieutenant de Grimont at Bizerta."

"He'll need it!" said a somewhat intoxicated voice, and the group broke up laughing to move to the anteroom where coffee and cognac were served. Then General Boulanger drew Alain aside.

"I've been meaning to tell you," he said, "that I met your uncle, the Duc de la Treille, many years ago. We were both hospitalised in Milan after the battle of Magenta, and even in the same ward. Charming man! When you write next, pray give him my best remembrances."

"He'll be honoured, *mon général*."

"He seemed to drop out of things after the war in Italy. Lives with his wife in the south of France, doesn't he? Have they a family?"

"Two sons, sir."

"In the army?"

"They both chose other forms of service. Maurice, the elder, is on the staff of the Governor-General of Cochin

China. He married the Governor's daughter about a year ago."

"With his parents' approval, I trust?"

"Oh yes! They were only sorry it was too far to go to Saigon for the *demande en mariage*."

"I should think so! And the other boy? Is he older or younger than you?"

"Armand? He's two years older than I am, and he's in the navy. He distinguished himself in the naval action at Tamatave last year, when we captured Madagascar."

"The duke is fortunate in his sons," said the general with a sigh. He was the father of two grown daughters, who took their mother's part against him.

"I'm honoured by your presence here tonight, *mon général*," said Alain awkwardly. Now, he thought, *he* must say something, and he did.

"I came to wish you luck in your first command," said General Boulanger, and, dropping his voice, "It's a long march to Bizerta, but remember, you're on the road to Strasbourg now."

10

The road to Bizerta, over the muddy hills of Tunisia, seemed long to marching men under the desert sun, but it was entirely peaceful. The French contingent encounterd nobody except a couple of traders with loaded saddlebags, and two or three families on their way to Tunis. It was two years since the second insurrection had been put down, and there was nothing more to fear from the Tunisians, but Lieutenant de Grimont was so conscious of his command that he saw danger everywhere. His orders were to bivouac by night in an old stone fort, a relic of Turkish rule. He was glad of its stone walls, slit for weapons, because the fort was defensible, which Bizerta as he remembered it was not. It was a good moment when they came in sight of the town, and saw the Tricolore flying in the North African sunlight.

Lieutenant Fournier, who was guarding Bizerta with two platoons of what the late Baron de Grimont would have called sullen conscripts, was vociferously glad to see an old comrade in arms. He and Alain had fought side by side with the second expeditionary force and were good friends: now Lieutenant de Grimont's arrival with a relief force sent their friendship sky-rocketing. When Alain was washed and dressed in a clean shirt they sat down together to a most convivial meal.

"I don't mind telling you I was as near to having a go of the *cafard* as any of the men, and as you know that's the thing you've got to watch out for," said Fournier.

Alain nodded understandingly. He had seen cases of *cafard* even in Tunis, and in this desert outpost the danger must be twice as high. *Le cafard*, or 'the beetle' was the despair which burrowed into the brains of soldiers far from home, and made them a prey to violence or suicide.

"Well, that's all over now," he said. "You've done your three years' foreign service, one of them here in Bizerta; you should rate a good spell of home leave now."

"Three months, I make it. Lord knows what *you'll* rate after this tour of duty, with mapping and surveying thrown in. Remember to keep scouts out, if you're working on the road by day."

"Can't very well work by night, can I?"

"I meant you'll be using sentries at night instead of scouts. Just lately we've been having a little trouble with the old green flag brigade. The *sidis* in the town are all right, and Tripoli's a long way away, but the nomads are beginning to show their teeth again."

"Fournier! Not another *jehad*?"

"Nothing like '81, far from it. Just the occasional flash of green and the chanting — you know, Allah-el-Allah, when a man's trying to go to sleep."

"Is there a mosque in the town? A muezzin?"

"No mosque and no muezzin. Look, de Grimont, those night prowlers aren't Tunisians like the men we fought three years ago. They're Bedouin, desert nomads; when you try coming to grips with them they're as invisible as the wind."

Two mornings later Lieutenant Fournier and his men marched off to the sound of bugles, with the supply waggons carrying their kit, and Alain walked out of the Bizerta gate noting that it must be reinforced. Bizerta was not a fortified town, but a sprawl of native huts and the old Turkish buildings used as barracks. Alain's men were set to sandbagging the walls and building an extension to the *chambrée* or dormitory, too crowded for a half-company. They were not conscripts, but regular troops of the Line, obedient and well-drilled, and at first they had no complaints about the monotony and confinement of life in a command post. The two sergeants were reliable men, and the colonel had picked two men who had accompanied Alain when he was mapping the harbour of Tunis and the road to Algeria. One of them carried the surveying instruments not in use, and the other could write well enough to make notes to dictation. The calculations were Alain's task, and he worked them out in his own room after Lights Out.

Even the scouts were interested in the beginning, especially at finding themselves advancing on the road to the border. Alain started work there: he wanted to have something positive to show the colonel if and when he came on an inspection tour. It was too much to hope that General Boulanger would come to Bizerta too.

Alain de Grimont had a capacity for hero-worship. The circumstances of his childhood, with an indifferent father in the Baron de Grimont and a surrogate father in his uncle, had left a gap in his life, which the brilliant, authoritative father-figure of General Boulanger had begun to fill. In his few weeks as commander-in-chief the general had set a new example in looking after the welfare of his men. He learned all their names and where they came from, even a little – a very little, for they were reticent – of their family backgrounds. There was no doctor on the strength, but there were two medical orderlies, who assisted their officer in the inspection of the men's feet and also in the inspection of the army brothel. He checked the *pinard* rations, not even leaving wine and food to the quartermaster, and when he visited their mess at the time of the evening meal, first passing by the cookhouse to taste whatever was in the cooking pots, the men were quite sincere in the traditional reply: "*La soupe est bonne, mon lieutenant!*"

He became popular, especially when the garrison saw him coming in from 'outside' sweating under the blue cutaway which he might have put on only ten minutes earlier, when the surveying work was done. "The lieutenant is serious," they said (that high French word of praise) "he's a worker." Alain knew that it might be a race between his popularity and *le cafard*, for their lives were monotonous, and Bizerta had no form of entertainment to offer except the obvious one. It was long before the days of organised sport for the troops, and the only alternative Alain could offer was the physical training and fencing he had learned at St Cyr. His day with the garrison began with close order drill and ended when he checked the gates and posted the sentries, when he was nominally free to sleep until he inspected his picquets at 4 AM.

Some of his classmates at St Cyr would have consoled themselves by thinking of Bizerta as a cog in the wheels of the machine becoming known as the French Empire. But Alain de Grimont had never been interested in empire-building. He had read in his Clausewitz at St Cyr that 'the heart of France lies between Brussels and Paris'. That could mean Sedan, where the French had lost, or Verdun; it didn't mean along the Mekong or on the Nile.

Yet the Nile was at the centre of the news throughout 1884. The Khedive Tewfik ruled in name and the British in fact. Mr Gladstone, the Liberal prime minister, wished to evacuate the Sudan, that lost empire of slaves and ivory, and eventually to quit Egypt. He sent General Charles Gordon to Khartoum to liberate what he called 'a people rightly struggling to be free'. But the Sudanese were now the captives of a fanatic, the Mahdi, the Expected One, the Moslem Messiah, who from the month of March onwards besieged Gordon in the governor-general's palace in Khartoum, while Gladstone procrastinated in the despatch of a relief force. In January, while Alain was still in Bizerta, where the green flags fluttered in the light of the little fires kindled in the desert sand, the *jehad* triumphed. The Mahdi and his Dervishes stormed the palace, murdered Gordon, and drove the British from the Sudan.

Blanche de la Treille stood in the doorway of her home between the flower-filled Biot jars, and almost sobbed with pleasure as two young men came hurrying up the palm avenue. For one was her nephew Alain, back at last on three months' leave, and the other was her son Armand, home from sea to marry the girl he loved.

"*Voilà, maman*, he's got here, and just in time!" exulted Armand de la Treille. He had a loud voice, trained to speak through a gale, while Alain was whispering "Dearest Aunt Blanche," as he took her in his arms and kissed her.

"Both my boys!" she said emotionally. "If only dear Maurice were here . . . at least he came through the Chinese war safely . . . but you've all been in such danger . . ."

"I haven't been in any danger, darling," said Alain. "-Please don't cry!" and the emotional moment passed as a groom ran up to lead away the pony carriage and old Jacques, still in service, began to unload Alain's kit from the waggonette. "I'll take this stuff upstairs, madame," he said. "Monsieur Alain looks well, doesn't he?"

"Very well, Jacques." But when she had 'both her boys' inside the salon, still smelling deliciously of fresh roses and pot-pourri, she thought Alain looked more tired than the journey from Algiers warranted, and more like thirty than twenty-five. A moustache and side-whiskers aged him, and while both young men were bronzed, Armand's was the healthy tan of the sea while Alain's thin cheeks had the desert's brown aridity.

"And how's the charming bride?" he asked his cousin with a smile. "When do I get to see her?"

"When you can, is my own experience. Her mother and sisters keep fussing round her, worrying her to death about her trousseau and the wedding presents and the new house—"

"Monsieur Barthou has given them a delightful little villa, not five minutes' walk from here. So she'll be near all of us when Armand's at sea," said the duchess, beaming.

"I couldn't picture Henriette as a sailor's wife in lodgings at Toulon," said Armand. "*She* was willing enough, bless her little heart, but my father and Monsieur Barthou came to another arrangement."

"But where *is* my uncle?"

"He's with Monsieur Barthou now, but he'll be home in about an hour. They had a meeting with their solicitors — something to do with the new house, I think," said the duchess vaguely. "Henriette's parents have been very generous. They've invited all the guests coming from a distance to be their guests at the Hôtel de la Plage. Even Armand's other witness."

Alain smiled. He knew that his aunt, grown stout and lethargic, was not fond of house guests. He said, "Who is Armand's other witness?" and the bridegroom replied that it was *Capitaine de vaisseau* Plouvier, who had served with him in the Madagascar squadron.

"And are there many people coming from a distance?"

"Quite a few from Paris, and Henriette's godmother, of course," explained his aunt. "Then there's the young lady who attended the Couvent des Oiseaux with Henriette, Mademoiselle Lacroix. Her father's bringing her down from Paris to be Henriette's second witness along with Valérie."

"Look here," said Armand, obviously impatient, "why don't you come along with me now, and let's have tea at

Henriette's? She's dying to see you, and so's her mother."

"He'll do no such thing," said his mother indignantly. "How can you be so selfish, Armand? Go and see your fiancée by yourself, and leave Alain and me to have a comfortable tea together. Do you realise that this boy postponed his leave for four months so that he could be your witness at the wedding?"

"I do know, and I'm very grateful; thanks, Alain," said the impatient sailor. "How did you work it, by the way?"

"Through General Boulanger. He came up to Bizerta on an inspection trip at Christmas time, and we discussed leave then. The men *had* to get their leave in February, but I told him about your wedding and asked permission to stay on until the end of June. Well, he said No to that, because he wanted to move a company of Sappers into Bizerta, so he transferred me to the Topographical Engineer Corps at Algiers as soon as they started surveying the west opening of the road."

"Which is to run from Algiers to Tripoli, you said in your letter?"

"That's the idea."

"It'll take years."

"Shouldn't wonder."

"Armand, would you please ring for tea?" said his mother pointedly, and as the sailor obeyed and left the room smiling, Alain sat down beside his aunt on the sofa, and gave her another hearty hug.

"Armand's head over heels in love," he laughed. "So it was pretty little Henriette Barthou after all!"

"It's been Henriette for a long time, only poor Armand couldn't speak until he got his promotion after that horrid affair at Madagascar. It's been a long courtship, but at least it gave her time to grow up. They're both all the better for the waiting."

"So you and my uncle are happy about it?"

"Perfectly."

"I remember years ago, you were very angry because you thought I'd snubbed her."

"No, it was because I thought you were trying to snub me. 'Please don't pair me off with a girl of sixteen' — I thought it was very impertinent."

"So it was. Didn't I apologise then? I do now."

"Oh darling boy, I was very stupid. I didn't realise until next day that you only said that about a girl of sixteen because you hated to think of your mother's being married when she was a mere child."

Under the fair moustache Alain de Grimont's mouth tightened. He looked into his aunt's plump loving face and kissed her hand. But he made no direct response to what she had said except, looking at his mother's portrait on the opposite wall, hanging where the sun would fall upon it for many hours of the day, and with a bowl of roses on the polished table below:

"How very well you've hung her picture! I'm glad you didn't hang it on the staircase with the princes."

"Alain, how can you? When Gilbert brought the portrait home after your father died, he said to me, 'I'm keeping this in trust for Alain. It shall hang in a place of honour until he marries and has a home of his own.' I hope that'll be soon, my dear!"

"I haven't met the right girl yet."

These were the last serious words spoken in the Château de la Treille for more than twenty-four hours. After tea Henriette Barthou appeared, driven in the pony carriage by Armand, and primed with kisses for *Belle-mère*, as she already called the duchess, and 'dear old Alain'. She was certainly grown up, as luxuriant as a full-blown rose in her simple muslin dress and capeline straw hat tied with black velvet ribbon, and she was very much the bride, bubbling over with attentions for the duke and Captain Plouvier, who came in

127

soon after, and never letting go of Armand's hand. At last the duchess told her playfully that Armand must drive her home for an early dinner and an early bed. "Remember, you're being married tomorrow," she said, and Henriette blushed rosy red.

"It's only the civil ceremony," she said. "Mother has invited as few people as possible to the *mairie*, and for lunch after." *Le lunch* was now the fashionable term for the wedding breakfast, but the tremendous meal which was to follow the religious ceremony a day later was called *le déjeuner*.

More kisses, and the happy couple drove away, with Armand coming back in half an hour to pour drinks, to be very attentive to his mother during dinner, and when she had gone to bed to play billiards with Alain and Captain Plouvier. They got him through a fit of nerves and into his dress uniform next morning, and put on their own — there was never any relaxation of the rule about uniform — and took him to the *mairie* in good time. The *salle de mariages* of Hyères was light and gay, and there were flowers from the duke's carnation fields on the table behind which stood the mayor, impressive in his tricolore sash. The duchess and Madame Barthou were both crying quietly when the girls came in. Henriette was ravishing in peach coloured silk, with her dark head modestly lowered. Her elder married sister, Valérie, stood next to her as her first witness, and beyond Valérie — Alain caught his breath — there was someone very fair, with delicate features and a smile with — not mockery in it, but the faintest touch of scepticism in a face he seemed to have known since he was born.

In a boarding-school hand she wrote her name, Isabelle Marie Liliane Lacroix, which he thought lovely, above his Alain François de Grimont. She smiled at him again while the kissing and congratulating went on, but did not speak until Madame Barthou bustled up to introduce him formally to the young lady as the Baron de Grimont. Impossible to snub the good woman by saying that he preferred to be known as Captain de Grimont — he had been promoted after he left Bizerta. Alain guessed that Madame Barthou's mind was running on titles. Her tears had dried with speed when she hailed her daughter as 'Princesse Armand de la Treille'! and if Maurice and his wife continued childless, the girl might be a duchess yet.

By the rules of etiquette, Alain had to take her sister, Madame Valérie Ovize, across the way to the *lunch* for twenty people arranged on small tables in the Hôtel de la Plage. He was nowhere near Mademoiselle Lacroix, who had fallen to Captain Plouvier's share, and when Valérie's attention was engaged elsewhere (after all, they had known each other since childhood) he could look at the lovely girl who seemed unresponsive to the sailor's wedding jests. Once or twice she looked across at Alain with that shadowy smile, but the Château de la Treille party was at home again before he learned more about her.

"You had the prettiest girl in the room, next to Henriette, for your partner, Plouvier," he said, when they were all back in the salon and all suffering from a feeling of anti-climax.

"Pretty as a picture, but so shy I could hardly get a word out of her. Acted more like a schoolgirl than — how old is she, de la Treille?"

"Younger than Henriette, I know."

"Ought to be at home under her mamma's wing."

"Wasn't her mother there?"

"The mother's a semi-invalid, I gather. Not up to the train journey."

"I met her father." Alain thought meeting a tall bearded man had been a poor substitute for meeting his daughter. "He gave me his business card."

"His *business* card?" said Armand with a scowl.

"I thought myself it was rather odd. Fernand Lacroix,

stockbroker, and an address in the Rue du Quatre Septembre."

"They live in the Rue de Courcelles. Rich people, but old Fernand isn't the important one in that family. His brother is."

"What does the brother do?"

"He's an ironmaster," said Armand de la Treille. "He's exploiting the ironfield the Germans missed when they were drawing the new frontiers of Lorraine, damn them. Their geologists thought they'd included all the known iron deposits, but they missed out the biggest one of all, near Briey. That's the one Frédéric Lacroix's working on. Too busy to come to our wedding, of course."

Armand spoke savagely. He cared nothing for the Lacroix family, but was frustrated by being a married man and yet no husband. His wife had been taken home by her parents, and he by his: no consummation was permissible until after the religious ceremony next day. Captain Plouvier had been infected by his depression, and was now in the state when a French naval officer thinks sullenly of Trafalgar.

"I suppose we'd better go and knock a few balls about," said Alain. The others said it was a damned stupid way to spend another evening, but they rose, and were crossing the hall to the billiard room when the duke, with a newspaper in his hand, came out of the library.

"Billiards again?" he said. "Alain, I've hardly had a chance to talk to you since you arrived. Come and have a chat with me now. Your aunt's gone to bed with a headache, and I need company."

"I'm sorry, Uncle Gilbert, I thought you were reading the *Figaro*."

"Go ahead, Alain," said his cousin. "Go and cheer papa up, he's looking grim."

It was true that the Duc de la Treille did look strained, possibly as a result of being affable all day. Alain wondered how he looked himself, and what there was about him to make a young lady smile that little sceptical smile. He took the most unusual step of looking at his reflection in the long mirror between the bookshelves in the library, and there he thought he saw the answer. His side-whiskers were light brown, like his hair, but his new moustache had grown in as blond as his curls had been when he was a little boy. The effect was lopsided. Enough to make any girl smile. First thing in the morning he would go to the barber and have it off.

It was a very hot evening, and his uncle, divested of his wedding finery, was wearing a thin suit with a loose jacket, and standing between the open doors of the french window which gave on one of the many flowery terraces of his home. He seemed in no hurry to begin the chat, perhaps because they had all chatted about every incident of the civil marriage and the *lunch* since they came home. He was still holding on to the newspaper.

"Anything new in the *Figaro?*" said Alain de Grimont, lighting a cigarette. He had unhooked the collar of his tunic, and was very much at ease in a leather armchair.

"The government appears to be in difficulties."

"Did you ever know a government that wasn't? Who's in trouble this time? Monsieur Ferry?"

"Monsieur Ferry, the great coloniser, is heading for a fall."

"That Tonkin business did for him. Ah well, I suppose the president will send for de Freycinet. My father used to say French politicians always got a second time around; this will be Monsieur de Freycinet's third."

"Are you developing a taste for politics at last, Alain?"

"You can't serve in Algeria without being bitten by the political bug."

The duke folded the newspaper and laid it on a table.

"Monsieur Ferry's problems aren't the leading topic in this

Figaro. There's some disturbing news in it about General Boulanger."

"What's happened to him?"

"He's back in Paris – not on leave."

Alain's face lit up. "He's done it then, as he said he would!"

"How do you know what he said?"

"I saw him in Algiers three weeks ago."

"What was he doing in Algiers?"

"Having consultations with the Bureau Arabe."

Drumming up support, thought the duke. He was silent for a moment, and Alain said swiftly:

"Look here, Uncle Gilbert, I didn't tell you that I was in the general's confidence, because I gathered you didn't like him. He sent you a friendly message last year and you didn't acknowledge it, either to him or to me. But I meant to tell you, as soon as the wedding excitement was over, that I knew he was going to Paris, that I expect to see him there, and that I'm glad he's put an end to the intolerable situation in Tunis."

"You mean his quarrel with the Resident, Monsieur Cambon? We've been hearing a lot about that recently."

"We even heard about it at Bizerta."

"The general hasn't changed since I met him in a hospital ward in Milan, all bluff and braggadocio. He didn't do especially well at Magenta – like myself, all he did was get wounded – but he boasted to the doctors and the Sisters of Charity, and any Frenchmen silly enough to listen to him, as if he'd won the battle single-handed. As if he were the new Napoleon Bonaparte."

"He's scored a lot of successes since Magenta."

"And I have not. Now he's strong enough, and popular enough with the army, to set himself against the civil power. He wants to drive Paul Cambon out of office and make himself supreme in Tunisia. Two days ago, it says here, he took a very big gamble. He told the government that if Cambon remained in Tunis he, Boulanger, would resign. That's blackmail, Alain: how can you admire such a man?"

"He's going to lead us to victory, I know. He's going to give us back Alsace-Lorraine. It's no use, uncle, I'm pledged to him. He said that after he went to Paris he would send for me, and he asked me to be one of his aides-de-camp."

11

Captain de Grimont was early for his appointment with the general, so he walked from his Paris hotel to the place where the palace of the Tuileries had stood. He had not been in the capital for four years, and when he left the palace was a burned out shell, a hideous reminder of the Commune. Now there were flowerbeds, lawns, and gravel walks bordered with low boxwood hedges which gave out a pleasant scent under the September sun. Tourists were trooping along the paths on their way to the picture galleries of the Louvre.

Alain stood at gaze until the striking of a clock warned him to turn back to the Rue de Rohan and the Hôtel du Louvre. There was a small crowd of idlers round the door, and the desk clerk, giving him directions, said they were probably waiting for a glimpe of General Boulanger. In the general's suite the anteroom was also crowded, and an orderly whom he recognised was telling the group, most of whom were in uniform, that General Boulanger regretted he could receive no more of them that day. Then he saw Alain, and said with a bow, *"Entrez, mon capitaine!* You are expected."

"How are you, Keller?" asked Alain – the man was an Alsatian.

"Very well, I thank you, *mon capitaine*. One is very busy," the orderly said in a low voice, and as he opened the door of a small salon they heard Boulanger say:

"You'll stay here as long as I need you, is that understood, madame?"

Then he turned sharply, greeted Alain, and introduced him to Madame Boulanger.

She was a grim looking woman, knitting like a *tricoteuse* at the foot of the guillotine. There were two young ladies in the room, Marie and Marcelle Boulanger, who resembled her rather than their handsome father.

"You have come from the Riviera, Captain de Grimont?" said the general's lady.

"From the Sologne, madame. I've been shooting with an old friend of my father." And for the first time in his life he had been glad to leave Hyères, where his uncle never stopped criticising the general, and his aunt had been at her wits' end trying to keep the peace between them.

"You don't regret disposing of your own shooting?" asked Boulanger, and Alain said he never had. He was trying to make conversation with the girls, who seemed ill at ease, when the orderly announced Count Dillon. The newcomer entered, bowed to all the company, captured the knitting hand and kissed it, on which Madame Boulanger got up and stabbed her needles through her ball of wool.

"Come, my dears, it's time for us to withdraw," she said to her daughters, and sketched a sarcastic curtsey to her husband as he held the door open for them. Then, dropping his ceremonious manner, he said, "Arthur! This is my new aide-de-camp, Captain de Grimont. We mustn't work him too hard, because he's on leave till the end of September."

"*Mais, mon général* . . ." Boulanger held up his hand. "I know what you're thinking. You're afraid of being sentenced as a deserter if you're not back in Tunis by the thirtieth."

"Not as a deserter, but as an officer who's overstayed his leave."

"Then you can stop worrying. Your colonel has been informed that the War Ministry has agreed to your remaining in Paris as aide to me as a *général de division*. For that I have to thank Monsieur Clemenceau. We were at the *lycée* at Nantes together."

"Indeed, sir!" Alain had not realised that the formidable Georges Clemenceau sympathised with General Boulanger. It must be like two tigers inside one cage, he thought. He knew that Ferry, the prime minister, was on his side, but Ferry had fallen from power and instead of the experienced de Freycinet, had been succeeded in office by a man called Brisson.

"Count Dillon will tell you what has been done so far," said Boulanger, "and then you'll have some idea of what your new duties will be. By the way, where did you spend the night?"

"I took a room at the Hôtel Regina, sir. Just round the corner from the Hôtel du Louvre."

"Very convenient; stay there until you find a suitable apartment . . . Go on, Arthur."

Arthur Dillon intrigued Alain. Dillon was an Irish name (did they have counts in Ireland?) but the card he had put into Alain's hand bore an address in Neuilly, and what little he had said so far was spoken in perfect French. He wore an American businessman's sack suit and high button shoes, and had laid a derby hat on the sideboard.

He was older than Boulanger, whom he had met when the latter headed the French military delegation to the United States for the centenary of the British defeat at Yorktown. As a director of the Commercial Cable Company he had seen all Boulanger's possibilities in the world of communications, and when he retired, a wealthy man, to France — his native land — he got in touch with him at the crucial moment when the general was beginning his campaign against Paul Cambon. The press attacks on the luckless Resident in Tunisia had been orchestrated by Dillon, who knew that Paris pens were always to be hired.

"Do you know Paul Déroulède?" he began abruptly.

"The poet? I learned his *Soldier Songs* in the schoolroom," said Alain.

"His were the first poems, or songs, or whatever you like to call them, to praise our defeated army and turn our people's minds towards revenge," said Boulanger.

"Didn't he organise some sort of patriotic league, a year or two ago?" asked Alain.

"The *Ligue des Patriotes* – yes, he did," said Dillon. "Their office is in the Rue St Augustin, number 22, and I'm working there at present, in close co-operation with Monsieur Déroulède."

"But to do *what*, sir?"

"To make General Boulanger's name known through the whole of France. He has been lost in North Africa: now we must make everybody realise that he is the country's born leader: France's foremost soldier, the saviour of society."

Napoleon III, at the time of his *coup d'état*, had been called the saviour of society. "How are you going to do it?" Alain asked Arthur Dillon.

"By using modern advertising methods," said 'Count' Dillon. "They understand these things better in America. Take the case of the Statue of Liberty, for instance – "

"What about the Statue of Liberty? It's finished, isn't it?"

"Yes, thanks to the French. But on the American side it was found very hard to raise money for the pedestal, until a newspaper proprietor called Pulitzer offered to print the names of all the contributors in his papers. Then the fund was completed in record time, and they were even able to turn down an offer of $5000 from the Castoria Oil Company to put its name on the statue for one year."

"*My God!*" said Alain. He thought of the Head of Liberty which had thrilled him at eighteen – that calm face, that world's crown – defaced with an advertisement for a patent medicine.

"This idea you have," he said, "of making the general's name known all through France – unless he goes to war for Alsace-Lorraine and wins a victory – won't it cost a fortune?"

"The first subscriptions are very satisfactory."

"And – *monsieur le comte* – do you seriously intend to sell General Boulanger like Castoria Oil?"

"Why not?" said Arthur Dillon coolly. "It's the American way."

Alain had to admit that the American way worked. He knew nothing about the subscription lists, which were kept at the *Ligue des Patriotes* office, but he knew that the general entertained beautiful and wealthy women to dinner at the Meurice or the Splendide, sometimes with their husbands, and that cheques arrived later at the Hôtel du Louvre. Madame Boulanger was seldom present on these occasions. Count Dillon had decided, after her few appearances in public with her husband, that she was as necessary to his schemes as Castoria Oil.

Alain was not impressed by the *Ligue des Patriotes*, whose motto was 'France Quand-même, 1870–18 . .', whatever that might mean; but he was very much impressed by the increasing crowds of sympathisers who appeared in the anteroom of the general's suite. It was one of his duties to talk to the military men among them when the general was not 'receiving', and afterwards prepare a list of their names, rank and regiments. It was dull work, but the compensation was driving with his master in an open carriage when he went to one or other of the government offices, and listening to the cheers of the people in the streets.

He rented a small furnished apartment in the Cité du

Retiro, an ancient building in a courtyard with two exits, and arranged with the concierge to keep it clean and prepare his breakfast. His evenings were nearly always free that autumn, and he dined with old acquaintances from St Cyr or went to the theatre, but he was only marking time until the Lacroix family returned to Paris from a round of country house visits. He had danced twice with Isabelle in the Barthou garden after Armand and Henriette were married in church, and after the guests had enjoyed a *déjeuner* of fifteen courses, which put dancing out of the question for some of the company. Her father had watched them with great approval, and when Alain asked for permission to call in the Rue de Courcelles he said:

"*Enchanté, mon cher baron!* From the twentieth of October, Madame Lacroix will receive our friends every Thursday after nine o'clock."

It sounded like a regular salon, an unexpected pastime for a semi-invalid, but when he paid his first visit to the Lacroix mansion he found the mistress of the house in good health and spirits. Marie-Alice Lacroix had once been as pretty as her daughter, and still had an eye for a handsome young man. She made no demur when Alain asked Isabelle to show him the conservatory, divided by glass doors from the salon, and carried her off from the rest of the guests. They were all business people, heavy, pompous and conventional, and the pretty girl seemed glad to put her arm through his and lead him into a charming place of ferns and fountains.

"This suits you," he told her, "you ought always to be among flowers. What's that scent you're wearing?"

Blushing at such an intimate question, she murmured "'*Bouquet' de Guerlain*."

"I knew it was a flower scent." And he was sick to death of musk, chypre, 'Jicky' and all the perfumes fast women wore, to say nothing of the fierce African scents of Melissa and her kind. Isabelle was the sweetest girl he had ever met, and the happiest. She *adored* Henriette, she said, and was thrilled to be a witness at her wedding, because Henriette had been *so* sweet to her at the Couvent des Oiseaux, when Henriette was a big girl and she was a little one. She loved riding — not in the Bois, where people stared, but in the country, and she thought it must be thrilling to be an aide to General Boulanger, who was *so* handsome!

Her father, when they returned to the salon and Isabelle went to help her mother to 'receive', was less than thrilled. "No reflection on you, Baron de Grimont," he said, "but I wish I could see where General Boulanger was going. Paul Cambon says he's only interested in promotion and personal politics. What do you think?"

"You can't expect me to comment on that, monsieur."

"No, no, discretion, discretion! You're only doing your duty as a soldier, *I* understand."

"Thank you. And may I ask you a great favour, monsieur? When you introduce me to your friends, may it be as *Captain* de Grimont?"

"What's the use of having a title if you don't use it?"

What indeed.

Alain chatted for a while with Isabelle's younger brother Raymond, who was with his father in the *agence de change*, and then took his leave. He dared to kiss the tips of Isabelle's fingers, and imagined he could feel the blood throbbing under the white kid glove. She blushed as she said good-night.

Alain de Grimont walked back to the Cité du Retiro under an October moon, feeling happier than he had done for years. After the lonely celibacy of Bizerta, after the corruption of Algiers, he was ready for romantic love, and he believed he had found his ideal in Isabelle Lacroix. She was just the sweet, simple girl whom an intelligent man could mould as he pleased, and *mon Dieu*! she was beautiful! He did not perceive that her beauty was as chilly as the full moon riding high above the chimney pots of the Faubourg St Honoré, any more than he wondered why he felt no rage to possess her. He was in no hurry. He was prepared to embark upon a long, slow, delightful courtship: the engagement, the settlements, the decision on where to live in Paris, the question of a country house, would all take time. It never occurred to him that he might be asked to leave the army.

As the Baron de Grimont (he always thought they were talking about his father) he paid two more visits to Madame Lacroix's salon, and sent flowers to her and her daughter every week. On the third visit he found Isabelle a little capricious, a little inclined to pout because he talked more to her elder brother than to her, but that was only because he found Félix Lacroix's talk so interesting. Félix, three years older than himself, worked with his uncle in the iron works at Briey and was absorbed in technicalities like the Gilchrist-Thomas smelting process which had just come into use. Félix Lacroix wasted no time on 'the gap in the Vosges' or false sentiment about lost Lorraine: he was perfectly happy a few miles from Lorraine, exploiting the German geologists' mistake, and helping to lay the foundation of what would become the great iron and steel industry of France.

Alain planned to be more explicit in his wooing when he went back to the Rue de Courcelles, but the next reception was cancelled because Madame Lacroix had an attack of bronchitis, and in December there was an increase in the political tempo such as the French loved, which brought Boulanger's waiting to an end.

Monsieur Grévy's seven years' mandate was over, and as was generally expected he was elected President of the Republic for a second term. But there were ugly rumours afloat, not about Grévy but about his son-in-law, who was suspected of using his position to traffic in decorations. In this climate of unease the Brisson cabinet suffered a defeat, having survived a bare five months, and Charles de Freycinet, former right hand man of Gambetta and now an ally of Clemenceau, entered on his third term as prime minister. And on 8 January 1886, at Clemenceau's urging, he appointed General Boulanger Minister for War.

"Now," said the exultant Dillon, "we shall see what we shall see!"

The *Ligue des Patriotes* rejoiced, the general's female adorers sent him flowers and little lacy cards of congratulation, the Hôtel du Louvre was practically under siege by his admirers, and only Alain de Grimont, shuffling papers in embarrassment, heard Clemenceau say when he came to call on the new Minister:

"Now don't lose your head, Georges! Don't think so much about popularity, but work at bringing in the reforms you say you want! You're a member of the government now, not a playactor."

They moved to the War Ministry on the Rue St Dominique, and the reforms began, but they had no reference to the recovery of Alsace-Lorraine. Boulanger was being called *Général Revanche* now, but his reforming zeal had nothing to do with revenge. In spite of Clemenceau's warning, he was still playing for popularity and still showing off. He had a second aide-de-camp now, a handsome young cavalry lieutenant called Porges, and a Spahi guard, in their vivid uniforms, on duty at the War Ministry. Alain and Porges had new uniforms, with gilt *fourragères* round their shoulders, and when Isabelle Lacroix saw Alain for the first time wearing the *fourragère* and the gilt-edged képi she clapped her hands and pretended to be dazzled. Her mother admired him too, but she sent Isabelle out of the room on some excuse, moved her chair closer to Alain's and whispered.

"Is it true that General Boulanger is living apart from his wife?"

"He's left the Hôtel du Louvre, madame. He hadn't a

moment's peace there, because he was badgered by callers, and now the ushers at the Ministry take care of *them*."

"But he hasn't returned to the family home?"

"I know nothing about his private affairs, madame."

"You're very loyal, Baron de Grimont. But I have it on good authority that he's installed in a *garçonnière* at 128 Boulevard Haussmann. Not very becoming for a man of his age and position, is it?"

Alain shrugged. She was quite right, even to the street number, but Alain knew that some of the business men she 'received' in her home had the same sort of bachelor establishment. He didn't fault the general for that, because he had met Madame Boulanger, and in spite of his own reverence for Isabelle, he had had women up to his apartment in the Cité du Retiro often enough.

Madame Lacroix leaned forward in her chair, and just as Isabelle turned the door knob she whispered again:

"You mark my words, women will be his undoing!"

One thing was sure, whatever went on at 128 Boulevard Haussmann, the general put in a full day's work at the Ministry. He was showing the same concern for the troops as he had begun in Tunisia. They were to get better food served on plates instead of in mess tins, and they were to have free Sundays as well as special leave at Christmas and Easter. Regimental museums were to be opened in the principal towns of France, to make people proud of the glorious past, and provincial barracks were to be renamed after war heroes of the area. To publicise these 'reforms' General Boulanger installed his personal press office in the Ministry.

Once he threw a sop to Alain de Grimont by telling him about a new rifle that was going into production. The young man was beginning to be a bore since he took up with the Lacroix girl, parroting off the opinions of her uncle and her brother about the need to build up the French arms industry

— using their heavy metals, of course — and how the blast furnaces in the Ruhr were turning out steel for Krupp's big guns, which had already done fearful execution in the war. The Lebel rifle would be a big advance on the *chassepot*, and next year there would be a new weapon of light artillery — a 75mm quickfiring field gun was going into production.

"With great respect, *mon général*, I've heard it said the .75 has a flat trajectory which makes it unsuitable for use in hilly country like the Vosges," said Alain.

"Who did you hear saying that?"

"One of the permanent staff of the Ministry, sir."

"There's not an artilleryman among the lot. I don't want my aides fraternising with that bunch of civil servants."

"*A vos ordres, mon général.*"

"Now let me see the latest correspondence about the Cercle Militaire."

Alain saw Lieutenant Porges grinning at the snub, and reflected that the *fonctionnaires* of the War Ministry were not anxious to fraternise with the Minister's young officers. Cynics to a man, they knew that they would last while Ministers came and went on the ever-turning carrousel which gave so many men a second chance in office. He went to look out the files of the Officers' Club, or Cercle Militaire, which was Boulanger's latest enthusiasm. He intended to open officers' clubs in all French cities, but the club in Paris was naturally to be the most elaborate, the most expensive, and the best centre for Boulangist propaganda of them all.

The month of July promised to be so busy, and at the same time so brilliant, that Alain decided to bring his leisurely courtship of Isabelle Lacroix to the point. She was twenty-one now, twenty-one to his twenty-six — what could be more suitable? — and he had very nearly proposed to her on the night of her birthday dinner. He was glad he had delayed. A few nights later he took Isabelle and her mother to see *A Daughter of the Regiment* at the Opéra Comique, and when

Madame Lacroix fell heavily asleep in the cab going home Isabelle had allowed him to kiss her with a passion which she seemed to be on the verge of returning. He decided to speak to her father after the opening of the Cercle Militaire was past.

On both sides of the Atlantic an exceptional event was to be celebrated in the month of July 1886. In the United States the fourth of July was to see the unveiling, in New York Harbour, of the Statue of Liberty, exactly ten years after the event it was intended to commemorate. In France the fourteenth of July, the anniversary of the storming of the Bastille, was to be celebrated as the National Day for only the seventh time in the life of the Third Republic. "Festivities! Give us festivities!" Georges Clemenceau had cried when the Chambre des Députés adopted the fourteenth as the great date, back in 1880, and Clemenceau's protégé, the new Minister of War, was preparing to give the Parisians a festal military review, all brass bands and flying Tricolores. By way of a rehearsal of the *Quatorze Juillet*, there was the opening of the Paris Officers' Club on July first.

The club was to be inside the Hôtel Splendide, between the Avenue de l'Opéra and the Rue de la Paix, one of the most central and impressive sites in the capital, and these wide streets, as well as the great Opéra square, were capable of holding a multitude of spectators. The event had been well advertised through the general's press office, and two thousand Parisians had turned out to see and cheer *le Général Revanche*. He made his appearance at ten o'clock on a fine summer night, riding a black horse and escorted by a squadron of Cuirassiers and two detachments of drummers. Boulanger was wearing full dress uniform, his golden beard was glittering, he repeatedly raised his feathered tricorne hat to acknowledge the cheers of the crowd, and the crowd went mad.

Inside the handsome clubrooms which he had come to

inaugurate, there was the same tremendous enthusiasm. He made his way through the applauding crowd, a glass of champagne in his left hand, his right free to grasp another hand or pat a shoulder, and a well-turned compliment always ready on his lips. He was complimented himself on the cheering and singing which went on outside the Splendide, where the crowd loitered to gaze up at the lighted windows. His two aides-de-camp were close on his heels, leaving him of course to the high-ranking officers but ready to anticipate any of his wishes, and listening avidly to the praise.

"Congratulations, *mon général*! You have scored a great personal triumph tonight!" was what they heard most often, and Boulanger's reply never varied:

"This is nothing, *mon ami*! I've got to seduce the whole of Paris on the fourteenth of July!"

It was a delirious night for most of the young officers present; less so, perhaps, for Alain de Grimont. He wondered if the demonstration in the streets would appeal to Monsieur Fernand Lacroix, who had remarked more than once that he wished he 'knew where Boulanger was going'. He was going a long way, that was now obvious, but in what direction? Was it quite the right time for the general's aide-de-camp to ask the stockbroker's permission to propose to his only daughter? Alain decided to risk it. It was nearly a year since he met Isabelle, and her brother was beginning to look at him speculatively. If he dallied any longer, could her parents accuse him of trifling? He was in love with Isabelle, so he told himself a dozen times a day, and now he must make up his mind to tell her father. He sent Keller, the Alsatian orderly, to the stockbroker's office on the Rue du Quatre Septembre, with a letter requesting an interview.

"An unexpected pleasure to see you at my place of business, *mon cher baron*," said Monsieur Lacroix, when Alain presented himself. "And what can we do for you here that I can't do in the Rue de Courcelles? Are you by any chance in need of investment counselling?"

"Not exactly, sir. Monsieur Imbert of the Banque de France looks after my financial interests. He was one of my trustees while I was still a minor, after my father died."

Alain could have added that Monsieur Imbert had recently negotiated the purchase of a substantial block of stock in the Lacroix Ironworks, using Maître Leboyer as the nominee. Both men assured Alain that it was an excellent investment.

At the mention of Hubert de Grimont's death, or rather murder, Fernand Lacroix looked pious, and murmured, "That was a terrible affair! You must miss him very much," and Alain bent his head.

"I can't believe," he said, after a suitable interval of silence, "that you don't know why I am here, monsieur. I think you must be aware of my great admiration for your daughter Isabelle."

With a slight smile Lacroix said the baron's attentions had certainly been remarked by Isabelle's parents.

"I'm glad of that. Because I'm here to request your approval of my proposal of marriage."

He sat back with folded arms, an attitude copied from the general. Alain de Grimont was a little above himself that summer, a little drunk on cheering and army pride as the Great Unknown became the Known and Beloved, and he would have had to be a fool not to know what a good match he was. Young, handsome, and healthy, the master of an independent fortune and the nephew of a duke, he was one of the most eligible men in Paris society, and he waited for Lacroix's reply with assurance.

"Have you spoken to my daughter?" was what he heard.

"Certainly not, sir; I am waiting for your permission."

"Very correct, Baron de Grimont, very considerate. Will you be indignant if I ask you to say nothing at all to her at present?"

Alain dropped his studied pose and half rose from his chair.

"*Nothing*, monsieur? But why?"

"Because her mother and I decided, long before we met you, that a career officer would not be a suitable husband for Isabelle."

"I'm afraid I don't understand you," said Captain de Grimont haughtily.

"A girl brought up as Isabelle has been, to every luxury and refinement, would not adapt readily to life in a garrison town in France, or in Algiers, or Tunis, or anywhere in the new territories. If you were a civilian it would be different. We have welcomed you to our home; we would welcome you, and gladly, to our family."

"But the army is my life!"

"You could continue in the army — in the reserve of officers."

"I'm afraid the regular army doesn't think much of the reserve."

"You once told me your uncle the duke was a reserve officer when he was called up to fight in the war for Italian unity."

"But he had a place at the imperial court — it was quite a different matter!"

"And then there's something else."

"What more?"

"You can be proud of your record in North Africa, *mon cher baron*. Your present service ... at the War Ministry ... worries me a little."

With an effort Alain reminded himself that this maundering old fool was Isabelle's father and must not be antagonised. He said, "You have criticised General Boulanger several times in my presence, sir. May I ask if you have ever met him?"

"Never. I know a great deal about him, however — he takes

care of that. I know he makes a great appeal to the rabble in the street – he takes care of that too."

"If you saw, or realised, how he appeals to *all* his country-men – how they all hail him as a great leader, who has restored the French sense of patriotism – would you change your mind about my proposal?"

"I don't think patriotism has been restored by the gen-eral's order to paint all sentryboxes blue-white-and-red," said Lacroix drily. "Pray what occasion have you in mind to excite my admiration of General Boulanger?"

"The Longchamp review, monsieur, the national parade on the fourteenth of July. If you and Madame Lacroix would bring Isabelle – and Raymond too, if he likes – as my guests, I think you would see exactly what I mean." And knowing the stockbroker's inherent snobbery, he added recklessly, "I could arrange for you to have very comfortable places in the presidential box."

"Oh papa, oh maman, isn't this exciting!"

The whole vast concourse assembled on Longchamp racecourse thought it was exciting, this fourteenth of July of banners and music, of pretty women in elaborate *toilettes* and men in uniform, of working-class families in their Sunday best, with crying children. The President of the Republic, Jules Grévy, was there with his daughter and his suspect son-in-law. The prime minister Monsieur de Freycinet was there with most of his cabinet, and they were all, whether they showed it or not, excited because this was Longchamp, where the King of Prussia, after having himself proclaimed German Emperor in the palace of Versailles, had held a review of his victorious troops before sending them on a march through the defeated Paris of 1871. Fifteen years had passed and defeat was forgotten. A master showman was reassuring the Parisians: the world was theirs again.

For Isabelle Lacroix the excitement was not in the spectacle, thrilling though it was, nor in the fact that her papa had turned round in their box (and it was a real *tribune*, such as the cabinet had) to take off his tall silk hat to President Grévy and receive the president's bow in return. The excitement was that Alain de Grimont had made all the arrangements for them, and that Raymond, her favourite brother, had said, "Better put on your best *bibi* for the review, Isabelle! You may see your *soupirant* there, if he's not too busy with his famous general! Be prepared to say thank you prettily."

"My 'suitor'? Do you mean Captain de Grimont? He's not my suitor, you silly old Raymond!"

"If he's not he soon will be. He looked desperately serious when I saw him being shown in to father at the office. I'm sure he was going to ask for your hand in marriage – "

"Oh, Raymond!"

"Haven't you been expecting that?"

He was teasing her again about Alain while they waited for the parade to start.

"Don't be ridiculous, children! Don't make fun of serious things!"

The interruption came from their mother, who was looking uncomfortable, on such a hot day, in a dress of mauve moiré antique and a matching pelisse. The Lacroix men looked uncomfortable too in their heavy frock coats, while Isabelle, in white muslin, felt deliciously light and free. Her *bibi*, or tiny bonnet, was made of silk lilies of the valley springing from a bandeau of green satin. The pale soft green was the only colour she wore, otherwise she was in white like a bride. And perhaps very soon I shall *be* a bride, she thought exultantly. If Alain – Captain de Grimont – went to see papa, it must have been for that! Two of his business friends had already proposed for her on behalf of their sons – she knew that through the invaluable Raymond – and their offers had been declined because there was no title. This time there was, in spite of dear Alain's funny ideas, and that pleased

Isabelle as well. *Madame la baronne*, she thought contentedly. I shall outrank my mother.

"Daydreaming, Isabelle?" said her brother. "Here they come."

The massed bands, which had been playing a patriotic medley, broke into the *Marseillaise*, and President Grévy led the huge audience in rising to his feet. The national anthem was not being played in his honour, it was clear, because simultaneously, from the far end of the racecourse, the troops selected to pass the reviewing stand appeared.

They were all mounted. First came a platoon of Spahis in their brilliant uniforms, and last came no fewer than four hundred officers drawn from the cavalry, the Chasseurs, the Foreign Legion — Isabelle gasped at the impossibility of finding Alain among so many. But it was the man in the middle who seized and held the multitude's imagination. General Boulanger, riding alone, was the focus of all eyes. He was wearing a uniform of his own devising, with pink breeches and a turquoise blue dolman. He lifted his white-feathered tricorne high, like a field marshal's baton, as he passed the reviewing stand where President Grévy stood with bared head. His mount was a black stallion newly bought on the Champs Elysées, to which he had given the name of Tunis. It was a showy animal, and showy was Boulanger's gesture when he caracoled past the president.

There was no doubt which of the two men was the dominant figure. It was Boulanger, his face pale and set like the painting of Bonaparte at Arcola. Tunis pranced and curvetted beneath him, and the general's powerful body, gripping his mount between his thighs, roused quivering sexual fantasies among the watching women. Male and female, the crowd of thousands sang the *Marseillaise* again:

> *Allons, enfants de la patrie,*
> *Le jour de gloire est arrivé!*

12

The great review began at half past three and was timed to end soon after five, but at half past five, after the presidential party had left, the people swarmed over Longchamp racecourse, snatching at the flags and bunting, dodging the police in their search for souvenirs. Those who came on foot and brought their children started out for the city first. Those who could, crowded on to the lumbering buses; the rest walked, and were prepared to start carrying their young before they reached the Arc de Triomphe. As for the rich, who came in their own carriages, they found it impossible to move until the police began to direct the traffic. Then, according to the ideas of their coachmen, they began to crawl up one or another of the great avenues along which, fifteen years earlier, the government troops had marched from Versailles to crush the Commune.

The Lacroix coachman took the line of least resistance and the Avenue de Longchamp, the most obvious exit, and thereby condemned his employers to more than an hour of misery under the late afternoon sun. They rounded the Arc de Triomphe at last, and made their slow way down the chain of avenues and boulevards which led them to the Rue de Courcelles and home, whereupon the ladies went upstairs and the father and son went into the library, where they thankfully took off their frock coats. It was unheard of for the stockbroker to sit in his shirt sleeves, but the heat and the fatigue were overpowering. They drank brandy and soda, and began to relax.

Raymond asked his father 'what he thought of that performance'. Lacroix snorted. "Performance was the right word. My God, the fellow was dressed up like a circus rider."

"It was an unconventional uniform, certainly. But the people liked it — this afternoon."

"What does that mean?"

"It means that kind of popularity doesn't always last."

"That's what Félix said when he was here on Thursday. I told him what I told you yesterday, about de Grimont's proposal and my answer, and today's invitation which was to show me how Boulanger was loved by all. How I'm going to reply to *that* after what we saw today, I don't know."

"What did Félix have to say?"

"When he heard the settlement de Grimont offers — far superior to Isabelle's dowry — he said we should accept the proposal, because we'd never get a better."

The young stockbroker shifted uncomfortably. He was very like his sister, blond, with a fair complexion, now flushed.

"Good old Félix," he said, "always an eye to the main chance. I'm not so much interested in the business side as I am in Isabelle's happiness. I don't see why it should be dependent on the ambition of General Boulanger. Give the poor girl a chance to speak for herself."

"You think her happiness depends on Alain de Grimont?"

"Yes I do."

Both men were startled when Joseph, the elderly manservant, with the look of one who had huddled on his livery coat, opened the library door to announce:

"Captain de Grimont, monsieur!"

"*Mon cher baron*!" Startled though he was, the familiar locution came all too easily to Lacroix's lips. "This is – a surprise."

"And I apologise for it," said Alain, advancing to shake hands with the father and the son. "I was so – exceedingly anxious to know how you – enjoyed the review, that I came as soon as we escorted – the general to the War Ministry."

"You must have ridden the devil's own pace to get here so fast from the Rue St Dominique, through the crowds in the street tonight," said Raymond Lacroix.

"I know all the short cuts. But I'm afraid I'm not very presentable." There was dust on Alain's uniform, in the gilt of his képi, in the loops of the *fourragère d'honneur*. "Well, sir?" he said imploringly. Monsieur Lacroix still temporised. He said, "I thought you would be celebrating, this evening, with the hero of the day."

"The general is doing his celebrating at the palace of the Elysée."

"Oh? Oh indeed! The guest of the president, is he? General Boulanger's star is certainly in the ascendant." Lacroix paused, seemed aware for the first time that he was in his shirt sleeves, and asked Raymond to hand him his coat. "Well, monsieur, to answer your question, we did enjoy the review. You showed me what you promised: your master cheered by the highest and the lowest, a leader in the land. I withdraw my objection to your addressing my daughter." At Alain's exclamation of delight he held up his hand. "Wait! I make one absolute condition. If she accepts you, there is to be no public announcement of the betrothal. We shall inform the members of our immediate family, and you of course will do the same. And there is to be no question of marriage until

154

next year, perhaps until Christmas of next year . . . depending on where you are stationed."

"I hope to be still with General Boulanger," said Alain stiffly, and Raymond thought, "What an obstinate devil he is! Doesn't he know he could ask for another posting, if he wanted to?"

"Do you accept these conditions, *mon cher baron*?" persisted Lacroix.

"I do, monsieur – if I may speak to Isabelle tonight."

"Ring the bell, please, Raymond, and tell Joseph to ask your sister to come down."

When the message reached Isabelle's bedroom, Raymond had added the words 'Captain de Grimont is here,' and the girl started up from her dressing table in delighted surprise. She had had a bath and put on a silk peignoir, and her mother's maid was brushing her fair hair with slow, soothing strokes, while in the darkened room next door her mother was sound asleep, recovering from the heat and discomfort of the long drive home.

"Oh quick, Suzanne! Help me to get dressed! What shall I wear? No, not the white chiffon, it's too – too grand. Not the eau-de-nil taffeta, it's far too new. Nor the pink. Yes, the blue, I think that's just right. Don't you?"

"If mademoiselle pleases." The smart Parisienne had her own view of mademoiselle's dresses, which she thought too *jeune fille* for her age, but she scented romance in the air, and her fingers flew as she laced Isabelle's satin corset and drew the laces tight. When the draped forget-me-not blue dress was over her head and the finishing touches had been put to her hair, Suzanne felt she did her dresser credit. She watched approvingly as Isabelle pressed two leaves of *papier poudré* to her burning cheeks, and hung over the baluster to see her walk downstairs. The tiny train of the blue chiffon broke like a little wave behind her on every step.

It was bright daylight outside, but dark in the curtained

library which smelt of brandy. Alain hastily put down the glass Raymond had given him when the lovely girl came in. She came straight up to him and gave him her hand.

"Captain de Grimont, thank you for this afternoon. Only we couldn't see you anywhere!"

"Did you look for me in that huge troop? I saw you, but then of course I knew where you would be . . . "

"Isabelle," said her father, as the young man's voice died away, "Captain de Grimont has something to say to you."

"Yes, papa?"

An embarrassed silence fell.

"Well, come on, papa, let's go and change," said Raymond robustly. "Let's give the man a chance to say it!"

But Monsieur Lacroix was not to be deprived of his moment of importance. He kissed his daughter's forehead. "God bless you, my child," he said. "Remember, what you will hear has papa's approval."

The door closed behind the father and son. And Alain de Grimont took Isabelle's hand and said with the utmost simplicity, "Darling, I love you. Will you be my wife?"

He saw her lips shape the word Yes, and then he was kissing her fiercely, with all the pent-up longing of months in his mouth. She seemed to melt in his arms with a molten softness, and between his kisses she whispered all the words he hoped to hear. Yes, she loved him too, would try to make him happy, they would be together always . . . He felt, and heard, that she was ready to adore him. But Alain wanted more than adoration. His father's cruel words had festered in his mind for years. Suddenly he held her away from him, looked into her dark eyes and quivering lips, and said hoarsely, "Isabelle! Swear to be a faithful wife to me!'

At about the same time that evening a popular music-hall singer called Paulus was having a last-minute look through his repertoire to see if he had anything to celebrate the principal event of the day. The crowds had come back from Longchamp and the boulevards were swarming with people shouting the praises of Boulanger, the theatres and restaurants were packed. Even in Red Belleville the fourteenth of July was being celebrated with the usual horseplay. Bands of youths would suddenly surround a couple with cries of "Kiss her! Kiss her!" and there was no escaping the dancing ring until the kisses were sheepishly exchanged. In all the fire stations there were firemen's balls to which all passersby were welcomed and given wine from barrels standing in the courtyard. Only in the Faubourg St Germain were royalists doors shut on the *fête* of the Republic: the owners of the once-great houses had left the city for their country estates. At the Elysée General Boulanger, who had exchanged his review apparel for a dress uniform, outshone all the other guests at the president's table.

Paulus was hunting through the song sheets which reached his dressing room at the Scala every week of his life. There was one he had glanced at a few days before which might have been written, and probably was, in anticipation of this day's great event, but it had sunk to the bottom of the pile. His manager helped in the search. "Good title," Paulus explained. " 'Coming back from the Review' — just what everybody in the theatre did today, I'll bet!"

"Here you are, then, *En Revenant de la Revue*," said the manager, dusting his hands as Paulus stood humming over the words of the new song. "Better start your make-up, hadn't you? I'll call the *chef d'orchestre* — you haven't got much time."

The band leader was co-operative. He played the new song over on a battered rehearsal piano, and said if he could run through it once with the orchestra they could vamp the accompaniment when Paulus came on stage. It was an easy tune; catchy. "You've got a hit there, monsieur," he said, and ran to assemble his musicians in the big room under the stage.

The men were not so sure about the hit. "Trying to put a song over at a moment's notice," they grumbled. "But if Paulus wants to take a chance . . ."

He did. He had memorised the words of 'Coming back from the Review' before the call boy summoned him to head the second half of the show. Exhilarated as always by the faces staring up at him from the great amber bowl of the theatre, he warmed up his audience with two popular songs, and then he made himself over into a little fellow, just like one of the crowd, who had taken his wife and family to the great review that day.

> We went
> To see and compliment
> The army!

It was a sentiment which had not been heard in Paris for many a long day. Then Paulus told how they all reacted:

> My sweet wife clapped and gasped
> When the St Cyr boys went past,
> Her mother seemed at ease
> Making eyes at the Spahis,
> All *I* did was shout hurray
> For brave General Boulanger!

It was a hit all right. The band leader nodded to his musicians as the cheers came rolling in from the curved shell of the theatre. The audience demanded encores. They were singing the song as they spilt out on the boulevard.

> All we did was shout hurray
> For brave General Boulanger!

"*Vive Boulanger*! *Vive le Général Revanche*!"

Le Boulangisme had found its anthem at last.

Arthur Dillon could hardly believe his luck. Here was the perfect means of propaganda, discovered without any effort on his part. The poems of Paul Déroulède had reached literate people, but the songs of Paulus and his imitators reached the people of the streets who could neither read nor write. Soon the whole of France was singing the review song, errand boys were whistling it, barrel organs were playing it, and again and again the one name was repeated, *'Not' brav' général Boulanger!'*

Dillon was on his mettle, and he produced a new device: the Red Carnation. It was presented as General Boulanger's favourite flower. To wear it proved that you were his man, or his admiring lady. The Red Carnation was sold in silk or cotton in the streets, along with other objects adorned with the image of Boulanger. It was very clear now that the general would not be satisfied with the Ministry of War. His ambition was to be the President of the Republic.

The review song, introduced by Paulus, remained the prime favourite. Another song of the streets, even more explicit than the appalling doggerel of the first, was

> It's Boulange, lange, lange
> It's Boulanger that we need
> Oh! Oh! Oh! Oh!

Need for what? For the liberation of Alsace-Lorraine? There was yet another song, more sinister than the others, to reach the streets, which implied that the lost provinces were already free:

> *Regardez-le là-bas!*
> *Il nous sourit et passe*

Alain heard a beggar woman singing it one morning in the courtyard of the Cité du Retiro, and felt a chill as he listened:

Come see him as he goes
Come see him smile and pass
He's just set free for us
La Lorraine et l'Alsace

It was a lie, of course. Boulanger had not taken one step towards the liberation of Alsace and Lorraine, but it was not so ominous as the end of the song:

You'll be more than a king, you'll be more than a god
Because you will be France
O *Général Revanche*!

Suppose the man began to believe it?

Alain said nothing to the girl he loved about these new anxieties. His time with her was too precious for talk about anything except themselves and their future life. Early in their unofficial engagement Isabelle's uncle the ironmaster and his wife came from Briey to meet the Baron de Grimont. Monsieur Frédéric Lacroix was less pompous than the stockbroker, but being aware of his own importance to French industry he seemed pleased by Alain's genuine interest in the new technical processes in use at the Lacroix Ironworks.

"My brother was impressed by you," Isabelle's father told Alain later. "He asked me to find out if you would be interested in joining him in the near future."

"Joining the firm, you mean?"

"Exactly."

"But I don't know enough about iron."

"He doesn't want to employ you as a labourer. After a little training he thinks you would do well as head of his new Paris office."

"What would Félix say to that?"

"Félix has his own place at Briey. He knows Isabelle's husband will have his share in the family fortune."

"That's very generous, sir. But I'm a soldier."

"I hope you know what you're doing."

Alain was beginning to wonder what he was doing in anything so vague as an unofficial engagement, but he put the best face on it when he wrote to Henriette to tell her how happy the friend of her schooldays had made him, and of course when he wrote to his aunt and uncle at the château.

"Well, what do you think?" said Aunt Blanche anxiously, when her husband finished reading the letter and put his spectacles back in their case.

"Think? It seems to be an excellent match. I remember the young lady from Armand's wedding – very pretty, very well brought up, and shy. That's my only criticism. I should have thought Alain would have chosen a girl with more spirit, more to say for herself, but that'll come with time. He says no date has been set for the wedding."

"And the family connection is quite suitable?"

"Every bit as good as the Barthou connection, and we didn't object to that, did we? Personally I didn't care for Monsieur Lacroix, a typical Stock Exchange man, calculating and heavy in hand, but now I learn he's opposed to that mountebank Boulanger we might get on quite well together . . . What's the matter, Blanche?"

The duchess had turned her chair away and was holding a silk fan between her face and the fire. Her husband thought he saw tears on her cheeks.

"Nothing's the matter," she told him. "I just wish I could be sure that Isabelle Lacroix is the right girl for our boy. He'll always be our boy, Gilbert, no matter how headstrong he is."

"What makes you think she isn't the right girl?"

"Because – you felt this yourself – because there's so little *in* her. I hardly noticed her at Armand's civil marriage, because dear Henriette was the bride, but the boys raved so about her beauty that I made a point of watching her at the *déjeuner* next day, and when she was dancing with Alain. Then I had a talk with her."

"So did I. I told you, she was very shy."

"Didn't she remind you of anyone?"

"Nobody in particular."

"She reminded me of Alain's mother."

"Of Elvire!" The duke looked at his sister's portrait on the wall. He had become reconciled to the manner of her death since her husband, whom he held morally responsible for it, had met his own end by violence. He studied it now with renewed attention.

"I suppose there is a certain resemblance," he said doubtfully. "Elvire was about the same age as that girl when Cabanel painted her. Only there's more spirit, more of the devil if you like, in poor Elvire's face. Blanche! Are you saying that's what attracted Alain to Isabelle Lacroix?"

"I'm saying he hasn't got over his mother's murder," said Blanche de la Treille. "He never will until he finds himself."

13

One who had found himself was General Boulanger. He was the idol of Paris, and as opinions regularly taken at the officers' clubs showed, the idol of the army. His goal was his recognition by the whole of France as the liberator of the territory and the man called by a plebiscite to be the chief of state.

First he intended to get himself elected to the Chambre des Députés, and he was already a prospective candidate in the Department of the Nord. It was the day of multiple candidatures, when a man could present himself for several seats at once, and Boulanger wanted more contacts in the south, among those fiery *méridionaux* who all seemed to model themselves on Gambetta. As a start he told Lieutenant Porges to invite an old school friend from Toulouse to luncheon at the Ministry of War.

Monsieur Théophile Delcassé was a man in his early thirties, who had come to Paris like a character from Balzac or Zola, very poor and very ambitious, at the age of twenty-three. Beginning as a free-lance journalist, he became the secretary of a Deputy called Massip, and when Monsieur

Massip died he married Massip's rich widow and succeeded to Massip's seat in the Chamber. He was a dapper little man, with black hair and keen black eyes behind gold-rimmed spectacles. Boulanger did not find him congenial, but Delcassé wrote for important newspapers and the general was always ready to give a vivid personal interview. Théophile Delcassé's special interest was foreign affairs. He advocated an alliance with Russia as a bulwark against Germany when the time came to reclaim Alsace and Lorraine. Did not *'Général Revanche'* agree? This of course excited Alain de Grimont, who was in attendance, and gave General Boulanger the idea of opening relations with the Czar.

He had gone some distance down the road to megalomania before the New Year of 1887. He now felt that he *was* France, ready for his great destiny – if only he had what seemed to be required of public men these days! A wife fit to stand beside him in the full glare of the limelight, to receive his guests graciously, to listen to his confidences – this fate had not granted him. He had summoned his wife to the Hôtel du Louvre when his adventure began, but she was worse than useless with the people she met there, and their meetings since she returned to Versailles had been few and far between. The President and Madame Grévy had invited her to dinner on the night of the grand review – which of course she had not attended – and she had very nearly ruined the occasion. Surly, apathetic, ignorant – Louise Boulanger had been all three in turn, and as for looks and charm, with her broad bosom and broader beam swathed in red velvet she had looked like an upholstered sofa. Damn Louise, and damn his own folly in agreeing to marriage with a cousin!

Now their daughter Marcelle was going to be married to a young army officer, Captain Driant, and bowing to the hypocrisy of weddings and funerals in society, he would have to be present to give the girl away and propose the health of the happy couple. Within a year he might expect to be a grandfather. He, the *beau sabreur*, the idol of the drawing rooms, to be called *grandpère*! He was depressed, he had been depressed ever since de Freycinet, who had put him in the War Ministry, fell from power in December. He was an able man; the carrousel might bring him round again for the fourth time, but it might be too late for Boulanger's master plan.

In this mood of pessimism he accepted an invitation, one January day, to a private dinner party at which the hosts, he knew, would never dream of pestering him about the Lebel magazine rifle, which was not yet in production, the .75mm gun, which was, nor the need, in the name of *élan vital* and *furia francese*, to keep the French infantryman's red trousers, which young de Grimont insisted made him such a mark for the enemy. There would be congenial men and pretty women present, and one piquante as well as pretty, a real attraction to a man of the world: a divorcée who, so far from hiding her shame, frequented and was welcomed in the best society.

Marguerite de Bonnemains was a beautiful brown-eyed blonde. Born Marguerite Bouzet, she had been the victim, like the general himself, of an arranged 'cousin' marriage, and had divorced her cousin six years before the night when in a Paris drawing room she heard her hostess say, "Madame de Bonnemains, may I present General Boulanger?" and laid her little gloved hand in his. He took her in to dinner. He was within a few months of his fiftieth birthday, and before they rose from table he was as much in love as any lad of eighteen.

Since her divorce, Madame de Bonnemains had lived with great discretion. If she had affairs, they were not known. She never discussed the failings of her former husband, whose settlement was so ample that she was able to live in great comfort in a charming house at 39 Rue de Berri, just off the Champs Elysées, with a capable staff, and no boring widow for chaperone. When her butler brought her General

Boulanger's flowers next day — a flamboyant bouquet of orchids and camellias — she found that the accompanying note was only six words long:

"May I see you very soon?"

Marguerite's reply was even shorter:

"Come tomorrow at five o'clock."

She was as sure then as he had been the night before that they would be lovers.

When he arrived, tearing off his greatcoat in the hall and entering her pretty drawing room as a supplicant and not as a star, he found her standing near the log fire, wearing a sophisticated gown of peacock blue in which she looked — to him — like a little girl dressed up, with one of his camellias in her hair and another at her breast.

"Madame!"

"General, I must thank you for the lovely flowers."

"It was nothing. I want — I must tell you — "

She held up her hand, not authoritatively, but in a gesture of defence. "Was it still snowing when you came in?" she said.

"Snowing? I — didn't notice. It's a cold night — "

The white hand dropped, the last defence was down. The *coup de foudre*, the thunderbolt, had struck them both.

"But it's warm where you are," said Boulanger, and took her in his arms. "Marguerite, Marguerite, share your warmth with me!"

He felt her slender arms go round his neck, consenting; her lips open beneath his own. Gently he parted the laces at her throat, and his kisses fell blindly upon flowers and flesh. The petals of the camellia were no softer than her breast. It was a supreme moment for them both; for the woman it was the happiness she had missed in life, for the man it was ruin.

Within two weeks they were the talk of Paris. This was the doing of Boulanger, who refused to content himself with discreet visits to the Rue de Berri, where Marguerite's faithful servants would have kept their secret. He was so much in love, so proud of his beautiful mistress that he paraded her everywhere, at the theatre, at the famous restaurants, and when the weather grew springlike in February the most conspicuous man in Paris rode beside her hired carriage in the Bois. She was infatuated enough to accept it all.

She never heard any of the new songs which were being rushed out for the amusement of malicious and cynical audiences in the little intimate *café-concerts* like the *Lapin Agile* up in Montmartre. The General and the Lady – *there* was a theme for hacks who never feared the law of libel! Marguerite only knew that the review song, and the god song, as she called them, were still being whistled and sung every morning by the delivery boys bringing milk and croissants down the Rue de Berri. Sometimes she whispered the words of one of them to her lover when he was in her bed, with his golden mane and golden beard flickering along her naked stomach:

> You'll be more than a king, you'll be more than a god
> Because you will be France

and then he would call her his queen of pleasure, his goddess of delight, until the rage of love possessed them once again.

The clubs made the most of the scandal, and bets were laid on that old battleaxe, Louise Boulanger, for or against her giving her husband a divorce. "If she does, they've got it made," said educated opinion, "but it'll cost Boulanger a pretty penny to make Marguerite his wife."

"The *Ligue des Patriotes* can afford it," said opinion more educated still. There had been a good deal of gossip recently about the swelling funds of the League, and the use Count Dillon was likely to make of them.

The Lacroix men heard the talk, of course, and Fernand

Lacroix had to tell both his sons not to say a word about it at home. Marie-Alice Lacroix was in bed with another bronchial attack— "Mother's not to be excited," said her husband, "and of course it's not a subject to be mentioned to your sister."

"Do we mention it to Alain?" Raymond wanted to know.

"Say nothing to Alain either unless he alludes to it himself. Something must happen soon to discredit Boulanger. I can't imagine the government is happy with this state of affairs."

The government was far from happy. The general's folly was not discussed at presidential level, for Monsieur Grévy had his own problems. There was now a considerable body of evidence to prove that his English son-in-law (perfidious Albion again) had been using his privileged position at the Elysée to sell decorations, especially the coveted Légion d'Honneur. The net was closing round Monsieur Grévy too. But in the conference rooms of the Chambre des Députés the new premier, René Goblet, and his colleagues discussed Boulanger tirelessly.

"He never attends a cabinet meeting," complained Monsieur Goblet.

"He's neglecting his duties at the War Ministry," said another.

"Dancing attendance on that woman."

"He ought to be replaced as Minister for War."

"Gentlemen!" said Georges Clemenceau, by far the most forceful person present, and to whom Boulanger owed his position, "we can't disgrace a popular hero because he's taken to behaving like a second lieutenant. Just give him enough rope and he'll hang himself, as the saying goes. Sooner or later there'll be an incident which will bring him down. And at all costs he mustn't appear at another Longchamp review."

The incident came sooner rather than later. In April there was a scuffle at the Alsace-Lorraine border when a French customs officer, who happened to be a cripple, was arrested on some trumped-up charge by the guards on the German side. He was soon released, but the honour of France had been insulted, a disabled man had been brutalised, no apologies were acceptable from the German bullies, no financial arrangement could be considered, and so on. The Minister for War demanded a general mobilisation.

The government was appalled. Go to war with Germany because of an insult offered to Customs Officer Schnaebele? Go to war at any time when the army was under strength and not equipped for war? All for the glory of *Général Revanche*? It was unthinkable. The man had gone too far. He was removed from the Ministry 'pending a return to active duty' (but not on the German border) and replaced by the harmless General Logeret.

General Boulanger took the news of his dismissal with his usual bravado. He had his Marguerite for consolation, and he had Arthur Dillon by his side to tell him that this was only a temporary setback, because after the elections next year he would be able to face his enemies on their own ground. The electors of the Dordogne were eager for his candidature, and under the changed circumstances he might be wise to let his name go forward there as well as in the Nord. Now was the time to begin spending money seriously.

He took it for granted that Lieutenant Porges would accompany him to the Hôtel du Louvre and the old suite of rooms on the day he cleared his desk at the Ministry, and told Captain de Grimont he could take the afternoon off. Alain had been very silent since the bad news came. For a few days after the Schnaebele incident he had given way to the old fantasy of an invasion of German-held Alsace and Lorraine; when the mobilisation order was sent up to the government he had pictured Boulanger riding across the Rhine on Tunis, with himself close behind, but when the refusal was received he admitted for the first time that he was getting too old for that sort of dream. He went off as in duty bound to the Rue de Courcelles, wondering how Isabelle would take the news.

Her mother, though hoarse and wheezing, was out of bed and sitting with Isabelle in the salon. Isabelle was sewing, making a present for her godmother. It was a set of table napkins in drawn thread work, although what would be the use of napkins with a lot of holes in them was more than Alain could see. She put down her work and kissed him tenderly, saying "Poor darling, it *is* a shame!" though her face had fallen at the first sight of him without the *fourragère* and the gilt-laced képi.

"We read it in the *Figaro*," said Madame Lacroix in a bronchial whisper. "A message from yourself would have been appreciated."

"I'm sorry, madame, but things were chaotic at the Ministry for the last couple of days."

"I can imagine."

"What are you going to do now, dear?" asked Isabelle.

"I'm hoping the general will take command of troops, darling. I'd like to get back with troops again."

"Oh, Alain! Does that mean leaving Paris? We're to be married at Christmas, and you haven't found a place for us to live yet!"

It was a sore point with his fiancée that he had 'sold the old family home – it would have been so nice to live there' and he had explained in vain that it was a gimcrack affair, 'bastard Louis Philippe on mock Middle Ages' was how he had described it. Now he said it wasn't his fault that Christmas was the date. If her father had let him have his way they would have been married months ago. This sent Isabelle behind a screen of blushes, and her mother intervened.

"Monsieur Lacroix thinks this would be as good a time as any for you to leave the army and go on the reserve officers' list."

"Madame, I've already explained to him that that's impossible."

Isabelle's mother fell into a paroxysm of coughing, and when it was over asked her daughter to fetch her a clean pocket handkerchief. The girl left the room with a backward look at Alain. She knew, and so did he, that something was to be said which a young person ought not to hear.

It was said as soon as the door was shut.

"Alain, I heard something very unpleasant when I came downstairs after my illness."

"What was that, madame?" But he knew, it was going to be the story of the *garçonnière* on the Boulevard Haussmann over again, only worse.

"I heard that General Boulanger was — was cohabiting with the notorious Madame de Bonnemains. Is it true?"

"Cohabiting? He certainly is not living with her, if that's what you mean."

"You know what I mean."

"General Boulanger's private life is no concern of mine."

Madame Lacroix drew her shawl around her. "Perhaps not," she said. "But my husband and I would oppose our daughter's being placed in a situation where she would come in contact with depravity."

The crowds were still singing '*Général Revanche*' outside the Hôtel du Louvre, and so many red carnations, real and paper, were sold that the streets seemed to be lighted with little red lanterns, when a routine political crisis broke. The carrousel of office was creaking round as usual, and René Goblet fell from power at the end of five months. He was succeeded by Maurice Rouvier (first time around) and the new prime minister was determined to get General Boulanger out of Paris. At the end of June it was announced that Boulanger, Georges, demoted to brigadier-general, was to command the XIVth Army Corps at Clermont Ferrand, effective 8 July.

Clermont Ferrand? The idol of Paris railroaded to a garrison town in the Auvergne? They want to get rid of him before the Fourteenth of July, said the wearers of the Red Carnation. We'll show them!

But — "I'm off," said Lieutenant Porges. "He's finished, and I've got a new posting. You're a damned fool if you don't look out for yourself."

"I'm sticking to him."

"You're an obstinate devil, de Grimont!"

"What's your new posting?"

"Staff of the Military Governor of Paris."

Like Robert Scheffler, long ago. "How'd you manage that?"

"I went to Delcassé — remember Delcassé, the Deputy? He's got a line on Logeret, the new Minister, and he fixed it for me. You ought to have a word with Delcassé yourself."

"No thanks."

"If you stick to Boulanger too long, you may find yourself back on topography again. At Timbuctoo."

"I'll take a chance on that."

Porges and a few others like him disgusted Alain de Grimont. They reminded him of an English idiom Monsieur Scherer had taught him, something about mice leaving a sinking ship. He had forgotten most of his English. No matter! At the railway station he thought Porges and the rest of the mice (or was it rats?) had been egregiously wrong. The general finished? Not him! This was the grand review all over again, and better.

One hundred and fifty thousand people had gathered at the station to cheer their hero. They sang, they cheered, they clambered over the 8.07 to Clermont Ferrand until they had destroyed the whole traffic pattern of the night. The station staff were helpless, so were the police, and the engineer of the 8.07 finally jumped off the footplate, saying he dared not move the locomotive for fear of crushing the demonstrators on the track. Finally an ancient engine was hauled out of the sheds and left at 9.40, with the general and half a dozen officers in the cab. The engineer blew his whistle repeatedly, the fireman shovelled coal, and they were all covered with fine black dust when, some miles down the line, an equally ancient train consisting of three wooden compartments divided by a corridor was attached to the antique locomotive. The general, exhausted, got into the first compartment and tried to clean his face with his white handkerchief.

"I haven't got you any water, sir," said Alain de Grimont, returning from a trip down the corridor. "There isn't a lavatory on this train, nor any food or drink."

"That's all right, I have my flask. We're going to be more than two hours late at Clermont Ferrand. You must go forward later on and ask the man if he can stop somewhere on the outskirts, where we might all wash and make ourselves presentable. God knows what's happened to our baggage!"

"I enquired, *mon général*, it's following on the next train."

"Very good, de Grimont. Try to get some sleep."

Each of the two men, as they sat on wooden slats with a wooden partition between them, and watched the stars of a summer night come out over the fields of France, was thinking of a woman. Alain heard Isabelle's sobs as they said goodbye, and felt her tangled hair against his cheek as she shook her head when he whispered, *"Bon courage*, darling! It isn't long till Christmas!" If only her mother didn't fill her head with rubbish . . .

Boulanger too was thinking of a parting. But his sweetheart, who would never be his wife — Louise had sworn it — had been naked in his naked arms, in her bed, beneath the shaded lamp and the little statue of the Madonna.

"Georges, take me with you to Clermont Ferrand."

"Darling, if I could I would — "

"You must."

"My angel, I've told you it's impossible. But I'll come to

173

Paris whenever I can, and next year, after the elections, we'll be together always . . ."

"I can't wait till next year . . . Georges, I want to have your child."

Many women had said that to Boulanger, from society ladies intent on self-dramatisation, to whores in the exercise of their profession. He knew Marguerite meant it. Jolting in the ramshackle train, he remembered her tears when he told her, with caresses, that it was impossible.

14

Clermont Ferrand was not only a garrison town, it was a spa; the largest of the resorts on the high plateau of the Auvergne famous for their thermal springs. By the first week in July the town had begun to fill up with those who came to drink the waters and take the baths, and a number of semi-invalids and holidaymakers were at the station with the Prefect and his officials and the military who had come to greet General Boulanger. In the very early morning he stepped off the emergency train with his entourage, all of them shaved and immaculate, and was greeted with the same enthusiasm as he had left behind in Paris.

One week later the afternoon train brought a lady, heavily veiled and unattended by a maid or any other escort, who told the stationmaster her baggage would be called for, and walked quickly across the yard to a waiting carriage. It took her less than three miles to the outskirts of another spa called Royat, where the waters were good for a number of maladies, including arthritis, anaemia and respirational problems. The lady appeared to be in good health. She did not direct the driver to one of the first-class hotels of Royat, but to a modest inn called Les Marroniers, the chestnut trees, where the innkeeper, a woman, was curtseying in the doorway. The lady, at her direction, ran up a steep stair to a sitting-room just level with the tops of the chestnut trees. The door was open, and in a moment more, Marguerite de Bonnemains was in the arms of Georges Boulanger.

The innkeeper, Marie Quinton, went back to her kitchen, smiling at the thought of a romance.

"What a lovely place, darling," was the first coherent thing Marguerite said. The little sitting-room, with its First Empire furniture and its porcelain stove for the mountain nights in winter, pleased her at once.

"Will it really do?"

"Of course it will. Is this the bedroom?" Marguerite opened a door in the wall opposite the window, nodded, and went in to lay her bonnet, veil and light jacket on the curtained bed. "It's all perfect, Georges. So quiet and peaceful."

"It's not the place for you, my love. You ought to be in your own home in Paris, with your good servants to wait on you, and your friends to visit – "

"But in Paris I wouldn't have *you*."

"I'll come every day – every night, rather. It wouldn't be prudent in daylight."

"How did you come today?"

"I rode, darling. Tunis came down in a horsebox on the Paris train yesterday. Why are you laughing?"

"At your idea of prudence, dear. You on black Tunis – recognisable to everyone between Royat and Clermont Ferrand!"

"It isn't for long, Marguerite. I can't stand much more of garrison life. Dillon's looking out for a house in Paris for me. Oh for a by-election!"

"And I'm to go back to the Rue de Berri?"

"Where I'll know you're happy and comfortable. I'm afraid you'll be bored here, alone all day."

"I'll have so much to think about. You to look forward to."

He kissed her with a passion that demanded its fulfilment, but he commanded himself to remember that she had been on a long journey and must be tired. "I have to take care of you," he said fondly, and made her take off her dress and shoes and corset before tucking her up on the four-poster under a light blanket. "Till tomorrow night!" he whispered, and tiptoed down the steep stair, trying to soften the noise of his riding boots. At the foot he encountered the rosy-cheeked landlady and gave her money. "See that madame has everything she needs," he said. "Look after her well." Then he sent a boy to bring black Tunis from the stable, and rode back to Clermont Ferrand.

The general was in high spirits in the mess that night; Alain had not seen him so cheerful since they left Paris. On duty he was the same martinet as when he arrived at Tunis and had a trial of strength with the civil power in the person of Paul Cambon, and with the same concern for the welfare of the troops. He spoke to them, chosen at random, on parade, and remembered their names when he inspected the mess halls at noon. *"La soupe est bonne, mon général!"* The men said it as if they meant it.

It was a different story in the evening. There was no lingering over apéritifs in the anteroom, the meal was eaten quickly, and the general withdrew to his own quarters and from his rooms to the stables. There Keller, the tall, bearded Alsatian orderly was waiting with black Tunis, saddled and bridled, and in the summer dusk the general took the road for Royat and the waiting woman.

August had begun before Alain de Grimont realised what was going on. His hours off duty were fully occupied in looking for a house to rent. He was determined to marry

Isabelle at Christmas and bring her to Clermont Ferrand, and he wrote glowing accounts of the town and its fashionable society, its entertainments, balls and concerts, and its tonic, health-giving air. Isabelle wrote doubtfully back. No doubt the place was lively in August, high season for the spas, but what would it be like in winter? Snowed up, when all the surrounding resorts – La Bourboule, Mont Dore, Royat and the others – had closed down until late spring? How long did Alain expect to be stationed at Clermont Ferrand anyway? Was it possible to find servants there? Papa thought, etc.

Alain could afford to pay for half a dozen servants, and the local agents assured him that capable staff would be available as soon as the summer lettings were over. He was able to view a number of houses, and eventually found a charming place with a garden and a view over the wide Auvergne landscape. He put down a sum of money to secure it from November, and wrote in triumph to tell Isabelle.

Then he became fully alive to the gossip of the mess. At Royat Madame de Bonnemains had been recognised when walking in the very early morning by Parisians going to the thermal springs. General Boulanger, that too conspicuous figure, had been seen riding along the back roads in the evening. *Oui, monsieur,* he has the little lady tucked away at Les Marroniers, what d'you think of that? Hasn't the XIVth Corps got a spirited commander? Chuckles and digs in the ribs.

Marguerite and her adored Georges knew nothing of all this. Like all middle-aged lovers – she was in her thirties – they were pretending to be a boy and girl again, in a playhouse high in the branches of the chestnut trees. Marie Quinton guarded their privacy from the few local people who came to drink in the taproom below, lit fires in the porcelain stove as the nights grew colder, and brought them food and wine at midnight. "But madame should rest," she said, for Marguerite had caught a bad cold and coughed a good deal.

Marguerite grew fond of her landlady and took to calling her *la belle meunière*. "For she is like a miller's wife or a miller's daughter with those lovely rosy cheeks, isn't she, Georges?" she said.

"I'd like to see more colour in *your* cheeks, my love. Are you sure you're feeling better?"

"If I'm pale it's because I keep my parasol up when I'm in the long chair under the chestnut trees." She had missed the chestnut candles but not the fruit: the green spiky buds were swelling every day.

One Monday morning in the middle of September General Boulanger entered his office before lunch to find his military secretary with an open letter in one hand and a startled look on his face.

"Something the matter?"

"An urgent message from Paris, *mon général*."

The man handed over the letter. Written in the third person, it announced that the new Minister for War, General Logeret, would inspect the XIVth Army Corps at Clermont Ferrand in ten days' time. Copies were being sent to the colonels of the regiments which made up the corps.

Boulanger was furious. It was a deliberate provocation – an inspection by the man who had superseded him, with himself subordinate if not subservient. He refused an acknowledgement and went to luncheon in an evil mood. After the silent meal was over he rode to Royat. Marguerite's cough was worse, and she was so feverish that red spots of colour had appeared on her pale cheeks. The doctor was sent for, sounded her chest and looked grave. He prescribed a linctus and a sedative which soothed her into a restful sleep. Boulanger sat by her bedside until six o'clock, and then rode back to his command.

His ADC was with the military secretary when he appeared in his office and asked if there had been another signal from the Ministry of War.

"Nothing from the Minister, sir, but Colonel Chautemps has asked to see you about arrangements for his visit."

Chautemps was the senior colonel at Clermont Ferrand, a lickspittle timeserver if ever there was one, Boulanger believed.

"Where's Colonel Chautemps now?"

"In the waiting room, *mon gènèral*," said Alain de Grimont.

"Show him in."

Colonel Chautemps came in, but he was not alone. He was accompanied by two officers of his own rank, Colonels Mirepoix and Fremineur, and all three saluted respectfully.

"Good evening, sir," said the spokesman, "we missed you this afternoon. We were anxious to hear your views on the War Minister's visit."

"My views?"

"On the ceremonies of his arrival. The honour guard, the band, the luncheon for the Minister and the Prefect, the reception for the mayor and councillors — "

"All that for General Logeret?"

"Sir, for the Minister for War."

"Colonel, *I* was the Minister for War until a few months ago, and I never expected my official visits to be treated like the Second Coming of Our Lord."

Boulanger had risen to his feet, and the veins on his forehead swelled alarmingly.

"Sir, you are not yourself!" exclaimed Alain de Grimont.

"Yes, God damn you, I am myself! I refuse to be hunted and hounded by those jacks-in-office in Paris! You can tell Logeret to go to hell! I won't permit that incompetent, stupid bastard to come spying and prying in my command! Let me go, de Grimont. Let me go, I say . . ."

He never knew who sent the telegram to Paris — Chautemps probably — but the reply was promptly received.

"Boulanger, General Georges, is hereby condemned to

fortress arrest for thirty days, on a charge of insubordina-
tion and verbal insults to the Minister of War. Effective
immediately."

15

Fortress arrest, with its sinister implications of dungeons, fetters and leg irons, sounded more alarming than it actually was. General Boulanger was confined to his own quarters, with a sentry on the door for the sake of appearances, and he was supposed to stay for four weeks in the pleasant, sunny rooms in a far wing of the barracks. His rooms were on the third floor and there was only one exit to the stair, but there was a dovecote so close to the rear window that any man in good training could scramble out in the darkness, swing himself over and grasp the shelf of the dovecote, and then use the footholds to reach the ground. Boulanger achieved this on his first night in custody, and reached the thicket where his orderly was waiting with Tunis. Before anyone thought of checking he was at Les Marroniers, where he spent the next month helping to nurse his mistress back to health.

Tunis was back in his stall by morning, and the faithful Keller set to work to cover his master's flight. He was seen carrying trays to the 'fortress' three times a day, and he had been given money to bribe the sentries not to look inside the rooms. Keller brought out lists of books the general wished to read and Colonel Chautemps provided them from his own library. Quite possibly he was not fooled by the elaborate charade and the breach of regulations, but he never sought to visit the prisoner, and seemed satisfied with saying, after an evening patrol of the lamplit building, that he had seen the general's shadow on the blind. Alain did a patrol on his own, and saw that the bearded shadow was unmistakably Keller's, but he said nothing to Chautemps. Let them do their own dirty work. His own position in the mess was very difficult, and the only ray of light was that General Logeret had cancelled his visit to Clermont Ferrand.

A week had passed, and the nights were drawing in, when Alain received a letter from Raymond Lacroix, terse and to the point. "Dear Alain," it ran, "if you mean to marry Isabelle at Christmastime or any time, you had better come to Paris and set a date. Your general's latest escapade has infuriated my father, and mother preaches morality to Isabelle by the hour. Remember 'the absent are always wrong.' Yours, RL."

Ten minutes after reading Raymond's letter, Alain put in a request for Paris leave.

"This might be as good a time as any for you to go on leave," said Colonel Chautemps with a slight smile. " 'Urgent family affairs' eh? Of course. Can you settle them in a week? Very good, Captain de Grimont. Your pass and travel warrant will be ready this afternoon."

"Thank you, *mon colonel*." Alain went straight to the telegraph office and wired to Isabelle, 'Arriving tomorrow four afternoon *tendresses* Alain' and then tried to be patient until the night train came in.

When he reached the Rue de Courcelles next day they were all waiting for him in the salon, Raymond and his father in black cravats with crêpe on their sleeves, Madame Lacroix and Isabelle in black dresses and shawls. With the addition of a jet necklace and earrings, Isabelle's dazzling fairness was set off by the black frills.

Alain looked from one to the other and asked if anything had happened. Monsieur Lacroix, as usual the spokesman, said his wife's third cousin Albert had passed away at the age of eighty-one. "Sit down, Alain," he added as an after-thought.

"My condolences, madame," said Alain courteously. "Cousin Albert. I don't think I ever heard of him."

"He lived in Lille," said Raymond. "He was bedridden for the past ten years," and his mother sobbed aloud.

"I'm very sorry," said Alain again. "I didn't mean to intrude on your family mourning, but I had to take leave when I could get it — "

"When your general was in prison," said Lacroix.

"On a technicality, sir, and only for four weeks."

"And a blot on his record for the rest of his life."

Alain ignored him. "Isabelle darling, how are *you*? It's you I came to see."

"I'm pretty well," she said without meeting his eyes.

"I've brought some papers for you to look at. Full descriptions of the house I've taken at Clermont Ferrand, and a plan of the garden. There's an inventory, too, of all the stuff that goes with it, like pots and pans and china, and linens, so you can decide what you want to bring from Paris . . ."

"I don't want to live with other people's furniture and linens."

"But darling, we must begin somewhere, if we're to be married at Christmas, that's only three months away. And it's really a very nice house."

"How can you even *think* of a wedding at Christmas, now that we're in mourning?"

"For Cousin Albert."

"Yes."

"The truth of the matter is, *mon cher baron*," said Lacroix,

"I cannot give my consent to your marriage with my daughter as long as you are an aide-de-camp to that reprobate Boulanger."

"Or while she runs the risk of coming in contact with — *cette créature*," said Madame Lacroix. She meant Madame de Bonnemains, of course, *créature* was what every bourgeoise called a woman of easy virtue.

"Well, make up your minds, both of you," said Alain, "I shall stay with General Boulanger as long as he needs me. What's the alternative?"

"You could send in your papers and leave the army."

"I'm twenty-seven now, monsieur. What do you suggest I should do with the rest of my life?"

"Become a landed proprietor like your father before you, *mon cher baron*."

"No thanks."

"Then, Isabelle, I think you should tell this gentleman what you have decided."

"Yes, papa." she looked at Alain at last. "We have talked it over and papa thinks — "

"Isabelle!" warned Lacroix.

"I mean I think — I think it would be best to break off — our unofficial engagement now." She had got so far in her rehearsed speech when Alain rose and stood over her; one look at his puzzled, desperate face and her courage nearly failed her.

"Dear Alain, I don't think we would be happy together. We have — have different views on so many things, and so I want — I want to set you free."

"Isabelle!" He pulled her roughly from her chair and crushed her in his arms. "You know we've been happy! You know we'll be happier still after we're married! You know I'm madly in love with you!"

She lifted her tear-stained face and whispered, "No, not with me. Only with your idea of me."

185

He looked over her golden head at the three black figures of mourning, and a weary hopelessness overcame him. He took Isabelle's hand, kissed it, and stood back.

"Very well," he said, "I have received my *congé*. Madame, messieurs, permit me to make my adieux." He bowed and turned to the door. Raymond got up quickly, saying "I'll come with you."

In the tessellated hall Isabelle's brother took his arm, and said "Alain, I'm desperately sorry about this — "

"Thanks, Raymond. You've been a good friend."

Old Joseph was shuffling forward to help him on with his greatcoat, give him his képi and gloves.

"Goodbye, Raymond. Don't come any further." It was all he could trust himself to say before the door opened, and the autumn wind was blowing down the Rue de Courcelles.

Alain had kept on his *pied à terre* in the Cité du Retiro when they went to Clermont Ferrand, and he was glad of it now. It was better than a hotel room, it was a place to hide. He had left his valise there when he came off the train, and the concierge came up the stairs with him shrilling that if he had only let her know she would have had the place aired and dusted for him. She had been in the apartment while he was out, for the window was open in the living room and still the place was warm. They must have turned on the *chauffage* early this autumn. There were clean sheets on the bed (other people's sheets) and some groceries in the kitchen which also held his hip bath. He didn't intend to go out to dinner. A little bread and cheese and a lot of wine would be all he needed.

He took off his uniform and put on an old shirt and trousers before he went back to the living room and sat down on the daybed with its faded rust velvet cover. It was directly opposite the window through which could be seen the deep archway which led from the Cité into the Rue du Faubourg St

Honoré. What Alain saw was the Lacroix salon with those four black figures like funeral mutes, ready to fling gravel on the grave of his hopes. He saw the husband and wife mourning Cousin Albert (he must have left them money) who had stuffed Isabelle with their own hypocrisy, their own false morality – damn them! damn them! He heard Isabelle parroting off her lesson and felt her fragile shoulders under his hands. She had sworn to be a faithful wife to him, and now she was insisting that theirs was an 'unofficial' engagement, meaning not binding. He hated those hair-splitting distinctions between *officieuse* and *officielle*. He hated them all.

He felt as if he had boxed himself into a hopeless situation. His general was in prison – *officiellement* – and who could tell where he would go when he was released? Would he stay on at Clermont Ferrand as if nothing had happened, or take his mistress back to Paris? What about the rented house? He had lost the deposit on it, of course, and there was enough of old Henri Grimont in his grandson to make him regret the fact. Worst of all, he had lost Isabelle.

You weren't in love with me, she had said. 'Only with your idea of me.'

What if it were true?

He expected to lie awake all night, but the concierge told him he was 'sleeping like a happy man' when she brought up his coffee and croissants, and that made him laugh. He still felt as though he had been hit on the head with a sledge-hammer, but not having dined he began to think of lunch soon after he had bathed and got back into uniform. He could go to the Cercle Militaire or the Jockey Club, see his friends, and hear the reactions to the general's fortress arrest, but he shrank from all the questioning and possible ribaldry about the events at Clermont Ferrand. He decided on the Continental Hotel, and about midday set out for the Rue Royale, not happy but not quite broken-hearted, to enjoy the superb vista of the Place de la Concorde.

There he saw a strange sight. Gustave Eiffel, who had once had trouble with the framework of the Statue of Liberty, had undertaken to build a tower which, as the highest structure in Europe, would grace the International Exhibition planned to open in May 1889. Alain knew that work had begun on the thing, beginning with eight piers uniting at five hundred feet to support a single shaft as high again, but the work in progress had not been visible when he went away. Now the tip of the piers had risen above the skyline – the harmonious skyline of Paris, which they ruined of course – and squatted like a great animal, destroying the symmetry of the dome of the Invalides. And they called that progress! When the single shaft was erected he thought, as so many born Parisians did, that the Eiffel Tower would be a disaster.

It took his mind off Isabelle.

The Continental luncheon was excellent, and it was soothing, after a succession of mess halls, to sit at a table with flowers and starched napery, without having to jabber and make conversation as at Clermont Ferrand. He knew nobody in the restaurant until, just as he was paying his bill, a short dark man detached himself from several others and came up to Alain's table holding out his hand.

"*Bonjour, Capitaine de Grimont!*"

"Monsieur Delcassé!"

It was the Deputy who had been Lieutenant Porges's schoolmate at Toulouse, and had got Porges posted to the Military Governor's staff.

"I'm delighted to see you, Captain de Grimont. Are you in a hurry or have you time for a chat?"

"I'm in no hurry, but what about your friends?"

For answer the Deputy turned and waved his hand at the group with a brisk "See you later!" He said to Alain, "We'll be confronting each other from different sides of the Chamber in an hour's time. Let's go into the smoking room and have a cigar."

When the cigars and another pot of coffee were brought into the quiet smoking room, Delcassé continued, "I'm very glad to see you, *mon capitaine*. You were one of the few people who really understood what I was trying to do when I proposed a formal alliance with Russia."

"You didn't get it through the Chamber, though. And I was enthusiastic only because you convinced me it was important for the recovery of Alsace-Lorraine."

"No, I didn't get it through the Chamber – this time – and I know I didn't convince *Général Revanche*. Tell me about him. Frankly I thought you'd be in Clermont Ferrand by his side."

"I'm on leave. Did you think I'd be under fortress arrest too – on a technicality?"

"Are you worried about that? It hasn't done him the slightest harm politically."

"So the morning papers said. But I'm afraid I'm no politician, Monsieur Delcassé. Have you seen our friend Porges lately?"

The abrupt change of subject caused Delcassé to raise his eyebrows. He said, "Porges is getting married to a doctor's daughter in Toulouse. The wedding will take place at Christmas."

"Lucky Porges!"

"Yes, he left Boulanger in time," said Delcassé, wilfully misunderstanding. "Are you planning to follow his example?"

"I'm not much use to the general at present. But I'm staying as long as he needs me."

"You're very loyal. I only thought, since you're not interested in politics, you might find yourself less comfortable in General Boulanger's entourage in future. I suspect his life is going to be all politics from now on."

"Hadn't I better wait for him to tell me so?"

"*Touché!*" Delcassé was astute enough to smile. "But

perhaps I could be of service to you if you were looking for another post. No, I'm *not* trying to drum up recruits for the Military Governor's staff!"

"I didn't think you were, monsieur. Only—things haven't turned out quite as I expected when I was in Tunisia."

"An able man is lost in Tunisia. How about a posting to Egypt? I've acquired some influence in Egypt."

"My father proposed a civilian job for me in Cairo, during the Dual Control. I turned it down when I was just a kid."

"Why?"

"It was one way to annoy my father. Sooner than go to Egypt I'd go back to the Topographical. You see results for your work there."

"Permit me to say, *mon cher capitaine*, that you don't make the best use of your opportunities. You don't put yourself forward enough. After all, you're the man who saved the life of Marshal MacMahon. You were a brilliant student and instructor at St Cyr, you fought in Tunisia, and your work at Bizerta earned you a decoration. Remind people of that! Don't stay forever in the general's shadow ... Have I offended you?"

"Not at all. I know you're only trying to give me good advice."

"I'll give you some practical advice. Write something for my paper."

"What could I possibly write for *La Petite République*?"

"Your opinion of the French Army."

Alain laughed aloud. "And get myself cashiered? You know we're not allowed to write for the newspapers."

"You don't have to sign your own name to it. But a good hardhitting article would be something you could quote one day in the right quarter. Try it and see." The Deputy rose to his feet and took out his card case. "If you produce anything, don't send it to the paper, but to myself at home. This is my private address. And good luck!"

At St Cyr Alain had been trained in good clear *précis* writing, and he had no difficulty in putting his ideas on paper. In his quarters at Clermont Ferrand, with the door locked, he found it took his mind off Isabelle to write a challenging essay on the new ideas beginning to infiltrate the Great Unknown. Gambetta had believed in 'a fight to a finish', while Colonel de Picque, killed in the war, declared that 'to win you have to advance'. Captain Gilbert believed in what he called 'the French fury', and the philosopher Bergson swore by 'the vital impulse'. It was all philosophy, wrote Alain de Grimont, everything in the mind and nothing in the guns. The army chiefs failed to realise the technical advances in weaponry, or understand that no amount of *élan*, fury or advance could stand up against heavy artillery.

Alain was rather pleased with his effort, and signed it with the initials HG in honour of his Grimont grandfather, the cobbler's son. Delcassé was delighted with it, gave it prominence in his paper and asked for more. About this time, however, General Boulanger's 'imprisonment' came to an end, and he was formally released by Colonel Chautemps from the room which he had not occupied for thirty days, and to which he returned as he went under cover of night.

He met his officers with his usual swagger, and ordered the whole corps out on autumn manoeuvres. He spared neither himself nor his men but flung himself into the exercise with enthusiasm, for he, like his ADC, had something on his mind.

Marguerite was pregnant, and her lover was torn between tenderness at the sight of her joy, pride in his own virility, and pure terror at the effect of scandal on his career. The first by-election would put him into the Chamber, or so Arthur Dillon wrote, for the money was rolling in, and so were the supporters, for the 'fortress arrest' story had brought in a lot of waverers of the liberal sort, opposed to any form of 'government tyranny'. Dillon wanted to see the hero of the hour in Paris soon, and Boulanger was ready to start as soon as the manoeuvres were over, taking his mistress with him. He wanted to go to his house in Versailles and ask Louise again for a divorce; he wanted Marguerite to be surrounded by all the comforts of the Rue de Berri. The little country doctor was less enthusiastic. "The greatest specialist in Paris would agree with me," said Dr Ribot, "that there's nothing like the early stages of a pregnancy for starting up a latent lung complaint. Keep your lady in our pure mountain air for another couple of months before she attempts the journey to Paris – if it really is indispensable – and bring her back to us for her confinement."

Boulanger thought the idea had its merits. The *Ligue des Patriotes* had not taken his liaison with Madame de Bonnemains too seriously, because it might not last, and for a public man to have a mistress was a tradition which had lasted since the Second Empire, and long before. But a bastard child! He imagined the cabaret songs and jests, the cartoons in the gutter press. Even if Louise granted him a divorce, he would lose the Catholic vote for certain . . . He saw his election campaign in ruins before it began.

Marguerite, always docile, agreed though with tears to the solution he proposed. After a short stay in Paris, she would return to Royat and await the birth of her child, whom Marie *la belle meunière* would pass off as her own and bring up until . . . until such time as its parentage could be acknowledged. She would of course be paid well for acting nurse. Marie, who had always been in their confidence, agreed to the price, but demanded some recompense for what she called 'the slur on her reputation'. She accepted Boulanger's gift of a gold link bracelet, set with a medallion of St George, his patron saint. In December, before Marguerite's condition became too obvious, she travelled to Paris on the same train as her lover.

The event which took the general away from XIVth Corps, without the trifling formality of asking permission, was the resignation of the President of the Republic. Monsieur Grévy's son-in-law had brought about his downfall, and a new president was to be elected by the Deputies and Senators who constituted the electoral college of the Republic. Boulanger, determined to make his presence felt, made for the Chambre des Députés as soon as he had seen Madame de Bonnemains safely to her own comfortable home. He wanted to 'collect opinions' — and to give them — on who should be Grévy's successor. It was a rehearsal for the great day when he himself should be the sole candidate for the presidency.

Boulanger might have been hoping for a popular demonstration in his favour, but it was not known that he was back in Paris, and the city was in one of its Red moods that day. The crowds massing in the Place de la Concorde, threatening to march on the Chamber and string up certain Deputies to the most convenient lamp posts, were only imitating their forerunners of the Commune and the revolution of 1848. Alain, from a vantage point on the northern embankment, saw that the police had the situation well in hand. They had stopped all traffic and all foot passengers across the bridge, making the Chamber impregnable, when they were suddenly challenged by a grey-haired woman in a ragged gown of rusty black, with nothing but a thin shawl to protect her from the December wind.

"Hireling of capitalism!" the woman shrieked at a sergeant of police. "Let the People pass! Follow me, comrades! Storm the Chamber of corruption as our forefathers stormed the Bastille!"

There was a roar of applause, and a rabble of youths ranged themselves behind her.

"Who the devil is that?" said Alain to a man beside him, who appeared to be calmer than most of the spectators.

"Don't you know?" said the man. "That's Louise Michel, who led the Women's Battalion in the Commune, and served a sentence in New Caledonia—" The pressures of the growing crowd forced them apart.

Alain grasped the coping of the embankment to keep his place. So that was Louise Michel, one of whose devotees had murdered his father! He had made it his business to find out a little about her after the amnesty allowed her to return to France. She lived in two rooms in a miserable house at Neuilly, with a collection of dogs and cats and monkeys. Some said she tried to help the poor and even served them as an untrained midwife, but the truth was that she still lived by the politics of the Commune, and was currently agitating for the victims of what she called the Haymarket Massacre, a recent fight between anarchists and police in Chicago.

Now she was inciting the Paris crowd to sing the Carmagnole, the song of the great revolution which she had so often led during the Commune. They sang with her, they pressed on behind her; Comrade Louise Michel might well have led her 'troops' to victory again if a resourceful sergeant had not seized her in his arms and bundled her into a police van waiting at the far side of the bridge. She was rattled away to face one more charge of inciting to riot, and without her inspiration the crowd lost heart. The gendarmes came forward swinging their batons, and to the familiar order *"Allez, allez, circulez!"* the would-be demonstrators began to retreat across the square and filter off down the Rue de Rivoli and the side streets. The intervention of Louise Michel was all Alain had to report of interest to his master, and Boulanger shrugged it off. He had no belief in women as a political force.

On 3 December 1887 François Sadi-Carnot was elected President of the Republic. More sensational than his election was the murder, on 10 December, of Jules Ferry, the great coloniser. "Let's go back to Clermont Ferrand, we'll be safer there," joked Boulanger. "We might take another little trip in the New Year."

*

There was no fanfare when General Boulanger returned to his command, as if the senior officers realised that his presence was a mere formality. The ranks on parade were diminished because with his insistence on the welfare of the troops he had instituted five days' leave at Christmas as a reward for good conduct, and for those still in barracks he paid out of his own pocket for a special Christmas dinner and a bottle of wine for each man. He was cheered as he walked through the mess halls on Christmas day, and Alain smiled as he followed his master. It was the last time he was to hear Boulanger cheered by enlisted men.

Very soon after that he told Alain he was going away again, officially to Paris but in fact to Switzerland. Alain was to buy the railway tickets and book a room in his own name at the Hôtel des Bergues in Geneva.

"Am I to accompany you to Geneva, *mon général?*"

"I shan't be staying in Geneva. I want you to stay here and deal with all my correspondence. I expect a telegram from Count Dillon about the impending by-election in the Nord; send it on to me without delay at Prangins."

"Very good, sir." They were in Boulanger's bedroom, and Alain noticed that Keller, the orderly, was packing a valise with civilian clothing. It was Keller who ordered a carriage from the town which took the general to the station after dark.

It was not until later that Alain de Grimont remembered that Prangins was the name of the Swiss estate owned by Prince Jérome Napoleon, the most unpopular member of the Bonaparte family, whom the young Prince Imperial had refused to recognise as his heir. Why should Boulanger put on civilian clothes to visit him?

The answer was obvious: he had gone to solicit money. Although the royalist aristocracy of the Faubourg St Germain had contributed generously to Boulanger's political fund, desiring to punish the republican government by supporting the man who was planning to overthrow it, he had not yet tapped the Bonapartist resources, hence his approach to the disreputable prince known as 'Plon-Plon'.

Alain de Grimont had explained away Boulanger's evasion of 'fortress arrest' by telling himself that the sentence was unjust and prompted by jealousy, but with the furtive visit to Prangins his last illusion was shattered. *Général Revanche* had no intention of liberating Alsace and Lorraine. He had recently been adopted for three more constituencies, and if he were elected for only one he could make his voice heard in the Chambre des Députés and perhaps through the whole of France. He might be a hero to the voters but he was no longer a hero to his ADC.

It was a miserable New Year for Alain, and he had to force himself to share in the artificial jollity of the officers' mess. He had expected to be married by this time and on honeymoon with his lovely bride. All he could do to banish his dismal thoughts was to draft another article for *La Petite République*, this one in support of a Colonel Philippe Pétain, who said the army was too slow in adopting the new Maxim-Nordenfelt gun. It was a dreary task with the snow falling outside his window, and Alain welcomed the break when Keller came in with a telegram. The expected message from Count Dillon, of course. The date of the Nord byelection must be fixed.

It was not from Dillon. It was signed Dr Thomas and was very brief.

"Madame had serious accident advisable you come."

Boulanger knew what he would hear before he reached the Rue de Berri. Haggard and unshaven, sleepless for all the forty-eight hours after he received the telegram forwarded by his ADC, General Boulanger knew by the sympathy in the face of the butler who opened the door, and the tears of the maids in the background, what the doctor had to tell him.

Dr Thomas, waiting in the salon, was urbane, sympathetic and explicit.

"Madame has lost her hopes of maternity," he said. "The unfortunate consequence of a fall."

"A *fall*? How?"

"She caught the high heel of her slipper in the frilling of her skirt as she was coming downstairs, and fell heavily to the next landing. No, nothing was broken – a great mercy – and she was only bruised, but the mischief was done, and she suffered a miscarriage about an hour later."

"How is she now?"

"As well as can be expected, but very much distressed."

"Can I see her?"

"Not at once, sir. She is sleeping naturally for the first time, and I want her to have her sleep out. A nurse is sitting by her bed, of course, to let me know of any change . . . and dare I suggest that you make some alterations in your dress and general appearance before you go to her? Remember she depends on you for comfort now."

"I need a brandy."

He poured the spirit with an unsteady hand from the cellarette – Marguerite's cellarette, from which she delighted to serve him! – and said hoarsely, "Will she live?"

"My dear sir, of course she'll live!" said the doctor robustly. "Physically it was a routine mishap, and the real damage is to the poor lady's nerves. Also, I can't conceal from you that I'm not satisfied with the condition of her lungs. She must not be allowed to catch cold or cough. I should prescribe a fortnight's bed rest, another two weeks downstairs, and at the beginning of February you should arrange to take her to a Swiss sanatorium, to spare her the remainder of the Paris winter."

Switzerland – not Royat, where they had pretended to be children in their playhouse in the treetops, and where she had planned to give birth to their own child! He longed to go to her, to hold her in his arms, but the doctor was right, he must shave at least before he saw his darling. He said, "Doctor, one more question. Was it possible . . . could you tell . . . what it was?"

Dr Thomas said gently, "It was a male child."

A son. Years before, while he was still living with his wife, Boulanger had hoped for a son, a boy to follow in his footsteps from St Cyr to the General Staff, a brilliant boy unlike his stupid sisters, the boy Marguerite's son would have been. He covered his face with his hands. And yet, even when the painful tears came to his eyes, and he felt the doctor's consoling hand on his shoulder, the unworthy thought came to Georges Boulanger, the man of destiny:

Perhaps it's better as it is.

16

Eighteen Hundred and Eighty-eight was to be Boulanger's Year, he had told his followers so, and his promise came true. In February he was returned to the Chambre des Députés for all the five constituencies in which he had been nominated, on a platform which was not always solid, but on which he would be tackled plank by plank by the professionals sharpening their claws in Paris. Dillon's promotion, and his American-style campaigning, had worked so well that for the provincial voters it was enough merely to see the general about whom they had been told so much. When he appeared at election meetings, in full uniform and wearing all his campaign medals, they were prepared to vote for him from the moment he threw his arms wide as if to embrace them all, and cried *"Chantons la Marseillaise!"*

With six million francs to spend, Boulanger, Dillon and Déroulède were able to open the 1888 campaign in style. Photographs of the general riding Tunis, the archetypal Man on Horseback, were distributed along with booklets about his life and aims, which not all the country voters were able to read. Pipes in which the bowl was the general's head, watch-chains, canes and tie-pins similarly ornamented, even soaps and cheeses with the general's face stamped on them, found a ready sale for profits ploughed back into the campaign fund. When he returned to Paris in triumph the majority of men were wearing the Red Carnation.

He had left the Hôtel du Louvre (and since Madame de Bonnemains entered his life, he had abandoned the *garçonnière* on the Boulevard Haussmann) for an imposing house at 11 Rue Dumont d'Urville near the Etoile. It had a huge reception room with a table at the far end behind which he sat to receive his supporters and petitioners, thus making sure they would have a long way to walk before they reached him. There were a few chairs, which were genuine antiques from the period of Louis XV, but the men in and out of uniform who crowded into the room to pay their respects to Boulanger seldom sat down. They were delighted to stand, talking to each other, exchanging the latest gossip from the Chamber, the Bourse, the *Ligue des Patriotes* and the other nerve centres, while all the time watching him.

He could afford to live well, for money continued to flow into the fund administered by the *Ligue des Patriotes*. The principal subscriber was the Duchesse d'Uzès, a widow of right-wing convictions, but money also came from America, notably from the publisher of the *New York Herald* and the Commercial Cable Company founded by John Mackay, the Silver King. What Boulanger could not afford to do was live without Marguerite. She knew it, and when he made a half-hearted attempt to send her to a Swiss resort she said, "Not without you, and you have your election."

When she had wept in his arms, wept until she was more like a suffering animal than his beautiful mistress, Marguerite de Bonnemains showed courage a soldier might have envied. She swore not to worry and weary him with the lamentations of a grieving woman, and when she was allowed to come downstairs she blessed her skill in the use of cosetics. She could blend rouge and powder skilfully enough to disguise the slight hectic flush on her thin cheeks, and she coughed as little as possible. By the time the election was won and the Deputy for the Nord took his seat in the Chamber, she was even able to preside at a dinner party at the Rue Dumont d'Urville, given in honour of the inner circle of his supporters. Rochefort had joined him now, Rochefort the ex-Communard, and Mermeix who was to edit the Boulangist newspaper *La Cocarde*, and Georges Laguerre, Freemason and Socialist, with Nagret, once an anarchist, and a young writer called Maurice Barrès. There was room for all who wore the Red Carnation.

One who was not present was Alain de Grimont, for a Deputy was not expected to have an ADC in the Chamber, and with well-expressed regret Boulanger told him that his service was over.

"I hope this isn't an unpleasant surprise," the general said.

"Well, no, *mon général*. When I realised you would soon have no more need of my services, I arranged to be posted to the Topographical Section of the War Ministry."

"To the War Ministry!" Boulanger was dumbfounded. "And General Logeret endorsed an appointment for *my* aide-de-camp?"

"I don't believe the general knows I exist – a mere captain – and Topographical has always been a specialist section."

"But how was it arranged?"

"Monsieur Delcassé arranged it, sir."

"Delcassé! The little Deputy from Toulouse? I didn't know he had any influence at the Ministry of War."

"Apparently he does."

"You often gave me the impression that you wanted to be back with troops, de Grimont. Have the fleshpots of Paris been too much for you?"

"I'd go back to the Ninety-third tomorrow if there were any prospect of combat action, but there isn't, except for an occasional *razzia* in the desert, and the Foreign Legion takes care of that. So I thought I ought to stay in Paris, not so much for the fleshpots as to see what happens next."

What happens to you and your ambitions, was what the fellow meant. The general felt with fury that behind the controlled military mask the young man (whom I, *Moi Boulanger*, picked out of that dump in Tunis when he was a mere lieutenant) was laughing at him.

"I wish you all success," he said coldly. "As far as I'm concerned you've only one failing: you've never realised the importance of the *Ligue des Patriotes*, nor worn the Red Carnation."

"*Mon général*," said Alain, "may I say one thing, with the greatest respect? That night in the mess at Tunis, before I left for Bizerta, you said to me, 'You're on the road to Strasbourg now.' I would have followed you through fire and water on the road to Strasbourg. I'm not prepared to follow you on the road to the Elysée."

Boulanger's principal worry, of course, was the Chambre des Députés. There he not only was not allowed an aide-de-camp, but he was not allowed to appear in uniform. Without the uniform and the medals he was curiously diminished; no longer the Man on Horseback but merely a good-looking, middle-aged man in a black frock coat, without the experience or the knowledge of the protocol of the Chamber. He was also a man without a party, with only the rump of the extreme right – royalists or the few surviving Bonapartists – to come to his rescue when the debate went against him.

He proposed to get round this by founding a party of his own, though he had come out against the party system and the jockeying for office which had given France eleven prime ministers in ten years. His National Republican Committee would organise a monolithic party, 'uniting the hopes of all'. But first the Chamber must dissolve itself, and meet again to revise the Constitution of 1875 and draw up a new one, in which the President of the Republic should be chosen, not by the Deputies and Senators, but by universal manhood suffrage. The President of the future should have powers in the American style, including the power of veto – Boulanger got no further before the Deputies howled him down with a mixture of boos, jeers and whistles. They had heard enough of the fantasies of *Moi Boulanger*, the man who believed he was France. Early in March the new War Minister relieved him of the command of XIVth Corps, which he still nominally held, and put him on the retired list.

This of course created a sensation at the Ministry, where Alain de Grimont had slipped quite naturally into a place in the Topographical Section. Nobody asked what he thought of Boulanger, or associated him with the fallen commander, because the topographers were a race apart, and when Alain had to analyse mapping and surveying reports from the southern desert of Algeria, he was glad to be working in Paris and not in Timbuctoo.

There were many new faces at the Ministry, some of them belonging to old friends from St Cyr, with whom it was pleasant to lunch or dine. Alain soon found that while there was a strong anti-Boulangist party at the Ministry of War, there was an equally strong and now overt element of anti-semitism. 'International Jewry' had reappeared as the faceless enemy. One day Alain encountered Edmond de St Etienne, with whom he had had words at St Cyr at the time of the Prince Imperial's death. He was a major now, working in Records, and they had barely exchanged greetings before they were on bad terms again.

"I hear you were Boulanger's ADC for a couple of years, de Grimont," St Etienne began. "Many Jews in his inner circle?"

"None that I know of."

"This fellow who calls himself Count Dillon – he's a Jew, isn't he?"

"I don't believe so."

"Too bad. You must have missed your Jewish friends."

"Look here, St Etienne," said Alain. "I only had one Jewish friend in my life and I never knew him well, but he was killed in action, *mort pour la France*, while you and I were sitting on our backsides in comfortable desk jobs — "

"Speak for yourself," growled the other. "I went ashore with the first assault wave at Sfax when you were an instructor at St Cyr."

"All right, I'm not at St Cyr now, and we're neither of us cadets to be expelled for duelling. If you go on with this antisemitic stuff I'll meet you any morning in the Bois de Boulogne, swords or pistols, whichever you like, whenever you care to send your friends to me."

St Etienne backed down, of course, as bullies always did, and contented himself with cutting Alain dead from then on. One of the topographical officers, who had listened to Alain's outburst, told him he was a fool to get across a man in Records. "They've got access to our dossiers," he said, "they can fix them any way they want."

"I don't give a damn." Captain de Grimont didn't give a damn for much in those days, and it was a welcome break when he got summer leave. He went off to a grand family reunion at the Château de la Treille.

Two days before he left, General Boulanger formally moved the dissolution of the Chamber, and in the ensuing tumult played his old game of threatening to resign unless his wishes became law. In some fierce exchanges with the latest prime minister, an elderly lawyer named Charles Floquet, he challenged the man to a duel. Floquet, who probably had not handled a foil since his student days, accepted the challenge, and when they met next morning succeeded in wounding the general, so near the jugular vein that the great swordsman, the *beau sabreur*, was not out of danger for three days. Paris rang with the story. It was the joke of the boulevards and the *chansonniers*, and the Duc de la Treille's first words when he met his nephew at the Hyères railway station were *"Vive Floquet!"*

Not that they wasted much time on politics. Maurice de la Treille was on leave from Saigon with his wife and the baby son who would one day be the nineteenth duke, and they had brought with them three Annamite servants: the baby's nurse, the lady's maid, and Maurice's valet. The château, with the arrival of Alain, would be full. Maurice had promised to be the godfather of Armand's second daughter, three months old, and Armand himself was on leave while his ship was in dry dock at Toulon.

Maurice de la Treille had gone to Saigon for one year and had stayed for ten. He had risen from the secretaryship of a trade commission to the Governor-General's staff, married the Governor-General's daughter and fought well in the war with China. He was now a very able administrator, and in ten more years would probably be the Governor-General himself.

"They scare me," confided the duke as he drove his nephew home in the pony carriage. "Not Maurice alone, he's still the same good-natured fellow, but Maurice and Eugénie together frighten me, and I know they terrify poor Blanche."

"Stand on their dignity, do they?"

"I've seen nothing like it since I was a young fellow at the court of the Tuileries. I suppose you know that the Empress Eugénie was my daughter-in-law's godmother? I don't think anyone in Saigon is allowed to forget it for a moment, and Saigon is fast becoming the Paris of South-East Asia. They're a new breed of French men and women to me, *les colons*."

"Algiers is full of them."

"Maybe you can handle the lady, then. I can't."

Maurice's wife was not so intimidating at close quarters. She was a pretty women, beautifully dressed, and when Alain addressed her as *Princesse* she warmed to him, and took him to see her infant son in the old schoolroom, now transformed from a sewing room into a nursery. He was a nice little boy, and Alain patted his small hand with the feeling that here was a new generation, and that he was somehow left behind. No one mentioned his broken 'unofficial' engagement, though Aunt Blanche kissed him with especial warmth, and Uncle Gilbert congratulated him on getting free from that charlatan Boulanger. It was not until Henriette came across from the Villa Rivabella next morning that anyone mentioned the name of Isabelle Lacroix.

Henriette and her little girls, Armande and Marie-Blanche, were like a painting by Renoir, as pink and white as a bunch of roses. When she took them up to the nursery her plump babies shone by contrast with the pale little colonial boy, lively and engaging though he was. She left them in the care of the Annamite nurse, and declaring that she wanted to hear Alain's news, carried him off for the obligatory tour of the rose garden.

As soon as they were out of earshot of the house and within sound of the sea, Henriette said how sorry she was that Isabelle Lacroix had broken off the engagement.

"I never thought she would do a thing like that," she said. "She wrote to me when you were first engaged – "

"Unofficially," said Alain.

"Oh yes, she insisted on that. It was unofficial for the time being, and you hadn't been allowed to give her an engagement ring, but Alain, she'd given you her promise, and she seemed so *happy*! She *thanked* me for inviting her to be in the wedding where she met you!"

"I suppose everybody knows about it?"

"I don't know about everybody. I told Armand, of course. I wouldn't dream of telling Eugénie! I hopeyou don't mind, but – Armand's mother showed me the letter you wrote her."

"I don't mind at all." Who could be vexed with Aunt

206

Blanche for showing anyone those two lines, impersonal as a notice in the papers, in which he told her that 'Mademoiselle Lacroix has decided to bring our engagement to an end'. "Did you know Isabelle's parents well?" he asked.

"Not very well. Why? Do you think they had something to do with it?"

"They had everything to do with it! Her mother told her Boulanger was immoral and her father wanted me to leave the army, and between the two of them they persuaded the poor child that the whole thing was a mistake."

"But you're not General Boulanger's ADC any longer!"

"No, that's the crazy part of it. If Monsieur Lacroix had been patient just a short time longer, the whole problem would have settled itself." He hesitated. "Unless of course he'd found a better match."

Henriette flushed. Whatever she was about to say, she changed her mind.

"Did you never try to see her again, Alain— afterwards? To ask her to reconsider?"

"I wasn't going to beg."

His cousin's wife nodded, as if he had given her the right answer. "Then, my dear," she said, and stood on tiptoe to kiss his cheek, "I think you've got over it. And I know you'll meet the right girl some day."

General Boulanger lay ill in his own house for the last two weeks of July, smarting from the wound to his body and the wound to his self-esteem, both administered by the elderly civilian named Charles Floquet. He kept asking for Marguerite, but Dillon refused to bring her to him, because there were never fewer than a dozen reporters keeping the death watch in the Rue Dumont d'Urville. At last he made his getaway in a closed cab from the stable entrance, and was driven to the Rue de Berri. In Marguerite's bedroom, with Marguerite whispering, "I'm going to nurse you like you nursed me at Royat!" he was soon on the way to complete recovery.

The dog days began in August, and the English trippers sweltered their way across the Champ de Mars, where once the Head of Liberty had stood, to look at the slender shaft of Monsieur Eiffel's tower beginning to rise from the first platform on the base. It was to be ready when the new exhibition was opened on the first of May, and Boulanger intended to be an American-style President of the Republic by then, so as to declare the *Exposition Universelle* open to the world.

Count Dillon thought he might just do it. The Deputies had gone on holiday and the humiliating duel would soon be forgotten, while in no fewer than three by-elections the general was returned to the Chamber without being seen or heard by the voters. He now represented eight constituencies, all in the provinces. The supreme test was approaching. He could carry the backwoods, but could he carry Paris? In the coming January, would he be elected Deputy for the Seine? If he were, Monsieur Sadi-Carnot might have to consider evacuating the Elysée.

His principal supporters made the greatest effort of their lives that autumn. The Duchesse d'Uzès contributed another half million francs to the campaign fund. Dillon brought the total number of photographs distributed to three million. Mermeix, editing the Boulangist paper *La Cocarde*, had the assistance of the biting pen of Henri de Rochefort, back under amnesty from New Caledonia. De Rochefort, a brilliant journalist, had only one principle, to be against the government – any government. He had been against the Emperor when Napoleon III ruled France, against Thiers when the Versailles troops destroyed the Commune, and now he was pro-Boulanger and against the government of the celebrated duellist, Charles Floquet. Paul Déroulède was bringing out a new volume of poems called 'Military

Refrains' and writing election speeches about the need of a plebiscite to elect a Leader for the nation. Finally, Dillon hired an army of men to cover Paris with billboards bearing the words:

Révision
Dissolution
Constituante

BOULANGER!

The sight of his own name so many times repeated, and of his photograph given away free at the street corners, in the newspaper kiosks and also in the toilets of the cheaper restaurants, seemed to increase Boulanger's megalomania. He now believed that he had a Star guiding his career like the two Bonapartes, the greater and the less. He also wrote, as one monarch to another, to the Czar Alexander III, saying "I will destroy the pestilential parliament!" There was no reply from St Petersburg.

The officers at the Ministry of War were laying bets on the outcome of the election in the Department of the Seine, due to take place on 27 January. Alain de Grimont thought Boulanger was certain to be elected; the real issue was what he would do with his victory. He knew from Captain Porges, whom he saw occasionally, that the Military Governor of Paris had been ordered to provide a bodyguard for President Sadi-Carnot inside the Elysée on election night, in case of an attempt at kidnap or murder. It was to be hoped they would do better than MacMahon's bodyguard on a memorable night in the Rue Tronchet.

Alain had had a short-lived affair with a dancer from the *Variétés*, his first theatrical encounter since the night in the Rue d'Amsterdam, just before the arrival in Paris of Prince Maurice de la Treille. He had been summoned for consultations with the Minister for the Marine and Colonies, while his wife took little Guy to show to her parents, in retirement

like so many of *les colons* at Aix-les-Bains. "Eugénie dreads
the Paris climate in winter, for herself and for little Guy,"
said Maurice. "Besides, she wants to break in the new
nursemaid in France, before we take her to Saigon."

"Why, what's happened to your Annamite?"

"She married one of my father's gardeners."

"Married, eh? That'll start a cross-breed in Hyères!"

"Henriette found us a nice little French girl. If *she* gets
married in Saigon, let's hope it's to a Frenchman. Plenty of
choice out there."

It was great to see old Maurice alone, without Eugénie's
oppressive dignity, and Alain gave a dinner for him at the
Jockey Club. He was staying at the Hôtel Meurice, and by
contrast to the Meurice Alain's cramped apartment in the
Cité du Retiro looked very shabby.

"What the devil are you doing in this dump?" asked
Maurice, with all the freedom of their young days at Hyères.

"It's very convenient for the Ministry. Nice walk across
the Seine to the Rue St Dominique."

"Convenient for a lot of things." Maurice's nostrils
twitched, and Alain knew he had caught the lingering scent
of the dancer's patchouli.

"Look here, Alain, why don't you volunteer for Saigon?
There's a big French force there now, and new drafts are on
their way. The Minister says the whole of Indo-China will
soon be in French hands, and new garrisons will have to be
established."

"Indo-China," said Alain. "That's a new one. It's usually
Egypt people want to ship me off to."

"Never mind Egypt, think seriously of Indo-China.
Eugénie and I will make you very welcome – "

"I appreciate that. I know it's time to be moving on. It's
back to the desert for me, one of these days."

"You're in the desert here, *mon vieux*."

*

Paris was very far from being a desert on the night when the result of the Seine election was made known. The polls were closed when Alain de Grimont fought his way along a crowded pavement of the Rue Royale to dine at the Café Weber. It was about nine o'clock, and the result was expected about eleven, but already thousands were massed in and around the Place de la Madeleine, where the general was dining at Durand's restaurant. The spectators were excitedly telling each other that two companies of the Republican Guard had been seen riding up the Rue du Faubourg St Honoré, to defend the Elysée Palace from the Boulangists who, with the general at their head, had sworn to overthrow the Third Republic.

Alain, at a table near the front, was enjoying the commotion in the street when someone wished him good-evening. He looked up, it was Raymond Lacroix, last seen more than a year ago.

"How are you, Raymond, won't you sit down?"

"I can't, thanks, I'm here to meet a lady."

"Not many ladies would care to be out tonight."

"I know, that's why I'm early, to be here when her cab arrives. She's coming from the theatre. Well, I'll just sit down for a minute—" He pulled up a chair. "No, nothing to drink, thanks."

"How are they all at the Rue de Courcelles?" Alain asked with constraint.

"Quite well. Look, Alain — when I saw you sitting here alone I thought I'd speak to you . . . ask you, I mean . . . if you knew Isabelle was married?"

"No, I didn't. When?"

"Last August. It was in the *Figaro*."

"I seldom read the social columns of the *Figaro*. Who's the happy man?"

"The Comte de Marigny. Do you know him? He's a member of the Jockey Club."

"There was a Comte Henri de Marigny in my topography class when I was an instructor at St Cyr. It can't be him!"

"No, it's his father, Claud. He was a widower."

"Interesting," said Alain. He caught the waiter's eye and called for his bill. "I must be moving on, Raymond. I'm going round to Durand's to see what happens when the Seine result comes out."

"You're still loyal to your general?" asked young Lacroix.

Alain smiled. "Not exactly loyal," he said. "Merely curious. Good-night, Raymond. Be sure to give my best wishes to Madame la Comtesse de Marigny."

Alain walked up the Rue Royale, devoid of feeling. Isabelle married in August, and to an old widower with a grown son! I believe Henriette knew, when we talked in the garden, that it was going to happen, and didn't want to hurt me. Why should it hurt me, after more than a year? She couldn't keep her word to me, and her father sold her to the highest bidder, as my mother was sold before she left the schoolroom. Isabelle! When she spoke of love, happiness, fidelity it meant no more than that gimcrack adventurer, round the corner at Durand's, means when he talks of *Honneur et Patrie.* Isabelle de Marigny, Georges Boulanger, what they both mean is *Moi*.

A great burst of cheering, loud enough to lift the roof off the Madeleine church, broke out as Alain turned the corner into the square. From the shouts of *"A l'Elysée! A bas Carnot! A bas Floquet!"* which rose from the mob, he knew the result was out, and Boulanger had won. He pushed his way into Durand's restaurant. A waiter tried to stop him, but fell back before the tall man in uniform, who snapped "I'm late!" and ran upstairs to the packed private rooms on the first floor.

There were three long windows, wide open to the January night, and Boulanger was out on the balcony of the middle window, opening his arms wide to the ecstatic crowd. A

Spahi officer whom he knew embraced Alain, another put a glass of champagne into his hand.

"He did it, de Grimont! A landslide victory in every ward but one! And now we're off to the Elysée, to throw those pettifogging lawyers out! Just listen to them!"

> C'est Boulange, lange, lange,
> C'est Boulanger qu'il nous faut!
> Oh! Oh! Oh! Oh!

The police had given up trying to control the crowd, who had climbed the trees in the square to see inside Durand's and knocked over most of the stands in the flower market. That's where it all began, said Alain to himself. That's where the clowns were talking to the men from the van, and over there is where I kissed the little street-walker, Alice or Annie, whatever her name was. Schoolboy stuff! What happens now?

"A l'Elysée! A l'Elysée!"

Boulanger came back inside the room, smiling. He was wearing what Ouida and other lady novelists liked to call faultless evening dress, the white tie and tails which suited his golden hair and beard, now artificially brightened. He saw Alain at once and greeted him cordially.

"De Grimont! This is a pleasant surprise."

No more snapping to attention, no more à vos ordres. "Good evening, monsieur. Congratulations."

"Thank you. Have you experienced a change of heart? Are you going to join us now?"

"Not exactly, monsieur. I came to watch your departure for the Elysée."

"Good! Good!" "What are we waiting for?" "Let's go!" the murmurs began in the crowded room. In the restaurant beneath they were singing the Marseillaise.

"Yes," said Boulanger, "it's time to go. Somebody fetch my hat and cloak. And excuse me for a few minutes while I speak to those good folks downstairs."

He hurried away, and his hat and cloak were brought. The singing stopped, the general's voice was heard and then there was silence. The few minutes became ten, became fifteen, while the crowd in the square grew restless. In Durand's private room the men looked doubtfully at the gibus hat and the opera cloak.

"He ought to be in uniform, riding Tunis, when he goes to the Elysée," said an Engineer officer.

"*If* he goes," said Alain de Grimont.

His disillusionment with Boulanger, his disgust at the general's little treacheries, like the evaded fortress arrest and the clandestine intrigue with Prince Napoleon, had made him suspicious of the man, even in the moment of his political triumph. He was half convinced that Boulanger's nerve would fail him at the last moment. He lacked the ultimate courage to storm the Elysée. Even the opera hat and cloak spread carefully on a sofa seemed to symbolise the end of his military bravura.

"My God, look here!" cried a man at the window. They crowded round to see.

In the street below, General Boulanger's carriage had been brought up to the door of the restaurant. The man himself ran across the pavement, jumped into the carriage and slammed the door. Some of the startled bystanders heard him give an address on the Rue de Berri.

The man of destiny was in full retreat — to the arms of his mistress.

At one o'clock in the morning the Place de la Madeleine was bare of everything but scavenging dogs and tattered red carnations. At the Elysée the Garde Républicaine was stood down and trotted back to barracks.

The Republic was saved.

During the election campaign Count Dillon had organised *claques* to gather at the street corners Boulanger was timed to pass each day and applaud him as he went by. For this each man was paid from one franc fifty to two francs per day. In the week after the fiasco of the *coup d'état* that failed, ten francs would not have bought a single burst of cheering. There was no more applause for the Man on Horseback.

"Why did you do it, Georges?" lamented Dillon at a meeting of the cabal next day. "Why did you desert us in the hour of victory?"

"Why did you rat on us?" growled the outspoken Laguerre.

"Because I saw no point in taking by violence what will be legally mine at the general election in six months' time," retorted Boulanger.

"Don't be too sure. The government can do a lot in six months."

The government was prepared to act without delay. The general returned to the Chamber a discredited man, rejected by the fickle mob, and ostracised by Deputies who would have followed him if he had brought off a *coup d'état*. As quickly as possible a case was prepared against him, accusing him of an attempt on the security of the state, the employment of secret agents, and embezzlement of military funds. The last charge was unlikely to be brought home, for the funds Boulanger had spent so lavishly were freely given by men and women willing to back their fancy, who in the end had backed a loser.

Without the money raised by the *Ligue des Patriotes* he was a poor man, comparatively speaking, entitled only to the 8000 francs a year due to a general on the inactive list, plus the 2000 francs pension of a *grand légionnaire*.

"They can't call me an embezzler," said Boulanger to his mistress. They were in her boudoir at the Rue de Berri, embraced on a favourite sofa before the wood fire, while she stroked his hair and tried to comfort him. "In any case there's no more money left. The Paris election took every last *sou*."

"Of course you're not an embezzler, darling," she said. "Those men attacking you are only jealous of your election victories, your oratory, your heroism. It'll all come right quite soon, you'll see."

Marguerite knew how to feed his vanity, and to cheer him as he had never cheered her when her love and hopes were all frustrated; and she still excited him by her beauty and the delicate garments she wore to allure him. But tonight he refused her comfort, and said "Perhaps it won't come right this time."

"Then, Georges," she said, "there's something I have to tell you. Something I've been saving up as a surprise. You remember when my old aunt died a little while ago, I told you she had left me money?"

"Of course I remember." He hadn't paid much attention at the time for Marguerite had made light of the unexpected legacy, and he had been far too busy to attend the old lady's funeral.

Now his lover slipped from her place on the sofa, knelt on the white fur rug and clasped her hands on his knee.

"Darling, it was three million francs."

"*What?*"

"It's true."

"It's a fortune."

"And it's all for you. Yes, I insist. You must accept it, because everything I have is yours. You took half a million francs from the Duchesse d'Uzès for your last election, surely you can take more from me."

Boulanger lifted her back into his arms, calling her the best, most generous girl who ever lived, his only friend.

"Just promise me one thing, darling," she said with her head on his breast. "Promise you'll take me with you wherever you go."

"I don't have to promise that, Marguerite, I couldn't live without you. And I've no intention of going anywhere."

"You may have to, Georges."

"What makes you think so?"

"Those awful things the papers say — that you'll be arrested . . ."

"Oh! Those government hacks, ranting in the Chamber! They can't touch me, I've got parliamentary immunity."

"Are you sure?"

Two who were not sure were those not-so-secret agents, Messieurs Dillon and de Rochefort. "They'll find a way round your immunity, Georges," said the latter. "If a man who represents nine constituencies doesn't have parliamentary immunity, I don't know who does. But if the Deputies vote to raise your immunity, it's all up; and if they make the charges stick it's prison for sure. Better get out while the going's good; I will."

"What about me?" quavered Dillon. "Will they arrest me too?" He was an older man, accustomed to a soft life, and the thought of prison terrified him.

"What do you mean by get out?" said Boulanger. "Get out where?"

"Across the border," Rochefort said. "Belgium or Switzerland. England as a last resort."

A foreign land — with Marguerite and three million francs. It had its possibilities.

The lawyers in the government wasted no time. The Constitution of 1875 laid down that the Senate could function as a High Court of Justice to try the crime of an attempt on the security of the state. The Deputies voted by 383 votes to 199 to lift the parliamentary immunity of Georges Boulanger. Henri de Rochefort, an old hand, left Paris unostentatiously, while Arthur Dillon, a quivering mass of nerves, begged Boulanger to make plans for their escape. None of them knew that Charles Floquet, flexing the muscles of his duelling hand, had agreed with the Minister of the Interior that Boulanger must not be allowed to appear as a martyr.

217

"There's nothing he'd like better than the publicity of a state trial," said Floquet. "If we give him a good fright he'll cut and run, just as he did on the twenty-seventh of January. Let's go after some of the small fry first, and see what that does to *notre brave général*."

Warrants were accordingly issued for the arrest of Georges Laguerre, Alfred Nagret and Paul Déroulède, as secret agents engaged in a conspiracy against the state, and the press was informed accordingly in the evening of 31 March. On the morning of April Fools' Day Alain de Grimont's concierge brought a sealed letter upstairs with his breakfast coffee. "A boy brought this ten minutes ago," she said. "It's marked Urgent."

"My dear de Grimont," the letter began, "in the name of army loyalty and for the sake of an invalid lady I ask you for your help. Would you meet us at the Faubourg St Honoré entrance to the Cité du Retiro at half past eight tonight, and have a cab with a reliable driver waiting at the Boissy d'Anglas exit? In great haste, Boulanger."

He thinks I'm still his ADC, thought Alain. How did he know I still live here? Did I put him in mind of me by turning up at Durand's that night? And what's he running away from this time?

He understood better when he read the morning papers. With his friends under arrest, Boulanger evidently thought it was his turn next, and so by evening it might be. Alain might then be accused of aiding a suspect to escape from justice. But the day passed with no word of Boulanger's arrest, and at half past eight he was underneath the Faubourg archway when a man and a woman got out of a fiacre. The lady was heavily veiled and seemed to be half fainting. Boulanger, the Man on Horseback unhorsed, looked like a commercial traveller carrying a bag of samples. He wore a belted grey overcoat, a soft felt hat, and a heavy scarf to hide his beard. He gave his arm to Marguerite, who stumbled on the cobbles of the entrance and almost fell. Alain begged her to take his arm too.

"Madame is unwell," he said. "Would you like to come up to my apartment and let her rest for a little?"

"No time to lose. Got a train to catch," said Boulanger in a stage whisper, as if the ancient dwellings in the courtyard of the Cité were full of enemies.

They went as quietly as possible past the concierge's *loge*, which was at the other gate. The fiacre fetched by Alain earlier was waiting in the Rue Boissy d'Anglas. Whether the man were reliable or not, he was at least sober.

"Thank you, de Grimont," said the general. "I knew I could count on you. Please tell the driver to take us to the Gare du Nord."

Madame de Bonnemains lifted her veil, and in the light of the ancient oil lamp opposite the gate Alain saw a face from which all the beauty had been drained, and heard her whisper, *"Merci, monsieur."*

Boulanger lifted her into the cab and took his place beside her. Then there was nothing but the clip-clop of an old horse's hooves, the creaking of wheels, and the sight of a red tail light like a faded red carnation.

Alain turned back into the dark yard. He felt as if he had lived a page from Dumas or a scene from a Feydeau farce. The Gare du Nord — that meant Brussels. Wherever they were bound for, it was the end of the glory road for Georges Boulanger.

PART THREE

'A Girl of Sixteen':
Interlude at Cap Martin

17

Sarah Colt woke up at a quarter to seven in her bedroom at the Hôtel du Cap Martin. It was not a drowsy awakening, for she always awoke briskly, ready for anything the new day might bring, and she was out of bed in a moment and hurrying to the window. It was her ambition to see the outline of Corsica on the southern horizon, although her governess had told her that very few of those born along the Ligurian shore or in the town of Menton had ever seen the island in their lives. There was nothing to see today, no violet silhouette, no mystery: the Mediterranean lay with hardly a ripple on its silken surface, deep indigo to where it met the orange line which heralded the coming of the sun.

A soft breeze blew in through the open window, bringing the sound of birds rehearsing their morning songs, and Sarah hurried to get dressed. Not the *grande toilette* of the hour after breakfast, but enough to go outside and enjoy the best hour of the Riviera day. A short cotton dress and heavy shoes were produced from the back of a cupboard, a brush dragged through the long brown hair, and – since the March mornings were cool – Sarah's London school cloak was put on above the dress. She had outgrown it; the cross straps on her bosom were uncomfortable.

Her coffee and rolls would not be brought to her room until eight o'clock, so since she was only sixteen and had a healthy appetite, Sarah found a tablet of chocolate by way of provisions and put it in the pocket of her cloak.

She let herself quietly out through the sitting-room, glad to hear no sound of movement from her governess's room on the other side, and went down in the lift to the great marble hall, where the porters had finished washing and polishing the floor and maids were plumping up the cushions and dusting the woodwork of the heavy mahogany chairs. A clerk at the reception desk gave her a respectful good-morning, and shook his head as the American young lady, after a blithe *bonjour monsieur*! began whistling as she ran down the wide steps under the glass fan which protected ladies getting in and out of their carriages. Down and then up, still whistling, went Sarah, for the hotel was built on a slope, and a broad path opposite the entry led to a network of narrower paths through four hectares of gardens, carefully tended by a team of gardeners, and already glowing with the flowers of spring.

There were tall trees round which wisteria vines were twining, palms with coronets of white blossom, and orange and lemon trees which would bear fruit later on. There were almond trees, mere balls of rosy blossom, and in the grass beneath them lingered enough white narcissus, the first flowers of the year, to leave their sweetness on the air. Freesias added their own perfume, and in the rockeries which defined each path dwarf lavender iris and many-coloured cyclamen grew between the stones.

Sarah Colt went along the topmost path, basking in light and colour and nibbling her chocolate, until she came to a lookout point with an arrangement of summer seats, from which the whole coast could be seen from Monaco on the west to Italy on the east, and the sea broken by nothing but a few belated fishing boats making for the market of Menton. There was no time to sit and watch them; Sarah took one of the downward paths which wound round and round the slope, down through rougher ground where rosemary grew, until she came to a broad alley bordered with mimosa, giving out the most evocative scent of all.

There she stopped, and looked back at the hotel. Built of white stucco and white marble it topped the cliff of greenery like a gigantic wedding cake, a place of luxury, meant for holiday and happiness. But there was sorrow behind the roses growing in pots behind the wide white terrace. In the royal suite, so called because it had hidden the grief of the Empress Elizabeth of Austria after her only son Rudolf had shot himself and his mistress in the hunting lodge at Mayerling, there were now other sorrowing royalties. The Prince and Princess of Wales had lost their eldest son, dead of pneumonia a few weeks before his wedding to Princess May of Teck, fixed for 27 February 1892. They came to Cap Martin on 9 March, for a stay of six weeks, a rest from the demands of their life in London, and Sarah Colt's father arrived a little later, to play poker with the Prince of Wales and his equerries. Sarah had not been presented to the Princess, she was too young, not 'out' – "That'll come later," said her father, "after you've been to see the Old Lady at Buckingham Palace, with three feathers in your hair and a grand court train. We're going to do the thing in style, Baby!"

Sarah had seen the Princess of Wales twice, leaning on the arm of her younger son Prince George as he led her through the hall of the hotel for an airing in her carriage. She had curtseyed, as all the ladies did while the men bowed, without seeming to stare or pry, while yet watching every move that incomparably graceful figure made and speculating on the romance said to be preparing for Prince George.

There was no one on the balcony of the royal suite, nor did

225

Sarah expect to see anybody at that hour, but it was unusual to meet nobody in her ramble down the gardens. There was no gardener rolling the new lawn tennis court or marking the white lines, and no cleaners to be seen round the Moorish kiosk where afternoon tea was served and male guests went to smoke cigars after dinner. Beyond the kiosk there was only a fence separating the hotel grounds from a public path, and then the limestone crags, covered with samphire, which marked the point of Cap Martin. The sea was fretting at the crags like yards of blue silk flung across a draper's counter. As Sarah watched, breathing in the salt air, a gate in the fence opened and a man came up from the rocks, stepping warily as if not quite sure of his balance, and as he came nearer she saw that his left arm was in a sling.

The man was wearing a French army uniform which had obviously seen hard service – maybe the whole length of his military career, because he was not a young man. She was unable to read the insignia, but she recognised – she had seen it in Cairo – the new scrap of bright red ribbon on the breast of his faded blue tunic. At the point where their paths crossed there was room for four people to walk abreast, but the soldier stopped and stepped back a pace, as if to make room for Sarah Colt to pass. She murmured, *"Merci, Monsieur,"* saw his hand flick up to his képi, and hurried by him to enter a short avenue of oleanders from which another path led uphill to the hotel.

She had just time to take off her schoolgirl clothes and put on a new blue satin dressing gown before the maid brought in her breakfast. The woman looked concerned.

"Mademoiselle Garrigue is very unwell this morning, mademoiselle," she said. "She doesn't even want a cup of coffee. She would like to speak to you when you've had yours."

"I'll go to her room right away." Sarah did delay five minutes after the maid had gone, for there was a letter in her father's handwriting propped up against the silver coffee pot, and she tore it open to read the few laconic lines with shining eyes before she went to mademoiselle's bedroom. Her governess was lying in semi-darkness, and it was warm enough already for the room to be stuffy. Sarah approached the bed on tiptoe.

"Another wretched migraine, Mademoiselle Garrigue?"

"Yes, another. I'm so sorry, Sarah!"

"Don't be. Is there anything I can get you? Shall I send for the doctor again?"

"He didn't do me any good before. I know how it goes: if I stay in bed today I'll be all right tomorrow. And I've sent a note to the duchess asking her to look after you at lunch time."

"You mean you've *already* sent it! Oh, I wish you hadn't! The duchess was expecting her nephew from Algeria last night. She won't want to be bothered with me at lunch."

"She's very kind, and you can't be cooped up in the sitting-room all day. Don't make difficulties, Sarah, please!"

Her voice trailed away, and Sarah Colt shrugged her shoulders. Impossible to argue with someone whose face showed her pain. She whispered, "Ring for anything you want. I'll look in again after lunch."

Sarah was cooped up in the sitting-room for most of the morning, writing an essay mademoiselle had set her the night before, and when it was finished spending an hour on the private balcony before getting ready for lunch. She had already a light tan, which was more than any girl or woman in the hotel had acquired. They all went out sheltered by large straw hats and parasols, and anointed themselves with lemon and cucumber skin creams at bedtime. Sarah's tan was becoming, it suited her brown hair and brown eyes and the crisp white blouse and skirt she wore to luncheon. It was still a *jeune fille* outfit, for the skirt was calf-length and her shoes and stockings were black, but her hair had been plaited into a

227

smooth braid, doubled under and caught at the nape of her neck by a black silk bow, the unmistakable sign of a girl who was half-way along the road to young ladyhood. The guests already lunching in the hotel dining-room, a huge semi-circle opening on the marble terrace, were surprised to see a *jeune fille* come in unchaperoned, and Sarah heard the name 'Colt', 'Charlie Colt's daughter' whispered at several tables. Even the Duchesse de la Treille, who knew her, was surprised at the child's composure as she made her way, with the *maître d'hôtel* in attendance, across the big room. As for the duchess's nephew, recently arrived from Algeria, he stood up at a word from his aunt, looking as amazed as he felt.

"Madame, I hope I'm not late. Your note did say to join you in the dining-room." The girl dropped a schoolgirl curtsey.

"No, no, my dear, you're not late. We've been out driving, and only just got back. Miss Colt, may I present my nephew, Captain de Grimont?"

"*Enchanté, mademoiselle!*"

"You were the soldier at the shore!"

The duchess's nephew looked better than the soldier at the shore, for his hair blown by the sea wind was brushed smooth, and he was wearing a new uniform. Only the black silk sling and the new red ribbon of the Légion d'Honneur were the same, but now he was smiling, which brightened a serious face.

"Have you two met already?" asked Blanche de la Treille, looking from one to the other.

"Our paths crossed this morning down by the sea," said Alain de Grimont.

"Out for another of your solitary rambles, you naughty Sarah?"

"Oh please madame, do call me Sadie. I hate my real name! Sarah makes me think of Sarah in the Bible. You

228

know, Sarah and Abraham, and being about a hundred years old."

"I don't think you need worry about old age yet, Mademoiselle Sadie," said Alain with a laugh, and changing the subject with the aplomb of an older woman Sadie asked, as soon as she drank her soup, if he felt tired after his trip from Algeria.

"I did when it was over, but I haven't come directly from Algeria, mademoiselle. I spent two weeks with my uncle at Hyères first."

"Oh, then you have the latest news from home!" exclaimed Sadie, turning to the duchess.

"Yes, and it's good news. The work on the drains is nearly finished, and my husband will be here next week for the holiday he richly deserves."

"I'm so glad for you!" Then, rather shyly, Sadie added, "I have good news too. A letter from my father – he's coming back next week."

"His Royal Highness will be delighted. The princess told me when I had tea with her yesterday that he was missing his poker games."

"I thought baccarat was the Prince of Wales's game," said Alain.

"Not when he plays with Monsieur Colt, it seems. Your father isn't coming to take you away, Sadie dear?"

"Not yet!" She turned to Alain. "I'm going to Paris after Easter, to live in a family where they take foreign girls to 'finish' and learn French. Not only the language, but French art, music, literature – everything."

"Your French is very good," said Alain kindly.

"Oh thank you, but my Aunt Liz says it has to be much better. She's my mother's sister, Elizabeth Otway, and she teaches French in a girls' high school in Kensington. I lived in London with her after I came back from America."

"Sadie is a much travelled young lady," explained the duchess. "She spent last winter with her father in Cairo, before that she lived in London, after – how many years in America?"

"Ten years in Old Harbour, Connecticut," said Sadie, smiling. "After my mother died my father took me to live there with *his* mother, and I loved it." She declined the waiter's offer of coffee and got up. "Duchess, will you excuse me now? I must look in on Mademoiselle Garrigue, and then it'll be time for my tennis lesson," she said to Alain, who had risen as well. "I play every day at three o'clock. Thank you both for letting me have lunch with you."

"Shall we see you at dinner?" Alain asked.

"I don't come down to dinner yet. We have schoolroom supper upstairs. Thank you again, *chère madame. Au revoir.*"

"Well!" said Alain expressively when she had gone. "There's an independent young lady for you!"

"But you thought she was amusing, didn't you?"

"Amusing? I suppose she's what I've heard called the Girl of the Period – something new to a backwoodsman like me. And would you kindly explain, my dear aunt, what you meant by telling me we would have a child for luncheon?"

"A child? I never said that!"

"Forgive me, but you did. *'Cette chère enfant'* was what you called her. Goodness knows she looked about twelve this morning, when I saw her down by the sea. What is she really? Seventeen? Eighteen?"

"Sixteen last month."

"She's very – self-possessed for her age."

"Not really." The duchess yawned. "I'm sleepy after our drive, Alain, and oh! my bones are aching! Give me your arm, dear boy."

The duchess heaved her considerable bulk from the table, and Alain gave her his arm all the way up in the lift to her room. "I know I'm a self-indulgent old woman, but I must

230

have my siesta," she said at the door, and her nephew, walking back down the silent corridor, thought most of the guests of the Hôtel du Cap Martin were enjoying their siestas. He felt wide awake. He went down to the empty hall and smoked a cigarette. Then he looked at his watch, went out by the marble terrace, and down through the gardens to the new tennis court.

Captain de Grimont had never seen tennis played. There were courts in Algiers, but when he rejoined the 93rd of the Line in May 1889 (by which time Boulanger and his mistress had moved on to London, where he tried to drum up support from the British) he was ordered to Bône, a port town with few luxuries. On the grass court at Cap Martin, where Sadie greeted him with a cheerful wave of her racquet, the professional was instructing her in the underarm service used by ladies. He was a good-looking fellow of about twenty, wearing white flannels, a white shirt, a stiff collar and a striped tie, and Sadie had changed into another white dress, with white stockings and white rubber-soled shoes. The pro, confound him, was using every excuse for touching her, placing her hands in the right position, and once even putting his own hands on her waist 'to demonstrate flexibility'. So this was what the Girl of the Period got up to, independent and unchaperoned! It was a relief when they began to play. The pro placed Sadie with her back to the sea, so that it was his eyes the afternoon sun would shine into, and served – overhand – very gently. *"Bien! Très bien!"* he called again and again, and Alain could see that she was getting the ball across the net and moving to and fro over the lawn with grace and speed. What a picture it was, the grassy lawn, the running girl and the blue sea beyond! What a contrast to the battleground of El Djezir where Captain de Grimont won the Légion d'Honneur *à titre militaire*! He couldn't wait to see the end of the lesson, with that fellow pawing her again, showing her what she did wrong! In an agony of frustration Alain left the seat where he had been watching and walked up to the hotel.

That evening when they met for dinner he alarmed his aunt by appearing without his black silk sling.

"But Alain, your wound!"

"It's healed long ago, Aunt Blanche. Yes, I know what the Bône doctor said. But it's a mere affectation to go on wearing the sling, at least until I've seen the doctors at Val-de-Grâce."

18

"Now it's your turn," said Alain de Grimont. It was his third afternoon at the tennis court, Sadie's lesson was over, and he and she were settled on one of the wooden seats beneath a flowering bush of rose laurel. "Yesterday afternoon you made me tell you about soldiering in Algeria, a dull topic if ever there was one, and then you promised to tell me how your father became a cotton magnate in Cairo. I'm interested."

"What I promised," said Sadie, "was to tell you how it came about. He didn't make a fortune with a snap of the fingers. It took years and years and a lot of hard work."

"Begin, then."

Before Sadie could begin her governess rose from an adjacent seat, where she had been supervising the tennis lesson over a lapful of fancywork. "Sarah dear," she said. "Put on your shawl. You've been overheated and you mustn't catch a chill."

"Catch a chill on this warm day!" Sadie protested, but she took the white bag Mademoiselle Garrigue held out to her and flung a brightly-coloured wrap round her shoulders. "Thank you, mademoiselle." When the fussy, grey-haired

Frenchwoman had gone back to her seat, shaking her head, the girl commented, "Overheated indeed! Monsieur Paul doesn't keep me running hard enough to get overheated. But I'm glad she remembered the bag, because there's something in it I want to show you – a photograph of my father."

"Your father was a soldier in the American army, I think you said?" prompted Alain. "He fought in the Civil War?"

"In the Union army," she corrected him. "He was twenty when the war began and twenty-four when it was over. He was wounded at a battle called Gettysburg, have you ever heard of it?"

"Yes," said Alain. "And he was an officer?"

"Not when he enlisted, he was just a farm boy from Old Harbour, Connecticut. He was a lieutenant when the war ended, and that was very important for getting to Cairo. But he didn't know about that at first, when he got a job as a learner in a cloth commission house in New York. He worked there for nearly four years. Then the Khedive Ismail advertised for experienced American officers to train officer-candidates for his army. My father had to get a certificate of service from the War Department and another from the colonel of his regiment, the New York Zouaves. In 1870 he took the oath of allegiance to the Khedive and signed a five years' contract to work in the military college at Abbassiya. This is what he looked like then."

She produced the photograph from her bag, a sepia print in a silver frame, and held it out to Alain. It showed a tall man of about thirty, with a shrewd cleanshaven Yankee face, in Egyptian court dress: a black frock coat buttoned to the throat, black trousers and a fez, presumably red.

"The outfit was called a *stambouli*, for Stamboul, Constantinople," said Sadie. "To show that the Sultan of Turkey was still the boss in Egypt."

"That's very interesting," said Alain slowly, handing back the photograph. He remembered the dinner party for the

Egyptian officials in the Grand Hotel, and his father talking of what he called American mercenaries and their speculations in cotton futures in the Egypt of 1878. "Your father had more initiative than me. I was offered a job in Cairo before I entered St Cyr, and I turned it down."

"In the army?"

"No, it was in the days of the Dual Control. In the Commission of the Public Debt."

"I don't remember the Dual Control," said Sadie Colt, and Alain reflected that when he was eighteen this enchanting girl was two. She said, "I can't picture you in a *stambouli* and a red fez!" Sadie thought Captain de Grimont was the handsomest older man she had ever seen, although his desert tan (faded in hospital) showed up the little white fan of wrinkles at the corners of his eyes. No! she couldn't picture him in a fez, the army képi on the seat beside him was the right wear for him. She replied primly to his continued questioning. When the contract with the Khedive expired in 1875 Colt married and set up in business as a cotton broker, long staple cotton introduced from India being Egypt's principal export. Now Charles Colt had a cotton manufactory, producing sheeting for export, and that was one reason why her father had taken her away from her London school last year, because her Aunt Liz kept heckling him about the health and wages of the *fellaheen* who were his workers.

"Aunt Liz is very strong on the rights of man, and votes for women and the right to strike," she said. "Father took me to Cairo because he thought she was making me strong-minded."

"But before your father took you back to Cairo he left you with other people after your mother died, didn't he? With your grandmother in America and then with your mother's sister in London? Didn't you resent it?"

The candid brown eyes reflected none of the resentment which had marred his own adolescence. "No, why should I?"

said Sadie Colt. "He had his own work to do, and I had to start growing up before I could be any use to him. He's nice, my father, you and he would get on well, I know. I wish you weren't going to Paris next week."

It was the avowal no older woman would have made, but before Alain could reply Mademoiselle Garrigue was upon them again, insisting that her pupil must come indoors now and rest. Sadie protested that she wasn't tired, and Alain, as an alternative, suggested they both come to tea with him in the Moorish kiosk, where a piano and violin had begun to play.

"Oh, lovely!" cried Sadie. "Mademoiselle, do let's!"

"Thank you, monsieur," said the governess. "I'm afraid we could only accept your kind invitation if *madame la duchesse* knew and approved. Sarah, say goodnight to Captain de Grimont."

"It was four in the afternoon," fumed Alain to his aunt, "and that poor kid was dragged away to write an essay or some such rot. Will you tell me why the Garrigue woman treated my invitation to tea in the hotel grounds as if I were asking them to a Port Said opium den?"

"She's a silly woman," agreed the duchess, "but she does feel responsible for the child. She has to follow her every-where – "

"When she's not incapacitated."

"True. When Monsieur Colt comes back I'm going to drop a hint about the migraines and the sick headaches and all the rest of it. He engaged her in a hurry, and she's not the right governess for a girl like Sadie. Of course her scruples this afternoon may have been on my behalf. She may have thought it rude to enjoy a tea party without me."

"But darling aunt, if you would only have tea at the kiosk it would be wonderful – "

"I think you might get me down there on your arm, but I don't think you could get me uphill again, and I'd rather not try . . . It's very sweet of you, Alain, to think of an entertainment for that poor child."

"Why poor?"

"She won't find it easy to be Charles Colt's daughter, when she goes back to Cairo."

"Is he such an ogre? How did you get to know him, Aunt Blanche?"

"He was a friend of Armand's at Alexandria," said his aunt vaguely.

"And the Prince of Wales?"

"He likes Americans, especially when they can make him laugh and play a good game of cards. Alain, I've had an idea! Why don't I propose a visit to my brother at Laghet? You've never seen the old château, and," the duchess was counting the stitches on the baby sock she was knitting, "Sadie might like to see it too."

"You mean you'd take Sadie on a visit to your brother? You're being awfully nice to her, Aunt Blanche."

"I always wanted a daughter," said his aunt. "Especially when I had to bring up wild boys like you three. Perhaps that's why I'm glad to take Sadie Colt under my wing."

"Henriette's a very nice daughter-in-law, and now you've got three granddaughters. The new one's a little pet."

"Marie-Rose. We gave her Madame Barthou's name, and it suits her, doesn't it? As for Henriette, she's my right hand. I could never have had this holiday if she hadn't been at the Villa Rivabella to look after your uncle, and see him through this nasty business of the drains. But they all spoil me, Alain!"

"You deserve it, dear."

"Tell me something. Why are you in such a hurry to go to Paris? I thought you meant to keep me company until your uncle came."

"He may arrive before I leave. I'm sorry, aunt, but my friend Delcassé advises me to get to Paris quickly if I want promotion. At present I'm in line to be the oldest captain in the French Army."

"After six months in action against the Touaregs?"

"That doesn't count. What does count is what a contact of Delcassé's saw on my file at the War Ministry. It's stamped *Esprit Politique Suspect*, which means I'm considered politically unreliable."

"You? Politically suspect?" The Duchesse de la Treille sat upright on her sofa, shocked out of her usual indolent calm.

"The army is riddled with antisemitism, aunt, and I'm supposed to be a Jew-lover." He guessed it was the hand of Major Edmond de St Etienne, Records clerk, which had added *Esprit Politique Suspect* to his dossier.

"But that's crazy!" His aunt hesitated. "You don't suppose your being with Boulanger had anything to do with it?"

"I don't think so. I was his ADC, I never was a Boulangist. And anyway, that's all ended now."

"And what an end!" The duchess shuddered. "That poor infatuated woman — "

"He dragged her everywhere with him, but at least he never left her, aunt. Not even when he was offered one million francs to do a lecture tour in the United States, riding Tunis on to the stage . . ."

It was just eight months since Marguerite de Bonnemains died of tuberculosis in Brussels, less than six since Boulanger shot and killed himself on her grave in a Belgian cemetery.

"We were talking about it one night at Hyères," said Alain, clearing his throat, "and my uncle Gilbert said a curious thing. He said he thought a statue to Madame de Bonnemains should be erected somewhere in Paris, because she saved France from dictatorship. He said if ever again there's a French general who wants to be an American-style president, who believes in his own publicity and who thinks he *is* France, we should pray for a Marguerite de Bonnemains in his life too."

"Gilbert was teasing you, dear. It can never happen again."

"Let's hope so. Now we ought to start planning the trip to Laghet."

"You may find my brother rather gruff at first," said the duchess to Sadie Colt. "Since his wife died ten years ago he has lived pretty much as a recluse."

"I can't remember when I saw him last," said Alain. They were driving north into the hills above Monte Carlo in the carriage and pair he had hired from the hotel's livery stable, on the other side of the Roman road where a tramcar plied between Nice and Menton.

"Had they no children?" asked Sadie.

"Yes, one son. He's a banker in Geneva, married to a Swiss girl. I don't think they'll ever want to live at the Château de Laghet."

"I'm so excited about seeing it." Sadie was excited about everything that day, twisting round in the carriage to see the ever widening view of the Mediterranean shore from St Jean Cap Ferrat to Bordighera, exclaiming at the quaint village of La Turbie, and silent when they came in sight of the ruined Trophée des Alpes, erected to commemorate Augustus Caesar's victories in AD 14. When they passed the point where the Via Julia and the Via Aurelia had met in Caesar's time, they were only five miles distant from the château of Blanche's ancestors, which should have been called as it once was the Tour de Laghet. It was nothing but a thirteenth-century tower, built to keep watch when the Saracen pirates out of Tripoli were ravaging the coast, with a low two-storey building of small dark rooms built on three centuries later, but at the sight of her birthplace, and her white-haired brother standing by the door, the ready tears came to Blanche's eyes.

Comte Lambert de Laghet was anything but gruff: he

greeted his guests enthusiastically, and took them indoors to drink iced white wine and seltzer water to refresh them after the drive, while through the door of the small dining-room two elderly maids could be seen setting the table for a tremendous luncheon. He told his sister she was looking well, congratulated Alain on his part in the battle of El Djezir, and was obviously delighted with Sadie. In her white school prize-giving dress, with the straw hat wreathed with silk poppies instead of the striped school ribbon she looked so fresh that the elderly gentleman twisted the ends of his white moustache, yellowed by the nicotine of innumerable cigarettes, and Alain thought that recluse or no, the old boy still had an eye for a pretty girl.

Monsieur de Laghet wore a white tussore silk suit also yellowed with age, white spats to his calves and a floppy panama hat. Sadie thought he looked like the pictures of Tartarin de Tarascon in the Daudet book she had read with Aunt Liz. The only thing she dared to ask him when they were outdoors again, and the smooth turf of the plateau stretched around them for mile on empty mile, was if it wasn't sometimes lonely at the Tour de Laghet.

"Not at all," said the recluse briskly. "Any day now the pilgrimages will begin. I see them passing and hear them singing on their way to the Carmelite sanctuary of Notre Dame du Laghet, and they're all the company I need."

"It's a beautiful place," said Blanche, "but it lies in the valley, Sadie, you can't see it from here."

"Is that where you were married, duchess?"

"No, my dear, we were married in Paris, at St Louis des Invalides, with the Emperor and the Empress present, and half of Gilbert's troop as the guard of honour."

"How marvellous."

"Come now," said de Laghet, "we ought to make the *tour du propriétaire* before we sit down to lunch. Blanche, you'd better take my arm, and the young people can follow."

"The schoolroom set!" said Captain de Grimont with a grin. But Sadie did not smile. As they set off down the narrow path to the flower garden she said softly, "What about *your* arm? I notice you keep your hand in your pocket all the time since you took off the sling."

"It's all right, thank you. Just gets a bit tired . . ." Not for worlds would Alain have told her that he had tried rolling a sheet of paper into a ball and throwing it up with the arm that had been wounded, and sketching an overhand serve with his right. The left arm was too feeble to throw up a tennis ball.

The brother and sister, each believing the other to be hard of hearing, were talking loudly just ahead of them. Wasn't that where the rabbit hutches used to be, and Why did you cut down that fine old cypress were some of Blanche's nostalgic comments.

The flower garden and the kitchen garden, both in apple pie order, were duly admired, and the Comte de Laghet, piloting his sister back to the house, told Alain to show Sadie a new fir plantation where jonquils and narcissus were growing in the rank grass beneath the trees.

"I don't remember this little wood. It's pretty, don't you think?"

"It's lovely, but it's dark." Sadie shivered. "Something about this place scares me."

"*Scares* you?"

"It's all so old. That Saracen watch tower is like the Trophée des Alpes down yonder. It's — outside the world I know."

"Then what about Egypt? You saw sights far older than those in Cairo."

"Yes, I did. I've been to Luxor and the Valley of the Kings, and last winter we lived at Mena House, with the Pyramids and the Sphinx for our nextdoor neighbours. But that's antiquity, and frightening in another way. How I wish

241

I didn't have to go back to Egypt and keep house for my father!"

"But I thought you were so fond of your father! You're very proud of him — "

"I *love* my father! I only wish he could meet some nice woman and marry her, so I could be free to live my own life!"

Alain put his arm round her shoulders. He was falling in love with this child against his better judgment, and he thought he had learned everything about her. She had described her gentle English mother, coming to winter in Egypt for her health, staying with friends until she met and married Captain Charles Colt, and then dying when their little girl was barely three. He could picture the spirited American granny, who gave her a childhood at Old Harbour as idyllic as his own at Hyères. It was not so easy to visualise the strongminded schoolteacher aunt, and impossible to understand that the sum of all of them had made Sadie Colt, in 1892, a girl of her own time.

"What do you mean by living your own life?" he asked.

"Not having to waste two years at finishing classes in Paris. Being properly educated instead. Not like those ladies at Mena House, who lived for fashion, and spent hours every day with their hairdressers and manicurists — "

"In a few years you'll enjoy being fashionable too."

"Not if it means being so trivial. I want to do something real with my life."

"How do you propose to set about it?"

He was laughing at her. Sadie pulled away from Alain's encircling arm.

"I asked my father to let me go back to the United States and study at a college for women called Bryn Mawr, and he refused."

"He wouldn't want to let you go so far away alone."

"That's what he said." She looked at him defiantly. "What I want is to be a doctor."

19

Sadie woke to the misery only possible when a girl of sixteen believes she has made a fool of herself in the eyes of an attractive man. Not 'an' attractive man, but the most attractive male she had ever seen, the French officer with the wounded arm and lined, handsome face who made his counterparts in Cairo look like popinjays. And she had done everything wrong in that sinister fir wood: derided the fashionable women he probably admired, and tried to make herself important and interesting by parading her superior intellectual powers. "I want to be a doctor" — it wasn't a lie, but Sadie knew that her father would no more consent to her medical training than he had agreed to her enrolment at Bryn Mawr. It was Aunt Liz, that resolute feminist, who had told her about Elizabeth Garrett Anderson and Sophia Jex-Blake, the pioneers among medical women; it was also Aunt Liz who would have called her fine speeches to Captain de Grimont showing off. "That's your besetting sin, Sarah, showing off," Aunt Liz had said it often enough, and now Mademoiselle Garrigue, in French, said the same.

In the grey dawn of a cloudy day — for she had awakened

early — Sadie Colt accused herself of another fault, intangible but positive. What had she done to make Alain de Grimont think he had the right to put his arm around her? Did he think he was comforting a child or embracing a woman? Had she thrown herself at the head of the first exciting man she met? Lying in bed, she put her own hand on her naked shoulder, and tried to imagine it was his strong hand which gripped her there. At least she had had the strength to break away from his clasp when her own body, in the grip of an elemental urge, wanted to be held still closer to his own. Darling, my darling, she whispered to her pillow. What shall I do when you have gone?

At least he *was* going, no later than tomorrow, and she wouldn't have to live through another day like yesterday. At Laghet she had learned an adult lesson, how to dissemble. She had acted the part of a happy girl, *une jeune fille comme il faut*, from the moment they had heard the Comte de Laghet calling to them in that horrible dark wood. "Come along, children, lunch is ready!" Alain had laughed, he thought it was funny to be called a child. Back in the shadow of the tower built against the Saracens, she had hardly been aware of pain, of the knowledge that she had made an abject fool of her self-important person; it was not too hard to be bright and interested and speak when she was spoken to. The drive home was worse, with Alain sitting opposite, his back to the horses, smiling at her in that — that patronising way, at the silly girl who said she wanted to be a doctor. At least the duchess did the talking for the three of them. She was far more animated than usual in her pleasure at seeing her brother and getting his promise to hire a vehicle at La Turbie and come down to the hotel to see her husband when 'dear Gilbert' arrived at the end of the week. Everybody was moving on. Alain was going to Paris, and when her father took Sadie to Paris he would have returned to finish out his leave at Hyères. They would never meet again, and with the tragic diction of sixteen Sadie told herself that she 'must learn to live without him'. Beginning today. It was beyond her power to face him again today.

With this in view she set herself, at breakfast time, to persuade Mademoiselle Garrigue to spend most of the day in the town of Menton, three miles away by the little tram.

Mademoiselle objected on principle to the tram, where one rubbed shoulders with working people, but otherwise she was persuadable. She had been impressed by Sarah's docility on the previous evening, which she had spent reading *Eugénie Grandet* aloud while the governess corrected her pronunciation. Mademoiselle, who also wanted to buy silks for her own fancy work, finally agreed that they might leave the hotel at eleven, and Sadie went down to the reception desk to cancel her tennis practice. Then there was an unexpected delay. The Prince of Wales, who had never left the royal suite since his arrival at Cap Martin, was going to Cannes with his son Prince George. Everybody knew what was afoot when the great carriage with the royal arms on the doors was brought round to the gravel sweep in front of the entrance. It had been sent out from England, like the prince's yacht, the *Nerine*, which was lying in Cannes harbour, so far never used. Two footmen in the royal liveries of scarlet and gold, with powdered hair, were seated at the rear of the carriage, while a third footman sat beside the driver on the box and jumped down to open the carriage door when the future king emerged from the hotel.

Such a sight brought a little crowd into the lobby and the gardens, and Sadie watching from behind a pillar thought the Prince of Wales did not look unduly grief-stricken at the death of his elder son, whom he had teased and called Prince Collars and Cuffs from his exaggerated tastes in haberdashery. He was very stout and also very affable. He raised his silk hat in acknowledgment of the bows and curtseys of the hotel guests, and actually laughed when two young

Englishmen shouted "Good luck!" when Prince George appeared. The prince, looking sheepish, climbed into the carriage and took his place beside his father.

The splendid carriage drove away, and Sadie, using the dispersing crowd for cover, piloted Mademoiselle Garrigue down the drive edged with purple iris and bushes of tea roses already in bud to the wooden hut on the Roman road which marked the tramway halt. The tram from Nice came along before mademoiselle had time to do more than complain of the rising wind and carried them downhill and along the curving promenade where one or two villas had been built on the shore of the beautiful Bay of Peace, and so into Menton, a short distance from the Italian border.

Menton had been a favourite winter resort of the English, whether invalid or healthy, for nearly fifty years, since the benefits of its climate had been discovered by a London doctor. There were not many people about as Sadie and her governess walked under the plane trees of the main street, for the shops shut at noon, but they saw the English Church, the English library, the English grocer's, and fortunately an English tearoom, which was open. Mademoiselle approved of its genteel furnishings of chintz and bamboo, and the equally genteel spinster who brought them a menu, and their choice of poached eggs on toast and slices of dry Madeira cake with cups of China tea exactly suited her difficult stomach. Sadie ate and drank without enjoyment, thankful only to be out of the grand dining room at Cap Martin, where Captain de Grimont would have risen from his aunt's table when he saw her come in with her governess, and bowed . . .

And bowed, tall and distinguished, the best looking man in the room, respectful to a schoolgirl . . .

A little fool who said she wanted to be a doctor.

Mademoiselle Garrigue ordered a second pot of tea while they sat on in the creaking basket chairs, watching Menton wakening from its siesta and the shops opening in the Rue St

Michel. When they left the wind was still rising, and the shopkeepers were predicting a mistral, the master wind of the Mediterranean, and although Sadie got her as far as the Old Town, where the fishermen's nets lay on the beach, the governess absolutely forbade her charge to walk on the high parapet of the Bastion. They returned to the shelter of the shops. The embroidery silks were bought, and Sadie played for time by lingering over the purchase of some English magazines (*Chambers* and *Blackwoods* passed the Garrigue censorship) and a bottle of the lemon eau-de-cologne for which Menton was famous. By then the mistral was well established and brought rain with it. The governess, predicting earache, rheumatism and lumbago for herself, hurried Sadie to the tramway terminal. By the time they reached the Hôtel du Cap Martin a pouring rain and a lashing wind turned them into a pair of drowned rats, who left puddles of water on the carpet when one of the smart little pages, wearing immaculate white gloves, stopped them in the hall.

"Mademoiselle!" He spoke to Sadie. "Madame la duchesse de la Treille has been looking for you everywhere. She is at tea in the hall now, and hopes you will join her."

"Go and see what she wants," said Mademoiselle Garrigue, with unusual decision, "but don't stay longer than five minutes, Sarah. You must get into dry clothes at once."

"Yes, mademoiselle." Go and get it over — that was good advice, and she had the perfect excuse for escaping to her room. Sadie threaded her way among the tea tables brought in from the marble terrace before the rain began, and saw the duchess sitting alone. No tall figure in army blue rose to greet Sadie; only the smiles of the other guests followed the forlorn little figure whose plaited hair dripped on her sodden frock.

"*Bonjour, madame —* "

"Sadie! My dear child, where have you been? How did you get into such a state?"

"Mademoiselle and I went to Menton for lunch and got caught in the rain."

"I'd no idea where you were, and Alain was gone too when the message came — "

"Has Captain de Grimont left for Paris already?"

"No, no — he rode over to Monte Carlo with one of the prince's equerries. They meant to have lunch there and try their luck at the Casino — foolish fellows!"

"But what was the message, madame, that came too late?"

The duchess glanced around and lowered her voice. "You're shivering, you silly child, I won't ask you to sit down. Go and change, look out your prettiest dress and wash your hair. The message was from the empress — the ex-Empress Eugénie. She arrived at the Villa Cyrnos two days ago, and she sent a note by messenger inviting me to bring Alain and you to an alfresco luncheon there tomorrow. An imperial command," said Blanche de la Treille with satisfaction, "so Alain will have to postpone his trip to Paris."

"But — *me*, duchess? Why should the — Her Majesty think of inviting me? She doesn't even know I exist!"

"Oh yes, she does. She particularly said in her letter, 'I shall be glad to meet the daughter of Monsieur Charles Colt.' I didn't know your father knew the empress!"

"My father knows everybody," said Sarah Colt.

It was a very different Sadie who waited in the hall next morning for the hired carriage that was to take the guests of the former Empress of the French to the Villa Cyrnos. She had spent some of the previous evening in altering her prettiest dress without the knowledge of her governess. It was a new dress, not meant to be altered, but the skirt was only calf-length, for a schoolgirl, and Sadie let it down six inches to touch her ankles. The chambermaid took it away to press the new hem, and attached puffs and bows of tulle to Sadie's Leghorn hat.

248

While Sadie sewed behind a locked door the mistral blew itself out and the rain ceased. When the windows were opened a delicious scent of freesias came up from the gardens and Sadie's spirits rose too. When the duchess told her Alain had gone off with another man to gamble at Monte Carlo she had felt a fool again, but in a different way: a fool for making such an elaborate attempt to avoid him while he, completely indifferent, had gone off to pursue pleasure in the opposite direction. In the light of a clear sunset, she changed her mind, and began to wonder if Captain de Grimont had been as anxious to avoid a meeting, following the scene at Laghet, as she was herself?

Certainly he looked amazed and pleased when they met next day. Sadie's long dress, of a pale blue-green, made her look taller, and though it was not as elaborate as adult fashion demanded, it had an embroidered bodice draped over the tiny waist, and leg-of-mutton sleeves which, at the elbows, met her long white kid gloves. Her hair was 'up' for the first time, coiled into a shining knot on the nape of her neck beneath the sophisticated hat, but when Alain said "Sadie, you do look marvellous!" what he meant was that beneath the grown-up disguise she was still the schoolgirl who showed her naked feelings, who spoke without thinking, who was still, this girl of sixteen, too young for a veteran like himself.

Aunt Blanche, when she appeared, was dressed in her best mauve silk with a feathered hat to match, and giving thanks for the beautiful day. The distance between the hotel and the Villa Cyrnos was so short that an active person could have walked there in less than ten minutes, but the duchess thought the carriage as much due to the empress's dignity as to her own comfort. The gates of the Villa Cyrnos were guarded by two men, not in livery, who appeared to be employed as gardeners.

" 'Cyrnos' is the Greek for Corsica, the birthplace of the Bonapartes," the duchess instructed Sadie as they drove along the empty road across Cap Martin, under the drooping branches of pine and eucalyptus, fragrant after yesterday's rain. "It was only built three years ago, and very few people have been inside."

"Mademoiselle Garrigue told me the Bonaparte family were not allowed to own property in France," hazarded Sadie.

"Much she knows about it," sniffed the duchess. "The law of sequestration was lifted after the death of the Prince Imperial. The empress was allowed to sell the villa at Biarritz, the chalet at Vichy and the farms in the Landes. She says she prefers the Villa Cyrnos to all of them."

"But she doesn't live here all the year round?"

"Her real home is at Farnborough in England, where her husband and her son are buried in the church. She often goes to Spain, where her late sister was married to the Duke of Alba, and when she passes through Paris she stays at the Hôtel Continental."

"I've never understood that," said Alain. "I've stayed at the Continental myself. And how *she* can live there, opposite the Tuileries gardens, and see nothing but empty space where the palace was, is a mystery to me."

"You'll understand better when you see her."

They had arrived at the Villa Cyrnos, and the gardeners were opening the gates. The house was built in the Italianate style suited to the Ligurian shore, with a flat balcony along the roof of the wide white building, and a high top storey, glassed in, at the centre. Two Bonaparte eagles stood on pillars at the entrance door, and these, with the name of Cyrnos, were all that was left of the imperial legacy.

Sadie Colt had seen a coloured print of the famous Winterhalter painting of the Empress Eugénie in her radiant twenties, seated in the middle of her beautiful maids of honour, all their crinolines flowing about them like flowers. The whitehaired woman who came to greet them at the door of the Villa Cyrnos was dressed in black silk, and at sixty-five her shoulders were bent by increasing years and sorrows. The only beauty she had retained was in her eyes, vivid and piercingly blue.

"Dear Blanche, how glad I am to see you!" she said in a sweet, caressing voice, while the two women curtseyed and Alain de Grimont saluted. "You are all so welcome, pray come in! I expect you to admire my new salon."

The salon, furnished in good taste with some Bonaparte memorabilia, was chiefly admirable for its magnificent view of the sea and the principality of Monaco, where every building could be seen in the brilliant light. Eugénie motioned Blanche and Sadie to comfortable seats while Alain remained standing — almost at attention.

"So you are Elvire de Grimont's boy," said the sweet voice. "I remember her well — she was so lovely." Eugénie gave Alain her hand. He went down on one knee and kissed it.

"You have your mother's grace, and the de la Treille good looks," she went on. "And you are a soldier, too. Forgive my curiosity, but how old are you?"

"Thirty-two, *Majesté*."

"Four years younger than my poor boy."

"I was at his thirteenth birthday party — at the Tuileries."

"Were you really? And you remember it still! I'm deeply touched, Captain de Grimont."

The Prince Imperial's portrait, painted while he was still a cadet at Woolwich, hung above the fireplace where a small log fire burned, and held the eyes of everybody in the room. The emotional moment passed when a manservant, more formally dressed than the gardeners, came in with a salver laden with bottles and glasses, and proceeded to serve apéritifs.

"I was really nervous after I wrote to you yesterday, dear Blanche," confided the hostess, "proposing an alfresco luncheon. When the mistral and the rain began I thought it would be impossible to eat outdoors today. Not that we'll really be outdoors, we'll be well sheltered. I'm rather proud of my new summer-house."

"I'm sure it will be delightful, Madame."

She was only natural when she was talking about the weather, thought Sadie, silent and watchful on a low upholstered stool. She's sitting down now — and made Alain sit beside her — but she might just as well be up and walking round and round, or whatever it is royalties do when they *faire cercle*. Every guest gets the same amount of attention, and the empress says the right thing to everybody. The little prince's birthday party — that took care of Alain. Now it's his aunt's turn; how is dear Gilbert? Expected in a few days? I didn't know that, but you must come back again and bring him with you, to see my new home. Now me. Mademoiselle, I saw your father in Paris a week ago, and he gave me quite the wrong idea of you. He said you were very studious, almost a bluestocking. He didn't tell me you were a budding beauty.

Sadie blushed and hung her head. Blanche de la Treille said kindly, "Fathers are not always the best judges of their daughters. May I ask where you met Monsieur Colt, Madame?"

"At a dinner at the Comtesse de Lhomond's — you remember Sylvie, don't you? She came to me in England, in the first terrible winter, and I often visit her when I'm in Paris."

"You are faithful to your friends, Madame."

"When they have been faithful to me. But now tell me about your sons, Blanche. Armand is still in the Navy, and Maurice — they say he'll be the first Governor of Indo-China."

"So he tells his father and me, Madame. They're building a new Residence for him at Saigon."

"He'll be a great proconsul. France is fortunate to have men like him." The empress looked wistfully at her dead son's portrait, and they knew she was thinking of the man

252

France lost. They were not prepared for the shriller tone, the almost hysteria, of her next words.

"And I gave France Saigon! My enemies said I interfered too much, forced the Emperor into wars of conquest: it isn't true. The Crimea, Italy, Mexico, Prussia, those wars were not of my conniving. But Cochin China, yes. Some day to be the whole of Indo-China — French, because of me. And Saigon, which I have never seen, is *my* capital! Mine still!"

Eugénie seemed to command herself, and smiled at Sadie Colt.

"Do you find my recollections tedious, mademoiselle?"

"I think they're fascinating, Madame."

"And you, Captain de Grimont?"

"More than fascinating, *Majesté*." There was a grimness in his voice and in his look which made his aunt shake her head in warning, but Eugénie only smiled. "Two young people ought not to be kept indoors on such a lovely morning, and lunch will not be served for half an hour. Take Miss Colt out to see the gardens and the summer-house, and we will follow you. I want to have a little talk about old times with your aunt."

"*A vos ordres, Majesté*." It was what he had said a thousand times to Boulanger, *à vos ordres*. Now he held the glass door open for Sadie to precede him on to the terrace, where young plants of wisteria and bougainvillea had hardly had time to twine.

In the salon the former empress pulled a chair close to Blanche de la Treille's *bergère*, but not to discuss old times. It was new gossip which made her blue eyes sparkle and brought a little colour to her pale face.

"Blanche dear, do tell me what to do about the Princess of Wales. I wrote a letter of condolence to Sandringham, of course, as soon as I heard the shocking news of Eddie's death — poor Alix, now she too knows what it is to lose a son — and an acknowledgment came from a lady in waiting. Now, this very morning, I had a letter from the princess herself inviting me to dinner, but not till next week. Why the delay? What's been decided about Prince George?"

"Why, Madame, you must accept the invitation – for next week. By that time the prince's position may be quite clear. He and his father went to Cannes yesterday."

"To propose to Princess May? To take on the girl poor Eddie was to marry?"

"I don't know about a proposal, but to call on the young lady, certainly. And to stay for a few days, to let nature take its course."

"Mary Teck will be overjoyed. She saw her daughter as the future queen, and then the cup was dashed from her lips. Paris was buzzing with the rumour that she was ready to follow the Waleses to Cap Martin, is that true?"

"Not quite to Cap Martin, but the next place to it. She got her friend Lady Wolverton to rent a villa at Menton, and invite all the Tecks to be her guests. It really was too blatant, and they say the Prince of Wales was furious. Lady Wolverton gave up the Menton idea and took a villa at Cannes, which is where they're staying now."

"Poor Princess May – one fiancé dead and his brother hanging fire. I really feel for her, saddled with that fat silly mother. But she was Queen Victoria's choice for the next heir to the throne, so I suppose the match is bound to come off after a decent interval of mourning. What a farce the whole thing is!" She got up impatiently and walked to the window. "Come and look at this, Blanche. Here's a couple ready to let nature take its course without any manoeuvring or contriving."

The Duchesse de la Treille rose with difficulty from the deep *bergère* and joined Eugénie at the window.

"Alain and little Sadie!" she exclaimed. "You must be dreaming, Madame!"

The two had not gone very far in their exploration of the

garden. They were standing by a newly planted hedge of agave cactus, and Sadie was rubbing one of the coral coloured berries in her fingers. Her face was turned up to Alain's, who was bending over her in what seemed to the two experienced watchers to be a loverlike attitude – protective and imploring at the same time.

"I knew he was in love with her the moment they came in," said Eugénie, and "Alain!" said his aunt again. "I *have* thought once or twice that she was ready to hero-worship the wounded soldier with the black silk sling, but he – never! She's a mere child and he knows it – "

"How old is she? Eighteen? Nineteen?"

"She put up her hair and let down her skirts today to seem grown-up, but she's just turned sixteen. Exactly half his age."

"There's a difference in ages, certainly, but we saw the same thing often enough at the Tuileries. It would be a very good match, Blanche. The Baron de Grimont, with an independent fortune, and Monsieur Colt's daughter with a handsome dowry – it's a marriage made on the Bourse if not in heaven!"

Eugénie's little flippant laugh jarred on Alain's aunt. She had always defended the boy she brought up against his uncle's criticisms, for of recent years the duke had taken to saying that Alain had handled his army career badly. He ought to have entered the reserve and settled down on his family estate with a wife and family, finding as much satisfaction in the Sologne as the Duc de la Treille found in growing carnations for the Paris market. Her serious objection to a match between Alain and Sadie – now that she was forced to think of it – was not the disparity in age but the difference in character. How could a young American girl adjust to a man whose strong opinions had made him more enemies than friends, and who had never once acted to his own advantage? Thank God he's going away tonight, she

255

thought, and to the ex-empress said, with a light laugh to match her own:

"There may have been a little holiday flirtation, dearest Madame, but after all they've only known each other for a few days!"

"Sometimes it only takes a few hours."

This was precisely what Alain de Grimont was thinking, as he stood with Sadie Colt in the garden of the Villa Cyrnos. It was the first time they had been alone together since the fir wood at Laghet, and perhaps tactlessly he spoke of Laghet first.

"Do you feel scared here as you did two days ago?"

"Scared at the Villa Cyrnos? Where everything is fresh and light and new?"

"Including the lady it was built to please?"

"The empress? I think she's wonderful. Listening to her talk is like reading a page of history."

"Unfortunately," said Alain, "the page isn't ended yet."

He knew she didn't understand him. How could this child, who knew no other war than the Civil War, realise the shock effect of Eugénie's cry, *I gave them Saigon*! Saigon and the war of conquest, the war with China, the guerrilla fighting in the paddy-fields, the Paris of South-East Asia built on an insecure foundation! He said "Never mind," when she asked him what he meant, and told her they must go and find the summer-house so as to be ready with their compliments when the older ladies joined them.

The summer-house, half way down the garden, was built of logs with a thatched roof, and mounted on a swivel which allowed it to be turned with its open front always following the sun. Servants were busy inside, setting out glass and china, so Alain led the way downwards beneath the trees, through newly planted flower beds arranged by an Italian designer. As at the hotel, a carpet of wild freesias spread between the beds.

"Do you know which of these flowers is the deathless asphodel?" asked Sadie, trying to speak without constraint.

"I'm afraid I don't know all their names."

"Persephone married Pluto, the king of the underworld, who allowed her to go back to the upper regions every spring to visit her mother Demeter. And wherever she walked, spring flowers appeared. Some say they were anemones, some the deathless asphodel; I like to think they were freesias, because they smell so sweet."

"I'll think about the freesias and their scent tomorrow, under the rain and the sooty skies of Paris."

"Will you really be in Paris tomorrow? I thought . . . the duchess . . . said you would stay here a little longer . . ."

The beseeching look on her young face told him he was right to go, had been right to spend yesterday away from her, in the gambling rooms at Monte Carlo.

"I think my aunt only meant that instead of taking the morning train I would take the night express."

"I see."

The next words were forced out of him. "Sadie! Do *you* tell me to stay?"

She put up her hands defensively — and when the white gloves were off they were still a schoolgirl's hands, with the mark of a penholder on the fingers of the right — and whispered "I mustn't tell you anything."

"Then kiss me goodbye, my darling little girl . . ."

She came into his arms and took his kisses, not once but many times, with lips as cool and fresh as the sea on the rocks below the villa named for Corsica. She felt the uncontrollable thrust of Alain's body as he, in a passion of regret, felt the wild beating of her heart.

PART FOUR

*The House of
Islam*

20

After the crystal clear light of Cap Martin, the rain and sooty skies of Paris predicted by Alain were depressing indeed as he made his way to the military hospital of Val-de-Grâce for an examination of his wounded arm. Next morning the rain had turned to sleet, and the first flakes of snow were falling as he found a cab to take him to Théophile Delcassé's apartment in the Boulevard de Clichy.

Delcassé had lived in the same apartment, once Monsieur Massip's, ever since he married Massip's widow; quite content, in spite of his increasing power and influence, to remain in bourgeois comfort on the very frontier of Montmartre. Up that northern road, where he travelled by cab, Alain reflected that in 1871 the National Guard had dragged the cannon abandoned by the government, the cannon which had sparked off the carnage of the Commune. Now on the slope of the Butte Montmartre a great church had been built and called the Sacré Coeur as an expiation of the Communard sins. It was already open for worship, and in the falling snow a line of pilgrims was toiling up the great staircase leading to the white mass of domes, pillars and buttresses, neo-Greek, neo-Byzantine, neo-Paris, completely 1892. To make way for the Sacré Coeur much of old Montmartre had been swept away.

The Boulevard de Clichy had grown shabbier, more of a tourist trap in the way of bars and 'dancings' since Alain first visited Delcassé there, but the politician's apartment building was well maintained and freshly painted and in the warm hall a neat parlourmaid, with a look of concern, helped Alain off with the greatcoat he was now obliged to wear round his shoulders. His left arm was back in a sling again, on doctor's orders, and it was the first thing Monsieur Delcassé remarked upon when the greetings were over in the comfortable library.

"Still having trouble with the arm, eh? Not better yet?"

"A long way from better, according to the surgeons at Val-de-Grâce," said Alain. "Seems there was more damage done to the shoulder than the medics at Bône realised. It's an infernal nuisance, but — "

"But here's someone who's been waiting to meet you. Captain de Grimont, I don't believe you know Captain Marchand?"

"I'm very glad to meet him now," said Alain, shaking hands with a young man who had been standing near the library fire. "Even in a *bled* like Bône we've heard of your exploits, Captain Marchand."

Delcassé's other guest was slim and dark, with a neat pointed beard. Like Alain, he wore the ribbon of the Legion of Honour, and held himself with a quiet intensity like a greyhound on a leash. He murmured polite condolences on Alain's wounded arm.

"It was the Touareg, wasn't it?" he asked. "I've had a *razzia* or two with them myself, but more with the Toucouleur."

"It was a surprise ambush, when my company was out on patrol. We didn't expect the Touareg to come out yelling

Allah and waving the green flag. They didn't used to be among the Sons of the Prophet . . . Are you on long leave, Captain Marchand?"

"I'm going back to the Côte d'Ivoire at the end of the month. After that — who knows?"

"What I know is that you're going to be late for your luncheon engagement," said Delcassé. "Unless we can persuade you to cut it and stay to lunch with us?"

"Oh no, I couldn't do that, but thanks! Captain de Grimont, I'm sorry we haven't had more time to talk. But I hope we'll meet again, in Paris or in Africa!"

"I hope so too."

"So that's the man," Alain exclaimed, as soon as his host returned from seeing Captain Marchand to the door, "that's the man who explored the Ivory Coast, and traced the Niger River to its source! He looks hardly old enough to have done all that — more like a boy than an explorer — "

"He's twenty-nine."

"Three years younger than I am, and famous already!"

"Don't be depressed, Alain. I want to congratulate you on your promotion. Your majority will be in the *Gazette* tomorrow."

Alain flushed with pleasure. "I'm glad," he said simply. "Sometimes I thought it was never going to happen. Now I can face up to the future, whatever it is."

"Let's drink to your promotion first, and then we'll talk about the future." He poured two glasses of dry vermouth. "Here's to you, Major de Grimont!"

"Here's to you, Théo, and — thanks." When the glasses were empty he added slyly, "What about Marchand? Is he one of your protégés too?"

"He consults me from time to time. You must remember, Jean-Baptiste Marchand was never at St Cyr. He enlisted as a private in the Marines and rose by sheer merit, but he has always known how to make useful friends. Today he's lunching at the Bristol with Gabriel Hanotaux, whose ambition is to be our foreign minister: that could be helpful to young Marchand's career."

"So he's going to the Bristol via the Boulevard de Clichy. You must have been really anxious for the two of us to meet!"

"There you have me." Delcassé smiled. "Alain, sometimes you're too sharp for your own good. Yes, I did want you to meet Marchand, however briefly, because I think you might make a good team. This is the era of the young professional soldier. Boulangism is as dead as the general, and now better men are coming along. Mangin is younger than Marchand, while Joffre, Philippe Pétain and Ferdinand Foch are barely forty. Those are the men who'll get us back Alsace-Lorraine, without sporting the Red Carnation."

"Fighting Germany?"

"Yes."

"From which I gather that a military alliance with Russia is as good as signed and sealed already?"

"It's only a matter of time."

"And you've worked hard for it. But do you really think France and Russia together can beat Germany, where the young Kaiser is panting for war – "

"Against England."

"Yes."

"Which means," said Delcassé, "that once we're sure of Russia, we must make England our Ally too."

"An English alliance? You must be dreaming, Théo!"

"You've never been an anglophile, Alain. That's the one thing I hold against Marchand – he hates the British. No – not for the old defeats, Trafalgar, Waterloo, perfidious Albion – you know the hymn of hate; but for the new defeats in the scramble for Africa . . . Alain, forgive me. I'm putting the cart before the horse. Before I tell you what I want of you, I should tell you of the new posting which goes with your majority."

"Which is?"

"You're to be seconded for special service to the Bureau Arabe in Algiers."

"The Bureau Arabe!" said Alain in surprise. "I thought it was completely out of date since Algeria was divided into three Departments and declared an integral part of France. When I was in Algiers in the Topographical, people spoke as if it was just an administrative anachronism left over from the Conquest."

"Not where the Arabs are concerned, and that's where you'll be valuable. You proved it as soon as you came in today, when you talked about the Touareg ambush, and the green flags, and the Sons of the Prophet. You know the difference between a *razzia* and a holy war."

"I do, but I've never known a desert tribe to be proclaiming a *jehad*. In Tunisia, yes; but never so far west."

"The *jehad*, the war against the Christians, has been spreading westward ever since the Mahdi drove the British out of the Sudan."

"You may be right," said Alain slowly. "It always comes back to Egypt, doesn't it?"

"Egypt is the key to the Near East, and to North Africa as well," said Delcassé gravely, "and the Bureau Arabe in Algiers is a counter-intelligence agency, where your long apprenticeship will be put to good use. For instance, there's a bad situation developing between the Jews and the Arabs in Algeria, and you are known to be essentially fair towards the Jews — "

"Also as 'politically suspect', don't forget."

"That's been stricken from your records. And Major St Etienne, who falsified them, has been transferred to Madagascar."

Alain's worried look gave way to laughter. "You're a good friend, Théo," he said. "All right, I'm delighted with my new posting, even if Algiers is a long way from *jehad* headquarters at Khartoum. Was that what you wanted to hear me say, or is there something more?"

"A rather pleasant something. How much of your sick leave is left?"

"Six weeks."

"And what do you want to do — go back to Cap Martin?"

"*No!*" He saw Delcassé's surprise, and softened the explosive negative. "I had a good rest there, and at Hyères too. I'd rather stay in Paris for a bit."

"You'd have to do that anyway, to settle your posting at the War Ministry, and you ought to pay a duty call at the Ministry of the Marine and Colonies. After that I'd like you to spend a month in London."

"In London!"

"You speak English, don't you?"

"Not very well." He remembered the gardens at Cap Martin, and Sadie's insistence that he tell her about the desert fighting in her own language. He remembered how politely she had tried not to laugh.

"You'd soon pick it up."

"But what do you want me to *do* in London? I don't know a soul in the place."

"That's easy to arrange."

"Through our embassy?"

"No, keep away from the embassy. You mustn't be identified with politics in any way. I hope some day Paul Cambon will be our ambassador, but at present he's in Constantinople, watching the Sultan's reactions to Abbas, the new young Khedive of Egypt."

"Paul Cambon, who was in Tunis, and had the row with Boulanger?"

"The same. Another mistake by *Général Revanche*."

Alain was silent. Completely disillusioned with Boulanger though he was, he still disliked to hear the man disparaged.

"If Lord Lansdowne were in London, I would write a personal introduction to him, but as Viceroy of India he's necessarily absent. Besides, Lansdowne is like Cambon, a man for the future. For the present, I suggest you get your old friend Monsieur Imbert to take an interest in your visit to London, and open an account for you with Baring Brothers. An introduction to the senior partners will open doors for you everywhere, and allow you to get the only thing I want – the feel of England."

"Why Baring Brothers in particular?"

"Because one of the family, just created Baron Cromer, is the man who runs Egypt for the British."

"And holds the key to the Near East," said Alain. All roads led to Egypt, even via the Bureau Arabe at Algiers! Delcassé, who knew his man, decided to say no more at present. While they talked, a pleasant domestic odour of roast lamb had pervaded the library, and a gong struck just outside the door summoned them to lunch.

"Think it over, Alain," Delcassé said casually, as they both got up, "and let me know what you decide." He laid his hand on Alain's uninjured arm. "But if you relish the idea, remember the English are very strong on class. Take back your title for the occasion. Get out of that eternal uniform and go to a London tailor for the kind of clothes they wear themselves. I guarantee you'll be a great success. Now come to luncheon; Madame Delcassé doesn't like to be kept waiting."

Madame Delcassé was not a martinet, but a good housewife anxious that her excellent food should be eaten hot. She was all smiles and congratulations for 'Major de Grimont', and her mild conversation demanded no intellectual effort on Alain's part. Watching his host expertly carving the *gigot* of lamb he had time to marvel that those huge projects, a French alliance with Russia and one with England, were coming slowly to fruition not in palaces or parliaments, but in the brain of one unassuming little man in a Montmartre flat. There was no more political talk that day, for Delcassé rose from the table as soon as dessert was served, pleading an early engagement at the Chambre des Députés, while his wife, no doubt coached in advance, asked Alain to keep her company for a little while and have a cup of coffee in the salon. His account of the visit to the Villa Cyrnos kept the good lady entertained for half an hour.

Alain was glad to get out of the 'eternal uniform' when he returned to the Continental, although one of the hotel valets had to help him out of his tunic and into his comfortable dressing gown. The new massage treatment given to his arm at Val-de-Grâce seemed to have made it worse instead of better, and he decided not to go out again that day. The snow was still falling, in big soft wet flakes, and the pavements were a mess of brown slush.

The valet put a pillow in an easy chair between the fire and the window, and brought Alain a brandy and soda. He sat sipping it and looking out at the bare trees in the Tuileries garden, which were what the ex-Empress Eugénie saw when she came to the Continental, and remembering her cry of "I gave them Saigon!" which had chilled his spirit at the Villa Cyrnos. Saigon had been won by a war of conquest, and wars of conquest brought wars of revenge. Major de Grimont's boyish dream of marching across the Rhine and into Germany was as dead as Boulanger, but what about Delcassé's dream of an Anglo-Russian alliance with France against Germany? Austria would come in on the German side, which would fire the Balkans; Egypt and the Ottoman Empire would be involved . . . the price of recovering Alsace and Lorraine would be a full scale European war. "This is why I became a soldier," he said to himself. "This is what I'm supposed to want." The victory of France, the glory road — at whatever cost.

Delcassé had left too much unsaid or unexplained. How or when could Captain Marchand and Alain de Grimont become a good team with half of Black Africa between Algiers and the settlements on the Ivory Coast? What was the connection between the Viceroy of India and a mere Deputy of France? And how could the savages who had driven the British and the Egyptians out of the Sudan send the idea of a holy war, Islam against Christianity, across the Libyan desert into Tripoli, Tunisia and Algiers? He was pretty sure that his new posting to the Bureau Arabe was only a stepping stone on the road to Cairo.

In two years' time Sadie Colt would be in Cairo with her father, Sadie eighteen years old and adorably grown up — if her Paris education hadn't turned her into a cold coquette like Isabelle Lacroix. Or if his own abrupt and passionate approach hadn't put her off the very idea of sex.

He had been sitting in the firelight, but now the street lighting came on outside, and an electric standard beyond the window shone full into his room. Alain got up with an oath as his arm was jarred against the back of the chair, and went to look out. The Rue de Rivoli was seething with traffic, buses with bad-tempered drivers and pedestrians snarling as their umbrellas collided, but beyond the garden railings the spring snow was falling pure and white on the empty flower beds and the untrodden walks. He thought of the carpet of white freesias at Cap Martin which Sadie thought were Persephone's flowers marking her footsteps when she came back from the underworld. Now he was going into the underworld, where Sadie would forget him. In his heart Alain knew that he would not forget.

Next morning the sun was shining, the snow in the gardens had melted, and in the clear air Alain saw the Eiffel Tower, needle-slim and aspiring against blue skies. He was starting to like the thing, perhaps even more than he had once admired the Head of Liberty. People were beginning to say it was a symbol of Paris – that old Paris in which Alain de Grimont must try to make a new beginning.

After another visit to Val-de-Grâce he sent a note to Delcassé, saying the military surgeons had ordered daily massage treatments for the next two weeks, after which he was looking forward to 'a short holiday in London'. The two weeks gave him time to have a civilian suit made by the English tailor on the Boulevard des Capucines, to meet old friends at his clubs and see the new Feydeau farce at the Théâtre du Palais Royal, but he never had any of the hoped-for explanations from Delcassé. Foreign alliances and Islam were alike eclipsed by the latest Paris sensation: the return of terrorists to the boulevards.

Who flung the bomb into Véry's well-known restaurant? The police could not identify the criminals who had killed and maimed to no apparent purpose. The Russian Narodniki had not been active in France since the failed attempt on the life of President MacMahon, though they had been more successful in the homeland, where the Czar Alexander II had died in a bomb explosion. The home-grown anarchists had been relatively peaceful since Louise Michel was deported to England. But the dead and injured were at Véry's in the rubble and the flames, and violence had come back to Paris.

The Duchesse de la Treille, who had written at once to congratulate Alain on his promotion, wrote again about the Véry bombing, with the addition of a romantic note. "After the Prince of Wales left Cap Martin with his family," the letter ran, "Mr Colt and Sadie came to spend a few days with us at Hyères. Clever little Sadie tried to use the Véry episode to get her papa to send her to London to continue her education instead of Paris, but of course Mr Colt was adamant. Sadie consoled herself on the tennis court which Valérie Ovize has had made for her young people, and played there every day. She looked so pretty and happy, and was much admired."

This letter reached Alain just before he left for London, and he read it more than once on the packet boat to Dover. Sadie on the tennis court — how well he could picture the graceful girl in her white dress — and Sadie arguing about her education: he knew about that too. But she was happy, that was what really mattered, and he could stop feeling that his kisses were somehow equivalent to the rape of a child. Happy and admired, he would remember that.

Perfidious Albion, whatever she thought of France, was most amiable to one individual Frenchman, when he happened to be Major the Baron de Grimont, armed with impeccable letters of introduction and staying at the Savoy Hotel. His mistakes in spoken English and his attractive foreign accent endeared him to the ladies, of whom he soon met many, for the English habit of entertaining in their own homes was a surprise to the man from France. His social life began at Baring's Bank, where Monsieur Imbert's influence caused him to be taken in hand by a young Baring, who invited him to lunch at a St James's Street club far more silent and far more impressive than the Jockey. The young Baring was quite ready to talk politics in a muted voice, and Alain's first impression, from which he never wavered during his visit, was that Egypt and the reconquest of the Sudan mattered more to Britain than the blustering of the Kaiser or terrorist attacks directed at mere foreigners.

After that he was invited to dinner in several houses in Mayfair and Belgravia, and once with young officers on guard at St James's Palace. He spent a countryhouse weekend where one of the guests was a member of Lord Salisbury's cabinet, and by contrast he was a silent patron of the pubs in Soho and the Strand, listening to the opinions of 'the man in the street' which were chiefly concerned with sport.

One day he went to Hyde Park to watch a review of the

Household Cavalry by Prince George, last seen at Cap Martin, and recently created the Duke of York. Society ladies tittered that this was the incentive to propose to Princess May of Teck, still in mourning for his brother, but as yet no marriage announcement had been made.

The Val-de-Grâce treatment was so successful that Alain's arm was out of the sling for good, and strong enough for him to learn to drive a horseless carriage with the engine in front, and a man walking ahead carrying a red flag as the law required. He travelled in the new Underground trains, which took passengers any distance in London for twopence, and wondered when Paris would introduce a similar system.

As his English improved he read the newspapers from the halfpenny press to the *Times* leaders, and his holiday impressions of Merrie England were corrected. When he saw Delcassé again he told him that France was a great deal more unpopular in Britain than Germany was, and quoted the cabinet minister as saying any French advance towards the Nile would be regarded as 'an unfriendly act'.

"That's very strong language in diplomacy."

"It means 'war', doesn't it?"

"It could, in a bad situation, but that mustn't be allowed to happen."

"No, but Théo, I don't see how a formal alliance between France and Britain would ever be possible."

"But you got on well with the people you met? Would you like to go back to London?"

"When?"

Delcassé laughed. "Not yet," he said, "but I gather you enjoyed yourself. You didn't find the language a problem?"

"Not after the first few days."

"You must have a language brain. Did you pick up any Arabic in Tunisia?"

" 'Pick up' is right," said Alain. He grinned as he remembered the words Melissa had taught him in their love-hours

272

on her silken couch. "The Arabic I learned in Tunis is hardly the language of diplomacy."

"You might try some serious study in Algiers, it would do you good at the Bureau Arabe. Algiers has changed a good deal since your last posting to the Topographical."

Algiers, seen from the sea, looked the same as always, a mass of white buildings with the Tricolore flying from the old fortress, and a crowd of men in white *galabeyeh* and red fez thronging the waterfront. Ashore, Alain saw that the European quarter had been greatly extended. There were shops and hotels which had not existed seven years earlier, and in front of one garden hotel he saw a party of tourists collecting round a Thomas Cook guide. He commented on this as soon as a cab and two porters had delivered himself and his baggage to the Bureau Arabe. It was as good a way of breaking the ice as any.

"I've been living in an hotel since my wife died," said Monsieur Monnet, who was to be his immediate superior, "but really the swarms of tourists are getting on my nerves. They're a perfect pest to the police — always giving their guides the slip and sneaking off to the Casbah to see the belly-dancers, which means they're found next morning in some back alley, drugged and robbed. Disgraceful!"

"Is the Casbah out of bounds now?" asked Alain, amused. He had spent some voluptuous evenings in that congeries of dwellings on the hill, which had been the old Turkish quarter in the days before the Conquest, and was still a citadel of the House of Islam.

"Only to the troops," said Monsieur Monnet, with a sidelong glance at Alain's uniform which betrayed that he, as a civil servant of long standing, had his doubt about the wisdom of seconding an officer to the Bureau Arabe for special service. He was a man of sixty who had been with the Bureau for thirty years, and was unable to make up his mind to retire to some pleasant spot in the South of France. The Bureau was his life, but he was perfectly affable to the newcomer, and putting a panama hat on his bald head he personally escorted Alain to his quarters.

It was clear that Major the Baron de Grimont rated better treatment than young Lieutenant de Grimont, down from a tedious command at Bizerta to do a temporary job in the Topographical, and living in barracks. He had been allotted a two-roomed cottage in what the British would have called a cantonment built round an attractive park, and the elderly Arab couple who were to be his daily servants were waiting with an assortment of wines and fruit set out on a low brass table. Alain drank a glass of the local red wine with Monsieur Monnet, and promised to be at the Bureau punctually at eight next morning.

At that hour Alain met his new colleagues and then settled down to a harangue by Monsieur Monnet which reminded him of listening to a lecture at St Cyr. The older man denied that the Bureau Arabe was out of date, or less important since Algeria, a country four times the size of France, was politically integrated with the mother country. It had supervised the education of the city Arabs, *les évolués*, some of whom had actually gone to study in Paris, and was still responsible for the nomads, who were gradually being weaned away from desert warfare and settling down into village life.

"Not in the neighbourhood of Bône," said Alain ruefully.

"That was where you were wounded? We still have the occasional rebellion among the Kabyles, but the Foreign Legion is always prompt to put them down."

In his early days in Tunis Alain would have said "I don't blame the rebels. After all it's their country we've annexed!" It was the kind of remark which annoyed senior officers and caused his record to be marked Controversial even before he was Politically Suspect. He had learned enough wisdom to say only:

"The Berbers at Bône weren't rebelling against France. They believed they were fighting a holy war."

"The *jehad*? One hears more of it than one used to — "

"Is the inspiration coming from the Sudan?"

"Partly, but in Algeria the real war is not the Arabs against the Christians. It's the Arabs against the Jews, who can be very aggressive —" Monsieur Monnet broke off and Alain knew why. He was about to betray the covert anti-semitism which existed in the French Army.

In Algeria the Jews had full citizen rights, thanks to a bill pushed through the Chambre des Députés by Adolphe Cremieux, himself a Jew, whereas the Arabs were forbidden by their religion to accept the Code Napoléon and with it citizenship. There had been Jews among the political deportees from France after the *coup d'état* of Napoleon III, and Jews among the refugees from Alsace and Lorraine. Their hard work and keen business sense had contributed to the prosperity of Algeria, but in 1892 they were disliked by Christians as well as Arabs because of the collapse of the Panama Canal Company, promoted by prominent Jews, which had brought bankruptcy to many French shareholders. Alain heard many complaints in the homes of the French community, to which he was automatically invited.

His plan to study Arabic pleased Monsieur Monnet, who decided that 'young de Grimont was serious' and found the right tutor for him. This was an elderly scholar who had studied in Cairo at the great Moslem university of Al-Azhar, and spoke a purer Arabic than most Algerians. He told Alain that in the Moslem faith the world was divided into two: the House of Islam, inhabited only by the followers of the Prophet, and the dwelling of all the unfaithful, called the House of War.

"Alas, Grimont Bey," he said, "the black men, the Dervishes of the Sudan, are the masters now. The British dare not move against them, even to avenge the murder of General Gordon, because they know the Dervish chief, the Khalifa, can ruin Egypt by cutting off the headwaters of the Nile. The French have no more power in the land. I am a man of peace, and I dread war, but war is coming, and it will bring ruin to the East."

"I see no sign of war when I ride forth," said Alain in his careful Arabic.

On his tours of inspection, with a native escort and a lieutenant of Engineers to check the condition of the wells in the oases round which the nomads were creating settlements, Alain found no trace of the *jehad* mentality. There were complaints of petty thievery from the French settlers, called *les pieds-noirs*, who were producing corn and wine, but there was no religious rancour. Alain listened impartially to both sides, and his increasing fluency in Arabic endeared him to the *mudirs* of the new villages, who offered him many a feast of roast lamb, including the eyeballs, and *cous-cous*. He grew to enjoy these tours after the torrid summer ended in September, even when his little troop was battered by the stinging *chergui* wind from the west. He preferred the oases of the desert to the salons of Algiers, having no intention of starting a flirtation with a girl, or a liaison with a married woman.

Some of the French officers had native mistresses, as he had had in Tunis, others had set up house with young women from the *pieds-noirs* and led with them an entirely bourgeois and domestic life. The heir to one tiny European principality had been to the *mairie* to acknowledge the paternity of his young woman's daughter, a gesture which was to be important to the principality later on. Alain's reticence annoyed the ladies, who were piqued by his indifference. The most they could get out of him was some information about London fashions and London ways. They spent idle hours leafing through back numbers of *L'Illustration*, which carried pictures of the wedding of the Duke and Duchess of York –

the duke having done the expected thing and embarked, with his dead brother's fiancée, on what was to be a very happy marriage.

It was a vapid and introverted life these Frenchwomen led. They seemed to be remote, after two or three years as *colons*, from the affairs of the mother country, disquieting though these had become. Throughout the whole of 1892 there were bombings and other attacks on law officers, organised by an anarchist called Ravachol, who was finally brought to justice and guillotined, and at the end of 1893 another anarchist called Vaillant actually threw a bomb into the hemicycle of the Chambre des Députés. He too died by the guillotine.

It was to avenge Vaillant that the most sensational of all the anarchist crimes took place, when in June 1894, in the city of Lyon, an Italian called Caserio stabbed and killed the President of the French Republic.

21

The boat train for Calais drew out of a Paris in mourning for President Sadi-Carnot, and the passengers arrived some hours later in a London rejoicing at the birth of a son to the Duke and Duchess of York.

"Oh, how nice it is to see smiling faces," said Sarah Colt in her father's ear as he embraced her, "in Paris everyone was weeping crocodile tears for the poor president!"

"You don't seem overcome by grief," teased Charles Colt. He raised his voice. "I take it you had a good crossing! You too, mademoiselle, I hope?" he said to the undergoverness who had escorted his daughter across the Channel. She bowed and assented. Not all the girls who came to be finished at the Misses Monod's establishment had a father as impressive as this one – so tall, so courteous, so impeccably dressed – and she was flattered by the way he made sure that she had a lodging for the night before sending her off with a porter to find her a cab and pay the fare.

"Now let me look at you." In all the hubbub of Victoria the great American financier, the cotton magnate supreme of Egypt, took his daughter by both gloved hands and swung them to and fro. "You're Paris every inch of you—and haven't you grown a couple of inches since last year?"

"Good guess." She was tall and slender, this girl of his, with dark hair and eyes like her mother's, and there was a Paris finish to her grey travelling costume and the grey felt hat with a green cock's feather in it. Her shoes, like her handbag, were of the finest morocco leather.

The porters were hovering, but there was no need of their services, for all that Paris could provide for a girl's first London season had been sent on in advance, in portman-teaux, valises and dress boxes bearing famous names which had already arrived at the Savoy Hotel. "You'll hardly be able to get into your bedroom," said Mr Colt jocosely. "You'll have to sort the stuff out yourself and have some of it put into storage."

"I will," Sadie assured him. "Two of the biggest boxes are meant for Cairo, anyway. Mademoiselle Monod's maid packed them beautifully, they'll be all right till we get there. Oh, you brought an open carriage, lovely!"

In the two-horse carriage they were soon clear of Victoria, and at Mr Colt's order the coachman drove them past Buck-ingham Palace and down the Mall, where the trees were in the full leaf of high summer. The Sovereign's standard was flying over the palace, and Mr Colt pointed it out. "The Old Lady's in residence," he chuckled. "Come up from Windsor to see you make your curtsey. Nervous?"

"Not a bit. I feel like a princess myself today!" She was holding herself like a young princess, very erect, looking from side to side as if at a crowd of bowing subjects, but only seeing the London she had known as a child transformed in the eyes of eighteen into a magic city. Her father was silent as the carriage turned up the Strand. He had a thousand things to say to her, but they could wait. In spite of their long separations Colt and his daughter understood each other very well, and he knew how she was feeling. Free of the schoolroom, free of a great many restrictions, with a new life opening before her, Sadie was tasting what her father had known in his own youth – a moment of felicity.

"There's a pleasant surprise for you in our sitting-room," said Mr Colt, when they had arrived at the Savoy and were being escorted upstairs to his suite. Sadie had no idea what it might be, and was genuinely surprised when a little lady in black rose from a sofa behind a tea table and came hurrying across the room to kiss her.

"Aunt Liz!"

"Dear Sarah, I'm so happy to see you! And at the very moment . . . I was so pleased when your father suggested . . ." For a very precise woman, Elizabeth Otway was almost incoherent with emotion.

"I'm pleased too." Sadie kept one of her aunt's hands in her own and stretched out the other to her father, so that she held them both in her clasp. "But look here! Does this mean you two have buried the hatchet? Are we all going to be friends? No more quarrelling, like that awful time at Easter a year ago?"

There had been a spectacular row in Paris, when her mother's sister, that distinguished teacher and feminist, had come over in the Easter holidays to find out for herself how her niece was thriving and learning in the establishment of the Misses Monod. Taking a room in a modest *pension de famille* in the Rue de la Pompe, she was a daily visitor to the charming house at Auteuil where the Monod ladies 'finished' to a very high standard the girls entrusted to their care. The sisters, Republican, Protestant, and covert feminists themselves, approved of Miss Otway, and spoke so highly of Sarah Colt's capacities that her aunt began to talk of the old plans for a college education, or better still a medical training at Dr Sophia Jex-Blake's School of Medicine for women in Edinburgh. Their castles in the air were knocked down by the expert hand of Charles Colt, who arrived unexpectedly to see his daughter. He stormed at his sister-in-law and threatened to withdraw his daughter from Auteuil if there was any more New Woman nonsense, and Miss Otway, as quick-tempered as himself, cut short her visit to Paris and returned to Kensington. Now his smile was the smile of the victor as he said, "Of course we're the best of friends, my dear, and your aunt's coming to see you in your court dress on Thursday, aren't you, Liz? . . . They brought you tea, I see — that's right. Shall we order fresh tea for you, Sadie?"

"Oh no, thank you, it's nearly six o'clock, and I had some tea on the boat train." A pot of strong Indian tea and a thick wedge of plum cake, very British, very filling and not at all like a dainty Savoy tea, she was sure! "What I would like to do is take off my hat and jacket, and wash my hands — will you excuse me, please?"

When she came back from her bedroom, which had a fine view of the Thames, and where a maid was only waiting for her keys to start unpacking, she said to her father, "I see what you meant about the baggage! Did Lady Stewart get here safely?"

"Of course she did." Colt smiled at Miss Otway. "Sadie's excited about her presentation."

"Naturally."

"Lady Stewart will present her, along with her own daughter. Mary, I call her, but they spell it in some crazy Scotch way, with an 'h' in it."

"Lady Stewart's husband's on Lord Cromer's secretariat," Sadie explained with a knowledgeable air. "His parents have a house in Chester Square, haven't they, father?"

"They have, and that's where you're expected for lunch tomorrow to meet Miss Mhairi, if that's how you pronounce it, and some other girls who'll all be going to the palace on Thursday night."

"I hope Mhairi Stewart's nice," said Sadie.

"Do you hear from that nice Austrian girl who was with

you at Auteuil?" asked her aunt. "The Gräfin von Rorschach? She was no scholar, but very sweet and charming."

"Rosmarie? She was a darling, and I missed her when she left at Easter. She was the one who insisted with the Monod ladies that we should have riding lessons in a *manège* and then go riding in the Bois. What a fuss there was about chaperones for that!"

"Glad to hear it," said her father, who had his own views on foreign riding masters, and Aunt Liz chimed in:

"But I thought you could ride, Sarah."

"I rode the farm horses bareback when I was a kid at Old Harbour," Sadie laughed. "Not quite the style for Rotten Row!"

"Or for Gezira," said her father. "Did you get a decent habit, like I told you?"

"Oh yes, thank you, a lovely habit, made of white piqué."

"Just the thing for Cairo," said Mr Colt, and Aunt Liz with a dry smile, observed that "it all came back to Cairo. Have you told Sarah about her new home, Charles?"

"There hasn't been time yet."

"He's been very mysterious about it in his letters," Sadie said.

"I'm always mysterious while a deal's pending," retorted her father, "and I only signed the deed of purchase the day before I left Cairo. Now I'm ready to tell you the whole story."

He leaned back in the corner of the sofa, and Miss Otway thought how well this man whom she had never liked was bearing the burden of the years. At fifty-four Charles Colt was grey-haired, but his lean Yankee face had hardly changed: it still bore the eager look of his younger days, when he was out to make his fortune. It was reflected in the pretty girl who sat beside him on the sofa in her attractive green blouse and long tailored grey skirt, and they were smiling as they looked at each other. "They're two of a kind," thought Elizabeth Otway, "they're going to get on well."

"*Please* tell, father," Sadie implored. "*Where* are we going to live in Cairo?"

"Fifteen miles outside Cairo, at a place called Helwan. Hélouan-les-Bains, the French call it, because it's a spa like Aix-les-Bains, and the old Khedive, Ismail, developed it before he was forced to abdicate in favour of Prince Tewfik. There's a train service from Cairo now, but of course we'll have a carriage, and I'm thinking of buying one of the new automobiles."

"But the house, father?"

"It's not too big, only fifteen rooms, and the gardens are in good order – they run right down to the Nile."

"*Fifteen* rooms!" Sadie gasped. "Are they furnished?"

"I ordered beds and tables, and for the rest it's up to you. Let's see how Miss Monod's lessons in domestic economy pay off."

"It's a big responsibility for the child," said her aunt, but Sadie was laughing, and they all talked about the house at Helwan until nearly eight o'clock, when Miss Otway got up to go. "This girl should have a light supper now, and go to bed early. Tomorrow all the presentation fuss begins."

"But you're coming back on Thursday evening, aren't you, Aunt Liz? Early, but not too early, because father says I must have my photograph taken before Lady Stewart comes to fetch me – "

"Just tell me when you want me, dear, and I'll be there."

She was there in good time to watch while the hotel maid helped Sadie into the dress which her father's money had bought and Mademoiselle Monod's trained good taste had helped her to choose in Paris. It had a sweeping bell-shaped skirt and a low-cut bodice embroidered with crystal beads, and it was made of white satin, as was the court train falling from the shoulders. There was some excuse for the maid's saying, as she fastened a pearl necklace round Sadie's neck,

"The young lady will be a beautiful bride some day soon, won't she, madam?"

"Not too soon, I hope," said Miss Otway repressively, and then the photographer was announced before the three white ostrich plumes, the Prince of Wales's feathers, were fastened in Sadie's hair instead of a bridal wreath. He was from Ellis and Walery, the fashionable court photographers of the day, but he was quite unorthodox, asking to work in the bedroom because of the backlighting from the window, and without the usual impedimenta of tripod, plates, dark curtain and clamp to hold the victim's head in place. He used a Kodak camera and moved about the room, taking pictures from several angles until Sadie was quite relaxed and natural. Then he said, "Very lovely, miss, I wish you a happy evening," and went out followed by the maid. Sadie said her long white gloves were too tight.

It was deliberately prosaic, for she saw tears in her aunt's eyes. They were both over-excited. Miss Otway said, "I wish your mother could see you now, Sarah. She would have been proud of you."

"Aunt Liz" — hesitantly — "do you think I'm like my mother at all?"

"You don't remember her, do you?"

"No. And I've only got a little daguerrotype picture, that's begun to fade already."

"You have her dark eyes and hair, my dear, but you're much taller, and thank heaven much stronger. You're really more like your father, and — look at the time! We'd better not keep him waiting."

Mr Colt was in the sitting room, immaculate in white tie and tails. He had planned a little supper party after the ladies came back from the palace, for Sir Ian Stewart, whose elder daughter had already been presented, told him the girls were too excited to take bite or sup in the royal dining-rooms. When he saw his debutante daughter in the doorway, regal in satin and pearls, there was a catch in his voice as he said "Wonderful! I'm afraid to touch you — you might break."

"Not I!" And Sadie, regardless of court train and feathers, threw herself into her father's arms and kissed him. "Thank you for the lovely dress, and thank you for my necklace," she said. "I'll try to be everything you want me to be."

The emotional moments ended there. What followed was more than an hour of tedium in a closed carriage with Lady Stewart and Mhairi, as they made their slow way down the Strand and along the Mall to Buckingham Palace. It was a very warm evening, which at least meant that only the lightest of wraps need be worn, but Lady Stewart insisted that the windows be rolled up to frustrate the cheerful Cockneys who liked to look in at the nobs going to the palace and comment on their looks and grand toilettes. "Coo, ain't she a daisy!" and "This 'un's a reg'lar stunner!" hardly compensated Sadie for the increasing discomfort of tight lacing and twelve-button kid gloves which were certainly half a size too small. She saw a faint sheen of perspiration come out on Miss Stewart's round Scots face and was thankful to have tucked a few leaves of *papier poudré* into the top of her bodice. At last the ordeal by spectator was over, the crowd in the Mall was left behind, and inside the palace all was a reverent hush, broken only by the music of a string band.

"I'm so nervous I know I'm going to faint," whispered Mhairi Stewart, one ahead of Sadie in the processional order as they moved slowly upstairs. Miss Colt was not nervous: she wanted to see everything, observe everyone, and most of all the Queen. In her long widowhood she had left many of the Drawing Rooms to the Prince and Princess of Wales, but she was in the throne room tonight, they said, to mark her pleasure at the birth of Prince Edward, the third heir in direct succession to the Crown. The Duke and Duchess of York would not be present, as it was only a few days since the baby was born, but the Wales couple would support Her Majesty, with other members of the royal family.

The procession of debutantes and the ladies presenting them entered the throne room, and Sadie saw Queen Victoria. She saw the little figure in an ample black silk gown, with a tiny diamond crown on a Honiton lace veil, and the blue eyes faded by age, studying the curtseying ladies with the authority of one who was the ruler of half the world. The American girl, Republican by conviction and training, knew that she stood close to the mystery, to the personification of the British Empire at the summit of its power.

An equerry took the train she carried on her arm, and spread it carefully behind her. Mhairi Stewart gulped and approached the throne. It was then Sadie became fully aware of the Prince and Princess of Wales: he resplendent in scarlet and ermine, with the Garter fastened round his enormous silk clad knee; she in a silver tissue gown covered with diamond ornaments and ropes of pearls which seemed almost too heavy for her slight figure to bear. They were not recognisable as the affable gentleman and the sad lady in mourning whom she had seen at Cap Martin, and yet . . .

"Miss Sarah Colt!"

She advanced to the steps of the throne, swept three perfect curtseys, and moved on.

. . . and yet it was of Cap Martin she thought as, smiling at Lady Stewart and Mhairi, she began to walk down another red-carpeted flight of stairs to the dining-room where, as Mhairi's father had predicted, the girls with their ordeal behind them were far too excited to eat or drink. From the staircase they were a very pretty sight, like a carpet of flowers in their white dresses, and the ostrich feathers in their hair were waving like freesia blooms. Like the freesias at Cap Martin, where Alain de Grimont kissed her for the first and last time.

22

He probably married ages ago. That was how Sadie rational-
ised her feelings when, the presentation festivities over and
the finery laid aside, she knelt on the window seat of her
bedroom and looked out over the Embankment and the
moonlit Thames. Big Ben struck half past one before she
planned a way of finding out, and composed herself to sleep.

Next day Alain de Grimont's image had receded in her
thoughts. It was such a busy day, with another girls' luncheon, a pink tea, and a fitting of the black riding habit for
which her father would only trust a London tailor. Then the
invitations began to come in, for Miss Sarah Colt was now
launched in London society under the chaperonage of Lady
Stewart, and was an instant success. Americans were in
fashion, thanks to the Prince of Wales, and Sadie was an
American whom young men admired and girls liked because
she was never jealous or catty. Mhairi Stewart was her friend,
and in a year when everybody was reading *The Prisoner of
Zenda*, liked to compare Sadie to the heroine, Princess Flavia.

"Flavia had red-gold hair, and Miss Colt is dark," objected
her mamma.

"I know, but it's something in the way she walks, and when she dances . . . I can just see her wearing a red rose for the Elphbergs, and having a tragic love . . ."

"Don't be silly, dear. You read too many novels." Later on, Lady Stewart observed to her husband that their little girl had a generous heart.

"That's fine, my dear, keep up the good work; I owe Colt for several first class tips in the stock market," said Sir Ian, a practical man. Several much younger men, also practical, paid what the dowagers, yawning through the nightly balls, called "marked attentions" to the cotton magnate's daughter, and were only important to her because they kept her rooms filled with flowers. She danced through three pairs of satin slippers in that month of July, when the window boxes of the great London houses were filled with flowers, and red carpets were spread from kerb to doorstep in honour of the beautiful gowns.

Mr Colt had no house in London, but he gave two dinner parties at the Savoy, and arranged two theatre parties, one to Shaw's new play, *Arms and the Man*, which vaguely troubled Sadie, and one to hear Madame Nellie Melba sing at Covent Garden. When the black habit came home he took Sadie riding in the Row, and declared she would 'hold her own at Gezira' with the best English horsewomen of Cairo. He showed her off at Ascot, where the Prince of Wales invited them into the royal box, but he 'drew the line', he said, at the Royal Academy. Miss Otway took her niece there, but the visit was not a success, for the schoolmistress's art appreciation had stopped at Millais and Rossetti, while Sadie had been taught to admire the French Impressionists.

"You're disappointed in me, aren't you?" she said to her aunt one afternoon about a week after the Academy visit. Sadie had come to tea at the Kensington apartment where Miss Otway lived alone with a fat conceited cat called Rab, short for Rabelais, as her companion and a daily cleaning lady, Mrs Prayle, to keep the four small rooms in order for the busy school teacher. The book-lined living room had two windows, one looking south down a quiet suburban street and the other looking west into Kensington Square. At a desk in that window Sadie had done her homework while she lived with Aunt Liz. Now her chair was drawn up to the tea table, and she was trying to protect her dress from Rab, who was in a perpetual state of shedding fur.

"What a silly thing to say, dear! Disappointed in you, just because we disagreed about the pictures?" protested Miss Otway, pouring tea.

"Not about the pictures. About everything."

"Well," said the censorious aunt, "I'm glad to see you looking so well, considering the hours you keep, but I didn't expect you to be so – so steeped in frivolity and fashion. It rather shocks me when the halfpenny press keeps calling you the American Beauty."

"What do you know about the halfpenny press, Aunt Liz?"

"Mrs Prayle brings me copies of the *Evening News*."

"The American Beauty is the name of a very pretty rose, dear aunt."

Miss Otway smiled grudgingly. Really the child was distractingly pretty, and her silk dress, with the high lace collar and the pin-tucked bodice, was just the colour of a tea rose bud. "You can't help what the papers say, I suppose," she admitted. "But when I think of what you could achieve – with *your* education . . ."

"Some of the men I dance with think I'm over-educated. The average Guards subaltern hasn't a very large vocabulary."

"Mademoiselle Monod wrote to tell me that two Sorbonne professors saw your written work, gave you a viva voce examination, and said you were quite up to baccalaureate standard."

289

"In French literature and philosophy."

"Does your father know that?"

"It wouldn't impress him if he did. Dear Aunt Liz, do try to understand. Father wants me to enjoy the London season and — and be admired and all that, but it's only a dress rehearsal for what he hopes I'll be in Cairo. And it isn't all frivolity, you know. Nearly every morning, when he isn't going to the City, we have very serious talks, mostly about Helwan House — "

"Is that what the place is called?"

"That's what my father's going to call it. And he likes to talk to me about Egyptian politics."

What Mr Colt had said only that morning was, "You'll find that Cairo's filling up with British troops. It looks as if the C-in-C, Kitchener, the new Sirdar, means to tackle the Khalifa at last. Only they're mortally slow, and no wonder, given the distance and the difficulty, *but* it's nearly ten years since General Gordon was murdered in Khartoum, and the Mahdi and his Moslem Dervishes chased the British out of the Sudan."

"The Mahdi died soon after, didn't he?"

"Or was murdered, as some say. But make no mistake about it, Sadie, his successor the Khalifa is as fierce a fighter, as completely dedicated to Islam, as the Mahdi ever was. He'll give the British a run for their money."

Back in the tranquil Kensington parlour, Miss Otway sighed. A Liberal and a Little Englander, she pronounced that Egyptian politics were no credit to Great Britain. "But you're a good girl," she concluded, "to want to do your duty by your father."

"It isn't just a duty, it's a pleasure," said Sadie. "You've seen yourself how generous he is to me. He keeps saying, 'This is *your* summer, darling; enjoy it to the full.' Why, he's even allowing me to go to Scotland with the Stewarts, to attend the Highland balls in August; the only invitation he made me refuse was from Rosmarie von Rorschach, the girl you liked at Auteuil. Her mother asked us to stay with them at Bad Ischl, but father feels he can't stay away any longer from the offices in Cairo. And I'm thrilled about going back, Aunt Liz, I really am!"

With that Miss Otway had to be content. Sadie went to Scotland when the London season ended, danced at the balls in Oban and Inverness, and refused one more proposal of marriage, from an impecunious Highland chieftain who hoped American dollars would regild his faded crest.

Ten weeks was as long as Charles Colt had ever been absent from his offices in Cairo, from which he handled the affairs of cotton in the fields and cotton in the factory which had made his fortune, and also his extensive interests in sugar and tobacco. He lingered in London because of a new project, to be financed by himself and a consortium of Englishmen, to start a service of pleasure steamers on the Nile, plying between Cairo and Luxor in rivalry with the excursion steamers of Thomas Cook. Because he wanted Sadie to arrive when the worst of the summer heat was over he was willing to stay in London until the first of September, and booked their passage from Marseille to Alexandria accordingly. There was enough leeway in the plan for him to ask his daughter, as the date drew near, if she wanted to stop in Paris on their train journey through France.

"Want to say another goodbye to the Miss Monods? Got all the dresses and falderals you need for Cairo?"

They were in their sitting room at the Savoy, and Sadie in a dressing gown, on her way to bed, had taken off her father's stiff collar and cravat and was rubbing the back of his neck in a way that soothed him when he was tired.

"I said goodbye to school in June, remember? And you've

given me so many dresses and pretty things already, I don't need any more. It's been a wonderful summer, father! No girl ever had a more glamorous season."

"You've done me credit, Baby. Proud of you."

The gentle massage continued. Sadie was leaning over the back of his armchair, and her face was hidden. Her voice was almost a whisper.

"If you want to stop on the way to Marseille, what would you say to going on to Hyères and visiting the de la Treilles?"

"The – "

"You remember. They were so nice to me at Cap Martin, and we stayed with them two years ago last spring – "

"Sure, I remember now, the duke and duchess, very hospitable. Good chap, the duke, but not too efficient. Been having trouble with the drains, as I recall."

Sadie giggled. "I don't think that was his fault, father."

"Didn't I see the duchess's name on the list of people you were sending your presentation photograph to?"

"I sent her one, yes."

"Well, dearie, I think the good lady'll have to make do with that, at least for this time. It's one hell of a side trip from Marseille to Hyères, changing trains and all that. I'd rather we went straight on to the boat . . . Excitable people, the French. I wonder how they're making out with their new president."

Jean Casimir-Périer, the president of the Chamber of Deputies, had succeeded to the presidency of the French Republic when Sadi-Carnot was assassinated. A millionaire and the inheritor of a great name, he did not enjoy the confidence of his Radical ministers, but in a year when the great topic appeared to be the cementing of the Russian alliance he would have been more than equal to the burden of his office, if –

If Captain Alfred Dreyfus, a Jewish army officer on the General Staff, had not been accused by Major Henry, of the

Counter-Espionage Bureau, of selling military secrets to the Germans, on the strength of a torn-up memorandum of the goods for sale found in the German military attaché's waste basket.

Captain Dreyfus, loudly protesting his innocence, was arrested 'in secret' in October 1894, and tried *in camera* in December. The file of evidence against him was not made available to the defence, by order of the War Minister, General Mercier, and graphologists did not all agree that the handwriting on the memorandum was his. Nevertheless he was found guilty, condemned to public military degradation, and sentenced to solitary confinement on Devil's Island, the terrible penal settlement off the coast of French Guyana.

The whole thing had been carried out so quickly, and the defence was so weakened, that the Dreyfus case did not cause much commotion in December. There were a few routine shouts of 'Death to the Jews' in the streets of Paris, a few extra-virulent attacks in the antisemitic press, and for the Army, as for most Frenchmen, the case was closed. Captain Dreyfus had not been a popular officer. In his thirties he was fussy, supercilious, sarcastic, and of course, being a Jew, he was 'too clever by half'. Nobody was going to miss him. Most officers enjoyed seeing his epaulettes and insignia torn off on the parade ground, to the roll of muffled drums, and would curse him, when they remembered him, unless –

Unless it were possible to prove his innocence.

Alain de Grimont missed the excitement of the arrest and the trial. He saw no newspapers in the great empty land in the shadow of the Djurdjura mountains, where he was on tour among the Kabyles who had so long resisted the authority of the French. He heard the whole story of Dreyfus's crime and punishment from Monsieur Monnet, a highly prejudiced source, and like most army officers was prepared to accept that the court martial of a traitor had been properly conducted. The verdict was now a *chose jugée*, 'legally over and done with,' and could not be reopened. Alain was far more interested in the preparation of his own report on Kabylia. He had found the tribesmen increasingly devout in the practice of their Moslem faith. In one place he had even found an *imam*, qualified to read and expound the Koran to the males of the community. In the House of Islam women had a lowly place.

From the headwaters of the Nile, across the Libyan desert and Tunisia, the winds of a holy war were blowing. Many of those most susceptible to the word *jehad* were uncertain of the name of the new Leader, still believing in the Mahdi as the Moslem Messiah, although the Mahdi had been dead for ten years. It was his successor the Khalifa and his Dervish troops who had defied the British in Egypt, but in the westward domains of the House of Islam the Khalifa was still an unknown quantity. Major de Grimont noted the fact in the private report he sent to Théophile Delcassé, for Delcassé was the Colonial Minister now, the Ministry for the Colonies having at last been separated from the Ministry for the Marine.

President Casimir-Périer resigned in disgust after only seven months in office and was succeeded by a business man from Le Havre named Félix Faure. The public was restless and weary of the constant changes, ripe for mischief as in the days of General Boulanger. Dreyfus had been a welcome scapegoat, but Dreyfus had been hustled off the scene before full value could be extracted from that particular circus, and the circus of 1896, the State visit to Paris of the Czar and Czarina of Russia, had not been a success. Nicholas II and Alexandra Feodorovna had been too unresponsive, too haunted by the thought of assassination to please the crowds.

Not long after the imperial couple returned to St Petersburg Alain de Grimont received a pleading letter from the Duchesse de la Treille. Why had he stayed away from Hyères for so long? Why had he taken all his leaves in Algeria, going on shooting parties with other men? He was needed at the Château de la Treille. The grandson from Saigon was living with them now, and was a problem. Only the other day Alain's uncle had had a heart attack . . .

Alain, alarmed and guilty, at once applied for emergency leave. He had stayed away from the Riviera deliberately, because it held too many memories, too many reminders of a love he had denied, and he trusted his uncle and aunt, growing old, to Armand and Henriette. But Armand was still at sea, determined to make that most difficult of all steps from captain to admiral, and Henriette, after ten years of marriage, was at last the busy mother of a baby son. And then there was the other grandson, probably a spoiled brat . . . Alain was on his way to Marseille within twenty-four hours.

The groom who met him at Hyères station with the old luggage cart set his mind at rest at once. *Monsieur le duc* was in good health. He had come over queer when he was giving Prince Guy a fencing lesson, but he was all right next day. All the family were well, and the men would be glad to see 'the major' again. The luggage cart turned into the palm-fringed avenue, and there on the steps of their home were Alain's aunt and uncle, beaming and obviously in excellent health.

There was a great reunion in the salon, where Henriette was waiting with her boy in her lap, and the three little girls offering sticky kisses to the new 'uncle' from abroad. Henriette was pale and drawn, in mourning for her parents, who had died within three months of each other, and full of a project to move into their big villa. "Rivabella's too small for us now, with such a big family," she said proudly. "Alain, I want you to look the place over, and give me your advice."

"I don't know much about house property, Henriette."

"Still an inveterate bachelor?"

"Still."

At the sound of a bicycle bell they all turned to the open french windows, and saw a man and a boy riding up the avenue on the latest cycle models. "Guy and his tutor," said the duke happily. "They've been down to the seashore and back. Come and meet your uncle Alain, Guy!"

The boy (he must be going on for twelve, Alain reckoned) came in and shook hands with a bow for *'mon oncle'* and answered, very politely, the routine questions about his father and mother's health. He was tall for his age and well built, with the fair good looks of the de la Treilles. His tutor was a plain sensible Swiss, about Alain's own age, who kept in the background while drinking a cup of tea.

"You're in your old bedroom, Alain," said his aunt when tea was over. "Would you like to go up now?"

"And mayn't Monsieur Epper and I show you your old schoolroom, *mon oncle?*" said Guy eagerly. "Where you used to do your own lessons?"

Alain laughed, and the three of them went upstairs together. The former sewing room had changed again, but not back to the schoolroom of Alain's boyhood, any more than the practical Monsieur Epper resembled the emotional Alsatian who had read *La Dernière Classe*. The walls, now covered with a light brown paper, were the background for pictures of all sorts, from mechanical drawings signed G. de la T. to photographs of motor cars by Daimler, Benz, Peugeot and many others. There were also snapshots of birds in flight.

"Guy is going to boarding school after the long vacation," explained Monsieur Epper. "I'm coaching him in philosophy and the classics, required subjects at the Ecole des Roches."

"But Guy prefers mechanics, I can see," said Alain kindly. "Those drawings are very good, Guy."

"I've done a whole lot more," said the boy eagerly. "Engines for cars and motor-boats, would you like to see them?"

"Gently, Guy," said the tutor. "We mustn't detain Commandant de Grimont now. Say goodnight, and have patience till tomorrow."

"Goodnight, Guy, goodnight, *monsieur*." Alain escaped to his own bedroom. It was more nostalgic than the old school-room brought up to date. He looked out at the familiar view. The scenery of Hyères was not really like Cap Martin: the red rocks and the islands came in the way, but the blue Mediterranean was breaking with the same sound as the waves on the samphire-covered point of Cap Martin, and the flowers in the grass might have been Persephone's footprints as she came back from the underworld.

When Alain emerged from his room the wide upper landing was coloured amber with sunset light, and his aunt was arranging carnations in a Chinese bowl on a flower stand. He saw that under her soft grey dress, on which the waist line was marked only by a loose bronze girdle, she was much thinner than before. When he put his arms round her the duchess rubbed her cheek against his and said,

"You've shaved your side-whiskers."

"My barber did that, last time I was in Paris. He said whiskers had gone out of style, except for older men."

"You look younger than you did at Cap Martin. Oh, my dear boy, it's so good to have you home again!"

"It's good to be back. How quiet the house is, all of a sudden!"

"Henriette took the children home, and Guy is somewhere with his tutor."

"And my uncle?"

"The doctor likes him to lie down for an hour before dinner."

"Ah! I want to hear about that."

"Come into my boudoir."

The familiar, pretty room where Alain had wept for his own mother's death now contained, of its old furniture, only a lady's escritoire and chair, and a chaise longue. The other chairs were child-size, the book case held toys and stuffed animals instead of books, and a huge doll's house occupied half a wall opposite the window. Photographs of the grand-children at all stages covered the wallpaper, the latest addi-tion being baby Gilbert's christening picture, and some of them were of the same face repeated five times over at different angles. The visitor could be excused for feeling hemmed in by children.

"You've turned your boudoir into a nursery," said Alain with a smile, taking the desk chair after his aunt had estab-lished herself on the chaise longue.

"I love having the children here, and at least it keeps their toys out of the salon. They're sweet little things, don't you think? The girls, I mean."

"Very sweet, and they make me feel my age when they call me 'uncle'. Now tell me about *my* uncle. Your letter said he had a heart attack, and the groom said he felt unwell during a fencing lesson. What did the *doctor* say?"

"Well . . . that it was only a threatened heart attack," said the duchess apologetically. "He was fencing with Guy, and he had a sort of faint. So the doctor said no more fencing, no more riding, and a great deal more rest for the future. It's been a very anxious time, Alain!"

"I'm sure," said Alain. "Now about Guy. Your letter said he was a problem. He doesn't seem much of a problem to me — and he certainly isn't shy!"

"Oh, my dear, the first few weeks were dreadful after Maurice and Eugénie sent him to live with us. Remember I wrote to you that they thought a colonial child should be in a warm climate for at least six months before going north to school? Well, poor Guy had been so dreadfully spoiled in Saigon — no, not by his parents, but by the native servants, and even by some of his father's staff — and he expected the same treatment here. He very nearly got it, too, because his grandfather adores him. Anything Guy wanted, Guy got, and of course he became insufferable. Then Monsieur Epper was recommended to us, and he really saved the situation. He's a clever man and a disciplinarian. All that stodgy Swiss commonsense was just what an excitable boy like Guy required."

"So Guy isn't a problem child at all, and all my uncle has to do is take reasonable care of his health," said Alain. "Thank God for that. Your letter gave me a bad fright, Aunt Blanche."

"I'm sorry," said the duchess unconvincingly.

"Why did you do it?"

"I don't understand."

"I think you do."

"Very well then!" said his aunt, rearing up on the chaise longue, "I wanted to frighten you! I wanted to get you out of that — that refuge you've made for yourself in Algiers, and back among us all! So that I could get rid of a burden I've been carrying for two years, and find out the truth about your feelings — "

"My *feelings* — "

"About Sadie Colt."

Alain was speechless. But his aunt watched his slow flush, and told him to open the top drawer of her escritoire.

"There's a photograph, Alain, in a cardboard folder — "

He opened the folder. He saw the picture of a tall girl in white, wearing long gloves and a court train, with three white ostrich feathers in her hair. The background, deliberately softened to look like morning mist above a silver streak of river, threw her lovely face into strong relief — eager, natural, happy.

"My God!" said Alain reverently, "she's beautiful! Sadie . . . grown up!"

"Sadie two years ago," said his aunt softly.

"You mean you've had this for two years?"

"That was taken when she was presented at the Court of St James in '94. There was a note inside with her new address, Helwan House, Cairo, and somehow I had the feeling she hoped I'd send it on to you."

"Why didn't you?"

"Because she didn't tell me to, Alain, how could I interfere? When I wrote to thank her, I mentioned your posting to Algiers, but she never asked for you, not then nor in any of a few letters I've had from her since. So I began to think the Empress Eugénie and I were mistaken, when we thought you and Sadie were falling in love."

"That day at the Villa Cyrnos? Yes, we were."

"But you went away."

"She was so young, and I — I'd made one mistake with Isabelle Lacroix, I couldn't risk another. But, Aunt Blanche, she writes to you, she tells you about her life in Cairo, she would tell you, wouldn't she, if there were — anyone else?"

"There's no one else," said his aunt positively. "In her last letter she sounded quite unhappy. She's been doing charity work among the *fellaheen* — is that what they call the natives? and it's not working out very well, I don't know why. I believe if you were to write to her, she would be glad — "

"No," said Alain decisively, rising to his feet as the gong rang downstairs for dinner. "I don't know yet what I shall do. But what I have to say to Sadie I'll tell her face to face, and with my lips."

The scanty emergency leave granted to Major de Grimont allowed him to spend only one complete week at Hyères, the rest of the time being spent in travel. During that week he avoided private conversations with the duchess, nor did she lie in wait for him as she had done on the night of his arrival. He was with his uncle as much as possible, driving him to the carnation fields to talk to his new manager, discussing the Dreyfus case with him in the library (neither of them had very strong views on the affair) and gently trying to persuade him that a man in his sixties ought to take reasonable care of his health.

Under the duke's critical eye he fenced with Guy every day, though it was years since he had held a foil. He looked at the boy's mechanical drawings, advised Monsieur Epper to give him practice in mapping, and, what delighted Guy, '*mon oncle*' sat tranquilly beside him while the boy drove a horseless carriage round a stable yard. Carriage and yard belonged to Monsieur Ovize, whose wife Valérie, Henriette's sister, was always up to date, and could even drive the thing herself, though not as well as Alain. He took the boy for a drive on the main road, well pleased to be rid, in France, of England's man-in-front-carrying-a-red-flag.

Guy developed a strong case of hero worship of the man who had fought rebel tribesmen and could drive a motor car, and Alain could only wonder what the Duc de la Treille would say when he found that his grandson, the future nineteenth duke, had at present no other ambition in life but to be an automobile engineer.

On his last day but one at Hyères Alain took Guy and his tutor for a picnic to Port Cros. Neither of them had ever been there, and were delighted to take the ferryboat to the island and walk along the path beneath the scented pines to the secret cove where Alain and his cousins had picnicked long ago. Alain was wearing an old pair of flannels and a checked shirt, and being at peace with himself felt like a boy again.

"It's meant a great deal to Guy, having this time with you," said Monsieur Epper, when Guy had gone off exploring. The Swiss had actually taken off his stiff collar and tie and undone the top button of his shirt. "You've entered into his enthusiasms in a way I couldn't do."

"I think you're doing pretty well," said Alain lazily, lighting a cigarette. "A few more off-the-post outings like this one won't do him any harm."

"Now we've found the way to Port Cros, we'll be back," said Epper, and added shyly, "and may I say on my own behalf, *mon commandant*, it's been a privilege to have met you. I already heard about you from my friend Herr Scheffler in Basel."

"Who's Scheffler?" It was a name from the long ago, of a friend *mort pour la patrie*.

"Saul Scheffler — he's a glass manufacturer, his parents came to Switzerland from Alsace. He's done very well in Basel — of course he inherited a thriving business from his father. He used to tell me a fascinating story, about how you and his late brother were involved in saving the life of the Marshal-President MacMahon."

"'Involved' is the right word," said Alain, remembering the sabre blow and the law courts. "Robert Scheffler was a good man. But that's nearly twenty years ago, your friend was only a youngster then. I suppose he's a married man with a family now?"

"No, Saul Scheffler's still a bachelor. Just as well, for he'd hardly have time for family life at present. He's deeply involved in the appeal to reopen the Dreyfus case."

"Really? In neutral Switzerland?"

"Saul was Alsatian-born, like Captain Dreyfus. He knew Mathieu Dreyfus, the brother who's trying to get the case 'revised', as they call it, on the grounds that the court-martial was illegal."

"I did hear that Dreyfus's wife was pleading along the same lines, but her arguments don't hold water."

"Not hers, perhaps, poor woman, but she and Mathieu got a very able journalist, Bernard Lazare, to write a pamphlet called A *Judicial Error*, and he put the arguments very convincingly indeed. Perhaps you've read it?"

"Never even heard of it."

"Funny. Three thousand copies were distributed free to all the centres of opinion in the country and overseas."

"Well, if one was sent to the Bureau Arabe it didn't come across my desk. Where does Herr Scheffler come into this?"

"He put up the money for having the pamphlet printed, along with Mathieu Dreyfus. Unfortunately there was no reaction to the thing at all."

"You say 'unfortunately'. You seem to take a great interest in the Dreyfus case, *monsieur*!"

"What you're wondering is, am I Jewish myself?" said the Swiss tranquilly. "No, I'm not Jewish. My interest in the case is purely abstract, as a question of justice. And if your friend Robert Scheffler were alive today, I think he would be interested in abstract justice too."

Alain remembered the scene in the Rue d'Amsterdam, and Faustine spitting at her lover, "Get out, you Jew!" He remembered almost the last thing Bob Scheffler had said to him, joking to the end:

"You're on the way to being General de Grimont, who catches all his trains on time!"

He was a long way from being a general, and there had been too many missed trains in his career. But he had just one more chance — if his aunt's intuition was correct — of being punctual to his destiny.

23

On the day before he left Hyères Alain took his aunt for a stroll in the rose garden, having privately instructed Guy to follow them in ten minutes. He had no intention of becoming involved in another sentimental scene; he merely told the duchess that when he got back to Algiers he would wait for a couple of weeks and then ask for leave on urgent personal business.

"It won't be easy, because I've had my regular leave for this year, plus the present 'emergency', but the Bureau chief's a good fellow, I think he'll let me off. And then I'm going to Cairo."

Aunt Blanche stood stock-still on the garden path, with one hand pressed to her heart.

"Oh, my dear boy!" she said, "I'm so glad! I've been so worried, thinking I'd offended you – that I'd been a meddlesome old woman – "

"No, you haven't. I think you'd be a marvellous liaison officer for a colony of spiders, because what you *have* done is spin a spider's web of intuitions and imaginations about the feelings of two human beings who saw each other for less than a week four years ago. I'll tell you this: if Sadie had been older I wouldn't have left Cap Martin, but stayed close to her until I was sure she cared for me. Only, I couldn't force myself on a schoolgirl."

"She's twenty now, Alain — "

"Yes, and I'm thirty-six, there's still that difference."

"Don't talk as if you were a worn-out *roué*."

"I haven't been leading a celibate life in Algiers, and she's an innocent girl. There's no use talking any more about it, Aunt Blanche. Sadie and I must settle it between us; I only ask you one thing, don't tell her I'm coming to Cairo. I mean to write to her father first."

He spoke in his parade-ground voice, and his aunt had only time to say submissively, "Very well, dear," before Guy was upon them, whooping,

"*Grand'mere! Oncle Alain!* Monsieur Ovize is here with his new *teuf-teuf*, you've got to come and see it!"

Even the duchess admitted that a *teuf-teuf*, or motor car, took precedence over an unresolved love affair when it was the latest model De Dion.

Monsieur Monnet and the other officials of the Bureau Arabe were kind and concerned about the Duc de la Treille's supposed heart attack on the day Alain reported for duty in Algiers. Concern of another sort was shown next morning when he asked if a copy of Bernard Lazare's pamphlet, *A Judicial Error*, had ever been received at the Bureau.

"Who told you about that piece of rubbish? Some fool at the Cercle Militaire?" cried Monsieur Monnet.

"No, it wasn't anybody at the club. It was a man I met in France. Why is there such a mystery about it?"

"Because the Dreyfus case is *une chose jugée*, and all Lazare's polemics can't alter the verdict. The chief glanced through the pamphlet, and so did I, after which we decided not to circulate it."

305

"Why? Is it so dangerous?"

"Don't be a fool, de Grimont. It's in my inactive file, if you're so anxious to read it."

"*A Judicial Error: the Truth about the Dreyfus Case*" was not a very long pamphlet, and Alain read it through twice. Written with professional clarity, it stressed the illegal action of the court-martial in withholding four documents, called the Secret File, from the defence. These documents, said to contain irrefutable evidence of Captain Dreyfus's guilt, had been shown only to the judges, and one of the judges talked. Lazare argued that the man condemned to solitary confinement for the term of his life should be brought back to France and tried again, with all the evidence made available to himself and his lawyers.

Alain took the pamphlet back to Monsieur Monnet without comment.

"Satisfied?" asked the latter.

Alain shrugged. "Not satisfied about the existence of the Secret File."

"Are you questioning the judgment of the Minister for War, Major de Grimont?"

"May I remind you, monsieur, that my father was the Minister for Justice? Perhaps I've inherited his interest in seeing justice done."

Next day Alain's planned tour of inspection was cancelled, and his desk was loaded with papers of no importance which caused him to work overtime through the sweltering August days. He was cold-shouldered in the Bureau and at the club, and when he applied for special leave for one month from 1 September, the application was at once turned down.

Whereupon he went over the head of Algerian officialdom, and applied directly to the Minister for the Colonies.

*

In Paris the Chamber of Deputies had as usual prolonged its session, and Théophile Delcassé was about to leave with his wife for a belated holiday in his native south-west. He did not reply directly to Alain's letter, but a message from the military governor of Algiers was received at the Bureau Arabe, announcing that orders had been cut for Major de Grimont to proceed to Marseille and report to the Minister for the Colonies at the Hôtel de Noailles.

When Alain entered the private salon, smiling confidently, Delcassé flew at him like a turkey cock, his black moustache bristling, his gold pince-nez gleaming, and his whole small body quivering.

"What the devil have you done now?" he barked.

"Done?"

"Turned Dreyfusard, that's what they say you've done. Insulted your superiors, questioned the legality of the court-martial – "

"I didn't question the legality, it was Bernard Lazare who did that in his pamphlet."

"Which you insisted on reading, though your chief had filed it as classified."

"It's not exactly a secret document, is it? Not in the same category as the Secret File."

"Don't argue with me, de Grimont! I had 'Politically Suspect' removed from your record once; I'm damned if I could do it a second time if you come out for Dreyfus."

"I haven't 'come out' for Dreyfus; I can't forget that the man never ceased to plead that he was innocent."

"So would any criminal." Delcassé's expression, like his voice, grew softer. "Listen to me. I've read Lazare's pamphlet myself. It's very persuasive as far as it goes. But the plea for a revision of the court-martial's verdict will never be granted as long as Mercier is Minister for War. What Mathieu Dreyfus and his friends ought to do is find out who did write the memorandum offering to sell military secrets to the Germans. If it wasn't Captain Dreyfus, who was it? Who's the traitor in the high command? Have you the means of finding out?"

Alain was silent.

"Of course you haven't, and neither have I. The only positive result of Lazare's essay is that it's made people suspicious — not of some mysterious criminal, but of each other. Paris is dividing into two sets, Dreyfusards and anti-Dreyfusards, and there's an undeclared civil war between the two. Don't get involved in it! Don't spoil my plans for you at the eleventh hour! Upon my word, I'm disposed to grant you leave, if only to get you out of Algiers until the fuss you've started dies down. Where is it you want to go?"

"To Egypt, on urgent private affairs."

"To *Egypt*! That's something new. I didn't know you had any ties with Egypt. Private affairs, eh? I suppose that means there's a — ahem! a lady in the case?"

"A young lady now in her father's care," said Alain, "to whom I was introduced by the Duchesse de la Treille."

"Very well, let's leave the lady out of it. But Egypt! It couldn't have fallen out better. It fits in very well with my plans for you."

"What plans?" said Alain roughly. "That's twice in three minutes you've talked about your plans for me, and you've been hinting for years about my great possibilities, while I go plodding on in the Bureau Arabe. I think you ought to tell me what you have in mind."

"Perhaps you're right," said Delcassé. "And it's too hot a night for quarrelling. Sit down and let's be comfortable, I'll order drinks."

While the waiter was in the room Alain asked after Madame Delcassé, and was told she had already retired, prostrated by the heat and the noise of the Canebière.

"Now," said the Colonial Minister, when the glasses of brandy and soda were full, "what I have to tell you is an

308

official secret. It probably won't be a secret long, but if *you* leak it I wash my hands of you, and you can go and join Dreyfus on Devil's Island for all I care."

"I'll be discreet, *monsieur le ministre*." Alain sensed that this was a time for formality.

"You remember Captain Marchand, the explorer?"

"Certainly, I met him at your apartment. You thought he and I would make a good team."

"That day he was going off to lunch with Hanotaux, who's now the Foreign Minister. Now Hanotaux has been smouldering ever since he went to the Quai d'Orsay, because just at that time the Anglo-Congolese Convention divided the Upper Nile, giving the right bank to Britain and the left to the Congo Free State, with France nowhere, as usual. So Hanotaux was ready to support Captain Marchand's latest project for exploration and military glory."

"Which is?"

"He's going to lead an expedition across Black Africa, from Senegal to the White Nile."

"Impossible!"

"Marchand thinks it isn't."

"A military expedition?"

"French officers and native troops."

"What are they going to do when they get there?"

"Take possession of the Sudan in the name of France."

"But what about the British?"

"Ah," said Delcassé. "That's the point. The British are starting out for the Sudan to beat the Khalifa and recapture Khartoum, and if they get in Marchand's way there'll be a row. Enough to end the hope of an English alliance, my dream for years," he concluded bitterly.

"Then wouldn't it be wiser to stop Marchand before he gets started?"

"He has started. Some of his picked men left Bordeaux for Dakar in Senegal as far back as last March, and they'll all be heading for Brazzaville in the French Congo in a few days' time."

"Then," said Alain, "do I understand you? Do you want me to join the expedition now?"

"No, no! Haven't I just said I'm pleased you're going to Egypt? In Cairo you can use the British contacts you made in London, so that you'll be given facilities to *meet* Marchand — carrying sealed orders from me. A very important diplomatic mission for the right man."

"I suppose I should be flattered," said Alain de Grimont, "to be a kind of glorified courier. But I'd still rather be with troops."

"You'll certainly be with troops when you go to meet Marchand," smiled the Colonial Minister. "Probably with Kitchener, the Sirdar, and his men."

"Do you know anything about this man, my dear?" asked Charles Colt, handing a letter across the breakfast table to his daughter.

Sadie had been deep in her own mail, a letter punctuated only by dashes and exclamation marks from her friend Rosmarie von Rorschach in Vienna, and hardly looked at the page her father gave her until she saw the bold signature of Alain de Grimont. Then she felt her cheeks grow hot, and held his letter up between her face and her father's observant eyes.

"Sir," the letter began, and went on in stilted English:

I had the honour to meet your daughter, Miss Sarah Colt, when I was staying at the Hôtel du Cap Martin with my aunt, the Duchesse de la Treille, in 1892. Being now on a short visit to Cairo, I should welcome an opportunity of presenting my respectful homage to Miss Colt and to yourself.

Please receive, Sir, the assurance of my distinguished sentiments.

Beneath the signature an engraved visiting card was attached, with the name of

Baron de Grimont
Commandant
Le Bureau Arabe
Alger

"He's staying at the Continental Hotel," Sadie said, and Mr Colt said yes, that was the name on the writing paper, and if he was the duchess's nephew he was probably all right. "It's a funny sort of letter, though. 'Respectful homage', 'distinguished sentiments' – phew!"

"He's only translating from the French."

"What does his card mean – that he's the commander of this Arab Bureau?"

"No, that he's a major now. He was a captain when I knew him at Cap Martin."

"One of your tennis partners, was he?"

"Oh no, he couldn't play tennis. He had an arm wound from the desert fighting."

"Well, do you want his respectful homage, or don't you?"

"I do."

"Funny the duchess never mentioned him, when we stayed at the Château de la Treille. They were very pleasant hosts, and we'll have to do something for their nephew. We'll give him a dinner party, first off; Sadie, make up a guest list. About ten or twelve should do."

"Father, I think he'd rather dine with just you and me before we plunge him into Cairo society."

"H'm, that might be best, give us a chance to size him up, eh? Perhaps I'll call on him when I'm in Cairo this afternoon and bring him back to dinner if he's free. You aren't coming up to the city today, are you?"

"I thought I might go down to Helwan."

311

"Be careful then, we don't want any more fuss with the *hakim*."

She only wanted to get away, to hurry through the cool colonnades of her home to her own room, still holding Alain's letter, to read it again and again. He was coming to Cairo! Coming to see *her*! Oh, the dear duchess! Just a whisper of Sadie's unhappiness, and she must have dropped a hint to Alain. Perhaps in a few hours they would be together again. She sent for the majordomo, quickly gave him her orders for the day, and too restless to stay indoors, she picked up a shady hat and went outside.

"Colt Bey has just left, ladyship," said Riad the head gardener, coming at once to her side.

"I know, I heard the Daimler," said Sadie. Riad was a Turk; there were Moslems of all races in the army of gardeners looking after the ten acres of grounds round Helwan House. The flowers and fruit trees were looking their best in the clear light, for it would soon be October and the heat of the year was over. But — "Why isn't the irrigation engine working?" said Sadie sharply. "Can't you hear that it's been stopped?"

"That fellow!" said Riad deeply, and hurried down the path which led to the stables and garages, with Sadie at his heels. There by the housing of the engine a man in a blue *galabeyah* was squatting, smoking a cigarette with a sweetish smell, who as soon as he saw them squealed and dived towards the engine, which began to hum.

"Filthy idler, you deserve the *courbash*!" Riad called after him, and turned apologetically to his mistress. "It's the new man, Moammer, ladyship. He's not accustomed to the engine yet."

"He looks like a Bedouin, just out of the desert," Sadie said. "Don't thrash him, Riad, but put another man on the job. The engine's too important to be neglected." She nodded as Riad saluted her with a hand to his heart, lip and

312

brow, and turned away. She wanted to be alone by the Nile with her thoughts of Cap Martin.

The great river ran at the foot of the garden, beyond the highway which ran between Cairo and Helwan. Nearby were Charles Colt's fields, where cotton picking would soon begin. At present the women who did the work were cooking in the mud huts of the *fellaheen* which surrounded Helwan, preparing for the return of their men from the Colt factory, five miles away on the road to Cairo. Sadie spoke to one or two of the women, who pulled the *burka* more closely over their faces as she approached, the *hakim* or village doctor and the *imam* too disapproved of the infidel woman who gave them ointment for their babies' eyes and medicines for their own aches and pains. The few men in Helwan on a working day were huddled round the railway station, for one of the local railways which seamed the Delta had a stop at Helwan, and the inevitable drink shop had been opened there by a Greek, who conducted a money-lending business on the side. The six hot sulphur springs were further away, near a good hotel, but Sadie was not interested in the sights of the spa that day. Alain was in Cairo, that was enough for her. Would he come that night? Was he thinking of her? What was he doing now?

Alain de Grimont was filling in time. He had sent his letter to Helwan House by special messenger, assured by the manager of the Continental Hotel that it would arrive at breakfast time, but aware that he could hardly expect an answer before the next day, or even the day after. He occupied himself by carrying out the instructions given by Delcassé when he came back from his holiday in the Ariège and set the wheels in motion for Alain's leave. First he signed the book at the British Residence, from which Lord Cromer virtually ruled Egypt, and then called on the French consul-general, Monsieur Cogordon.

313

The consul's door was guarded by two Spahis in thin red cloaks, and Alain, as he acknowledged their salutes, remembered the use Boulanger made of the Spahis in their vivid uniforms at the famous Longchamp review.

"The French presence is still powerful in Cairo," claimed Monsieur Cogordon. "I have only a total of four Spahis to stand sentry, but I have a hundred educated Egyptian friends. We are friendly and interested in individuals, which the British are not. The British treat them all as 'natives' and even call them 'wogs'. Egyptian law is French, founded on the Code Napoléon, and it is not forgotten that we built the Suez Canal. But we were done for, Monsieur de Grimont, when the British put down Arabi's revolt at Tel-el-Kebir and ended the Dual Control. Now they are planning to defeat the Khalifa and win back the Sudan; much good may it do them. Only six months ago the Ethiopians defeated the Italians at the battle of Adowa; perhaps the Khalifa and his Dervishes will defeat another white army when Kitchener finally moves against them!"

It was evident that the Frenchman hoped they would. Not much support for Delcassé and his British alliance there! At the consul's suggestion Alain walked on to the Kasr-el-Nil barracks. The British troops now massing in Egypt had overflowed into the courtyard, where they were camped in yellow tents. There was no weaponry to be seen, but the consul said their heavy artillery was stored up at the citadel. There were Highland troops on parade with their kilts swinging, and Major de Grimont thought they were a formidable force.

On his way back to his hotel he saw the most impressive sight in Cairo: Lord Cromer emerging from his Residence in a carriage and four, preceded by trumpeters and outriders in livery. 'Al Lurd', as the Egyptians called him, was sitting upright against the cushions, a handsome middle-aged man

314

solid with authority. His modest title was the British Agent, his deportment was that of a viceroy.

There was a letter marked 'By Hand' waiting for Alain at the Continental Hotel.

> Mr Charles Colt will do himself the honour of calling on the Baron de Grimont at five o'clock this afternoon, and hopes the Baron will be free to return with him to dinner at Helwan House.

This peremptory invitation, written in the third person, was Mr Colt's riposte for 'respectful homage' and 'distinguished sentiments', but Alain had no fault to find with the style. It was so much better than he had hoped for, this chance to see Sadie at once, and he lounged chain-smoking through the afternoon hours when Cairo slept until it was time to wait for her father in the hall.

Charles Colt had no need of a hotel clerk to point out Monsieur le Baron de Grimont. In the crowded lounge, where English guests were assembling round the tea tables, the tall man in the white summer uniform of the French Army of Africa was certainly he, and as they met and shook hands Colt was more impressed than he had expected to be. This was no stereotype of a dandy Frog, but a mature man whose handgrip made Mr Colt sum him up as a tough customer. Was he free to come to dinner? Yes, with the greatest of pleasure. Come along then. Dinner wasn't until eight, but the nights were drawing in, and the gardens were worth seeing before it was too dark.

The Daimler was at the door of the hotel, and Gaston, the elderly French chauffeur, was fending off the usual crowd of beggar children. He gave an old soldier's salute at the sight of the French officer, and pushed the Daimler into the judicious pace of ten miles an hour.

"Step on it, Gaston," advised his employer. "If mademoiselle were here she'd be running rings round you."

"Mademoiselle drives the car?" said Alain.

"Not this car, she has her own. A Benz. She says she'd be completely out of things without it."

"Helwan House is at a distance from the city?"

"Fifteen miles. Too far for a horse and dogcart, which is what those straitlaced Englishwomen think the only vehicle for a lady ... So what brings you to Cairo, Baron de Grimont?"

"Curiosity," said Alain blandly.

"Curiosity about what? Antiquities, or the Nile barrages? The past or the present?"

"Very much about the present. My cousin Captain Armand de la Treille has told me so much about modern Egypt, I thought I'd like to see it for myself."

"That's the duke's son in the navy."

They talked about the de la Treilles, and the life at Hyères, all the way to Helwan.

It was not an attractive drive. Mr Colt pointed out the Tura quarries, where the stone was used for paving, and then his own cotton factory, where a late shift of workers was answering the blast of a whistle, and then there was nothing but fields and water and railway lines until they came to an iron gate in a high wall. Beyond the gate, down a garden vista, Alain saw a long low house, in colour a warm ochre, with a colonnade, across a tiled court where a fountain played among flowers. There was nobody to be seen until suddenly, in the very moment he was stepping from the car, she was there.

"Mademoiselle!"

"You used to call me Sadie."

"You were a child then."

"I'm not a child any longer."

"What are you two talking about?" said Mr Colt. "Come

in, baron, and tell me what you think of our Egyptian home."

"Beautiful!" said Alain. But he looked at Sadie as he said it.

The sun was still shining when they entered the largest of three rooms which opened into one another, and which had tiled floors spread with Persian carpets and plain whitewashed walls. The sweet scent of Damascus roses came from crystal vases set on low tables, and outside, in a great fig tree which stood at the side of the courtyard, the birds were twittering themselves to sleep. Alain and Sadie stood in the middle of the room like sleepwalkers.

"Come on, come on, sit down!" said Charles Colt. "An occasion like this calls for champagne. Mehmed!"

The majordomo, who had been hovering, brought a laden tray. He wore a white robe and a red fez — the fez and his heel-less slippers were, with the roses, the only bright colours in the room. Sadie was wearing white. She had gone through her whole wardrobe that afternoon, resisting the impulse to dress in her best, to wear one of the new frocks just arrived from Paris. What a fool she would look if Alain didn't come, and she had to dine alone with her father in that extravaganza! So she put on a white chiffon, simply but gracefully cut, with her pearl string for the only ornament, and nothing could have charmed Alain more. It evoked Sadie present and Sadie past: the American beauty of the presentation photograph, and the schoolgirl of Cap Martin, running about the tennis court. . . . He asked her, when they had all raised their glasses to each other, where she played tennis in Cairo.

"The best courts are on Gezira Island."

"She's the woman champion of Gezira," said her father proudly. "You haven't been there yet? It's quite near the Kasr-el-Nil barracks."

"There's a good hotel on the island," said Sadie. "The

Gezira Palace. The Khedive Ismail built it for the Empress Eugénie's visit, when she opened the Suez Canal."

And then they were both back in memory at the Villa Cyrnos, and the fields of Persephone's flowers were lying at their feet. They hardly heard Mr Colt remark prosaically that the baron had done well to choose the Continental. But the Misses Monod's social training had been too strict for Sadie to let the conversation flag. She began to ask about the de la Treilles (certainly a hard-worked topic that evening) and then about Alain's work at the Bureau Arabe, and half an hour passed agreeably before Mehmed appeared to say that Colt Bey's secretary was here from the factory, with telegrams.

Mr Colt got up with a sigh. "You'll have to excuse me, baron. My man Naccache gets terribly excited about telegrams, and he's probably brought a batch for me to answer. Sadie, why don't you take our guest round the garden right now? It'll soon be too dark to see anything."

Servants were bringing oil lamps into the rooms, and when Sadie and Alain went out into the court with the fountain they saw in the sunset sky the thinnest silver rim of a new moon above the Nile, like the Crescent of the House of Islam.

They walked in silence down the main avenue, which was lined with date palms heavy with ripened fruit. On either side narrow alleys led to flowery roundabouts of tobacco plants and night-scented stock. The irrigation engine had been stopped for the night, and the only sound was the barking of two half-tame foxes which, Sadie said, slept in the cactus garden beyond the orange grove. Having broken the tense silence, she forced herself to go on:

"I think your aunt's garden at Hyères is far prettier than ours."

"Aunt Blanche has only roses and carnations, and you have everything."

"Too much, maybe. But that's the way my father likes it."

Alain looked back at the house, where lamplight bloomed in the windows and shone through the colonnade.

"You have a beautiful home, Sadie. But my God, it's isolated, with the Nile on one side and the desert on the other!"

"We've two night watchmen to protect us, and an army of house servants. We only had some trouble once, when the Bedouin raided our hen roosts."

At least he had got her to look at him and smile. He said, "Do I hear another fountain playing?"

"It's in the oleander dell, not far away."

"You have oleanders here, like at Cap Martin?"

"Come and see."

As they walked he took her hand, and Sadie's slim fingers twisted and locked between his own. They felt each other's blood begin to throb.

In the oleander dell the shadows had begun to gather, so that the rosy blossoms were indistinguishable from the white, and the mauve geraniums round the fountain had darkened to the colour of night.

Alain took the girl in his arms and kissed her gently.

"You smell of roses, Sadie."

"Attar of roses — they make it from the flowers." She sighed, and laid her head on his shoulder. "Why — why did you stay away so long, Alain?"

"Have I stayed away too long, darling? Is there — somebody else?"

"There's been nobody else ever. I've been faithful to memory."

Faithful — it was the word of all others to strike him to the heart. With a cry Alain seized her roughly, and now his kisses were not gentle, but savage and demanding. She took his kisses as eagerly as when she was a schoolgirl. But now it was a woman Alain de Grimont kissed.

319

24

Preoccupied by the contents of his business telegrams, Charles Colt was poor company at dinner, and paid no attention either to Sadie's nervous bursts of chatter or the Frenchman's silences. He apologised for his abstraction when Alain took his leave – Gaston was driving him back to the city – and invited him to luncheon at the Turf Club two days later.

He had no idea of the effort Sadie had made in the twilit garden to prevent the man who loved her from marching into Helwan House and informing its master that he wanted his permission to become engaged to Miss Sarah Colt.

"No, wait, darling! Let me do it, I know how to manage him. If you startle him, he'll say No right away, and he's so stubborn, it'll take forever to change his mind!"

"I hate being in his house under false pretences – "

"What's false about keeping quiet? Alain, let's have a few days to ourselves, after all those years, without all the fuss and explanations!"

"Yes, but I want to see you all the time, and how can we?"

"To begin with, we can have tea at Shepheard's tomorrow."

"We'll hardly be alone at Shepheard's Hotel. Doesn't the whole English colony go there regularly?"

"Yes, that's why; no one will notice us. We'll just melt into the crowd."

It was impossible to refuse her, of course, with the scent of roses in his nostrils and her soft lips parting beneath his own, but Alain had his doubts about Shepheard's at tea time, and he was quite right. They tried to look unconcerned, and at least they spoke French, which none of the British tea drinkers understood, but a handsome man in the distinctive French uniform and the American girl whom everybody knew by sight were conspicuous on the famous terrace.

Miss Sadie Colt had not had the same success in Cairo as she had enjoyed in London. Her presentation at the Court of St James, while important at the 'court' of Lord Cromer, aroused the jealousy of the wives of minor officials, and her enthusiasm for charitable causes enraged others. "No American chit is going to teach me my duty to my neighbour," fumed the women who refused to join a Ladies' Aid Society, American style, got up to help the patients in the Victoria Hospital, and even Sadie's father told her to 'take it easy' when with a Coptic Christian helper she tried to organise a dispensary and first aid station in the factory.

"My senior overseer says you're trying to convert his men to Christianity, Sadie, is that true?"

"Certainly not. Ali thought I was praying when I was only repeating the Latin names of some of the medicines."

"What the hell for? Lay off it, my girl, or out will come the green flags and they'll be preaching a *jehad* in my own factory. Better forget all those crazy notions you got from your Aunt Liz."

Sadie Colt drove a motor car, often — when her father needed the chauffeur — alone. She played tennis at Gezira without a maid to help her in the changing rooms. She came alone to watch the polo at Gezira, and joked with the players, and when she went to the receptions at the Beit-al-Lurd her only chaperon was her father, whose reputation as a fast man was established long ago.

Now here she was on the terrace at Shepheard's, an unmarried girl without a chaperon, and flirting with a French officer! Significant glances were exchanged and lips were pursed as the Frenchman leaned towards the girl and whispered something which made her blush.

Mon amour, mon adorée! They were the right words for the right day, but spoken at the wrong time, in the wrong place. Sadie should have been in Alain's arms in some secret place, listening to him tell how he had never ceased to think of her, never seen freesias in a florist's shop without thinking of the footsteps of Persephone. It was a time for tender nonsense, not for the serious discussion into which Alain plunged, of when they would be married, where they would live and how they would organise their future.

"Can't we organise a few days alone together first?"

He smiled at the innocent suggestion. "We wouldn't be alone, would we? Sadie, I'm having lunch with your father tomorrow. Let me speak to him then. Otherwise I'll feel we're meeting under false pretences. . . ."

"Oh, don't say anything at the Turf Club, he wouldn't like that. . . ."

"Do you really think he'll object to our engagement?"

"I know he doesn't want me to marry and leave him. He says he's been so lonely, all those years without me."

"So have I." Alain de Grimont doubted if Sadie's father, vigorous and attractive in his own way, had ever gone short of female companionship during his years as a widower. But he gave way to Sadie's plea for a few day's grace. She was nervous, poor darling, no matter how practical she tried to be!

Meantime she was saying, practically, "We can meet every afternoon in Cairo, and then there's Lord Cromer's ball on Wednesday — we'll meet at that, for sure."

"Do you realise we've never danced together, darling? I bet you're a wonderful dancer. As it happens, I'm going to the Residence tonight, so I'll learn my way about."

"I didn't know there was a party at the Beit-al-Lurd tonight."

"It's not a party. The card said just a few men invited to come in after dinner to meet Sir Herbert Kitchener."

"To meet the Sirdar, so soon! Darling, you must be someone terribly important now!"

"No, just someone who knows the Barings in London. And I won't be asked to advise the Sirdar. All any Englishman wants of any Frenchman these days is to heckle him about Captain Dreyfus."

"Still, my father will be terribly impressed."

Mr Colt was interested when they met at the Turf Club, the centre of an Englishman's social life in Cairo. Lord Cromer's officials worked from 8 AM to 1 PM, went to lunch at the Turf Club, played tennis or golf after the siesta and, if they had no querulous wives to go home to, went back to the Turf for dinner. Alain made a good impression on Charles Colt and his friends. Having been an adventurer himself, Colt had supposed that the French officer who turned up in Cairo for no obvious reason was on the make as well, and that afternoon he sent a couple of telegrams to Paris which Mr Naccache was not allowed to handle. The replies were satisfactory. Apart from the de la Treille connection, the Baron de Grimont was the third holder of the title. He was the owner of a considerable fortune and his father had been the Minister for Justice.

"So he won't touch me for a monkey in Egyptian pounds before he leaves," thought Mr Colt, and he told Sadie to write a note to the baron and invite him to lunch at Helwan House on Friday. Charles Colt made only one concession to Islam: he required his workers to be at their looms for only half the day on Fridays.

He never knew that his daughter was meeting the baron (funny, he liked to be called major) on three weekday afternoons, and had constituted herself his guide to Cairo.

Having heard Cairo described as 'a dying Mecca and a stillborn Rue de Rivoli' Alain was surprised by the vitality of the capital. As well as the suburban railways, a tramway system had been installed and every tram was filled, with the men in their *galabeyahs* and red fezzes clinging to the outside like bunches of human grapes. Alain and Sadie took a carriage to the citadel and on to the Mokattam Hills; they visited Coptic Christian churches and even mosques in the Old City, and on another day they explored the Mouski, that ancient commercial street of many *souks*, all smelling of sandalwood. They listened to the storytellers squatting in the shade of the *souk* of the tentmakers, and Alain bought Sadie a translucent jar of attar of roses in the scentmakers' *souk*. The music of the luteplayers made them think of the ball on Wednesday night, and Alain begged his sweetheart to wear the white dress of her presentation at the Court of St James.

"Oh, darling, I can't. It's two years old, and out of style."

"It can't be, not that dress, and it looked so lovely in the photograph."

"Where did you see the photograph?"

"In Aunt Blanche's boudoir."

"You know, I rather hoped she'd send it on to you."

"Yes, she wasted our time. But now I've got the girl, can't I have the dress too?"

"Alain, I wore it at court and at two Highland balls, and every woman in the room on Wednesday will have seen it at the first very grand ball Lord Cromer gave after I came back to Cairo. . . ."

"Do they matter more than me?"

She wore the court dress, to her father's pleasure, and though she had neither court train nor Prince of Wales's feathers she looked like a princess as she swept into the ballroom of Beit-al-Lurd. The satin shimmered, the crystal beads on the very low-cut bodice shone, and instead of the ostrich feathers Sadie wore a wreath of white oleander flowers which she had made herself. It was no wonder that Major de Grimont, when he came up to make his bow and write his name six times over in the dance programme attached by its silk ribbon to her white-gloved wrist, whispered, "Darling! You look like a bride – *my* bride!"

Lord Cromer's entertainments were always magnificent, and although this was a small dance, of only fifty couples, it took on the prestige of a court ball, with 'Al-Lurd' himself sitting on a small dais to survey the dancers. The pipe band of one of the Highland regiments at Kasr-el-Nil alternated with string music, and as all the dances claimed by Alain were waltzes it was to the sound of violins that her body swayed to his.

It was strange to go from the vigorous grasp of a Highland officer who, with kilt swinging, piloted her through a schottische or a quadrille, into Alain's arms. They danced with the beauty of movement which only sexual harmony can give, and Sadie's face grew as pale as her dress with the intensity of her emotion. She seldom spoke, and when she did Alain heard love in her whisper.

"Thank you for the white lilies you sent to Helwan, darling. They're beautiful, but I couldn't wear them in my hair."

"I couldn't find any freesias in Cairo, Persephone. So you had to wear oleanders."

"They smell of almonds."

"And you smell of roses."

They danced the last dance together, and it was a waltz. To a Viennese melody they clung closer and ever closer, and Alain kept his hand on Sadie's waist to steady her when the music stopped. To join in the romping galop which followed was beyond them, but the noise covered a few quick words:

"Swear that you'll speak to your father about us tomorrow!"

"I swear it. Oh, Alain!"

"And I'll come down on Friday by the twelve o'clock train."

"I'll meet you at Helwan station in the Benz."

The band played 'God Save the Queen', and Mr Colt, who had been playing whist all evening, came to take his daughter home.

Next evening, when her father came back from Cairo, he found the whisky decanter and the seltzer siphon on a brass-topped table in the tiled court near the fountain, where Mehmed had arranged two rattan chairs with footrests. "Good idea," said Mr Colt appreciatively, when he was comfortably installed with a glass in his hand. "It was as hot as hell in the city today. What's that you're drinking?"

"Lime juice and soda," said Sadie, perched upright on the foot of her chair.

"Are you coming to your dispensary tomorrow?"

"Yes, half past nine, as usual," Sadie said. "Why?"

"Not too tired after the ball?"

"Good heavens, father! Me, too tired after a few hours' dancing! You know me better than that, surely."

"Obviously de Grimont doesn't. I saw him at the Turf Club at lunch time, and he was very anxious to know if you were well."

"That was nice of him. Did he have luncheon with you?"

"No, he was at the next table. Lunching with Kitchener's military secretary, and asking no end of questions about the action at Firket last June and the progress of the Sudan Railway."

"Well, he *is* a professional soldier, father."

"He's a Frenchman, dear. Some of the men at the Club are beginning to wonder about him. We all know the French are trying to get a footing on the Upper Nile, and it's just possible de Grimont's a French spy."

"How ridiculous!"

"Now don't get me wrong, I like de Grimont. But I don't know why a man like that should spend his leave in Cairo, for no purpose anyone can see."

"He came to Cairo to ask me to marry him."

"*What?*"

"And I said I would."

Mr Colt, not without difficulty, levered himself upright on the chaise longue, and set his half-empty glass carefully on the ground.

"You're not serious, Sadie!"

"I've been in love with him since I was sixteen."

"When you met at Cap Martin." Then violently: "He didn't get fresh with you, when you were just a kid?"

"He went off to Paris as soon as he could. But when he came to Cairo we began where we left off."

"And he proposed to you at the ball?"

"No, it was the night you brought him home."

"Then," said Mr Colt, the veins on his forehead swelling, "he should have spoken to me next day."

"Oh!" cried Sadie, impulsively clasping her hands, "he wanted to, but I wouldn't let him. He's coming tomorrow, you can have it all out then, but I wanted us to have a few days alone with each other first. . . ."

"*Alone?*"

"Walking in the Mouski, and having tea at Shepheard's, once. You see, there's so much we have to find out about each other. We've got four years of talking to make up."

"Marriage isn't all talking, Sadie. My God, I wish your mother were here tonight."

Sadie launched herself out of her own chair and fell headlong on her father. With her arms round his neck and her cheek against his, she whispered, "But I've got *you*, father!

And you're going to be a darling, aren't you, and let me marry the only man I've ever loved — "

"Get up, girl, you're strangling me," said Charles Colt. ". . . Sadie, this'll take some thinking over. One thing I know, de Grimont's a very rich man; he's no fortune-hunter. But I never thought you'd want to leave your lovely home so soon, and I certainly never thought you'd marry a foreigner."

"My mother did."

At that moment Sadie believed she had won her battle. Her father kissed her roughly and went indoors without another word. At least he had not said No. Apart from that silliness about spying for France, he hadn't objected to Alain as a suitor, only to the suddenness of his proposal, and Alain would make that all right when he came next day! Dinner was served, and they exchanged pleasantries in front of the servants. Mr Colt ate voraciously and drank an extra glass of wine as if he were stoking up for another encounter. His objections began as soon as they were left alone.

He's too old for you; what is he — forty? Thirty-six, well, there's not much difference. Religion: we're Protestant, what's he? A lapsed Catholic? That's nothing to his credit. Does he expect to take you to married quarters in Algiers where they were rioting last week about that fellow Dreyfus? That's not good enough for my daughter, and I'm going to tell him so. The battering, unanswerable arguments went on for over an hour, when Sadie went to her room in tears. Next morning she was glad when Mehmed told her Colt Bey had already left for Cairo, and would pick her up at the factory at half past eleven.

That meant she had to get the Benz out for herself, for Gaston was the only mechanic on the staff. Sadie left at her usual hour, on Tuesdays and Fridays, of half past nine; it was one of the tactless mistakes she had made, to hold her dispensary on the holy day of Islam. It didn't seem to worry the workers who came for first aid, or to get simple medicines to take home for their families, chronic sufferers from bilharzia and female complaints aggravated by excessive childbearing. With the most prevalent ailment, which was drug addiction, Sadie was incompetent to deal. The overseers, complaining of work days lost, told her that the Turks had taught the *fellaheen* to use drugs. Hashish was smoked at home in the nargileh pipes, but heroin was smuggled in from Turkey in the soles of slippers and in the skins of live camels slit and sewn up again after a small package of the drug had been inserted. "Turkish dealers go free," said Mark, Sadie's Coptic Christian helper, "Egyptian smokers go to prison."

About three miles from Helwan House, and two from the factory, a plantation of acacia trees gave some shade to the brassy road, and in the shadow Sadie saw a man lying by the roadside who might well have collapsed from an overdose of drugs. She stopped the car and hurried to his side. He was wearing a dirty *galabeyah* with a hood which half covered his brown face, and appeared to be unconscious. She knelt beside him, and was pushing up his sleeve to take his pulse when she was seized from behind by two men who had come out from the shelter of the acacias and made her their prisoner. The 'unconscious' man sprang up and seized her wrists.

Sadie cried once for help before they gagged her with an evil-smelling cloth, and she fought them with all her courage, kicking and writhing until in the struggle the hood of one of her assailants fell back, and she thought she recognised Moammer, the Bedouin gardener who had neglected the irrigation engine at Helwan House. But in that nightmare of pawing hands and the smell of unwashed male bodies she felt her senses failing, and when they bound her wrists and blindfolded her she was conscious of nothing but that she was being dragged across the road and lifted up in a man's arms. By the change in his footsteps as they sank deeper into sand, she knew she was being carried away into the desert.

When Alain de Grimont caught the noon train for Helwan at the Bab-al-Luk station in Cairo, he was braced for his interview with Sadie's father. Since the night of the ball he had been sure that her passion matched his own, and he had almost come to the most important decision of his life. If Mr Colt consented to their marriage in the near future – and Sadie would be twenty-one, her own mistress, in February – he was prepared to leave the army. It had been his life for eighteen years, and he had no real hope either for his old dream of liberating Alsace-Lorraine, nor for his present advancement. Delcassé was full of promises like the carrots held before the willing donkey's nose, but when would they be fulfilled? The Marchand Expedition was no secret now. It was still in the French Congo, still 'preparing' for the great trek to the Nile. The British had re-entered the Sudan when they occupied Dongola, but they had a railway to build before they came within striking distance of Khartoum. Why should he and Sadie waste two more years in waiting for an event – a clash between the British and Marchand – which might never take place? If he bought Rivabella from his cousin Armand they could be living in their own home within months, and then they could decide what to do with the rest of their lives.

It was a disappointment not to find Sadie waiting when he arrived at Helwan station, but the Daimler was standing in the yard with an older boy, who had been given a few piastres for his service, keeping the thieving hands of his friends off such parts of the car as could be stolen. Then the chauffeur, Gaston, came out of the telegraph office in a hurry, saw Alain, and saluted.

"*Mon commandant*, thank God you're here! We're in great trouble at Helwan House – "

"What happened, man?"

"Mademoiselle – has disappeared."

Alain stood aghast, and the man went on, "We greatly

fear she has been kidnapped. Her car was found empty on the highway, and there were signs of a struggle – *O mon Dieu!*" Gaston had to struggle too, to control his hard-bitten features. "Monsieur Colt sent me here to telegraph to the chief of police in Cairo. . . ."

"The *Egyptian* police?"

"Yes."

"They'll take their time about getting here. When was the car discovered? Where?"

"About an hour ago, on the highway not far from the factory."

"Listen, Gaston. I'm sure you're in a hurry to get back, but I want you to drive me further on, to the place where it happened. I want to know all the details when I meet Mr Colt. And step on it!"

Alain got into the Daimler. With his hands clenched and his jaw set he tried to realise that Sadie had been kidnapped. By whom? and in God's name why? He did his best to concentrate on what Gaston was trying to tell him. Mr Colt returned to the factory at half past eleven. The manager of the Tura Quarries had just arrived. On his way to Helwan he had found the abandoned Benz with all its tyres slashed, and thought Mr Colt ought to know.

"What time did mademoiselle leave home?" asked Alain.

"At half past nine, as usual, *mon commandant*."

So she had been missing for nearly two hours; nearly three now. Alain remembered reports of the atrocities committed by the Berber tribesmen on European women who fell into their hands in Algeria. He groaned aloud. Then Gaston pulled up beside the Benz. It had been pushed in among the scrub trees before the tyres were slashed, and the ground beneath the trees, like the surface of the road, was marked with the footprints, shod and naked, of all the men who had surged out of the Colt factory when the whistle blew.

331

"Mr Colt looked everywhere for a ransom note, sir," said Gaston, "but there was nothing."

"I don't suppose those criminals can write."

There was, however, something Mr Colt had missed, but Alain's younger eyes caught: a flash of green between the cushions of the car's two front seats. He pulled at something silken and small, the green of an emerald, and showed it to Gaston.

"D'you know what this is?"

"Mademoiselle's handkerchief?" said Gaston doubtfully.

"It's the green flag of the Prophet Mohammed," said Alain. "Now I know where to look."

He plunged into the desert sand. Like the road, it had been heavily trampled, but only for a short distance. Beyond that he found the first droppings of horse dung, and further on the tracks he had been trained to read: three horses, shod for the desert, three riders, one carrying a heavier load than the others. Sadie in the hands of her kidnappers! He turned and stumbled through the drifting sand to the Daimler.

When Alain ran up the palm avenue at Helwan House with Gaston at his heels he found Charles Colt standing in the tiled patio with Mehmed by his side acting as interpreter while his master shouted at a small group of men in the garb of outdoor servants.

"You know what's happened?" he flung at Alain by way of greeting.

"I know; I've seen the Benz; I've seen a track into the desert," said Alain. "What I don't know is who did it. Have you any idea?"

"Someone who knew Sadie's timetable," said her father. His voice was exhausted, his eyes red; Charles Colt looked twenty years older than the day before. "I assembled all the men on the place and found there was one missing, a fellow called Moammer, who worked in the gardens. This" he pointed at a tall man in the group, "is Riad, my head

332

gardener, who hired him. I think he knows more than he's telling, but Mehmed can't seem to get it out of him, and I don't speak Arabic."

"I do," said Alain, and in the parade-ground voice of Major de Grimont he barked at Riad, "Speak up, man! The Cairo police will soon be here, and they have their own ways of making suspects talk. What have you to do with this terrible crime? Why should this Moammer wish harm to your young mistress?"

"*Effendi!*" cried Riad, "as Allah is my judge I had nothing to do with it! Except that one day I thrashed him with the *courbash* for neglecting the water engine, and he thought ladyship had ordered it, though in fact she forbade me to use it — "

Alain stopped him with a raised hand and said to Colt, "What's a *courbash*?"

"A whip made of a strip of hippopotamus hide. It was used in the old days for extracting confessions. I believe the police still use it, against British orders."

Alain repeated the words in Arabic. "You hear that, Riad?" he said. "You'll get a taste of the *courbash* yourself unless you talk. Quickly!"

"Protector of the Poor!" cried Riad, still on his knees, "all I can tell you is that Moammer hates women, but he hated ladyship most, and often said he wished to do her harm. Here is the boy Abdul, who knows more about Moammer than I do — "

"His brother?"

"His little friend."

And Riad, scrambling up, pushed forward a boy of about fourteen, with the fair complexion of an Albanian, dark sloe eyes and a lithe unformed body, who promptly burst into tears.

"*Effendi*," he sobbed, "do not punish me! Moammer is cruel when he is under the madness of drugs. He makes love

333

to me and then he strikes me—look!" He pulled his *galabeyah* off one shoulder and showed a purple bruise.

Alain paid no attention. He pulled the miniature green flag out of his pocket and showed it to the boy. "Do you know what this is?" he said.

The boy paled under the grime and tear stains. "It is the Flag of the Prophet," he whispered. "It belongs to Moammer. Sir, he is Bedouin by race and Shi'ite by faith; he used to show it to me and say the Khalifa Abdullah and his Dervish Emirs would come from the south to drive the Franks and the Turks from Egypt, and we would join in the *jehad* — "

"Enough," said Alain. "Is he a nomad, your Bedouin lover? Or does he pitch his tent along the track which runs west from the acacia trees on the highway?"

"At the oasis called the Wells of Elam," said the boy readily.

"How far is it to the Wells of Elam?"

Young Abdul fumbled with the distance, but they agreed upon ten miles. The next oasis, westwards, was twice as far away.

"Will you send this rabble away, monsieur?" said Alain to Mr Colt. "Take my arm and come indoors. I only want one thing more of them — I want Riad's *courbash*."

The majordomo hurried ahead of them and brought wine into the salon. The master of the house sat down upon a sofa, speechless.

"Well, now we've got the picture," said Alain, after a swallow of wine. "Islam in a nutshell. The hate, the lust for revenge, the desire to humiliate women — it's all there. And the Shi'ite Moslems are the most fanatical of all."

"What are we going to do?" Charles Colt could barely speak.

"I know what I'm going to do," said Alain confidently. "I'm going into the desert to bring her out."

"Alone?"

"Hardly. You forget, sir, I'm an old campaigner. I know where to get the troopers and the mounts, if you'll lend me the Daimler and Gaston to get me to Cairo. And when the police arrive, tell them to follow me to the Wells of Elam."

"You believed everything that wretched little catamite said about the desert oases and the Flag of the Prophet?"

"I've seen that emerald green too often to be mistaken."

"But why did the brute leave it in the Benz?"

"As a symbol. As a warning that the *jehad* is going to spread out of the Sudan into Egypt. Will you send for Gaston now?"

Mr Colt rang a handbell and gave an order to Mehmed.

"Before you go," he said slowly, "Sadie told me what you meant to say to me today."

"She did?" Alain's smile lit up his stern face. "You know, then, that we love each other?"

"De Grimont, if you love her, bring her back to me. She's all I've got in the world."

When Major de Grimont came back to the Benz and the acacia trees late that afternoon he was on horseback, riding at the head of his little troop of four Spahis, recruited from the French consul-general's house. The Spahis, who were Algerians, welcomed the prospect of a desert *razzia*; the consul, while concerned, was reluctant to let them go. "For God's sake, no shooting, major," he begged, "if any of those men are killed I'll be held responsible." He was equally dismayed at the idea of applying to the British commander at Kasr-el-Nil for mounts. Alain found the Englishman sympathetic and cooperative: he offered troops as well as horses, but the British soldiers who knew the desert were at the front in the occupation of Dongola, and the men at Kasr-el-Nil barracks were Engineers newly arrived from England to work on the Sudan Military Railway, who as yet knew nothing about desert warfare. The horses did; they were the tough

335

little Syrian animals, only thirteen hands high, which the British were forced to use instead of the great chargers brought out aboard the troopships, and now eating their heads off in their Cairo stables.

Before they left, Alain called on the Chief of Police and told him to enter the desert at the acacia plantation instead of going to Helwan House: the Egyptian's shrug and gesture as he flicked the *tesbih* beads on his wrist showed that he thought the expedition useless. The English doctor whom Alain visited next promised to go back with Gaston in the Daimler to care for Sadie when — if — she was found in the vastness of the western desert which stretched on into Libya. His speech was blunter than the police chief's. "Sometimes it's better if they're dead," he said to Alain. The hideous word *rape*, which nobody had dared to utter, was in both their minds.

The Spahis had taken off their brilliant scarlet cloaks and carried them in rolls on the cantles of their saddles. Inside the rolls were lengths of rope and cloth. They also carried canvas water buckets and their regulation weapons, sabres and Martini carbines. Alain carried two revolvers, his own and Charles Colt's, and the *courbash* knotted into his belt. His white uniform, crisp and freshly laundered when he left for Helwan, was dark and blotched with dust and sweat.

After riding ten miles south they stopped at the Colt factory to ask for news and water the horses: the heat, though dusk was beginning to fall, was still intense. Ali, the head overseer, came out to shake his head and lament. Mr Colt was still at home, but he had sent orders to have the Benz towed away and put into one of the sheds. Alain swore under his breath. The new Bertillon system of tracing a criminal by his finger prints would not be needed. Anyway the car had been well pawed over while it was still on the highway, and he wouldn't have to look at it, Sadie's car, when they reached the acacia trees. Alain had eaten nothing since the coffee and roll of breakfast, but he allowed himself time to smoke a cigarette while the Spahis wound cloth round the metal of the horse harness to silence jingling sounds as they neared the oasis.

"*Mon commandant*," one of the Spahis ventured, "what if there are honest nomads at the Wells, besides the men we seek?"

"That's the risk they run, and so do we." He gave the Spahis their final instructions: if sentries are posted, knock them out with the flat of your sabres, don't fire until you hear my first shot; and they set out. By his pocket watch it was seven o'clock when they left the highway for the desert, and Sadie had been missing for ten hours. They had ten miles and a good hour's ride, to go.

The moon, which had been a silver paring when he and Sadie watched it rise above the Nile, was now a quarter full, and by its light they could see for about a mile on their forward way some traces of the men they followed. Then the flat expanse broke into sand dunes of different heights, wave upon wave of tawny sand touched to silver by the moonlight, in which the little Syrian horses gamely kept their footing. They were travelling through a lunar landscape and saw no other creature, human or animal.

When over an hour had passed, and they saw the first signs of scrub vegetation, they knew the oasis was not far away, and a faint smell of wood smoke told them it was inhabited. Alain halted his men and spurred forward alone. Over the rim of a high dune he looked down on the Wells of Elam. It was a very small oasis, with the wells indicated by a circle of date palms, and the only shelters were three *tukls* made of four posts driven into the sand and roofed with straw matting. These were empty. There was one tent, completely closed, with the canvas secured to tent pegs, at the sight of which Alain's heart froze with hope and terror. If Sadie were anywhere, she was there, a prisoner, but – how?

As nearly as he could see, there were five men lying on the sand, asleep or drugged, and one in a hooded *galabeyah* sitting over the fire. Alain backed his horse down the slope, extended his left arm in the agreed signal, and watched while the Spahis moved off to right and to left. He gave them time to reach their places, rode up to the rim again and shook the *courbash* free. He drew his revolver and fired once.

Five French soldiers now attacked the Shi'ites camped at the Wells of Elam, the Spahis with drawn sabres and the frightening screams of the *razzia*, while their officer rode straight for the fire to scatter it. Swerving aside as if tent-pegging, he lashed the seated man with the hippopotamus hide. The man scrambled up, head and shoulders bleeding. There was a rifle in the folds of his *galabeyah*, but before he could fire Alan wheeled his horse and put a bullet through the man's right shoulder. The Bedouin screamed and fell forward into the wreckage of the fire.

At his scream the flap of the tent was ripped open, and a young woman in a blue robe, with a bead fillet round her streaming hair, rushed out to throw herself on the wounded man. "Moammer!" she cried. "O my brother! O Moammer!" Then she broke into the high-pitched 'Lu-lu-lu' of a native woman's lamentation, and Alain shouted to the nearest Spahi, "Tie them both up!"

One glance assured him that his men had the situation well in hand. Kicked to their feet by the horses, the Bedouin swayed in a huddled group ringed by the sabre points of their captors, and Alain, still grasping his revolver, dashed towards the tent.

There were two women backed up against the further wall, who had begun the chant of 'Lu-lu-lu'. Sadie lay on the desert floor, bound hand and foot but not gagged. Her face was bruised and her eyes were glassy and unfocused. Alain used the *courbash* to tie her jailers together at the neck. He was sure they had knives beneath their robes, and once

338

out of the tent were perfectly capable of hamstringing the horses.

Then, and only then, he cut Sadie's bonds and lifted her into his arms.

"My darling, can you speak to me?"

"Alain?" At the sound of his voice a glimmer of light came back into her eyes.

"Yes, it's Alain." He kissed her tenderly. "My love, are you all right?"

"Yes, I'm all right." Her voice trailed off on the word "please" and he thought she whispered, "take me home."

"We're going home now, sweet." He made her drink a little brandy from his pocket flask and carried her into the open air. The Spahis had efficiently roped their prisoners, and one had tied a rough pad and bandage over Moammer's wound. Another had spread his cloak on the ground for Sadie.

"We've saved the lady, sir!"

"Yes, we have. Now we turn all the men over to the police. How many horses had they?"

"Six, hobbled just beyond the well, *mon commandant*."

"Cut their hobbles and let them run free. Draw water from the well for our own mounts. There are two women in the tent; tie their hands and bring them out. We'll leave them behind with this girl on the ground. Burn the *tukls* and the tent before we go."

There was scorched earth round the Wells of Elam before long, and the curses of the native women followed the 'Frankish swine' as the little procession started, with Moammer, bloody and stumbling, bringing up the rear. Sadie, still wrapped in the Spahi cloak, had been lifted carefully into Alain's arms. He rode rearguard, his eyes moving from her unconscious face to the wretched group ahead of him. Four Spahis, Algerian by birth, urging on six Bedouin in tatters — it was not the brilliant French force of his imagination, riding with him into Strasbourg on the glory road! Then his left arm tightened round the girl he loved. The glory of his life lay on his breast.

25

When the 93rd of the Line, once stationed in Tunisia, was transferred from Oran to Algiers at the beginning of 1897, Colonel Chaudron was glad to find that a former subaltern had been posted to his command. The colonel, a widower, was within a year of his retirement, and after a lifetime in the Army of Africa he was looking forward to the tranquillity of a little property at St Raphaël. With the agitation about the 'Revision' of the Dreyfus case increasing every month, it looked as if Colonel Chaudron's last year in uniform would be a difficult one, and he was glad to have an experienced officer like Major de Grimont on his staff.

"I'm delighted to see you, my dear fellow," he said when Alain reported for duty. "Let me see; how long has it been since you marched off to Bizerta – thirteen years?"

"About that, sir."

Chaudron looked consideringly at the handsome man before him. He remembered the young lieutenant of Tunis, with his championship of the Tunisians, his native mistress, and his hero-worship of Boulanger. Chaudron himself had rather admired Boulanger, who as a subject of controversy was preferable to Dreyfus.

"How came you to leave the Bureau Arabe?" he asked. "I understand you had an excellent position there."

"I lost interest in Arab affairs, sir. I'd had enough of fraternising with the Sons of the Prophet."

"Because of that terrible affair in Cairo last October?"

"Yes, *mon colonel*."

"A mercy it turned out as well as it did. You'll find you're quite a hero to my subalterns."

The kidnap and rescue of Miss Sarah Colt had been fully reported in the *Journal d'Egypte*, and the story, copied into the French newspapers, made Alain de Grimont's name better known for a time than Captain Marchand's. The Marchand Expedition seemed to have bogged down in the Congo Basin. Marchand had mobilised a company of Senegalese riflemen and commandeered a little vessel, the *Faidherbe*, but was having great difficulty in finding porters. Given his temperament, he was soon at loggerheads with the commissioner-general of the French Congo, Pierre Brazza. The founder of Brazzaville was another prima donna of the exploration field, who resented interlopers in his territory, and Marchand's departure for the Nile was delayed until April.

This was one of the reasons why Alain did not consult Delcassé, who had placed him in the Bureau Arabe, before applying for a return to the 93rd of the Line. The Colonial Minister accepted the situation, and wrote nothing but compliments on Alain's courage and resource at the Wells of Elam — nothing which might annoy him into throwing up the whole adventure and sending in his papers. For the time being, regimental routine and the companionship of his brother officers were what his protégé required — always provided he could keep out of the Dreyfus controversy.

The younger subalterns stood in awe of Major de Grimont. They had expected him to be a flamboyant character instead of a grave officer who refused to be drawn about his own experiences, and whose presence at the dinner table – he always dined in mess – inhibited their skylarking and their arguments. He was only known to be violent once, when a young lieutenant jeered at the slowness of the British progress towards Khartoum, conditioned by the progress of the railway. Then he slammed his clenched fist on the table until the silver rang, and said loudly, "Good luck to the British! I hope they kill every damned Shi'ite Dervish in the Sudan!"

When Alain had stormed out of the mess, Colonel Chaudron himself reminded the lieutenant of the Helwan kidnapping and the effect it must have had on Major de Grimont, and administered another snub to the youngster who said unwisely, "I wonder why he didn't marry the girl?"

None of them had any idea that there was the crux of the matter.

None of them knew that when Major de Grimont was alone in his new billet, decidedly inferior to the quarters provided by the Bureau Arabe, his first act was to unlock his desk and read Sadie's latest letter, all the while thinking, "What a fool I was to believe her father!"

Mr Colt, after his first transports of relief and joy at Sadie's safety were over, had handled the situation like a master.

"My boy," he said, "no one has a better right to my daughter's hand in marriage than the man who saved her ·om those savages. But surely you must see that wedding plans or even engagement parties are impossible at present. Remember what Dr Dawson said. No excitement, absolute rest, until the effects of the drugging and the shock had worn off!"

"I wouldn't dream of pressing for an immediate wedding," Alain had protested. "But surely by next spring – "

Mr Colt shook his head. "A year from now is quite soon enough," he said. "The doctor advises change of scene, change of interests, foreign travel – "

"She can have all that on our honeymoon."

It was no use. Alain realised that Charles Colt's touching appeal, 'she's all I've got in the world', meant 'and I mean to keep her to myself'.

Sadie was unconscious when Alain carried her into Helwan House, and Dr Dawson's examination was easily carried out. He dressed the bruises on her face, the result of a scuffle with her women jailers, and those on her wrists and ankles where the rope ties had bitten deep. Then he came down to tell the anxious men that Miss Colt had not been raped or sexually molested in any way.

"What a blessing," said the doctor, "that the kidnapping swine was a queer and a drug addict who handed her over to the women, but if you hadn't gone to the rescue, major, God knows what might have happened the next day. She'll need some professional care; I'll send you down a nurse tomorrow."

The nurse from the Victoria Hospital put Sadie through the routine of emetics and purgings which were the doctor's drastic methods of dealing with an accidental dose of heroin, and Alain, invited to stay at Helwan House, spent the time in accompanying his host on a series of official visits. They saw Lord Cromer, the Chief of Police and the American consul-general, Mr Harrison, after Moammer, in a prison hospital, had declared that he and his friends were only acting for the sheikh of the next oasis, who hankered after a Frankish girl for his concubine. Colt wanted an expeditionary force sent out to capture the villain and bring him to justice. He was told that the man Moammer was sure to be lying, and no force was despatched on a provocative errand. The Khedive himself was appealed to, and refused to run the risk of a *jehad* so near the capital.

Mr Colt had to content himself with the Public Prosecutor's guarantee that even in a Native Court Moammer would be given an exemplary prison sentence and not the relative freedom of wearing leg irons and working for the British on the Sudan Military Railway.

Sadie was very subdued when she first came downstairs. Alain spent an hour sitting beside her as she lay on the chaise longue by the fountain, fragile in a teagown of pale green chiffon, wearing powder to hide the fading bruises and dark shadows beneath her eyes. Alain put bracelets of kisses round her abraded wrists. If he had dared he would have kissed her ankles, but he was too aware of her father's presence in the salon, from which he emerged to say, too genially:

"Now then, you two lovebirds! Dinner in bed for Sadie; that's what the doctor ordered!"

That brief hour of happiness encouraged Alain to make another plea for an early marriage, and when it was refused he was provoked into telling the American he must take better care of Sadie. She was not to be allowed to drive alone; Gaston or her father must go with her everywhere. She was not to be obliged to supervise the gardeners. The house staff, yes; they all seemed reliable, but — "Fire that Riad," Alain advised. "I know his kind and I don't trust him. Hire the gardeners yourself or get your man Naccache to do it. And no more stray Bedouin. Take on some of the *fellaheen* from Helwan, local men, and not too many of them. You don't need all the staff you've got, anyway. My uncle runs his carnation fields with half the men you've got getting up to mischief here."

"Any more criticisms?" growled Colt.

"I'm only criticising you for Sadie's sake."

"Sure you don't want to help me run my business?"

"Certain."

They were out of temper with each other, and when Sadie came downstairs, in a workmanlike skirt and shirtwaist instead of the trailing chiffon, she was in the querulous stage of convalescence. She wanted the Benz back, complete with

345

new tyres and a thorough overhaul. She wanted to see Mark, to plan new hours for the dispensary. To Alain's gentle protest she said the Coptic boy wanted to be a doctor, and she was going to help him every way she could. She didn't want to see any of the ladies from the Gezira Club, who had been ardent in their enquiries and sympathy. She even grumbled at having to acknowledge the flowers sent by everyone 'on the list' at the Beit-al-Lurd. She only wanted – she only wanted – and the bad temper ended in a burst of sobbing in Alain's arms, with promises to 'be good' and take care of herself for him.

With that he had to be content, though his heart was heavy when he left for Algiers. All he had of Sadie now was her letters, read and re-read. He had a copy of her photograph in court dress, which she had ordered from Ellis and Walery and Alain had set in a repoussé silver frame, and a whole line of happy Kodak snapshots, intended to show him how well she was. "My father tries to treat me like an invalid, but I'm not, darling, I'm not!" Sadie on horseback, Sadie holding a racquet. "I played tennis for two hours at Gezira yesterday!" Sadie at Luxor, where her father had sent her for a holiday with some people called Stewart. Sadie dressed as a bridesmaid for some English girl, enjoying the wedding reception given at Beit-al-Lurd.

"Really, darling, you are being a little unreasonable," wrote Aunt Blanche at Christmas. "Many people are obliged to have long engagements nowadays. Look at Armand and Henriette, they had to wait *two* years, not one, and Armand was at sea most of the time. Be patient, and go back to Cairo when your leave falls due in May. I'm sure Mr Colt will relent when he sees you both together. . . ."

Alain was reasonable, he was patient, and in May Sadie wrote to say that her father was taking her away from Cairo as soon as the great heat began. They were going to stay with her school friend Rosmarie von Rorschach and her widowed mother, first in their flat in Vienna and then at their summer house at Bad Ischl, "where the Emperor Franz Josef goes. Of course, it'll be lovely to see Rosi again, she's such a dear, but oh! how I wish I was going to be with you at Cap Martin! Shall we go there for our honeymoon?"

Honeymoon — that made it seem so near, but the Colts were travelling by boat to Brindisi in Italy, and from there by train to Vienna. Mr Colt was making sure that there would be no chance of a meeting with a soldier in Algiers.

Alfred Dreyfus, formerly captain, degraded, was still in solitary confinement on Devil's Island, shackled like the Egyptian criminals labouring on Kitchener's railway. But the pamphlet written by Bernard Lazare had struck a tiny match of suspicion in several minds. It was only a point of light in the darkness, but it flamed up when a new chief was appointed to the Counter-Espionage Bureau which had accused Dreyfus in 1894.

Colonel Georges Picquart was dedicated to the French Army. He disliked Jews in general, and he had disliked the supercilious and too-efficient Captain Alfred Dreyfus, whom he believed to be a traitor. But far stronger than his dislike was his love of justice, and when on taking charge at the Bureau he found that the leak of military information to the Germans was still going on, he began a personal investigation. He sent for the Secret File, which had been ordered to be destroyed and was not. In it he found, with the other documents not disclosed to the defence at the Dreyfus trial, a letter from Panizzardi, the Italian military attaché, describing Dreyfus as guilty *before* the discovery of the memorandum by which Dreyfus was condemned.

He sent for the memorandum, and found that the hand-writing, supposed to be that of Dreyfus, strongly resembled that of a French officer of Hungarian descent, one Major Esterhazy. While he was considering this, an intercepted

347

letter from the German military attaché to a French officer in a treasonable relationship, came into Picquart's hands. The officer's name on the cover of the postal express letter called a *petit bleu* was Major Esterhazy.

The last link in the damning chain of evidence was provided by Esterhazy himself. Anxious for an appointment to the General Staff, he wrote letters in support of his campaign which were seen by Picquart. The handwriting was the same as the handwriting of the memorandum which had sent Dreyfus to Devil's Island.

When Colonel Picquart laid the evidence against Esterhazy before the Chiefs of Staff, he was told to forget it. If the Jew had been wrongfully imprisoned it was unimportant. The *chose jugée* could never be revised. When Picquart refused to keep the dreadful secret of injustice he was relieved of his duties in Paris, and sent to command an infantry regiment on the farthest frontier of Tunisia. But before he went he had the *petit bleu* photographed, and left a statement of his discoveries with a lawyer friend. Before long the respectable *Matin* published a facsimile of the memorandum, in which many influential readers recognised the handwriting of Esterhazy.

At the mere suggestion that Dreyfus was innocent a wave of antisemitism broke over France. Far fiercer than at the time of the actual trial, the anti-Jewish passion rose. The Commune, which had caused more Frenchmen to die than in the whole of the French Revolution, was at least confined to Paris. The Jew-baiting spread through all the great cities, and was nowhere more violent than in the city of Algiers.

The mayor, Monsieur Max Régis, was himself a Jew-hater. He made no attempt to control the outbreak of lawlessness. Arsonists set fire to Jewish property, shops were looted and windows broken, graffiti were painted on the fronts of Jewish homes. Women were insulted and men were beaten, until some of the younger Jews turned on

348

their tormentors and with fists and sticks began a running battle from the Jewish quarter along the seafront to the civic centre.

The Prefect of Police had the command of over one hundred gendarmes. He ordered them out, swinging their loaded cloaks, and for a time they succeeded in containing the mob in the Place Bugeaud. But now others had joined in the riot: disgruntled *pieds noirs*, descendants of the settlers of 1830, Marxist agitators, even Moslems coming down from the Casbah carrying the Green Flag of the Prophet. Slowly the gendarmes retreated, while Colonel Chaudron, watching through binoculars from the barracks roof, observed to Major de Grimont that he didn't like the look of things at all.

"If they try to storm the *Gouvernement-Général* we'll be called out," he said. "Can't those fools in Paris understand that by refusing Dreyfus a retrial they're putting the Army itself in the dock? One little Jew against the honour of the French Army! It makes no sense, but look, de Grimont" (lowering the range of his binoculars to street level) "here comes the messenger from the Préfecture!"

The inevitable had happened. One of the rabble had flung a stone at the captain of *gendarmerie* which struck him in the stomach, and though doubled up with pain he raised his walking stick in self-defence. From somewhere in the crowd came rifle shots, and there was a rush towards the *Gouvernement-Général*. The Prefect, well aware that the nearest French regiment of Sharpshooters was fifteen miles away, proclaimed martial law and called out the 93rd.

The infantrymen, in their blue cutaways, red trousers, and white neckcloths flapping from their képis, dashed out into a downpour of September rain. The stable sergeant and the farrier sergeant brought up chargers for the colonel and his two majors, the bugles sang out *En Avant!* and the 93rd was on the march. The crowd in the great square seemed to hesitate. The bodies of several gendarmes lay on the ground.

349

Colonel Chaudron, in the high authoritative voice of St Cyr, ordered his men to fire one volley over the heads of the crowd, and then ordered the insurgents to lay down their arms.

The answer was a ragged burst of rifle fire.

"Forward the Ninety-third!"

The three mounted officers drew their sabres. The infantrymen behind them reloaded their rifles. Then they were in the thick of it, in a hail of bullets, in the driving rain, Frenchmen fighting Frenchmen in the streets of Algiers. Alain de Grimont had only time for one conscious thought, as the nightmare of his childhood was re-enacted:

"My God, it's the Commune all over again!"

Then he heard his colonel shout, "I'm hhh—!" the shout dying away in a gurgle as the blood gushed from his throat. Alain spurred up to catch the old man as he reeled in the saddle. Then he felt a searing pain in his own chest, and was the first to fall.

26

On the last day of December 1897 Sir Herbert Kitchener requested reinforcements in his advance against the Dervishes. In Cairo Lord Cromer amalgamated three British battalions into a brigade to be commanded by General Gatacre, who was hurried out from Aldershot, and in London the War Office moved the 1st Battalion of the Seaforth Highlanders from Malta to Cairo. Thereupon the Khalifa assembled his Emirs and his warriors, 60,000 strong, on the Kerreri Hills outside Omdurman, and awaited the attack on his capital.

Early in January the Marchand Expedition, on the move at last, halted at the place they called the Poste des Rapides. They moved on to Fort Desaix in February, and stayed there until the first of June, after which, though constantly receiving orders from Paris to make haste, they passed out of official knowledge and plunged on through the fever swamps and lethal rivers of darkest Africa.

Kitchener was moving from north to south to reach the confluence of the Blue Nile and the White, Marchand from west to east to reach the same goal. Sooner or later they would

351

meet and clash, to an extent which Delcassé dreaded. But for the moment the meeting of Kitchener and Marchand was of secondary consideration. The prime topic in France was the latest developments in the Dreyfus case, now known by the impressive name of *L'Affaire*.

Major Esterhazy, hearing the charges against him, demanded a public inquiry, and a court-martial declared him innocent in five minutes. It was much more a trial of Colonel Picquart than of Esterhazy, for Picquart, who had put his whole career at stake for the prisoner on Devil's Island, was recalled from Tunisia, tried for misconduct, broken out of the army and imprisoned.

Major Esterhazy was acquitted on 11 January 1898, and on 13 January the famous novelist Emile Zola published an open letter to the President of the Republic. It appeared in Georges Clemenceau's new daily paper, *L'Aurore*, and it was Clemenceau who found the perfect title for it: *J'Accuse!* Zola accused two Ministers of War, the Chiefs of the General Staff and the War Ministry of possessing and suppressing the evidence of Dreyfus's innocence, and he did so in the hope that by being tried for libel he would bring truth and justice to light. He was tried and found guilty by seven votes to five. He fled to England to avoid imprisonment. He left behind him a France seething with indignation at the attack on the army, the great and noble army, the country's shield and defender, and the attacks on the Jews grew wilder every day. In Algiers, where the year before the riot had lasted one day and caused one soldier's death, Colonel Chaudron's, the riots after Zola's trial in February lasted four days and caused many deaths and beatings in the streets.

J'Accuse made the *Affaire* a world topic. It tore France apart and set friend against friend; the intellectuals signed protests at the treatment of Zola and Picquart; the salons and the royalist faubourg protested against the insult to the army. "My father told me the French called their army the Great

Unknown," said Alain de Grimont; "it seems to me the army's too damned well known now!"

"You've been very patient, Alain, and very tactful, all things considered," said Delcassé. Alain was on 'extended sick leave' in Paris, and they were talking in the Colonial Minister's office. "You're anxious to get back to Cairo, and now I really think you might make a start. Kitchener obviously means to attack at the Atbara, and that's where your assignment ought to start. There's not much point in going back to Algiers. You'll have people to see in Paris, and then you can go straight to Cairo. How long is it since you saw Miss Colt?"

"Four months. She came to visit my aunt while I was convalescing at Hyères." He smiled at the recollection.

"How much does she know about your new posting?"

"Only that it'll be in Egypt."

"You didn't tell her that if all goes well you'll be our next military attaché in London?"

"No, I didn't."

"May I ask why not? Doesn't mademoiselle like London?"

"She likes it so well that I didn't want to raise her hopes. And the London job isn't really certain, is it?"

"It will be if I say so."

"Yes, Théo, you believe in me, and I'm very grateful, but what about the high command? Plenty of men there will say it's too big a step for Major de Grimont."

"You'd be surprised how many men at the War College think highly of de Grimont, who writes perceptive articles about the army and signs them HG. Foch, Joffre, Pétain are all among your admirers. Write as good despatches from the Sudan front as you write for me, and the London job, as you call it, is yours for the asking."

Alain supposed, as he left the Minister's office, that he should have told Sadie what was in the wind. But he was still very much of an invalid when he left the military hospital in

Algiers for his old sanctuary at Hyères after an attack of septicaemia, so that his thinking was confused, and he was completely dependent on his medical orderly until the day when Aunt Blanche came smiling in to say, "Dear Alain! Your Sadie's here!"

"Sadie? But she's in Vienna!"

"I telegraphed to tell her you were here."

Alain was so determined to be in a chair, with his bed properly made, his hair brushed and himself in a dressing gown, that he never asked how Sadie came to be there. It was a miracle that she was by his side, dressed in a beige travelling costume with a bow of blond lace at her throat, kissing him very gently but with lips that clung, and telling him in her forthright way: "I was worried sick when I got word that you were wounded, and that was all I could get out of those people in Algiers. So as soon as Aunt Blanche telegraphed I caught the express from Vienna to Basel, and then crossed to Marseille, and here I am."

"Oh, Sadie sweet! You travelled alone?"

"Rosi's mother wouldn't allow it. She made Stepan, her old servant, escort me, but he wasn't much use, so I sent him back to Vienna from Marseille. Now tell me about you."

When she heard his account of the Algiers riot Sadie said soberly: "There always seems to be one of us in trouble."

"But you're all right, aren't you, darling? No nightmares about the Wells of Elam?"

"I never even think about it."

He knew that this was true. Sadie Colt's steady nerves and splendid health had carried her through an experience about which most women would have been whimpering for years.

"You're a lucky girl," he said. "When I was your age I used to brood too much about the past — my own and other people's."

"'When I was your age' indeed! You sound as if you were my grandfather."

"What's your own father going to say to this?"

Sadie smiled cryptically. "He'll be mad because he won't be able to fetch me from Vienna. He was—very happy there."

"What does that mean?"

"It's not my secret, so I shan't tell you. But it might be quite important for you and me."

After his soldier-servant appeared to say *madame la duchesse* desired the company of mademoiselle at tea in the salon, Alain almost persuaded himself that Charles Colt (that old goat) was having a senile fling with Sadie's friend Rosi.

He was not allowed to see her again that day, but he slept without a sleeping draught for the first time since he was wounded, and insisted on being up and dressed and going downstairs after breakfast. His first visitor was Henriette, bustling and energetic, who told him she and Armand (who was home on leave) had taken Sadie to dine at Rivabella, that she was crazy about the place and sweet with the children, and that he wasn't to worry about her father. Armand and she would leave the kids with their Aunt Valérie and take Sadie back to Cairo themselves. It would be fun to see Helwan House and visit Armand's naval friends at Alexandria.

"That's very sweet of you, Henriette. And you deserve a holiday if anyone does. But where's my girl?"

"Helping *Belle-mère* in the little flower-room. She won't be long."

She came in five minutes, as fresh as the morning in an Austrian peasant blouse and a dirndl skirt, carrying a bowl of roses to put beneath his mother's picture. She set it down before she came to kiss him, and said with a look at Elvire's portrait, "Aunt Blanche told me about her. She was very lovely."

"Yes, she was a pretty woman. I don't remember her very well."

If Aunt Blanche had overheard that, she would have said Alain had found himself at last. He was only interested in kissing Sadie Colt breathless before he asked her, "So you like Rivabella?"

"I've seen it before, you know. Yes, I like it very much. Henriette says it's too small for them now — "

"I know she does. I think they'd be glad to sell it to me, if you wanted to live there."

"Us live there? Oh, darling, could we?"

"Simplest thing in the world to arrange."

"Then are you going to be . . . invalided out of the army? Your uncle said last night you could be, now."

"I suppose I could. But they've got another posting in mind for me now. In Egypt first, and then in the Sudan."

"In *Egypt*! Oh, Alain!"

Then came the peal of delighted laughter he remembered. Before it was cut short. Before she said, "In the Sudan too. That means with the armies, I suppose."

"Something like that. As a non-combatant, of course."

"But you'd be in danger?"

"No more than any other man."

She sighed, and laid her cheek against his. He took her chin in his fingers and tilted her face towards him.

"Listen, Sadie. My life belongs to you. If you tell me to give up this — this idea, I'll do it. Discharged by reason of wounds received in action — it's perfectly respectable. Then, if you want London or any other place, we can travel as civilians. We can see the whole world, if we want to."

There were sudden tears in her dark eyes. "No, Alain, that won't do. That's not the soldier talking, who saved me from the Bedouin. The army is your life, I know. Stay with it while they need you."

That was what Sadie had said to him in October, and that was what Alain remembered in the closing days of February as he went around Paris, talking to Delcassé's friends and to General Billot, the War Minister who had sued Zola for libel, and paying an important visit to Cartier, the jeweller of the Boulevard des Italiens, who was moving into new premises on the Rue de la Paix. Then came the familiar night journey to Marseille, the boat to Alexandria, and the dusty carriages of the Delta Railway jogging him into Cairo.

There had been an exchange of telegrams with Helwan House, but he had a duty to perform before he went to Helwan. In his room at the Continental Hotel Alain had a bath and a shave before he put on the new uniform of his status as Colonel (brevet rank) the Baron de Grimont, acting member of the General Staff, accredited to accompany the forces of the Sirdar as the official observer of the French Army. "Put on everything you've got," Delcassé had said. "Remember, you've got to outshine the German fellow, von Tiedemann, and whatever other observers there may be."

So Alain put on his African decorations, with clasps, and the one that outshone them all, the Cross of the Legion of Honour; took up his new gloves and képi and had himself driven to the Beit-al-Lurd. There he was not kept waiting: it was a distinct advantage to have known Lord Cromer already, and even to have met Sir Herbert Kitchener. It was disconcerting to learn that he would have to leave for the front within thirty-six hours, because it might take two weeks, by varied means of transportation, to reach the confluence of the River Atbara and the Nile, where the most important battle for a year was expected to take place. The necessary documents would be sent at once to the Continental Hotel . . . and Lord Cromer wished Baron de Grimont the best of luck.

He had kept his taxi, not an easy vehicle to hire in Cairo of the donkeys, the camels, and the *faytons* lined with unsavoury rugs, and was driven to Helwan House. Sadie was watching for him, and in a moment she was in his arms again, kissing him, 'prettier than ever', as he had just time to whisper before her father hurried out of the house to shake his hand.

"You're looking well," was his greeting. "Quite got over

357

that nasty affair at Algiers? Good! Now come in and meet our visitors from Vienna."

Alain had known that Rosmarie von Rorschach and her mother were expected at the end of the winter season, but as he bowed over the Gräfin von Rorschach's hand he wished the pair at Jericho. There was so much he had to say to Sadie and her father before he left for the Sudanese front. They were charming women, the countess in her middle forties, her daughter of Sadie's age, both purring compliments when he explained that he had come to Cairo as the official French observer with the Anglo-Egyptian Army.

"And did you have a pleasant journey, Baron de Grimont?" asked the countess. She had a smiling way of talking, with her dark head slightly tilted to one side.

"Very comfortable, thank you, madame."

"Is an observer the same as a war correspondent?" asked Rosmarie with a great air of knowledgeability.

"I don't have to write articles for the newspapers, mademoiselle, but I do have to file despatches."

"It's a great honour," said Sadie proudly. She was a little overcome by Alain's parade uniform and his medals.

"That it is," said Charles Colt heartily. "Conferred on a colonel, too! I'd have thought they'd send a general on a job like that."

"The general officers are all too busy in Paris now."

"Ah! *L'Affaire!*" exclaimed the countess. "The trial of Zola — what a disgrace!"

Then they were off full gallop on the Dreyfus case, and Alain reflected that Colonel Picquart, now in prison, had done his work well. Most Europeans outside France had come to believe that the prisoner of Devil's Island was innocent. "That poor, poor man!" sighed the countess; she was watchful in a well-bred way, and Alain thought she would always agree with the last speaker. Her dark-eyed daughter was wearing an engagement ring. Was it possible that old Colt had proposed to her, and was this the reason for her visit to Helwan?

He began to change his mind when Mehmed announced dinner, and 'old Colt', with an authoritative "Come, Luise," offered his arm to the Viennese lady. Rosmarie sat on his left, and Sadie at the foot of the table with Alain by her side. She was wearing a dark red dress, and she had done her hair in a new way, with curls and tendrils dressed low on her forehead. Also she was wearing a new scent — tuberose, he thought it was, heady and sophisticated. He ached to be alone with her.

"Have you good news of my old friend Armand de la Treille?" asked Mr Colt while the obligatory champagne was being poured. "It was very pleasant to have him and his charming wife here when they brought this — this wild girl home."

"Very good news indeed, sir," said Alain. "Armand has got the step he well deserves. He'll be Admiral de la Treille at the beginning of next month."

The Austrian ladies bubbled over with compliments for a man they had never met. It was Sadie who said eagerly, "And what'll happen to the Villa Rivabella?"

"Well, that's just it, they'll have to live in Toulon, because a fine house goes with the job. But they've decided not to sell Rivabella, first of all because Maurice and Eugénie want to rent it for their next three months' leave, and then Armand and his family can go there for weekends. They don't want to be too far out of touch with my aunt and uncle."

There was no need to stress the point, as the champagne went round, that the Duc and Duchesse de la Treille were growing old and in failing health. Only Sadie said, almost defiantly, "I love your aunt and uncle, Alain. I hope we get to see them soon."

Charles Colt held the floor during dinner. Speaking directly to Alain, he boasted that in spite of the war the

359

Anglo-American Line, in which he held an interest, had begun operations in January. The *Columbia* and the *Mayflower* – "no finer vessels on the Nile, sir" – had been carrying passengers from Cairo to the First Cataract until the end of March. He spoke of Kitchener's engineering triumph, the Sudan Military Railway, on which Alain would soon be travelling, and he remarked that a desert railway had been one of the poor old Khedive Ismail's costly dreams. "It never got past Wadi Halfa," he said. "The Dervishes tore up the rest of the permanent way."

"I must admit," he went on generously, "the British have done a far better job of training the Gyppy army than we did. Did you know that nearly thirty years ago I was one of Ismail's Americans, under contract to turn a rabble of *fellaheen* into an army fit to fight the Turks?"

The Austrian ladies cooed their admiration, and Alain said, "I knew, sir. Sadie told me."

He and she exchanged glances. They were both thinking of Cap Martin, and the seat beneath the oleander flowers.

"We didn't do too well," said Mr Colt, launching like all elderly men into his reminiscences of the war before the last, "but there were only fifteen of us volunteers to be chosen, and all but four were Johnny Rebs. Well, *I'm* not complaining, I got a whole new life out of it, but the one who really scored was General William Tecumseh Sherman. The Khedive gave him a bag of diamonds for promoting the enlistment, said to be worth sixty million dollars."

"Sherman must have found that more profitable than marching through Georgia," said Alain drily.

"And no wonder Egypt went bankrupt," said Sadie tartly. She was as restless as he was, Alain thought, and this too-elaborate dinner seemed to be going on for ever. Soon Gaston would be announced, ready to drive *monsieur le colonel* back to Cairo. He was damned if he was going to sit over wine with old Colt –

— Who, instead, rose from table with the announcement that they would all go back to the salon together and have some music.

"Forgive me," said Alain, "but Sadie and I would like to have a talk. Remember, we have wedding plans to discuss."

"I will gladly play for you, dear Mr Colt," said the Gräfin von Rorschach swiftly, and Colt said, "Oh, very well. But have your talk in the library, it's too cold to go out of doors."

The library, which contained only French paperbacks and yellow railway novels, was charmingly lit by lamps and the flames of a wood fire. Alain drew Sadie into his arms in the depths of a leather sofa. A Chopin waltz began in the farther salon.

"Madame plays well," said Alain.

"Better than Rosi *or* me."

"'Luise', eh? She seems to be on very good terms with your papa. Was that the secret you wouldn't tell me at Hyères?"

"He's told me he wants to marry her. Oh darling, I do hope she'll accept!"

"She'll accept all right. But when I saw Rosi's ring tonight I thought *she* was the favoured lady."

"Silly! Rosi's engaged to a dashing Hussar, back in Vienna. One of the Empress Elisabeth's favourite showjumpers."

"Talking of rings," said Alain, "here's something you ought to have been wearing for a long time. But it had to come from Paris — and luckily you're wearing red tonight."

On a bed of white satin lay the ring from Cartier. Instead of the conventional half-hoop of diamonds it was a half-hoop of rubies, "Burmese stones of the first water," Alain had been assured by Louis Cartier himself. It fitted smoothly on to Sadie's finger.

"Oh, Alain! It's too lovely! Oh darling, I adore it!"

"And I adore you."

He kissed the hand that wore his ring, he kissed her lips, and Sadie asked how he got the size exactly right.

"Took a chance, and got one that fitted just below the nail of my little finger. Good! Now I know what size to get for your wedding ring."

"Oh, Alain! Are we really going to be married soon?"

"Just as soon as . . . as the battle's won."

"Father wants an enormously impressive wedding in All Saints. You don't mind, do you?"

"Of course I don't. But perhaps we'd better not set a date with the *curé*, or whatever you call him, just yet."

"Everybody says the war will be over as soon as the Sirdar comes face to face with the Khalifa, and then you'll be free to come back to Cairo, won't you?"

"Perhaps not quite at once, my darling."

"Why, who's to prevent you, when the battle's won? Not Sir Herbert Kitchener?"

"No, not the Sirdar, I'm not under his command. A man called Captain Marchand."

"You mean that French officer who's lost in the jungle?"

"He'll turn up."

If Colonel de Grimont, as a neutral observer, succeeded in reaching the Khalifa's stronghold at Khartoum, he could count on a journey estimated at between 1,150 and 1,200 miles long. The Nile would be in flood for the second part of the journey, and the ascent of the cataracts would have to be accomplished by the portage of horses. That it was possible at all was due to the construction of the Sudan Military Railway, or desert railway, as it was sometimes called, which would take him close to Berber, where the Sirdar at that time had his headquarters.

A neutral observer was not entitled to top priority by the Director of Transport, so Alain had to wait for two days at Wadi Halfa, the frontier between British-controlled Egypt and the Dervish-dominated Sudan. North of that frontier lay the Dar-el-Harb, the House of War, the dwelling of the infidel, and south lay the Dar-el-Selam, the House of Islam.

At the Hôtel des Voyageurs, once a tourist attraction but very much run down, Alain met several neutral observers from foreign countries, and also some British war correspondents who depressed him by announcing that instead of going close to Berber the railway stopped short of Forward headquarters by nearly seventy miles. The most optimistic of them all was Steevens of the new *Daily Mail*, and also the most knowledgeable; long before he and Alain boarded a supply train at midnight on the second day he explained to the French 'observer' that the Khalifa had massed his troops at Omdurman, near ruined Khartoum, but had ordered one of his best warriors, the Emir Mahmud, to give battle to Kitchener on the line of the River Atbara. The British, said Steevens, regarded this as a dress rehearsal for the big show.

The supply train jogged on across the desert. The passengers played cards, ate and drank and dozed. They got out at the many halts to stretch their legs, and were in good spirits until the last halt of all, when the track ended in a hill of sand which the labour gang were shifting at top speed. It was dark, and Alain had a few hours' rest in a *tukl* made of four posts and a straw roof, which made him think of the Wells of Elam. In the livid dawn he bought food from the Greek trader in the next *tukl* and arranged with the same businessman to hire a horse and a groom to take him on to Berber, beyond the Fifth Cataract of the Nile.

The Sirdar, Sir Herbert Kitchener, disapproved of married officers, disliked war correspondents, and forced himself to be civil to neutral observers. Alain de Grimont, having made himself presentable, was glad of his parade dress and row of medals when he entered the Sirdar's tent and found him immaculate in white. Kitchener greeted him with what amounted to affability and recalled their meeting at Lord

Cromer's Residence. He then introduced "Your German colleague, Baron von Tiedemann". Delcassé had been right: the German ('colleague' indeed!) was wearing all *his* medals, including the Iron Cross, first class, and the Pour le Mérite.

"Gentlemen, we have established contact with the enemy, and believe him to be stalemated on the river line. I intend to advance slowly, to allow for reconnaissance, and then give battle." That was all Kitchener told the observers of his plan of attack, and the war correspondents heard less, except that they would not be allowed to accompany the reconnaissance patrols.

Mahmud stood at Nakheila on the River Atbara with a force of 12,000 Dervishes, 4,000 being cavalry, and he had ten guns. They were protected by a *zariba* or fence of camel thorn and furze, bound with branches of wild mimosa, the scent of which, intensified by the desert heat, reminded Colonel de Grimont of the Riviera. Inside the *zariba*, it was afterwards found, there was another stockade and then a triple trench, with the Green Flag waving over all. The Anglo-Egyptian Army consisted of the British Brigade and an Egyptian infantry division, all *fellaheen*, with English officers; eight squadrons of cavalry, the Camel Corps and an artillery force equipped with Maxim guns. The total strength was the same as Mahmud's, 12,000 men, who on the night of 7 April began a seven-mile crawl or march through scrub to take up their positions opposite the *zariba*.

The bugles sounded the general advance on Good Friday, 8 April, at 7.40 AM, and by 8.25 all was over. The British, not without serious losses, had stormed their way through the *zariba*, Mahmud was taken prisoner, and the French official observer, so well accustomed to the little *razzias* of the desert, had witnessed the mass slaughter of three thousand men. He heard the Arabic exultations of the *fellaheen* — "a very good fight, a very good fight!" and the rejoinder of their English officers — "But not the big show. Not yet."

If not the big show it was a decisive victory, and the Sirdar was justified in sending his army into summer quarters at Fort Atbara. He paraded his troops and was cheered by them; they all believed in the infallibility of the big man with choleric red cheeks, drooping dark moustache and strangely penetrating eyes. He had done the impossible when he set his engineers to build the railway, and by mid-June the Railhead was at Fort Atbara, bringing letters, newspapers, hospital supplies, food, and drinks for the officers' club. The telegraph lines, which the Dervishes had often cut, were restrung, and Fort Atbara was in communication with the world.

Writing to Sadie, saying a great deal about the humours of life in camp and nothing about the bloodshed of Nakheila, meant more to Alain de Grimont than reading the news which arrived by fits and starts. He would, however, have been very interested to know about an event in Paris, which happened after they left Fort Atbara on 18 August.

The prisoner of Devil's Island had a new champion in the Socialist leader, Jean Jaurès. Convinced that the Army had rigged the evidence against him, Jaurès published a series of articles called *Les Preuves*, bringing new charges of blackmail and forgery against the army chiefs. The new War Minister, Godefroy Cavaignac, was incensed enough to order a new examination of the Panizzardi letter, one of the crucial documents in the case. The officer ordered to examine it by lamplight found that the writing paper was gummed together from two halves of the same brand of paper ruled in slightly different lines. Major (now Colonel) Henry, the original accuser of Dreyfus, had used two blank parts of real letters from Panizzardi to construct a forgery.

The horrified Minister — the sixth since the *Affaire* began — whose speech attacking 'Revision' in the Chambre des

365

Députés had been posted outside every town hall in France, now saw that he had been a party to a great wrong. He ordered the immediate arrest of Colonel Henry, who was taken to the Cherche-Midi prison in Paris on 31 August. That night, his guards having thoughtfully left a razor in his cell, Henry committed suicide.

Alain did know, though no one else at Fort Atbara was at all interested, that there had been a general election in France in May and his friend Delcassé had achieved his life's ambition of becoming Foreign Minister. What he did not know, and neither did Delcassé, was the whereabouts of Captain Marchand. Yet the 'emissary of civilisation', as Delcassé called him, was a great deal nearer Fort Atbara than the Cherche-Midi prison. After the long halt at Fort Desaix, after all the horrors his little force had undergone — the swamps, the flooded rivers, the reptiles and wild beasts, the hostile natives and the malaria — Captain Marchand had reached the White Nile. On 10 July he arrived at a ruined fort called Fashoda, and took possession of the fort and the whole territory of the Bahr-el-Ghazal in the name of France.

When the Tricolore was raised the halliard broke, and the bright flag fell to the ground.

Alain ended his last despatch to Delcassé before the Expeditionary Force set out for Omdurman and Khartoum with the words 'all seem very cheery and confident'. The same thought had been recorded by a new friend with whom Colonel de Grimont went off to have a drink and a cigar. He was only a subaltern, whose mother had used her influence with the War Office to overcome Kitchener's refusal to employ such a brash young man who, while a serving officer in India, had written about the army for the newspapers. Alain found the red-haired kid good company. Some of the British officers laughed at him because when he arrived at Fort Atbara a week after Mahmud's defeat he jumped off his horse in a hurry, crying, "Lieutenant Churchill, Twenty-first Lancers! Am I too late for the battle?" They told Winston Churchill, prophetically, that he was in good time for the big show.

The Khalifa was believed to have 60,000 men inside Omdurman, facing 8,000 British and 16,000 Egyptian soldiers. Kitchener also commanded artillery armed with howitzers and Maxim guns, a flotilla of ten armed gunboats and five steamers. As they marched to the shout of 'Farther South!' and reconnoitred, they saw and sometimes clashed with enough Dervish patrols to be certain that the Khalifa meant to give battle along the line of the Nile about seven miles north of Omdurman. There a vast plain extended between the Kerreri Hills to the north and the Surgham Heights to the south. When the day broke on 1 September, Kitchener's army could see from the high ground the confluence of the White Nile and the Blue Nile on the horizon, and also the yellow-brown pointed dome of a tomb among the mud houses of Omdurman. It was the grave of the Mahdi, the Expected One, the Moslem Messiah, who had brought about the death of General Gordon, the conquest of the Sudan and the triumph of the House of Islam – and it was their goal.

A day of sporadic contacts with the enemy ended in a bombardment by the gunboats, which after night fell played their powerful searchlights over the hills and the plain. To the Moslem army, which expected to fight for victory or paradise, it was an evil omen, and a powerful reason for postponing the night attack which was the only thing the British feared. The neutral observers were aware of that one dread, and when they were all together for a last meal Baron von Tiedemann tried to hearten them by exclaiming with Teutonic tactlessness:

"Tomorrow is the second of September, gentlemen! The anniversary of *our* great victory over the French at Sedan.

Sedan — Sudan! Let us drink to the new September second, and victory in the Sudan!"

Alain de Grimont got up and left the tent.

The battle of Omdurman was no forty-minute affair. The British bugles blew at half past four in the morning, and for seven hours a mass of eighty thousand men fought face to face on the great plain. Kitchener ordered the observers and the war correspondents to a place of reasonable safety on the west bank of the Nile, and as usual the British war correspondents disobeyed him. One Englishman rode with the 21st Lancers and was killed; two more were wounded. Alain kept as far from the German observer as their cramped emplacement would allow. Through powerful field glasses he saw the vast plain as a sea of colour. The Green Flag of the Prophet, the Black Flag which was the personal standard of the Khalifa and the white flags of his Emirs waved above the Dervish troops in their blue *jibbas*, while on the other side the Union Jack and the Crescent and the Star streamed above the khaki-clad men and the bright tartans of the Highlanders. Presently one colour dominated them all — the bright vermilion of spilt blood.

The Khalifa, who had been persecuting Christians and terrorising peaceable Sudanese for years, had never understood firepower, nor the withering effect of the long-range Lee-Metford rifles. In rank after rank his men stood up to die: savages and warriors dying valiant deaths. Alain remembered what he had said after Sadie was kidnapped, that he hoped the British would kill those Shi'ites to the last man — it began to look as if this would happen. Not until about ten o'clock was a mistake made which allowed the Khalifa to escape from the field and race for Omdurman. Without sufficient reconnaissance the 21st Lancers were ordered to charge from their position on the Surgham Heights. They were galloping furiously onwards when they ran into a Dervish ambush and met the enemy in an earth-shaking clash.

Lieutenant Winston Churchill, a troop leader and enjoying himself hugely, came safely out of the mêlée, but seventy Lancers lost their lives, and nearly half the horses were killed.

Alain de Grimont lowered his field glasses with a sigh. For those wild minutes, which the men around him were already comparing to the Charge of the Light Brigade, he had been lost in a vision of the past. Thus, in the war of his childhood, the French Cuirassiers had charged at Reichshoffen, the Lancers at Mars-la-Tour, and those fanatics screaming 'Allah-el-Allah!' were no more savage in his eyes than the Prussians of nearly thirty years ago. He followed blindly as his companions set off towards their tethered horses. They had permission to go forward, someone said; the Sirdar had decided to make straight for Omdurman.

He ordered three brigades to advance upon the city, but there was still fighting to be done as the Dervish army was driven away from the Nile and the gunboats and into the desert. It was not until half past eleven that Kitchener shut up his field glasses and remarked that the enemy had been given 'a good dusting'. The evidence of the dusting was strewn across the plain, which had become acres and acres of corpses, and the victors now needed to rest and eat the food they carried, and drink the water in their flasks. The Khalifa had fled on donkey-back, and his Black Flag became a trophy for Kitchener, who had it carried behind him, with his own banner in front, as he rode victorious into Omdurman.

The victors were soon sickened by the sights and sounds which met them in the conquered city. The Khalifa was now in full flight, while his Emirs lay dead with their soldiers. Many troops had deserted, while others, who had fled into Omdurman, were ready to fling away their arms and surrender. It was the filth of the place which was appalling: the human excrement, the bodies of unburied animals, and the condition of the women, three to every man, who had existed so long in utter slavery to their masters. They had begun their Lu-lu-luing hours ago, and were now ready to embrace the knees of their conquerors. The latter rode on behind Kitchener to the Mahdi's Tomb. That, for him, was the great symbol of his triumph: the vengeance for the death of General Gordon.

The war correspondents, obsessed as usual by transmission problems, were lamenting that the telegraph had not been poled further south than Nasri Island. All they wanted now was to get the horrible story out. They questioned the miserable prisoners, Christian for the most part, who had been shackled in the Khalifa's dungeons for years. The neutral observers wandered down the alleys between the roofless mud houses, and accosted any officer who might be able to give them a rough count of the casualties. Ten thousand Dervishes killed and twice as many wounded, was the first estimate. At nightfall Alain de Grimont was stretched on a stone doorstep, not so much asleep as stupefied by the day's work. His last rational thought, as rifle fire put an end to some defiant stragglers, was that twenty thousand Frenchmen had fallen on the field of Sedan.

27

Captain Marchand walked alone on the Nile bank several times a day. Although he knew the Senegalese sentry would report the slightest sign of human life as soon as it appeared by water or by land, the commander of Fashoda liked to keep a lookout himself, scanning the current which ran strongly between the banks of *sudd*, the belt of tangled weed from either shore, and the swampy grassland beyond. He sometimes saw a hippopotamus in the water or monkeys swinging in the trees: what he had never seen yet was any trace of Kitchener's army to the north, or coming from the south the Ethiopians on whom he had counted to be his allies.

On 18 September Captain Marchand had been in Fashoda for seventy days. In that time the old government building of pre-Dervish days had been strengthened enough to be called a fort, defensible against attack, the men were under canvas and in the wet fertile soil a vegetable garden had been laid out. Since taking possession in the name of France of the province of Bahr-el-Ghazal Marchand had accepted the homage of the Great Mek of the Shilluk tribe, but the Shilluks, while friendly, were lazy and not much inclined to work for the white men. They came to Fashoda by land, travelling silently along the forest tracks, and kept well out of the way when other visitors, not so silent, came by the river.

The French flag had been flying over Fashoda for about six weeks when two Dervish steamers, carrying five hundred men, came upstream on their way back to Omdurman after an expedition to collect grain for the Khalifa. They fired on the interlopers at Fashoda and got the worst of it, limping away after a twelve-hour fight from ship to shore leaving forty dead behind them, but also leaving the French danger-ously short of small-arms ammunition. That the Dervishes would return to fight again was Marchand's nightmare, and one reason why he had sent his own little steamer, the *Faidherbe*, downstream, ostensibly to collect grain or any other provisions, but in reality to look for and urge haste on the Ethiopians who never came.

Captain Marchand was only thirty-five, but he had changed very much from the handsome, fine-featured young officer whom Alain de Grimont had met in Delcassé's apart-ment in Montmartre. His face had fallen in because of hunger and fever, his body sagged from the sheer weariness of the long march through the jungle, and he was hagridden with the anxiety of his command. He had lost men on the way, some by death and others by desertion, and now he stood on the banks of the Nile without hope of help from friend or foe.

He had turned back towards the tiny settlement and was gazing downstream when simultaneously with the plash of oars he heard the sentry's cry:

"Mon capitaine!"

Marchand swung round. He saw two sailors in British uniform rowing a boat towards Fashoda.

His first instinct was to shout a welcome, his second to call for his officers, but Captain Marchand, mindful of the dig-nity of France, strode towards the tiny harbourage they had created until the sailors made their boat fast, stepped out on the jetty and saluted.

"Compliments of the Sirdar, mooseyoo," was what he understood them to say, and one of them handed him a letter which he tore open at once. It was written in English, but Marchand could make it out and knew it was from Kitchener. The writer announced a total victory over the Dervish army, the flight of the Khalifa, and his own progress down the Nile and approach to Fashoda.

The whole garrison was behind Marchand now, the Senegalese riflemen at a respectful distance and the officers at his back. The stolid British sailors looked at them all incuriously.

"Tell them to wait," said Marchand to his interpreter, who was more at home with native dialects than with English. "This must be answered very carefully."

He led the way back to the stone fort. Being Frenchmen, each of his officers was inclined to take a different view of the news. At least it was better than the return of the Dervishes. At least the Khalifa was defeated. But if Kitchener wanted to kick them out of Fashoda . . . ? "We'll fight to the last man," said Marchand hardily. "We haven't come so far to be deprived of our prize by those greedy Britishers. I'll show him who's the master here!"

He sat down at his hastily carpentered table and wrote a graceful note of congratulation on the victory of Omdurman, announcing the establishment of a French protectorate on the Nile, and bidding 'General Lord Kitchener' welcome to the Sudan.

A greeting which made the Sirdar's choleric face redder than ever when he received it a few miles upstream.

He had heard that there were Europeans in Fashoda as soon as the two Dervish steamers which had fired on the fort and been beaten off limped into Omdurman and found the Khalifa gone. He had very little doubt that it was the Marchand expedition, the only other possibility being Belgians from King Leopold's Congo; and when he sent for Colonel de Grimont he found that Alain had very little doubt either.

"Perhaps you were expecting to encounter Captain Marchand, colonel?"

"My Foreign Minister thought it was a possibility, sir."

"Was that why you were in no hurry to request transport to Cairo, like your colleagues?"

"I know communications are a great problem, sir."

Why, the fellow was talking like a diplomat! It was true the non-combatants had been falling over themselves to get out of the pestilential city of Omdurman as soon as the battle was won, the war correspondents being particularly vocal since the telegraph was still inoperative. One day to explore the battlefield, where the burial details and the vultures were working overtime, the next — a Sunday — devoted to a memorial service for General Gordon outside the ruins of his palace in Khartoum, and then they were agitating for a gunboat to take them back to the Railhead and civilisation. That was how they came to miss the story of Fashoda, which arrived via the Dervish steamers only a few hours after the non-combatants, with Kitchener's blessing, had left for the north.

"Is Captain Marchand a friend of yours, colonel?" the Sirdar asked Alain now.

"I met him once in Monsieur Delcassé's house, some years ago."

"I see . . . You'd better come with us to Fashoda, Colonel de Grimont."

"À vos ordres, mon général."

So the word was 'Farther South!' again, and it was an imposing force that set sail next day. Five British gunboats flying the White Ensign, two battalions of Egyptian infantry, two companies of the Cameron Highlanders, a battery of artillery and four Maxim guns accompanied the

374

Commander-in-Chief on his voyage of reconnaissance. When this formidable array anchored opposite the fort of Fashoda the British found drawn up before them eight French officers and NCOs and one hundred and twenty Senegalese riflemen, prepared to do the honours — or to fight.

Captain Marchand, with a guard of honour, was invited to go aboard the leading gunboat, where he was greeted by the Sirdar. He was wearing a fresh white uniform, with decorations, which like his brother officers he had made the bearers carry in tin boxes across the continent, in readiness for some great occasion. The white uniform hung loosely upon him now, but his salute was a model of military precision, and his Senegalese presented arms.

"Welcome to Fashoda, *Excellence*," he said. "Accept my congratulations on your brilliant victory."

Kitchener's French was rusty but adequate. In French he said the one deserving congratulations was Marchand himself, for his epic march across the Dark Continent. His bulging blue eyes surveyed, without expression, the ramshackle fort, the tent encampment and the Tricolore.

"Allow me to present my officers," he continued, and introduced the captain of the gunboat, his military secretary and a Colonel Jackson who, he said, "will command the garrison I shall establish here."

"With respect, *Excellence*," said Marchand, flushing, "*our* garrison was established at Fashoda on the tenth of July, when I took possession of the whole province in the name of France."

"And I," said Kitchener, "have taken possession of the whole Sudan in the name of the Queen-Empress and of the Khedive of Egypt. Come, Captain Marchand, we mustn't spoil this happy meeting by wrangling over precedence! Let us leave the matter in the hands of our two governments, and allow me to drink your health and sentiments before we all go ashore."

Marchand acknowledged the toast with a bow, but merely touched his lips to the glass which held whisky and soda. "I hope Your Excellency will allow us to entertain you at the fort," he said. "My own officers are anxious to be presented to the Sirdar."

"A pleasure," said Kitchener. "And here is an old acquaintance of your own, Colonel de Grimont, who has been with us for some months now."

Alain came forward with a smile and an outstretched hand. He had deliberately kept in the background, knowing as none of the Englishmen could know, the humiliation which Marchand must be feeling. He had not expected his hand to be ignored, nor the impression his khaki uniform, worn without insignia, must give.

"I met the Baron de Grimont in Paris some years ago," said Captain Marchand. "Is Your Excellency ready to go ashore?"

The disembarkation was as formal as the pathetic surroundings of the French force would permit. In what was little better than a swamp, with the curious eyes of the British and Egyptian troops watching from the river, Marchand presented the officers who had accomplished the tremendous journey. "It is these brave men, and not I, who deserve your congratulations," he said to the Sirdar, with a sweeping gesture which included the NCOs and the Senegalese riflemen. "Their courage has been exemplary. Would Your Excellency be pleased to inspect the troops?"

The commander-in-chief who had led twenty thousand men against the Dervish empire walked gravely down the ranks of one hundred and twenty who had left their homes in Senegal to follow the Tricolore. Then Marchand led the way to the fort, where champagne and glasses — also carried across the continent — were waiting for the men who had come from Omdurman. With the popping of corks a spirit of conviviality was at once established. The Frenchmen wanted

376

news of the campaign just over, the British wanted details of the long march and the dangers passed. In the babel of voices it was easy for Marchand to say coldly to Alain:

"Are you fighting with the British now, *mon colonel?*"

"Don't be deceived by the khaki," said Alain. "All the neutral observers with the Expeditionary Force, which is what I was, drew uniforms from the British stores when our own clothes were reduced to rags. Washerwomen are hard to come by on the Nile these days."

"A neutral observer!" echoed Marchand. "A very exacting service, I feel sure. You got your colonelcy out of it, anyway."

"Brevet rank," said Alain. "And let's not waste time in sarcasm. I have a letter from Monsieur Delcassé, now the Foreign Minister, for your eyes only, and I have his orders to remain with you until you receive further instructions from the government at Paris."

"And how the devil am I to receive them, tell me that!" said Marchand bitterly.

"By telegraph, of course."

"The telegraph is in the hands of the British. No one is looking at us. Give me the letter now."

Colonel de Grimont produced it from his breast pocket, and Marchand, turning his back on the company, read the two pages quickly.

"We'll talk about this later," he said. "I mustn't neglect our guests, *mon colonel*." Alain heard the suppressed rage in every word. He turned aside and began to speak to the French medical officer, Dr Emily, who asked urgently if *ces messieurs*, the British, could let him have a good supply of quinine. "Malaria is the curse of Fashoda," he said. "I never have fewer than six patients at a time."

"I'll ask Colonel Jackson," said Alain. "I don't know about their supplies, but I'm sure they'll let you have all they can. Here comes the colonel now."

377

But the colonel, giving a perfunctory "yes, certainly," had come to say that the flag-raising ceremony was about to take place, after which the Sirdar and his convoy would depart. If Captain Marchand wished to communicate with his government, now was the time to prepare his telegrams, which would be despatched via Cairo as soon as possible. "I believe Captain Marchand would appreciate your assistance in the matter," he said apologetically to Alain.

It was not assistance Marchand required. When all had left the room but himself and Alain, and writing materials had been placed among the empty champagne bottles, he merely said, "In view of your instructions from Monsieur Delcassé, I ought to show you the messages I want to send to Paris. I shall telegraph to the War Ministry and to the Foreign Minister himself. Does that meet with your approval?"

"Certainly."

Marchand wrote busily, and passed two sheets to Alain. The wording was identical in each. Captain Marchand had arrived at Fashoda on 10 July, had taken possession of the province in the name of France, had concluded treaties of friendship with the Shilluk and Dinka tribes, and had now been superseded by the British. He asked for instructions on how to proceed, these instructions to include Colonel de Grimont.

"Satisfactory?"

"Quite," said Alain. "If you're sure 'superseded' is the right word."

"What d'you call that?"

'That' was the skirl of the pipes as the Camerons disembarked, and with an Egyptian contingent formed a square round the spot where the flags of Britain and Egypt were to fly side by side, eight hundred yards south of the Tricolore. The two men inside the fort heard the proclamation of the Sirdar, the singing of the National Anthems and the cheers for that incongruous couple, Queen Victoria and the Khedive Abbas. Then they left the fort together, Marchand to give his telegrams to Colonel Jackson, Alain to find Kitchener, if he could, in the press of soldiers, black and white, who were fraternising where the hollow square had been. Gifts were being exchanged. Baskets of vegetables for the British. Quinine, cases of tinned bullybeef and bundles of old newspapers for the French. The language barrier was being successfully crossed.

"Colonel de Grimont!" said the formidable presence at the jetty. "Are you coming back aboard?"

"On the contrary, sir, I've just sent aboard for my equipment. With your permission I'm staying at Fashoda."

The Sirdar's heavy brows twitched. "You're not under my command, colonel. If you choose to be as foolhardy as Captain Marchand, it's got nothing to do with me."

"I'm under orders to remain here, sir. Captain Marchand knows that now."

"I assumed, from his attitude when you met, that friendship didn't enter into it."

"I hope his attitude will change in time."

"But how much time has he got?" growled the Sirdar. "He has provisions for three months, he says, and his position in this damned swamp is untenable. Well" – recollecting himself – "this wretched affair must be settled at government level. Good luck to you, de Grimont."

The entire French force except for three Senegalese in Dr Emily's hospital tent were on the banks of the Nile to see the Sirdar depart. Three British gunboats sailed for Omdurman, while the two left behind in support of Colonel Jackson's little garrison anchored in midstream between the unwholesome masses of water weed. The armed troops, and the guns visible on the decks, were intended to be a display of strength, and caused Captain Germain, Captain Marchand's second in command, to growl, "What an armada, to send against a handful of Frenchmen with hardly a cartridge in the magazine!"

"The flotilla didn't sail against the French, Captain Germain," said Alain coldly. "Hostile bands of Dervishes were attacked all along the Nile as we sailed south, and there was a ship-to-shore fight at Reng, with the same hostiles as attacked you here four weeks ago."

"So the Dervishes are still fighting back, are they? Omdurman was not a total victory?"

"It was a conclusive victory."

"But the Khalifa survived, and is still at liberty?"

"He may have been captured by this time, Germain."

"Or he may not, *mon colonel*. He may be able to raise another army, and march against the British in Omdurman."

"Is that what you want to happen?" said Alain. "Another victory for the House of Islam? You wouldn't say so if you'd seen Omdurman as I saw it, after the battle."

"A British defeat is what I want," said Germain, but he said it under his breath, and a French sergeant came up at that moment to say a room had been prepared in the fort for the colonel, if he would please to come and inspect it.

"It's hardly the Meurice," said Captain Marchand, who was waiting in the doorway. The little room had mud-covered walls, and contained a chair, a table on which Alain's canvas washbasin was filled with Nile water, and his sleeping bag spread on the mud floor.

"I've known worse bivouacs," said Alain de Grimont, and flung his képi on top of the sleeping bag.

"I want to apologise," said Marchand, "for my incivility to you this afternoon. At first I honestly thought you'd joined the British army."

"That was the uniform."

"Yes, and then I thought you'd come to take the command

of Fashoda away from me. You outrank me, of course – "

"Nominally, perhaps, but you are the leader of the Marchand Mission, and you command here. No one can take anything from you, certainly not the glory of a great feat of exploration, but – do you want to be the man to get us into war with Britain?"

"It's the British who want to take everything from us."

"But now you've read Delcassé's letter – "

"Now I understand that you're only here as a kind of gendarme, to keep me in line, to keep me away from the Ethiopians and make me defer to the British at the expense of our national pride. . . . Didn't I do well today?"

The tone was offensive, but Alain resolutely refused to take offence. He said, "Very well!" He saw the man was very near to breaking point.

"Marchand, Delcassé made the Treaty of Alliance with Russia, and he wants a similar treaty with Great Britain. He thinks it's for the safety of France in Europe. We have to obey orders, that's all, and remember they'll soon know in Paris where we are. We'll get our orders soon, and meantime it would help if you thought of me as a brother officer and not as a policeman. Delcassé sent me out to meet you because he thought we'd make a good team. Shall we try?"

That brief talk cleared the air with Marchand, and next morning Alain began to integrate himself with the life of the camp. It was not easy, because the French were a closed corporation of men who had been so long together and had suffered so much, but his great attraction for them was that he could give them news of Kitchener's campaign and fill them in on the news contained in the old papers and magazines the British had brought. The developments in the Dreyfus case divided the tiny community at Fashoda just as they had divided France: even perfidious Albion took second place to Picquart, Esterhazy and Zola. Captain Germain was vociferously anti-Dreyfus. Alain had placed him as the firebrand and troublemaker in the group. Lieutenant Mangin was the most soldierly, and Dr Emily the most intelligent. He lent Alain the diary of the March which he had kept since the previous November, a revelation of all the Marchand Mission had undergone. The little steamer, the *Faidherbe*, had been taken to pieces and carried on the shoulders of the Senegalese for fifty days, the boiler alone had been rolled on logs through the tropical forest, while sometimes the troop had advanced up to their necks in swamp water. After all that, to come to this anticlimax at Fashoda! It was no wonder that Marchand was nearly out of his mind with worry, and that they were all desperately waiting for a message from Paris.

The *Faidherbe* came back from her abortive errand, and the men aboard saw the British gunboats in mid-channel before a British steamer arrived from Omdurman on 9 October. She delivered a bag of mail and newspapers to Colonel Jackson, who had kept as much in the background as possible, and then sent one telegram from Paris to Captain Marchand. He read it in the big room at the fort with Alain by his side. It was very short. It congratulated Marchand on his magnificent achievement and announced his promotion to major, and that was all.

"They've forgotten us!" he said tragically, and with shaking hands dashed off a reply describing their plight, the sickness, the hunger, the need for reinforcements, their 'harassment' by the British – anything and everything that came into his head. "What do we do now?" he asked Alain.

"We go on waiting, of course, what else?"

"But what are they thinking about, in Paris?"

"Dreyfus."

Alain had told none of them about his approaching marriage. Sadie's name was not to be mentioned in the mess, even though there was no loose talk about women round that frugal table. The long march seemed to have killed the sexuality of these most volatile Frenchmen. But Alain cursed the War Minister for failing to issue some sort of movement order. Every day he spent at Fashoda was another delay to his long-delayed marriage – and he had heard nothing from Sadie since he was at Fort Atbara. At least she would have learned from the Cairo press that Marchand was found, and would be waiting for him. . . .

Colonel Jackson paid a formal call later in the day and was told of Marchand's majority. Congratulating him, the Englishman was too tactful to ask if there was any other news from Paris. He produced his own news instead. Kitchener had gone to Cairo, to confer with Lord Cromer about the Anglo-Egyptian condominium in the Sudan and the redevelopment of that devastated area after the Dervish rule. The Khalifa had been sighted in Kordofan province and plans were being made for his pursuit. There was dreadful news from Europe, where on 10 September the Empress Elisabeth of Austria had been stabbed to death by an Italian anarchist on the lakeside at Geneva.

"Another anarchist killing!" said Marchand. "Will they never stop?"

"Is there no news of Dreyfus?" asked Alain.

Then Colonel Jackson told them the story of Henry's forgery and his suicide in the Cherche-Midi prison.

"It's fully reported in the *Journal d'Egypte*," he said, "and in the London papers too. I'll send you them tomorrow, and one of the boxes of tinned foods the steamer brought. I imagine you can use them . . . Oh, and could you spare us a few of your splendid lettuces?"

Alain admired the tact of this English gentleman, who spoke excellent French, whose request for vegetables kept the French from feeling indebted for the food now badly needed. There was nothing more to be had from the native tribes who had made treaties of friendship with Captain Marchand. The inhabitants of Fashoda heard their drums beating from one side of the Nile to the other, and guessed correctly that the drumbeat was a warning to have nothing more to do with the white men who proved to belong to another and inferior tribe to the conquerors of the Dervishes who had tyrannised over the Dinkas and the Shilluks. The new major and his comrades were ostracised by the blacks, and their only lifeline was in British hands.

The second period of waiting for orders from Paris seemed far longer than the first. The absurd situation in which the soldiers of two Great Powers, each laying claim to the same mosquito-ridden swamp – virtually an island during the summer inundation of the Nile – were separated from each other by half a mile of marsh, was getting on the nerves of both sides. Health deteriorated, malarial attacks were more frequent, and water rats came out of the river to eat the precious vegetables. Men who had been friends and comrades on the long march began to quarrel over minor points in the news from home, such as they could decipher in the new batch of papers and magazines.

One piece of news which was entirely lacking concerned themselves. There was as yet no news of Fashoda in their British papers, although in London the halfpenny press was surpassing itself in invective – What! the British were to be robbed of the great victory, the reconquest of the Sudan, by the claims of a band of French adventurers, whose government should disown them – or else. ... The Paris rags replied in kind. Libellous cartoons were printed to the dishonour of the Queen and the Prince of Wales, perfidious Albion was insulted in every column. and the government was urged to mobilise for war – or else. Marchand had been quite wrong when he said they were forgotten in Paris. On the boulevards his name was on everybody's lips, and even the *Affaire* took second place for a time.

But part of the Dreyfus story which Colonel Jackson had delayed in passing on was that the result of Colonel Henry's suicide in prison was the new wave of demands for 'Revision', and a new trial for Captain Dreyfus. There was a clamour to have his case taken up to the Cour de Cassation, the highest court of appeal in France. The sick and weary men at Fashoda debated that with violence. Marchand himself took no part in the argument on one memorable night when two of his officers came to blows. He got up from the mess table and made for his room in the fort. Dr Emily followed him, came back and made a sign to Alain, took him aside and said, "*Mon colonel*, I'm afraid Major Marchand is in for another bout of fever. With him the onset is sudden and the duration four to five days. But the hospital tent is crowded out."

"I have the room next door, doctor. Tell me what needs to be done and I'll do it."

There was not a great deal that could be done but dose the patient with quinine and keep him warm. Marchand slept for most of the first two days, and then the fever increased with long bouts of shivering and garbled incessant talk amounting to delirium. For one long day Alain never left his bedside and Dr Emily was in and out, insisting that *mon colonel* should take the quinine medicine too as a precaution. "We can't have you going sick, sir," he said. "Colonel Jackson has sent some Liebig meat extract especially for you."

"I had all the Liebig I ever want when I was in hospital at Bône. Let's save it for Major Marchand."

On the fifth day Marchand drank some of the beverage, and then a glass of champagne. After that the fever departed as quickly as it came, and the hero of Fashoda (as they were calling him in Paris) thanked his nurse and asked if he had said anything stupid while his head ached so badly.

"Not a word," lied Alain. It was not the time to tell a convalescent man all that he had revealed.

After all, what Marchand said in his fever was only what Alain knew already: that this brave man had been incited to stir up trouble for the British wherever his great expedition

385

led him. Alain's support of Delcassé's plans for an *entente* with Britain, sometimes lukewarm, was strengthened from that night forward. As for Marchand, how far Alain's advice and Colonel Jackson's tact had brought him to a better understanding was revealed on the day, 23 October, when another British gunboat arrived at Fashoda with messages for both sides.

It carried telegrams for Colonel de Grimont and Major Marchand, couched in identical terms and signed Delcassé.

"Proceed forthwith to Cairo and report to French consul-general for further instructions."

After the first gasp of relief at the prospect of action, Marchand's dismay at the consequences were immediate.

"If I go to Cairo, Germain will be left in command, and God knows what trouble he'll make with Colonel Jackson!"

It was obvious that the English colonel, who called at the fort almost immediately, had the same reservations. His own orders were to expedite the departure of the two French officers so that they might return to Omdurman aboard the gunboat, and to Alain at least it was obvious that he knew what the 'further instructions' awaiting them might be. "Congratulations on getting out of this pestilential swamp," said Jackson, while Marchand was giving explicit orders to Germain, "it's not worth fighting over."

The scanty possessions of the two men were quickly put together, and after Marchand had made an emotional speech to his men the Egyptians under Jackson's command were marched down to the jetty to render military honours to the travellers. There was a touching attempt to play the *Marseillaise* with fife and drum, and the ready tears were in Major Marchand's eyes as he stood on the deck of the gunboat and saluted the Tricolore which still flew defiantly over Fashoda. A bend in the river and it was seen no more.

At Omdurman the Frenchmen were received courteously but impersonally, for Fashoda was not a burning topic there.

The Khalifa, at large for six weeks, was reported to be marching again on his former capital, and Sir Reginald Wingate was preparing to attack. Not many days were to pass before the Khalifa died in battle, but by that time Marchand and Alain were in Cairo and had entered on a new phase of the story. Their journey north was uneventful. The telegraph was in operation, the railway was in good running order, and soon they were at Fort Atbara, where the cry of 'Farther South!' had begun so many days of the march across the desert.

"What an achievement! What a great achievement!" Marchand kept repeating, as the desert miles were swallowed up by the Sudan Machine.

"They had a whole team of experts, and hundreds of *fellaheen* to lay the permanent way," said Alain. "Their achievement, as you call it, was no greater than your own."

"Only it was successful and mine wasn't."

As they neared Cairo Marchand grew more depressed. He had a premonition of the orders waiting for him there, and when they both sent telegrams from Fort Atbara to tell the consul-general at Cairo to expect them he seemed to regard it as a kind of defeat. The telegraph line was reserved for military use, but Alain bribed an Egyptian operator to send a message to Sadie, saying nothing but that he was on his way to Cairo and would be at Wadi Halfa within the next few days. Then he collected the kit he had left in storage at the fort, and they set out on the next stage of their journey across the desert.

When the watchword was 'Farther South!' Alain had shared a two-berth compartment with the man from the *Daily Mail*, who was certainly a livelier companion than Major Marchand. He alternated between worrying about Fashoda under the command of Captain Germain and the logistics of carrying out an evacuation, if that were ordered. To change the subject Alain told him that he hoped to be married soon, and wished to present Major Marchand to his fiancée while he was in Cairo.

"You are a lucky devil, de Grimont! You never said a word about your engagement at — back there."

"It hardly seemed the time or the place, somehow."

"Thank you for telling me now. How long is it since you heard from the young lady?"

"Over three months, but I know there'll be a message from her at Wadi Halfa."

It was waiting at the Hôtel des Voyageurs, and as Sadie was using the Eastern Telegraph Company and not a military wire, her message was less inhibited than Alain's.

"Welcome home darling father in Alexandria am Lady Cromer's guest at the Residence please come quickly to your loving Sadie."

Marchand seemed bewildered by the streets of Cairo. The noise, the trams, the street vendors and the smells seemed to overwhelm him, but at the same time he wanted to go direct to the French consulate. He had his beard shaved off and they both had their hair cut by a Greek barber at Wadi Halfa, which he seemed to think made them both presentable.

"We can't turn up at Monsieur Cogordon's like a couple of vagrants," said Colonel de Grimont. "We'll go to my hotel to shave and bathe while they press our dress uniforms. Medals and swords, I think. Whatever orders we get, let's receive them in style."

Once at the Continental Marchand luxuriated in abundant hot water, and Alain had time to send out for the *Journal d'Egypte*. The front-page stories were Major Marchand's arrival in Cairo, and the decision of the Cour de Cassation to accept the Dreyfus case. So the four-year fight for a retrial had been won, and the poor prisoner would be unshackled and brought home from Devil's Island! "It may take years," mused Alain, "because the army will fight to the last ditch, but God, how I hope they'll reinstate Picquart!"

"Isn't it time we went?" Marchand appeared in the bedroom, handsome and tense. "I want to hear the bad news and get it over."

"You've made up your mind it is bad news?"

"Haven't you?"

Alain gripped his friend's shoulder. "Marchand," he said, "remember this. Whatever the French government decide, you'll be hailed as a national hero. You've beaten the jungle and the elements; now you've only got to beat yourself."

They were silent as they drove to the consulate-general. There were two Spahis at the entrance — not the men who had ridden to the Wells of Elam — and as they presented arms the little crowd of loungers at the gates began to cheer.

"Vive Marchand! Vive le vainqueur de Fachoda!"

"What did I tell you?" said Alain under his breath. "It's beginning already!"

Then Monsieur Cogordon was on the doorstep, shaking hands, congratulating, and drawing them into his office, where two cablegrams were lying on the desk.

"These are your orders, gentlemen — "

"But they're sealed, monsieur."

"These are for you, from the Foreign Minister, who sent me duplicates. Colonel de Grimont — "

Alain opened the message. Congratulations — confirmed in the rank of colonel — three months' leave — then appointed military attaché at the French Embassy in London.

"Satisfactory?" said Marchand, watching him.

"I'm posted to the London embassy."

"Rather you than me." The man was shaking with nerves and the effects of fever. Cogordon handed him his cablegram without a word.

"Evacuate! Get my men out of Fashoda and get out!"

"With the cooperation of Sir Herbert Kitchener."

"Kitchener!" It was almost a sob, and Cogordon spoke quickly.

"The government has given in, Major Marchand. Lord Salisbury, the British Prime Minister, made it clear that the French presence would not be tolerated in the Sudan — that the only alternative was war. It's no reflection on your courage and daring. . . ."

"Steady, Marchand!" Alain was too late. The tormented man had flung himself into a chair with his arms across a table, and his wet face hidden from them both.

"I'd better leave now," said Alain to the consul. "He'll get a grip of himself when he's alone with you. And I'm expected at the Residence."

"I know," murmured Monsieur Cogordon, following him into the hall. "I saw Mademoiselle Colt yesterday — *en grande beauté* —"

"Nothing wrong at Helwan House, I hope?"

"Wrong? Oh, because of Mr Colt's absence? He had to attend a meeting of cotton brokers at Alexandria. Congratulations on all counts, Colonel de Grimont!"

Alain drove through the familiar avenues with his hand on his sword-hilt and his mind in confusion. So this was Delcassé's reward — London!

The Beit-al-Lurd was as imposing and as heavily guarded as ever, and the English butler, who prided himself on never forgetting a face or a name, said, "Welcome to Cairo, my lord! Her ladyship and Miss Colt are out motoring, they'll be back in a quarter of an hour. Will your lordship wait in the little salon? This way, if you please."

Alain had forgotten that a baron of Louis Philippe was entitled to so many 'lordships'. The butler, opening a door, supplied one more, almost with bated breath, "*His Lordship* is with the Khedive at the Abdin Palace."

The little salon was not the sort of waiting room reserved

for business visitors. It was a charming English parlour furnished in rosewood and chintz, with bowls of pot-pourri and gilt-framed watercolours. The only reminder of official-dom was a photograph of the Queen, signed with her own hand Victoria RI.

Alain had given his sword-belt to the butler with his képi, but even without its constriction he could not relax in the cushioned armchair. He was too keyed up for the meeting, too dismayed at the thought of the confusion in France. Yielding to Britain in the retreat from Fashoda, admitting the venerated army had erred in the prosecution of Dreyfus struck a double wound which would take years to heal. And the diplomatic posting which Delcassé had promised him was nothing less than an order to assist in the healing process! Would an alliance with Britain ever be possible now?

Subconsciously Alain de Grimont was waiting for the sound of a motor car. But he was on the wrong side of the Beit-al-Lurd, for the little salon faced the gardens instead of the portico, and only a murmur in the hall told him his love was near. He heard Lady Cromer's voice, almost outside the door, "Don't keep him waiting, dear!" and came sharply to his feet.

Sadie took her at her word. She ran to join Alain without pausing to look into the hall mirror when she pulled off her dust cloak and the hat tied with a silk scarf, and in her rumpled white dress and dishevelled hair she was the school-girl Sadie of Cap Martin, whom he now had the right to hold to his heart. There were no words of greeting after the long separation, not even the 'darling' or *'mon amour'* of their ritual endearments, just a sighing silence and deep exploring kis-ses, until Sadie whispered,

"Was it awful?"

"The campaign or Fashoda?"

"Both."

"Pretty bad."

"And Major Marchand?"

"He took it very hard. Our consul's looking after him. But it's over, and now we'll be married, Sadie; we'll never be parted again."

She had planned to tell him joyously that they could be married by special licence in All Saints' Church as soon as her father came back from Alexandria. Charles Colt planned to give them a grand reception in Shepheard's Hotel, a rehearsal for his own wedding to Luise von Rorschach in Vienna after Rosi married her Hussar. But Sadie's swift intuition told her that this was no time to chatter about her father's wedding plans or even their own. "We'll never be parted again" was all that mattered, and now Alain had relaxed his embrace to fumble in his pocket for a cablegram. "Read that," he said.

She read it, understood, and flung herself into his arms again. "Oh darling, it's wonderful! It's the best thing that could possibly happen! Now I understand what Lord Cromer meant yesterday — "

"Lord Cromer? Does he know about it?"

"Well, he's hardly talked to me since I've been staying here, you know he's always busy, but yesterday morning he asked me to walk in the gardens. Then he told me what was going to happen at Fashoda, and said a Colonel Jackson had sent messages to Kitchener about what a power for peace you'd been, and how your patience and forbearance had averted quarrels again and again — "

"Sounds more like Jackson himself than me."

"And that Kitchener said he didn't wonder Monsieur Delcassé needed your help in London."

"Would you like to live in London, Sadie?"

"With you? Wouldn't I just! And remember what Delcassé said when he became Foreign Minister: 'I shall never leave the Quai d'Orsay until I have brought about a cordial understanding between France and Britain!'"

"Fine words, darling, but you know in Paris ministries

can fall like snowflakes in winter. How long will Delcassé be at the Quai d'Orsay?"

The vivid face he loved grew almost stern.

"Alain, what are you afraid of?"

"Failure."

"Your own failure? Darling, that's impossible! You were made for the job!"

"Not really. I've been twenty years in the army without doing anything heroic, or taking a very definite stand on anything – unless it was on Boulanger, and that was my big mistake. . . ."

"But patience and forbearance are the very qualities you'll need in London. You may even be an ambassador yourself some day."

Alain actually laughed. "If you believe in me, my own love, then we'll tackle the job together. Because it'll be your job as much as mine, and you've been trained for the part you'll have to play. But before we begin, there's one thing I must be sure you understand."

"What's that?" she said, with her arms about his neck.

"That if by some miracle Delcassé and Cambon and Lord Lansdowne, perhaps the Prince of Wales too, combine in bringing off an *entente* with England, it'll turn into a full-scale alliance. France, Britain and Russia will be aligned on one side, with Germany, Austria and Italy on the other, and both sides spoiling for a fight. We want Alsace and Lorraine – I was brought up to want that – the Kaiser wants to conquer England, the Italians want Ethiopia, and Austria wants the Balkans. It may come to the point when only one shot may start a European war. Sadie, I've seen two pitched battles this summer, Omdurman by far the worse, and dead men in their thousands on the desert sand. I don't want to see that in Europe, not even for Alsace and Lorraine, so am I morally entitled to take this job I'm offered?"

"Would you rather grow carnations?" Sadie said. "D'you

want to duck out of the battle before the battle begins? Perhaps it'll never happen. Perhaps you'll be a power for peace again. Or maybe you'll be in the firing line. But whatever comes we'll be together."

It was a woman's reasoning and not a soldier's. But Alain de Grimont knew that with Sadie by his side he would follow the glory road to its bitter end.